UNNATURAL MAGIC

STACIA STARK

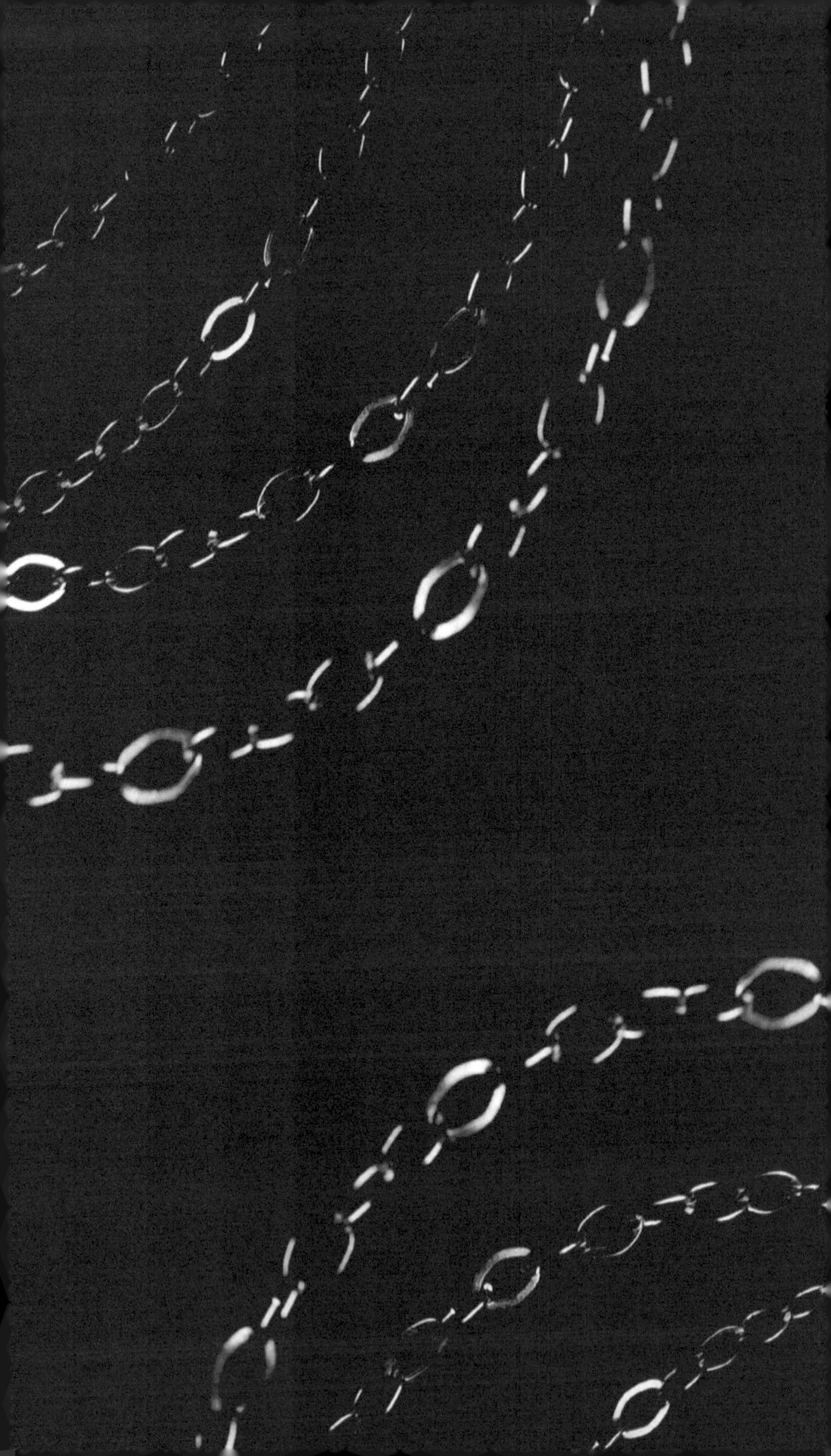

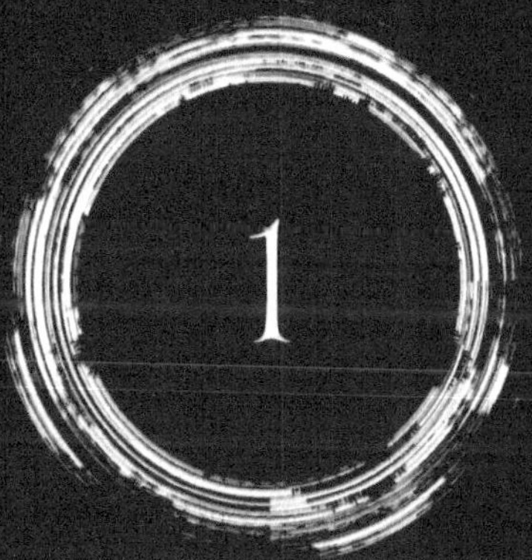

1

EVIE

I ducked, rolled, and lurched to my feet.

The roc swooped straight at me, stunningly fast.

It definitely had the advantage, what with its wings and all.

"I don't want to hurt you," I called. I was pretty sure it understood me. "But you can't terrorize the human kids."

The roc shrieked. It didn't like being told what to do.

I could relate.

"Lookit," I said, attempting reason. "You don't have to go home, but you can't stay here."

Truthfully, I had no idea which realm it had come from, or how it had gathered enough power to get through the portal. But it had been seen lurking outside the local elementary school. The kids were hunkered down inside the gym since rocs were known for carrying off small humans.

It must enjoy the *taste* of humans, because the creature was large and strong enough to lift an elephant.

I'd traced it back to its home base—the Occoneechee Golf Club. No one was playing today. Word had obviously gotten out about the killer bird. But the bird had cornered me in the parking lot, which was less than ideal.

I pondered my options. I could shoot the thing, but I didn't want to kill it. If someone had brought it through a portal to cause trouble, it wasn't the roc's fault. It was just doing as a giant bird did.

I could use my power, but recently, I hadn't been able to trust it all that much. It still worked fine defensively, but things sometimes went...wrong when I went on the offensive.

The roc shrieked and swooped once more. I threw myself to the left, hit the ground, and crawled along the pavement until I was stuck between two parked cars.

The roc dived at me again, its tail producing a drumming sound that made the hair on the back of my neck stand up.

"Come on, Evie. Badasses don't hide from giant birds," I muttered.

My sister wouldn't hide. *She* was a badass. Unfortunately for me, she was also currently in the underworld.

The roc landed on one of the cars, and we made eye contact. Shit.

Its wingspan had to be at least forty feet. It was red, black, and white, with a weird little collection of feathers on its head. The feathers bobbled as it moved.

Someone was screaming, drawing the bird's attention from me. The roc slowly turned its head, and I scowled.

"Shut up, dumbass," I hissed. "Unless you want to be bird food."

The roc launched itself into the air, and I crawled out from between the cars. If it attacked a human, I was going to have to kill it.

A human guy stood fifty feet away, pale and shaking.

"What the hell are you doing?" I called.

"Saving your life, ma'am."

"Oh no."

He'd ma'amed me.

We'd had a miscommunication here somewhere, likely because I was wearing a cute summer dress and strappy sandals. He thought I was human. Worse, he thought *he* was the protector in this situation.

I didn't know exactly what I was, but it wasn't all human. And I might have been dressed like I was on my way to a baby shower, but I could still kick ass when properly motivated.

The roc circled. I knew that move by now. It was

about to arrow toward the earth, shoving its huge claws straight into this guy's guts.

My vision narrowed, and I kicked off my sandals. Decision made. This bird was either going through the nearest portal, or I was shooting it straight in the head.

I slipped my knife from my thigh sheath. If the human guy had looked a little more closely, he would've seen a number of weird bulges beneath this dress. I no longer went anywhere unarmed.

I took a deep breath and mentally plotted out my route. I could cut across the golf course, but I'd have to hold my ward while I ran. Not the easiest, but it should enrage the roc enough that it stayed on me. This was going to suck.

I sliced my forearm with the knife. The roc whirled, scenting the blood.

I took off.

I didn't have to look over my shoulder to know the roc was hunting me. I could practically feel its fetid breath on the back of my neck. I was carrying a few charms and spells, but if I used them, the roc might decide to go hunt easier prey.

I charged across the golf course, hearing the human guy yell after me. Fingers crossed he wouldn't try to be a hero again. I dodged around a man-made pond.

Thwapp! Something slammed into my ward. My ears rang, and I stumbled, almost dropping to my knees.

If I lived through this, I needed to practice running while fully warded.

The roc screamed its rage, flapping its oversized wings. The wind pushed at me, and I aimed for the tree line. The brush would make it tricky for it to dive-bomb me again.

I weaved in and out of the trees, ignoring the sharp branches on the ground as they jabbed my bare feet.

In the distance, a busy road separated the golf course from Cates Landing.

I huddled under a low branch and bounced on the balls of my feet, waiting for the traffic to thin enough for me to duck out of the trees.

Bwark! The roc screamed its fury.

I shuddered, adrenaline coursing through me.

A moment later, a pickup truck slowed—the driver likely concerned by the giant bird swooping above us. I took a deep, steadying breath and ran like hell.

The warm concrete was rough on my feet, but I hurtled down the narrow entrance to Cates Landing. Ahead, the portal glowed welcomingly—no one was currently crossing between realms. I breathed a mental sigh of relief. It would really suck if someone crossed straight into the roc's claws.

Glancing over my shoulder, I grinned at the bird. It screamed at me, intelligent enough to understand I was taunting it.

The roc spiraled through the air toward me, and I somehow picked up speed. The portal loomed closer, closer, closer.

I threw myself to the side, rolling on the hard pavement. The roc screeched and thrust its wings out wide, attempting to slow its trajectory.

I focused, lifted one hand, and gave the wind a little help. The roc sailed through the portal. The knot of anxiety in my chest unraveled until I could finally take a full breath.

I groaned as I got to my feet.

My knee was scraped, bleeding enough that it had stained my dress. My feet were bruised, and stabbing pain shot through my wrist when I bent it.

Not a break, but it was definitely sprained. A little pain charm would fix that right up.

I glanced around at what had once been a luxury development for humans. When the portals first opened over seventy years ago, those humans suddenly became neighbors to the seelie realm.

House prices bottomed out, humans fled, and the only people who came to this area now were those who were planning to cross into the seelie realm.

I limped back to the golf course, letting out the occasional whimper since I was sure no one could hear me.

The human guy was pacing the parking lot, my purse clutched in his hand.

"You're alive," he blurted out. He snapped his mouth shut, and his cheeks flushed.

I grinned at him. He was cute. Geeky, but cute. I held out my hand for my purse, and he hurried toward me.

"I have your shoes too. Do you need a doctor? You're bleeding."

"I'll be fine. I have something that should do the trick."

That something was a low-level pain charm. He frowned, and I saw the moment he realized a normal human wouldn't have gotten involved with a paranormal creature.

He gazed at me and flinched as he put two and two together. He gave me a stiff nod and backed away as if I were contagious. I sighed, dug through my purse, and found my keys.

I should've been used to it by now, but never fitting in anywhere… It got old.

It was approximately three thousand degrees inside my car, and I turned the key, desperate for some cool air. My hand shook from leftover adrenaline as I pulled out my phone and called Detective Nelson.

Technically, this wasn't my kind of job. But Nelson had gotten in touch when one of his officers called him, screaming about the giant bird. Since Nelson had helped me with a recent case, ensuring we saved a pregnant light fae woman—and Kyla, Meredith, and I each receiving a hundred thousand dollars for our efforts—I owed him.

"It's done," I said when he picked up.

"Already? Good work. Where's the body?"

I sniffed. "I didn't kill it."

Silence. "Please tell me it's not hunting anyone else."

"Relax. I took care of the problem."

"How, Evie?"

"I sent it straight through the seelie portal."

Nelson laughed. "Evil. Thanks. I owe you."

My people were currently at war with the light fae. Their king had betrayed us, almost causing the deaths of everyone I loved. As far as I was concerned, the seelie had it coming.

By the time we ended the call, my car was cooling down, and I pulled out of the parking lot, heading back toward my office.

Technically, it was my sister's office, but since Danica was ruling the underworld for the foreseeable future, I'd convinced her to let me take over.

I pulled into the strip mall off East Main Street. The office was bracketed by a ballet school and an insurance firm, and one of the assholes from the insurance firm kept stealing my spot. I ground my teeth and waited for one of the ballet moms to pull out.

I let out a single pained moan as I got out of the car. Sitting down had made me stiffen up. Kyla opened the office door and took me in with a wince.

"The giant bird went that well, huh?"

"Should've just shot it," I muttered. She grinned at me and opened the door wider.

The werewolf was dressed in her usual uniform of leggings and a tank top, the mint color of the tank making her smooth brown skin glow.

Her light blue eyes gleamed in amusement as I riffled through my desk drawer. Those icy blue eyes were bleakly beautiful—and a constant reminder that she hadn't regained full control over her wolf.

Her eyes had been darker once, before she was imprisoned in the underworld, trapped in her wolf form.

When not even her Alpha had been able to bring her back, only a bargain with the unseelie king had allowed her to take back her human form. She still wasn't herself. She was doing better, though.

"Found it." I activated the pain charm and sank into my desk chair with a relieved breath. "Anything new?"

"Yes, actually," Kyla preened, and I sat up straighter. So far, we'd solved one case between us. Two, if you counted the roc. If this business was going to succeed, we had to do better than that.

"What is it?"

"A dark fae woman named Callula got in touch yesterday. She said she's looking for an important book that was stolen a few weeks ago. Knowing the fae, it's likely powerful. I got the impression Callula wasn't all that hopeful we'd be able to find it."

"We'll just have to prove her wrong. Where was it stolen from?"

"A silent auction. Callula brought it from her realm to sell it. But it was stolen at some point before the auction even started. Along with several other artifacts."

"Dark fae artifacts floating around the black market. Awesome."

"Exactly. We find the book, and we'll probably find the other artifacts too. I'm going to go interview Callula this afternoon."

"Let me know if you need any help." I turned my attention to the whiteboard, which we were using for my main project—finding the leaders of Humans for Equality—the people who'd killed my mother.

I'd already started the timeline of events.

Mom meets Lucifer's son. She has no idea the underking is his father. Gets pregnant with Danica. Learns Lucifer will kill Danica if he finds out about her. Begins hunting Black Books to take Lucifer down.

Mom leaves Danica with friends. Lured to HFE lab by promise of Black Books. Kidnapped. Gets pregnant with me. My father helps her escape.

Mom goes to Gemma's coven for safety.

Gemma's coven places a spell on me, tying me to their house.

I took a deep, shaky breath. I hadn't known it at the time, but Mom had left me to keep me safe. The coven had tied my power to their home, shielding me from Humans for Equality. Because those bigots would have loved to get their hands on one of the babies they'd created in that lab.

The problem? The spell required me to spend most of my time in that house. And it had changed my personality, turning me into a homebody. I'd had no real goals. No passions. I'd worked part time at various random jobs and never really noticed that my life was passing me by. It wasn't until the house burned down that I became *me* again.

"Are you okay?" Kyla asked, her gaze also on the whiteboard.

"Yeah." I had my own apartment now. It wasn't fancy, but it was mine. I made my own decisions. My own mistakes. And *nothing* influenced me.

I got to my feet, wrote *Danica and Mom leave,* and attempted to ignore the way my gut still twisted at the memory.

Mom returns to Durham. Murdered.

Danica returns to hunt murderers.

Danica bonds with Samael.

Coven burned to the ground. Witches slaughtered.

Seven words. And I felt like I'd been stabbed in the chest. Behind me, Kyla was silent.

My coven was targeted, because of me. My best friend was dead, because of me. My family was burned alive, because of me.

Because Humans for Equality had found me.

My phone buzzed, and I forced myself to step

away from the whiteboard.

"Hello?"

"Hello, Evelyn," a deep male voice said, and I raised an eyebrow at Kyla. Why exactly was her Alpha calling me? She gave me an I-have-no-idea shrug. I didn't bother putting the phone on speaker. She'd likely be able to hear both sides of the conversation from the parking lot.

"Are you looking for Kyla?"

"No."

I mirrored Kyla's shrug. I had no idea why her Alpha would be calling me, but I was officially intrigued.

"What can I do for you, Nathaniel?"

"I may have a task for you."

"A task, huh? What kind of task?"

"A well-paying task."

I narrowed my eyes. "Is this a pity job?" I wouldn't put it past the Alpha to get involved with Kyla's workplace. Dominant wolves couldn't help themselves, and they didn't come much more dominant than Nathaniel.

"No," he growled, and I grinned. Good to know I could still frustrate even the legendarily patient Alpha. Kyla shook her head at me.

"Okay, then. What do you need?"

"Meet me in my territory. It will be easier to explain there."

"Sure. Give me twenty minutes."

I ended the call and raised my eyebrow at Kyla. "Any idea what that's about?"

I caught a flash of something I didn't recognize in her eyes, but it was gone before I could ponder it. "Nope. Let me know how it goes. I better get going." She hauled her files into her arms and strolled out the door.

I was vain enough to detour to the small bathroom in our office, so I could wash some of the blood and dirt off my dress. My ex-boyfriend Liam was a werewolf, and knowing my luck, I'd run into him while I was looking like something the cat dragged in.

I bandaged my scrapes and sighed as I attempted to wrestle my blond curls into submission. It had taken me a long time to get to a place where I'd accepted my hair, but that didn't make it easier when I was running late and it was…misbehaving.

When it was dry out, strands stuck to my face like a disbelieving ex after a breakup. When it was wet, it kinked up so much it needed its own safeword. It was rare that it was anywhere between the two extremes, unless I jumped through several magical hoops. And I was out of one of those hoops.

I finally shoved my hair back in another *very* messy bun. Liam and I were over. It had been fun while it lasted, but…

"Put it away," I muttered to myself. I checked my weapons and locked the office door behind me.

The wolves lived on the edge of Duke Forest,

and I'd always loved the drive. My sister had made the mistake of visiting without an invitation once, and we'd ended up in a standoff with one of the sentries. When it came to protecting their territory, the wolves did not fuck around.

This time, a long howl sounded as I turned right onto Cornwallis Road. I took another right and slowed to take in a brand-new sign.

Wolf territory. Trespassers will be killed on sight.

"Jeez, Nathaniel..."

I turned right yet again, slowing my speed further, just in case the wolves decided to rescind their invitation.

When that didn't happen, I shrugged and put my foot down. The houses out here were mostly hidden by the forest. Still, I caught glimpses of the occasional home that peeked out of the trees.

Nathaniel lived at the end of one of the cul-de-sacs at the edge of wolf territory. It was as if he was the final stop before visitors could get near his people. His home was huge, and yet it somehow seemed like it was part of the forest too.

Nathaniel's house was set on a gentle hill—high enough that it seemed to meld into the forest around it. The walls were actually floor-to-ceiling windows—the glass tinted dark enough that no one could see in—and the curves and lines of his home blended seamlessly with the forest surrounding it. You could sit in Nathaniel's living room and practically be within the forest, the glass windows the only separation between the wolves' two worlds.

The wolves were predatory, paranoid, and private. They kept to themselves for the most part, but many of them had been cops, firefighters, and enlisted military before they'd been turned. That superhero gene tended to pop up when the wolves came across humans in danger.

Not that most humans appreciated it.

Nathaniel must've been told I'd arrived, because he was waiting for me outside his house. I opened my door and took him in.

The Alpha was a big guy, with shoulders like a linebacker. His hair was a deep brown and cropped close to his head, while his eyes were a dark blue. He stood statue-still, and when he moved, it was with predatory grace.

Those eyes lightened slightly as he ran his gaze down me. It wasn't sexual. The Alpha wasn't happy about my ripped dress, and he could likely smell blood from my scrapes. I placed my hands on my hips and waited for him to get a hold of himself.

The corner of his mouth lifted as if he was reading my mind.

"Evelyn." He was the only one who insisted on calling me by my full name. I narrowed my eyes at him.

"Nathaniel."

"Let's talk inside."

I followed him along the path toward his open

front door. I'd never admit it to Nathaniel, but I'd always had a big, fat crush on his house, with its swaths of glass, weathered wood, and stunning forest views.

The wide-open door welcomed me like a long-lost lover, and I stepped inside, inhaling the scent of chocolate chip cookies. One day, I'd own a house just like this.

Tobias stepped into the entranceway and beamed at me. Technically, he worked for Nathaniel in a butler-like role. All I knew was the submissive wolf managed to wrangle unhappy dominant Alphas, while ensuring Nathaniel stayed on schedule. He'd recently stayed at the demon's tower, and his cookies were so good, the demons had not-so-jokingly considered kidnapping him.

"Tobias." I grinned back at him.

"It's good to see you again, Evelyn."

I scowled. "Evie, please. Nate here just calls me that to annoy me."

Tobias lifted his eyebrow at "Nate," but humor danced in his eyes.

"Of course, Evie." His eyes gleamed at me. "Cookie?"

My mouth immediately started watering. A Pavlovian response, thanks to all the cookies he'd fed me when my sister was missing. I baked when I was stressed, but nothing I'd ever made came close to Tobias's chocolate chip cookies.

"I'll never say no to your food," I said.

He grinned at me and disappeared. Nathaniel took my arm and led me into a sitting room off the entranceway. The furniture was classy, obviously antique, and I took the sofa by the window, while Nathaniel sat in a chair that had likely been reinforced to take his bulk.

The last time I was in this room, Nathaniel scented something *wrong* with my scent. That had been awkward as hell when Liam watched his Alpha sniff at my neck. It was shortly after the coven's house had burned down. Once the spell connecting me to the house was gone, Nathaniel's superior senses had helped us find a tracking chip HFE had placed in my neck. The house had hidden my location from those paranormal-hating fuckers, and we'd managed to remove the chip.

I had no doubt that HFE knew where I was. But they'd get what was coming to them.

"Your wrist is swollen," Nathaniel said, and I blinked, pulling my attention back to the present.

My eyes dropped to my hand, sitting in my lap. Sure enough, it was a little swollen. That Alpha attention to detail at work.

"I have a pain charm," I murmured.

"It needs ice."

"It's *fine*."

We stared at each other, neither of us relenting. Finally, Nathaniel shook his head at me. Obviously, he'd decided to let it go. Smart man.

"So," I said. "What exactly are you hoping I can help you with?"

"I have a small problem with some of my juvenile pack members."

Ooh. I'd never seen any of the pack kids. The wolves kept them tucked away where they couldn't be targeted by either paranormals or humans.

"What kind of problem?"

"A group of them keep disappearing. They say they're going to their secret clubhouse, but their scents disappear."

I frowned at him. This was sounding more and more like charity. Sure, Kyla and I were new to investigations, but we didn't need the Alpha to hire us for meaningless work.

"You're their Alpha. Can't you just order them to tell you?"

Nathaniel frowned, shifting his attention to the window. "I could," he said thoughtfully. "I could make all of them drop to their knees and tell me anything I wanted to know."

My chest clenched. "But that would make them scared of you."

"Yes. I don't want a pack of slaves."

My estimation of Nathaniel increased several points.

"What about their parents?"

He stretched out his long legs. "Some of the older kids are currently being looked after by pack members.

Their parents are patrolling our borders. But it's not their job to deal with this. It's mine."

Tobias appeared with a glass of orange juice and a plate of cookies.

"Vitamins," he told me, tapping on the side of the glass. I couldn't help but smile.

"Thank you."

"And where are my cookies?" Nathaniel gave a mock growl.

Tobias rolled his eyes at him. "You've had more than enough cookies today." He turned and wandered off, and I grinned at Nathaniel.

"If you're nice to me, I'll share my cookies."

His eyes darkened, and I went still. Had I just... flirted with him?

"I'll be *nice*," he purred.

My heart tripped, my stomach swooped, and I stared at the werewolf Alpha.

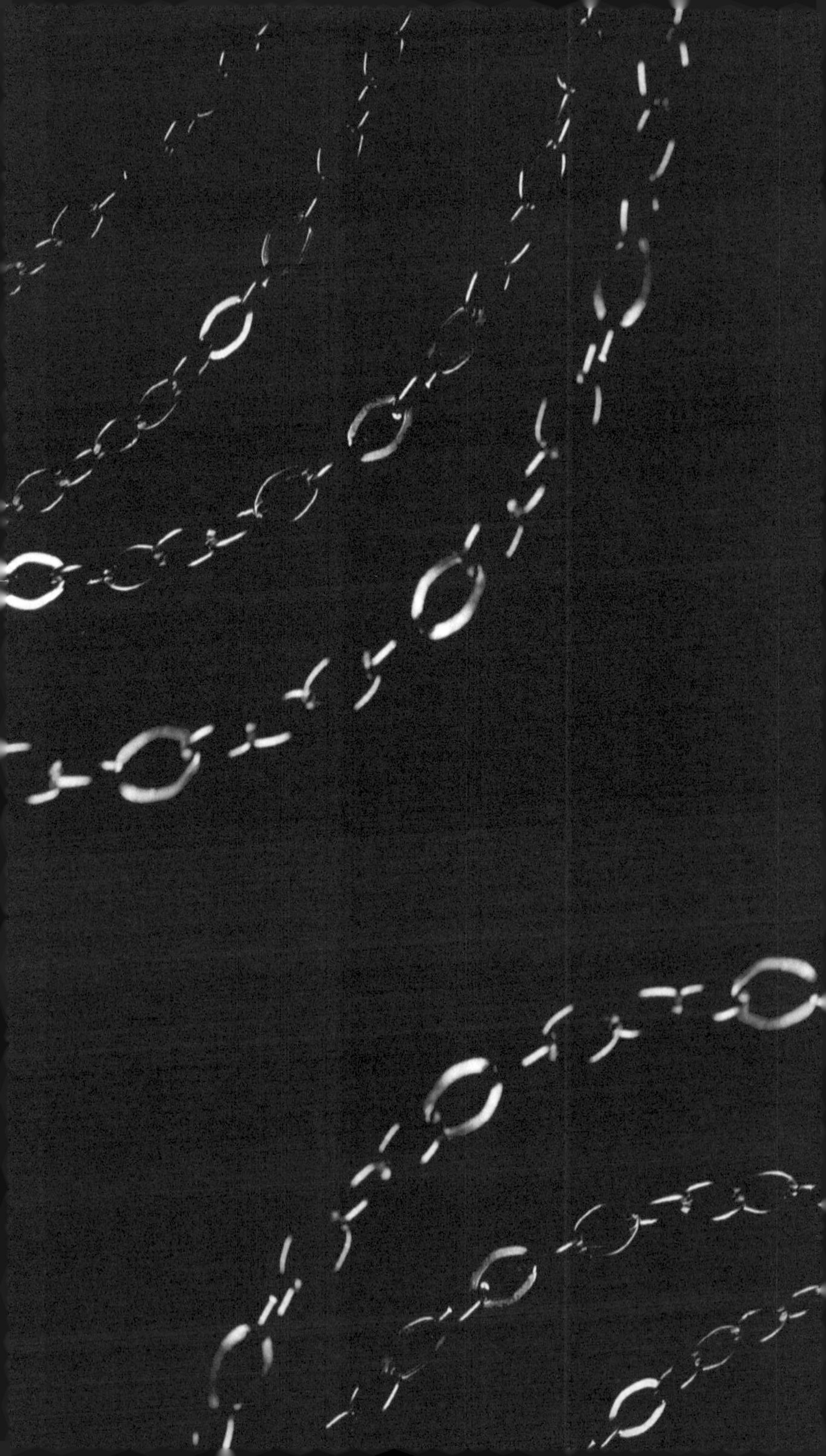

2

EVIE

My tongue was stuck to the roof of my mouth. I took a sip of orange juice while Nathaniel eyed me like *I* was the snack.

"Mine," I told him finally, pulling the plate into my lap.

The air turned thick, and I groped for something—anything—else to say.

"The parents," I got out.

Nathaniel nodded, the humor in his eyes disappearing.

"Three of my wolves were recently killed in fights with feral wolves. There has been an uptick in ferals on the outskirts of my territory. My pack is in mourning."

His expression turned bleak, and I stretched out my plate, offering him a cookie. His mouth quirked, and he shook his head.

"So you want me to figure out where the kids are going?"

"Yes. Hiring an outsider shows them I respect them enough to need help. Choosing not to order them to tell me shows I value their autonomy. But I need to know what they're up to."

"Do you really?"

He angled his head, and I took a deep breath. "If the kids are just hanging out..."

"They haven't gotten into trouble yet, but some of the younger kids have been following them around. It's only a matter of time before one of them gets hurt."

"Okay. I'll help."

Nathaniel nodded, as if he hadn't expected different. I got to my feet.

Tobias appeared, a plastic food baggie in his hand. He took the plate of cookies from me and disappeared. When he reappeared, there were even more cookies in the bag. "Kyla will want to share," he told me.

I leaned over and gave him a peck on the cheek. "Thank you."

I followed Nathaniel outside, along the path winding behind his house, and deeper into the forest.

We walked among towering trees, their wide trunks anchored to the ground with roots that could trip a city girl if she wasn't careful. I kept my gaze on the spongy forest floor, crunching over dried leaves and rotting logs as the wind whispered overhead. A bird screeched nearby, and I jumped.

Nathaniel sent me an amused look. "Out of your comfort zone?"

"Is it that obvious?"

Within a couple of minutes, we arrived in a huge clearing. It was surrounded by a ring of trees that were like living fence posts, a clear boundary between the wolves' day-to-day space and the forest itself. The air was heavy with the scent of greenery, and I took a huge breath, taking in the cabins. I'd been here before. One of those cabins had been a temporary home to my sister's bondmate while he lay slowly turning to ash.

And I hadn't been here.

I pushed that thought away. Now was not the time to get lost in guilt. Especially since the control freak Alpha next to me would be able to smell it.

I'd been here a few times before that too, while I was dating Liam. The pack had a cabin that could be reserved for non-wolves with approval from the Alpha, and I carefully avoided looking at that cabin as Nathaniel continued walking across the clearing.

I followed him along another narrow path. My skin prickled as I felt eyes on me, and I resisted the urge to raise a ward. I risked offending the Alpha, who was guaranteeing my safety by taking me deeper into his territory. Besides, no one would dare attack without his permission.

The constant surveillance still felt like an itch I couldn't scratch.

Nathaniel led me through a break in the trees, and my mouth dropped open.

"Wow."

It was a...neighborhood. Except it blended in seamlessly with the surrounding forest. No cars, but I spotted a café, a tiny convenience store, a huge playground, a long wooden building that looked like some kind of meeting hall, and more houses than I could count.

"While many of my wolves live on the outskirts of our territory, most people with families choose to live here. Where it's safer."

"This is incredible," I murmured. Some of the tightness disappeared from around Nathaniel's eyes.

"You have my permission to talk to anyone you need to. Everyone in my pack has been instructed to give you full access. See if you can get anything out of the kids."

I chewed on my lower lip. "I'm not that great with kids."

He merely shrugged. "You'll learn."

Nathaniel glanced at his phone, and his expression hardened. "I need to go. Spend as much time here as you need."

"Thanks."

He prowled away, and I took in the pack members who were going about their business. A group of human women was standing outside the coffee shop, cups in their hands as they chatted. These were the mates of the male werewolves, and the heart of the pack. I waved at them, attempting to show them I meant no threat. They fell silent as I passed, and I wandered down the narrow path.

A few kids shrieked and laughed as they ran around in the massive playground. I walked past it for now, continuing my walk. The path stretched out between more trees, before opening to another clearing where several more houses were nestled in the forest. This continued again and again. I'd never realized just how big Nathaniel's pack was.

A mile or so later, I came across a man-made lake. The water looked cool and inviting, and I wished I could take a swim.

Something rustled in the leaves a few feet away, and I went still. The hair on the back of my neck lifted, and I turned, my eyes meeting cold blue.

The wolf was gray, with a long stripe along its back. It was crouched as if readying itself to leap, and I pulled up a ward. It snarled at me, likely feeling the magic.

"I'm not here to cause any harm," I told it.

It merely stared at me some more. I swallowed and backed away, keeping my gaze on its face.

It snarled once more, this time enraged, and I sucked in a breath. Wolves saw eye contact as a challenge. For most people, dropping their gaze was instinct. My power gave me a leg up when it came to dominance games, but it meant I had to *make* myself play those games. I ground my teeth, and it took everything in me to slowly drop my gaze.

When I risked another glance, the wolf had

disappeared.

I strode back down the path toward the coffee shop. The Asian American woman behind the counter kept watching me curiously as she made my latte.

"I'm Evie," I introduced myself.

She smiled. "I'm Josephine. But you can call me Jo. Settling in?"

I couldn't help but laugh. "I thought I was about to be lunch."

She popped a lid on my latte and handed it to me. "No one would disobey Nathaniel. Especially on this. But people are curious."

"Do *you* know what the kids are up to?"

She shook her head. "Nope. And one of those little devils is mine." She grinned. "His name is Hugh, and you'll likely see him shadowing the older kids."

"Have you asked him what they're doing?"

"Of course. He wouldn't tell me. But he knows he can come to me whenever he needs me. Nathaniel said we can let this play out. Kids who grow up in the pack are a little different from most human kids. They see things... Well, let's just say most human kids don't watch their parents going furry."

"Aren't you worried about their safety?"

"Yes and no. We don't believe in helicoptering our kids. We know they'll get in trouble, but they'll never learn if we're continually there to pick them up when they fall down."

It made a lot of sense. "What would happen if you

guys knew without a doubt the kids were in danger?"

"We'd step in. And if the kids didn't talk to us, Nathaniel would make them tell him what was going on." Sadness crossed her face. "None of us wants that for him."

"Thanks for talking to me. Any tips for talking to the kids?"

"Don't be too eager. You have magic, which they don't see often. Let them come to you."

"I'd been planning to hunt them down and annoy them until they told me what they were up to. Your plan is better." I took a sip of my latte. "This is great."

"Thanks, good luck."

I stepped out of the coffee shop and wandered back toward the playground. Let them come to me, huh?

I sat on one of the swings, kicked off with my feet, and waited for my latte to cool. Across the playground, a group of young girls eyed me suspiciously.

I had a feeling this was going to take a while.

NATHANIEL

I glowered at the massacre in front of me. A family reunion. That's what these humans had been celebrating today.

Now, most of the members of that family were lying in pieces, organs strewn across the ground like carelessly tossed pieces of fruit. The stench of blood and viscera was overpowering, coating the air in a dense fog of death.

I took a deep breath, attempting to scent who had done this. Nothing.

Either too many people had wandered through the scene, or the murderers had managed to cover up their scents.

"What do you think, boss?" Ryker stood next to me, fury written all over his face as he stared at the bodies. "You think it's Frederik's pack?"

I glanced down. The ground was soaked with blood, the mud thick and tacky. The family had decided to have their reunion in a public park.

"I think too many people have wandered through here and I can't catch any familiar scents."

He nodded. "If I wanted to kill humans in the messiest way possible, and make it look like ferals were responsible, I'd find a way to remove any scents too. But what would Frederik be hoping to achieve with this?"

I scented a strange human and turned, right as a camera flashed. I narrowed my eyes at the woman. She was dressed in a pantsuit, her sleek red hair pulled back in a bun.

"*That's* what they're hoping to achieve," Hunter growled, stalking toward us. "What do you want to bet that reporter was personally invited to this little scene?"

Bad press. This many humans dead for a power play? Frederik had been slowly attempting to take parts of my territory. He'd been turned when the portals were first opened—just as I was—and he'd never reconciled the notoriety I'd received after I managed to make the rampaging wolves fall in line. Jealousy was a stupid reason to go to war, and yet Frederik had never been the smartest. But he was an idiot if he was hoping to make the humans turn on my pack in favor of his own. Humans wouldn't differentiate between packs of wolves.

One monster was the same as any other.

I stepped farther away from the reporter, gesturing for Hunter and Ryker to do the same. My wolf didn't like conceding territory to the reporter, but I couldn't risk her overhearing us.

"Any witnesses?" I asked, and Ryker shook his head. "We need to find out what the cops know. We can formally request the information, but we all know they'll delay it, releasing only what they have to."

"Your suggestion?"

He gave a languid shrug. "The demons have a human they use for this kind of thing. I met him when we were at the tower. Steve. He's hacked their systems more times than you can imagine."

I scowled at the idea of using one of Samael's people. Sure, our fates were tied together now that we were officially allies, but I didn't want any more ties than necessary.

Still, Todd—our own hacker—had recently relocated to San Diego with his husband. We needed the tech skills.

"Send a message to the demon king," I said. "Let's see if Samael's hacker can help us get our hands on the information without a request."

I took one last glance at the slaughter in front of me and gritted my teeth. "This is just the first," I said, and Hunter's eyes widened.

"Why do you think that?"

"Gut instinct."

He nodded. None of us ignored those instincts. "I'll keep you updated, boss."

"Alpha? A minute of your time?"

I ignored the reporter, sliding my sunglasses on as she continued taking pictures. I didn't need her getting a picture of me with my wolf staring back at her.

I heard her low curse as I slipped into my car. I had no time for those who would use the death of innocents for their own purposes.

My mind was only half on the drive back to my territory. Seeing Evie this morning had been… interesting. It still fascinated me, how she could keep her sense of humor after everything she'd been through.

Just months ago, most of her coven was slaughtered. The murderers mistook Evie's best friend for her—and killed her brutally.

Evie hadn't even had a chance to mourn before the remaining coven members had decided that, since she was the one who'd been targeted, she was too dangerous to have around. So they'd kicked Evie out.

Around the same time, she'd discovered exactly why she was targeted. Before Evie was born, her mother had been kidnapped by a human hate group and impregnated with Evie. She still had no idea what exactly she was, but her power felt like a mixture of several different factions—the scent changing depending on the magic she used.

No one would blame her for turning bitter and angry. But Evie refused.

I forced myself to push thoughts of her away as I parked outside of my house, preparing for a meeting in my home office.

Men like me—monsters who ruled other monsters—had no business thinking about fragile, *powerful,* curly-haired women with sharp tongues and a scent like sunshine.

And yet I couldn't seem to stay away from her. I wasn't a man who enjoyed lying to himself, but in my worst moments, I tried to convince the wolf inside me that we simply wanted to protect her. Because whoever had slaughtered her coven now knew where she lived, and independent Evie insisted on living alone.

The wolf refused to be convinced.

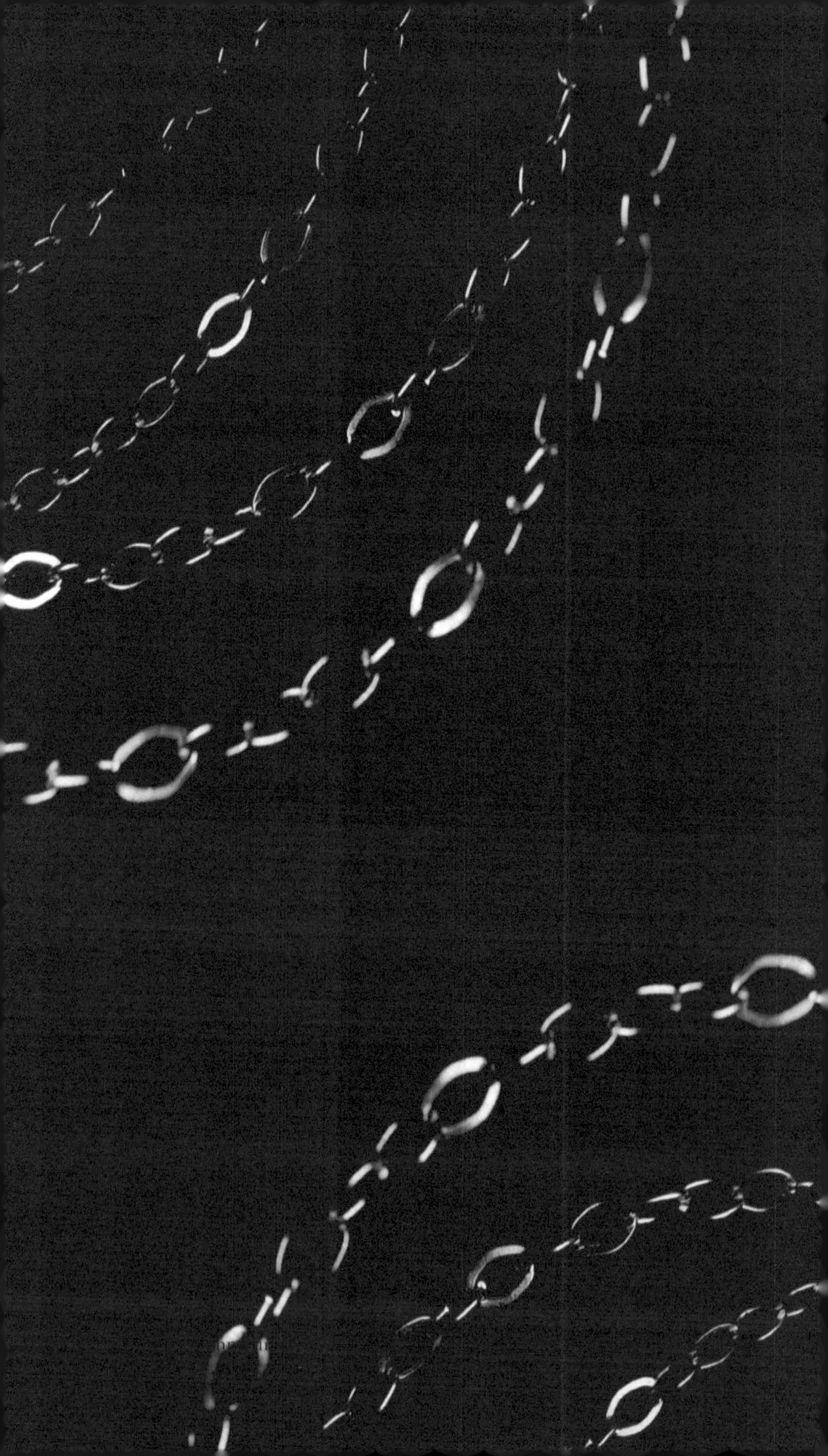

3

EVIE

"**L**et them come to me," I muttered as I started my car. "Yeah, right."

The kids had watched me from a distance for a while, then changed tactics and studiously ignored me. I'd resisted the urge to question them, but it was obvious I needed a new plan.

My phone buzzed, and I glanced down at it. Kyla.

Would love your opinion on the auction if you're finished for the day.

I messaged her back.

I'll be right there.

I mulled over my options as I drove down West Cornwallis Road. I took a left onto South Roxboro Street and followed it all the way back to Main Street, where it became North Roxboro Street. The building on the corner of Roxboro and Liberty had once been the Durham County Library. I'd seen pictures of the old building, with its sleek lines and large outdoor terrace.

When the portals opened, it was one of the first buildings to suffer catastrophic damage. A group of humans had stormed the building, where a group of lesser fae had been hiding. They slaughtered the goblins, who fought back, killing some of the humans.

Rumors were the building was cursed. Each time it was bought, the owners had possession of it for less than a few years before some calamity occurred. Floods, fires, a ward spell that had backfired, even a gas explosion. This building had seen it all.

I parked in the car park on Liberty Street and surveyed the building as I walked toward it. Kyla was waiting outside, sitting on the front steps with her face angled up to the sun.

"They ran the auction here?" I asked her.

She got to her feet. "Yeah. Some human billionaire bought the place a few years ago. He hires it out for paranormal events. Maybe he figures that'll help him dodge the curse."

I eyed her. "You don't really believe it's cursed, do you?"

A languid shrug. "Who knows better than us that there are some things that just can't be explained?"

She had a point.

"How did it go with Callula?"

Kyla scowled. "You ever meet someone who just seems beaten down by life? She lives in the unseelie realm, so she must have a decent amount of power, and yet she walked with her head down, eyes on the ground, as if she was expecting me to kick her."

I shook my head. "Someone's done a number on her."

"They have." Kyla cracked her knuckles. "And I'm going to find out who."

We walked through the sliding doors and into the lobby. Was I imagining the bleak atmosphere of the building?

"Can I help you?"

Kyla nodded. "Are you Elizabeth?"

"That's right. You must be Kyla." Elizabeth strode toward us on heels so high, my toes curled in sympathy.

She wore a sharp suit the color of cherries and a wide smile that looked pasted on.

"This is my colleague, Evie Amana," Kyla said. "We were hoping to get a look at the room where the items for sale were kept."

Elizabeth's smile dimmed slightly, but she waved her hand, gesturing for us to follow her.

"Of course. I've been working for this auction house for seven years, and I've never seen something like this happen. It's just terrible."

She continued chatting, and I tuned her out as I took in the glass windows and the wide, wood-stained steps. Elizabeth led us up the steps, and I counted off the security cameras in each corner of the room.

Tech could easily be fouled with magic. My friend

Meredith could do it with the blink of an eye, although she was somewhat of an exception. But even without the help of a tech witch, there were plenty of spells that could temporarily shut down the cameras.

"This is where the items for sale were kept before the auction," Elizabeth chirped as we stepped into a room the size of an auditorium. Long tables crossed over the center of the room, still holding a variety of human and paranormal treasures.

"The auction didn't go ahead?"

"No. After some of the items were stolen, we canceled the auction. Some of our patrons demanded their items back, no longer willing to trust our security. Others agreed to a later auction date after we slashed our fees. We've stepped up security as well."

"We're going to need a list of the other objects that were taken," I said.

"Of course."

I wandered down the long tables, stopping to gaze at a painting that was so lifelike, it could only have been painted in a fae realm. I felt as if I could step into it and dive into that pool, surrounded by an inviting forest.

From my experience with the inviting forest in the light fae realm, it was gleefully murderous.

I turned my attention back to Elizabeth. Kyla was prowling around the room, examining the remaining items. "Were the stolen pieces the most valuable items?"

"No." Elizabeth trailed one hand over a necklace that sparkled under the lights. "Take this, for example. It was right next to the book you were hired to find. Considering the rarity of underworld gems, many would consider this necklace to be almost priceless. And yet they left this and took the dusty old book next to it."

Insider knowledge. I glanced at Kyla and could see she'd reached the same conclusion. They'd had buyers lined up for everything they'd stolen.

"That dusty old book is my family heirloom," a low voice said, and we all whirled.

The dark fae king stood in the doorway, hands on his hips and wrath in his eyes.

Next to me, Kyla practically vibrated with tension. She glowered back at the king, and I couldn't blame her.

This was the man responsible for her most pressing problems. Unfortunately, he was also responsible for saving her life.

"Your—Your Majesty," Elizabeth stuttered.

"Silence," Finvarra said, striding toward us. He moved like a panther, and his eyes glowed bronze in his beautiful face. His dark hair was shorter than the last time I'd seen it, displaying sharply pointed ears. He didn't need his crown, and I'd never seen him wear it. No one who looked at him would have any doubt that he was a royal, powerful son of a bitch.

"What are you doing here?" Kyla asked, her voice carefully bored.

"The book that was stolen, the one you have been tasked with finding, has been in my family for centuries."

"How'd you lose it, then?" I asked.

He slowly turned his head. If my sister weren't mated to the new underking, I'd probably piss my pants. But I'd dealt with a number of over-powered males in the past year.

"I didn't—as you so succinctly put it—lose it. The book was tucked away in one of my estates. My cousin has fallen on some hard times after becoming involved with the wrong kinds of people. Evidently, she has decided to steal and sell anything she can find."

I swallowed. "Family, amirite?"

Finvarra just stared at me. I swallowed. "This is the same cousin who hired Kyla?"

"Callula?" Kyla asked, and Finvarra gave one nod.

"When you find the book, you will deliver it to me," he said. "*I* will deal with my cousin."

"Nope," Kyla said. "I have a signed contract stating I need to give it to Callula. Contracts take priority over your orders." She smiled sweetly.

Finvarra went very still. Elizabeth unfroze and began to back out of the room. I couldn't blame her.

The temperature dropped several degrees. "My cousin is a criminal," Finvarra said. "Earlier today, when she heard I was looking for her, she traveled to the middleground."

I winced. The middleground was dangerous as

hell and had always been the number one hiding place for creatures who were fleeing their realms.

And yet I couldn't blame Callula. Finvarra wasn't someone you disobeyed unless you had a death wish.

Or unless you were Kyla Hill.

She stared at him, icy eyes narrowed, hands on her hips.

He stared back, expression impassive with the knowledge that it was only a matter of time before she fell in line.

I saw her make the calculations. If her client had fled, the contract was no longer enforceable. Besides, the fae populations didn't live under a democracy. Finvarra could override any contract he chose.

Kyla would still make him pay for it, though.

"Since my client is no longer here, and it appears she won't be paying our fee, our business is concluded," Kyla said.

"And so you'd like to bargain." Finvarra raised one eyebrow. My heart thumped faster.

A few months ago, Kyla had made a deal with Finvarra. He'd been displeased when Danica bargained with his enemy—Taraghlan, the seelie king. When Samael was cursed by the Spell of Three, Danica and Kyla had given Taraghlan a sword in return for a cure.

Unfortunately, it wasn't just any sword. Taraghlan now owned the only sword with the ability to kill his greatest enemy...Finvarra.

On the brink of war, with Samael out of

commission and Danica desperately trying to save him, Kyla made a bargain of her own. She had six months to steal the sword from the light fae king and give it to Finvarra.

Of course, that was months ago. We still had no idea how the hell we were going to break in to Taraghlan's castle and steal a sword he'd been hunting for centuries. But if we didn't, Kyla had to leave her pack and join Finvarra's people.

Why that was part of the deal, I had no idea. There was no love lost between Nathaniel and the unseelie king. It was likely just another power play for a man who'd been around for centuries.

"You're damn right, I want to bargain," Kyla said. "I want an extra six months to get you the sword. In return, I'll find this book for you."

Finvarra laughed. It was the first time I'd seen true amusement on his face. Kyla looked like she'd been sucker-punched at the sound, but she recovered quickly, smoothing her expression into grim neutrality.

"The book is nowhere near that valuable to me," Finvarra said. "The sword remains my highest priority."

"I bet you don't want that book floating around where any criminal from any faction can find it, though," I pointed out.

He nodded. "Correct. I will give you two weeks longer to complete your task."

"Two months," Kyla countered.

"One month, and that is my final offer."

"Fine."

Finvarra gave her a slow smile. Kyla smiled back, but her teeth had sharpened. Her claws popped out, and all amusement instantly disappeared from Finvarra's face.

"How," he said softly, "do you expect to succeed at something as important as stealing my sword when you cannot even control your own form?"

Kyla went still. Her eyes flashed. Then she slowly angled her head in a way that was all wolf.

"Kyla," I murmured, and she glanced at me.

With a stiff nod, she stalked out of the room. The sheer willpower it must have taken her to turn her back on Finvarra...

Fury overrode any sense of reason. "*You* are the reason she's fighting for control," I snapped. "If Kyla goes feral for real, it will be because of you!"

"I saved her life."

"Yeah, for your *bargain*," I sneered. "Don't pretend you actually give a shit about her. She'll get you your sword, and she'll probably end up dead in the process. Not that you'd care."

"You know nothing, witch."

If he thought I was just a witch, *he* was the one who knew nothing.

He stalked toward the door, and I took a deep, shaky breath. By the time I followed him out of the room, he'd disappeared.

EVIE

Mere's bar was the only bar in Durham that was considered to be neutral territory. It was also the only place where you'd see werewolves, light fae, dark fae, witches, and mages all drinking together, with the occasional brave—or dumb—human dotted among the crowd.

You started shit at Meredith's, and you dealt with a crowd of pissed-off paranormals who were out for blood. That was if her demon bondmate didn't get to you first.

I parked on one of the side streets and hoofed it to Mere's. Kyla had said she'd meet me there, and after today, she'd be more than ready for a strong drink.

I glanced around, noting the group of mages loitering on the street outside Meredith's. They carefully avoided my gaze, and I memorized their faces.

The mages had once been one of the most powerful factions in Durham—thanks to Samael allowing them to go about their business. That was no longer the case.

"Evie."

Vas slung his arm around my shoulders and gave the mages a wide smile. They backed away.

I hadn't heard Vas drop from the sky, and I scowled. He reached up to ruffle my curls, and his hand hit my ward. A ward I'd created just for the demon who enjoyed messing up my hair.

"You're no fun," he said, dropping his hand and opening the door. We stepped inside. It was early enough that the music wasn't yet earsplitting, and we both wandered toward the bar, dodging a group of goblins arguing about politics, a trio of black witches likely up to no good, and a few werewolves I recognized.

I ignored the goblins, glowered at the black witches, and waved at the werewolves.

Mere was behind the bar, pouring a pint for a couple of high demons. Vas slapped one of them on the back and circled the bar, pulling Mere to him for a lusty kiss.

"Get a room," someone called, and Vas raised his hand, middle finger stabbing toward the sky as he laughed against Mere's mouth.

Orin, her light fae bartender, rolled his eyes and waved a hand, using his power to pour thimble-sized drinks for a group of pixies. The seelie was hot, in the almost-pretty way of the light fae.

"Evie." He nodded at me since Mere was still busy fending off Vas's roaming hands. "Drink?"

"Surprise me." I grinned at him.

He grinned back. "Staying out of trouble?"

"Now that would be boring."

I watched as he flipped a couple of bottles toward him, creating some concoction that would likely mean I'd be getting a Lyft in a few hours.

"Evie." Mere dodged past Vas and smiled at me. "How are you doing?"

"Not as well as you, obviously," I said dryly. Her face flushed, and Vas smirked at me. Contentment practically radiated off him. After everything he'd been through, he deserved it.

Orin slid a drink across the bar to me and I took a sip. "Delicious. What is it?"

"Harvey Wallbanger."

I took another sip. "Passion fruit vodka?"

"Good catch."

Someone called Orin's name, and he stepped away, giving one of the wolves a shy grin I'd never seen on his face before.

Meredith leaned over the counter. "They're going on their first date tonight."

I checked out the wolf. I hadn't met him before, but he looked at Orin like he was entranced. My heart melted.

The noise dropped a few notches, and I glanced over my shoulder. Kyla had walked in, and she prowled toward the bar. One of the demons stepped into her path. From her raised eyebrow, he was hitting on her. She gave him a feral grin and neatly dodged around him, then leaned against the bar next to me.

"We need a brainstorming session," she said to us.

Vas leaned on the bar and eyed all of us. "Is this a private party?"

Kyla sighed. "Mere will just tell you everything anyway," she said.

Mere grinned unrepentantly and glanced at Orin. They had some silent conversation, and he waved his hand in a way I assumed meant he had everything under control.

We all followed Mere into her stock room. Thanks to Vas's wings, which were currently hidden away, it was a tight fit.

One of them brushed my nose, and I sneezed. Vas flicked that wing, tickling my nose again, and I elbowed him.

"We need to talk strategy," I said.

Kyla nodded. "I don't have long left."

"I assume we're talking about the sword," Vas said.

"Yes."

"Finvarra gave us six months. Seven now. But that was…months ago." I needed to do the math and figure out exactly how much time we had left. The last few months had been one thing after another.

Mere had offered to help with this little task, but Vas's wings rustled in a way that told me he wasn't happy about it. He was silent for a long moment. Then he seemed to come to some kind of decision.

"Mere's pregnant," he said.

Mere's face turned bright red. "We weren't going to tell anyone," she muttered. "It's still early."

"Special circumstances, baby. You're not going on this little mission."

She frowned, and Kyla and I both shook our heads.

"You're out, Mere," Kyla said. "It's way too dangerous."

I leaned over and hugged Mere, holding out my free hand to give Vas a fist bump. "I'm so excited for you guys."

"I'll help with anything you need," Vas said. I glanced at Kyla, and we had a silent conversation of our own. The demons were at war with the seelie. There was no way we were taking Vas with us on this little mission.

"Sounds good," I said vaguely. Vas was too busy grinning at Mere to pay much attention.

"I can do any hacking you need," Mere said. "I doubt it'll help much, though."

Mere was a tech witch. Phones, laptops, tablets—none of it was safe around her. But that couldn't help us in the light fae realm. Still, maybe we could find someone close to the king who was in some kind of financial trouble and could be bribed.

"How's business?" Mere asked.

"I have a new case," Kyla said. "I thought it was for a dark fae woman and then found out Finvarra is involved. You can imagine how pleased I was by that."

Mere winced, and I couldn't help but laugh. The last time Finvarra stuck his nose into one of our cases, Kyla peed on his shoes.

While he was wearing them.

Mere had frozen like a rabbit, likely expecting the unseelie king to strike us all down.

"Evie spent most of the day out in wolf territory," Kyla said.

Vas raised one eyebrow. "What were you doing out there?"

"Kid-related. It's a pity case, even if Nathaniel says it's not. I'll have it wrapped up in a couple of days."

Mere nodded and opened the door. We all went still as a redheaded woman jolted back from us.

My gaze fell to the glowing rock in her hand. "Eavesdropping charm," I ground out.

Vas's face went cold. "Who are you?"

The bar went quiet, both paranormals and humans far more interested in our little drama than anything else.

"Human reporter." A succubus smirked as she strolled past us, on her way toward an unsuspecting group of human men.

"A reporter?" *Fuck, fuck, fuck.* How much had she heard? If word got back to the seelie king that we were planning to steal that sword...

The redhead's eyes flashed. "The people have a right to know..."

"She was standing there for about thirty seconds," Orin said as he strode toward us. He glanced at the woman's purse, and it opened, her wallet floating toward him before she could grab it.

"Ellen Harrison," he read. "Whatever you were speaking about right before you came out, she was listening."

Mere glanced at me, and I nodded. The reporter likely didn't hear anything about the sword. Still, an eavesdropping human wasn't welcome here.

"You were seen in wolf territory today," Ellen told me. "The people need to be informed."

"Informed about what?"

A smug I-know-something-you-don't-know smile crossed her face. I tensed, and her smile widened.

"Lifetime ban," Meredith said softly.

Ellen's smile disappeared as her mouth dropped open. "You can't be serious."

"Oh, I'm more than serious. People come to this bar to relax. To hang out with their friends. To let their guards down and create friendships across faction lines. They don't come here to have their business publicized."

Vas smiled over Mere's shoulder. "Get the fuck out. And stay out."

Ellen hesitated. Rage glimmered in her eyes. After a long moment, she snatched the wallet Orin held out and hurried toward the door.

The entire bar booed her as she left.

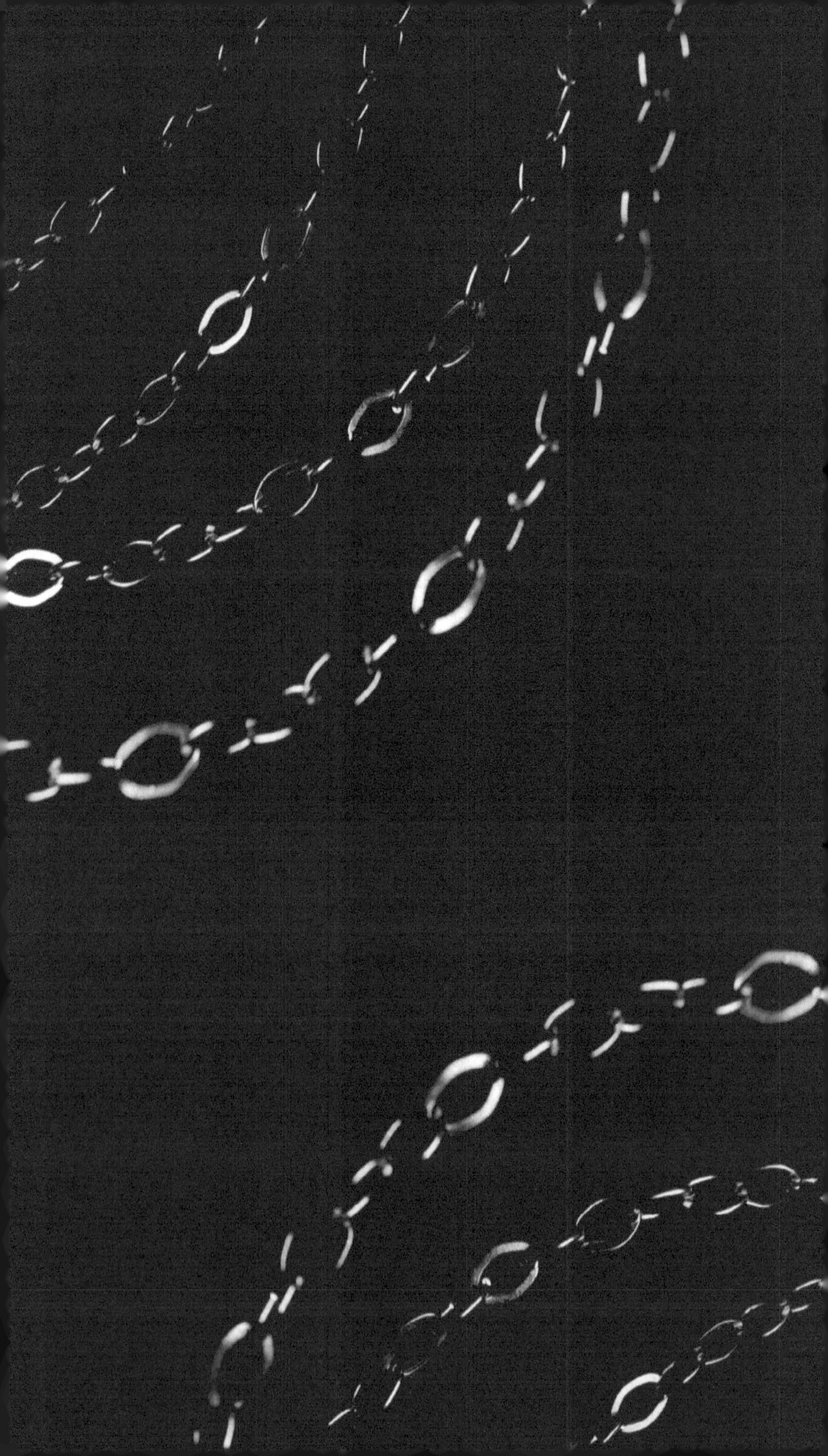

4

EVIE

I cracked one eye open as my phone buzzed. I pulled it toward me and forced my other eye open.

Why was Kyla calling me at seven a.m.?

"The fuck?" I mumbled as I answered the call.

"You need to look at today's newspaper."

"I don't have it."

"I'm sending you a picture."

I flipped to our chat and enlarged the photo of *Durham Denizens*—the paranormal newspaper read by every faction, including humans.

On the front page was a black-and-white photo of some kind of crime scene. It took my eyes a few moments to understand what I was looking at, and then it hit me.

Limbs were strewn across the grass, bodies ripped open, some of them left in *piles*.

Local investigator calls South Carolinian Werewolf Massacre "Kid-related." Vows to solve "pity case" in days.

My picture had been placed to the right of the massacre. It was an old headshot. In it, I wore a wide grin.

Beneath the picture was the article, with a quote from Albert.

"Unfortunately, this attitude is unsurprising, given the Amana sisters' casual disregard for human life. The Mage Council would like to assure human citizens that we continue to protect them from paranormals who slaughter them each and every day in this country."

"What. The. Fuck."

Kyla sighed. "You got to the addition from Albert, huh?"

I'd never fully understood the term "blinded with rage," but I got it now. The article blurred in front of me, and the entire room trembled. A stack of paperwork fell off my nightstand.

I took a deep breath and got a hold of my power. This was happening more and more often.

My neighbors likely thought we'd just experienced an earthquake. Oops.

I scanned the article again. "Albert's bullshit is on-brand for him. But the reporter is out of her goddamned mind."

"Yeah. I don't know if she actually thought we were discussing these murders or if this is her idea of revenge."

"Werewolf massacre?"

"I don't know. Nathaniel hasn't said anything to me about it."

My mind flickered back to the way his jaw had tightened yesterday. He'd strode away, and I hadn't seen him again.

"Your Alpha is going to fucking kill me."

Kyla was silent for a long moment. "Well…he's not going to be pleased."

Understatement. Harrison had implied werewolf children were responsible for this.

Everything the wolves did to protect the kids, and I'd just made them seem like they were murderous little beasts.

"Do humans know werewolf kids can't shift?"

"I doubt it," Kyla said. "I'm sure they imagine our kids are born as bloodthirsty puppies."

"So, people will actually believe this. That little kids could have done something this horrific."

"Yeah."

I swung my legs out of the bed. "I have to fix this."

"How?"

"I have no idea. I'll meet you at the office. But first, I need to have a little chat with Gary."

"Good idea."

I ended the call and dropped my phone on the bed before making my way to my bathroom. The trickle of water meant it took forever whenever I washed my hair, but this place was *mine*.

My apartment was a small one-bedroom on the outskirts of Trinity Park, close enough to the burned remains of the house I'd grown up in that I was careful never to drive down that street. The area wasn't the greatest. My car had already been broken in to twice, until I'd finally gotten the hint and warded it. But for the first time, I was living alone, responsible for paying my own bills, filling my own fridge, and learning about basic things like how to change air conditioning filters and the best places for takeout.

I loved every inch of it, from its peeling light-green paint to its thin walls, which let me know exactly how my neighbors' marriage was going at any given time.

It was a one-bedroom, though, which meant I had a pullout couch. I didn't exactly have a list of friends lining up to stay with me, but maybe one day the coven would forgive me.

A girl could hope.

I reached for leggings and a tank top, sliding my Applegate-Fairbairn fighting knife into my ankle sheath. I didn't have it in me to play hide-the-knife today, and really, who was going to notice another armed human strolling around paranormal-filled Durham? The A-F was my favorite—the six-inch blade designed for up-close fighting, with a weighted handle that seemed made for my hand. I'd replaced the sheath with a custom one of my own, and Edward had made me practice sliding it from that sheath in a variety of fun ways. One of them had been in the middle of a freezing lake when he'd set one of his selkie friends onto me.

Gary's store was located two blocks from the building that had once held the Mage Council. I parked on a side street, stalked into a nearby bakery and bought a few donuts, picked up a newspaper, and headed into Gary's.

Truthfully, I hadn't expected him to be open this early. Adult gnomes were mostly nocturnal. But he stood behind the counter on a step stool.

I glanced around the store, taking in the new shelves which held various weapons, spells, charms, and ingredients. "This place is looking good."

He smiled at me, revealing sharply pointed teeth. "Something tells me you're not here to admire my store."

"Nope. Where are the kids?" Cil and Zip were Gary's twin boys.

"School. Are those for me?"

"Yeah. Shameless bribery." I placed the donuts on the counter and opened the box so the smell would waft toward him.

His gray face creased as he smirked. "Bringing out the big guns."

"I need a favor."

He took a donut and gestured for me to do the same. I chose chocolate because, duh.

I pulled my copy of *Durham Denizens* out of my purse and slapped it on the counter, stabbing my finger at the tiny picture of Ellen Harrison. "Recognize her?"

Gary scanned the paper, and his eyes fired. "Yes."

"She used one of your eavesdropping charms to spy on us at Mere's."

"Lifetime ban?"

"Bet your ass. I need you to do the same. Please."

He sighed. "Word gets out I'm banning customers..."

"She's dangerous, Gary. And I don't just say that because I think she's a piece of shit for this article. Humans are going to think werewolf kids did this. She's putting actual children in danger."

Gary's mouth tightened, and I knew he was thinking of his own kids. Paranormals with silver-colored skin and sharp, pointy teeth.

"Fine," he said. "You want me to tell you what she tries to buy if she comes back?"

"That would be great. Thanks."

He slowly shook his head and took another donut, a smile playing around his mouth. "She's obviously new to town, or she would've known not to mess with you."

"Yeah," I said. "But she didn't. Now, it's war."

I left Gary's and drove toward Bethesda. The mages were working out of an old warehouse while they rebuilt their facility on Main Street. My sister had leveled that building when they'd attempted to take advantage of Samael's brush with death.

For a while, Danica had worked for the Mage Council. She'd been a contractor tasked with bringing in lesser demons who slaughtered their summoners and other paranormals who'd hunted humans. And as soon as she'd bonded with Samael—through no fault of her own—the mages had turned on her.

No one truly understood where the mages got their power from today. When the witches woke a demigod and the first portals opened, a human named Colin Smith had been traveling in Guatemala—close to the cave where the demigod had been sleeping. He'd been so close that he'd been hit with incredible power. Power that hadn't killed him but had instead allowed him to protect humans from some of the rampaging paranormals.

The council was incredibly secretive. No one knew how that power was distributed as lower-level mages worked their way up, attaining more and more power.

Gabriel—Colin's son—had eventually taken over the Mage Council, which had been formed to protect humans. He communicated only with the ten other members of the council itself, who were scattered throughout the country.

Albert was one of those mages. And I hadn't forgotten how his people had betrayed my sister in an attempt to deliver her to Lucifer, before the seelie king's adviser finally managed to get that job done.

Albert was obviously emboldened by the fact that neither Dani nor Samael were in Durham to keep him in line. I smiled as I parked my car, checking that my weapons were visible.

Two mages were on the door. Albert hadn't had any guards the last time I was here. I cocked my head and took them in. Albert knew they were outmatched.

Was he hoping to slow me down, or did he imagine I'd work out the worst of my rage on the almost powerless low-level mages?

I wouldn't put it past Albert to sacrifice his own people for the "greater good." It was just how he rolled.

"Move," I said.

Both mages stood their ground. The one on the left had blond hair so light it was almost white. The one on the right had the barest shadow of stubble, as if he was desperately attempting to grow a beard. He glowered at me.

I raised one eyebrow. "I hate to play this card, but do you know who I am?"

Stubble spat at my feet. "We know exactly who you are, mutt."

I laughed. Was that supposed to be an insult? Mutts were loyal, protective, and resilient as fuck. I brushed my hand over my chin. "You've got something on your face."

He raised his own hand automatically, then dropped it with a scowl. Blondie swallowed audibly, his feet shifting to point in the opposite direction. *He* didn't want to fight.

"Listen. I'm talking to Albert today. Period. He knows that, you know that. He's sent you out here to slow me down—and potentially to make me hurt you, so I'll look bad on your recordings." I flicked my gaze up to where a camera was watching my every move. "Do you really want me to do that?"

"I'm not afraid of you," Stubble spat.

"M'kay." I could feel eyes on me, and I had no doubt Albert was hoping I'd lose control, so he'd have proof that I was dangerous. He was right, but I was only dangerous to people who tried to hurt those I loved.

I concentrated. Levitating kids who wanted to fly was challenging, but moving a full-grown man who wanted to stay put was much more difficult. I didn't bother with any theatrics. I just narrowed my eyes and gathered the thread of my power to me. That thread urged me to pull harder, harder, harder, until it finally unraveled.

I shut down that urge and focused on coaxing out a few solitary drops of my power.

The mages cursed as they were pushed aside. Blondie landed on the grassy curb next to us. Stubble? He landed on the pavement with a curse.

Blondie crab-walked backward, staring wide-eyed at me as if I was his every nightmare come to life. Stubble raised his hand and channeled his own power. He didn't have much, and it hit my ward with a dull thump.

"Cute," I told him. I walked past them both and studied Albert's next line of defense. As far as wards went, Albert's was like a multilayered steel door on a bank vault. Impressive. Breaking wards wasn't my best skill—that was Danica's deal. But I studied it, examining the brown gleam of his power and the separate threads woven within the wards.

Behind me, Stubble attempted to hit me with his

power again. I ignored him and raised my hand. If I managed to break this ward, it would give whoever set it one hell of a headache. And I was willing to bet that person was Albert himself. I smiled.

I reached for the thread of my power once more, channeling it into the ward. My own power manifested as a rainbow of colors, representing the mix of my genes. I'd thought it was normal until I learned just how much of a freak I was.

I shoved that thought to the back of my mind. The thread of my magic touched the ward, licking along the door to the warehouse, as if tasting it. Then the thread turned brown.

I jolted, ripping my power away. Behind me, Stubble laughed. "Too much for you, mutt?"

I ignored him, attempting to understand what had just happened. I let a tiny bit of my power out once more, blowing out a relieved sigh when I took in its rainbow of colors. It was okay. Albert's magic hadn't infected me.

Reaching for the thread once more, this time, I didn't flinch when it hit the ward and darkened. Instead, I pushed harder, until my own power covered the entire ward like a shadow. It sank into the ward and continued to slowly, steadily channel my power, until I could feel Albert's power like it was my own. Until my own power mimicked his, melding with it until, for one terrifying moment, I didn't know where his power ended and my own began.

I shoved my power into the ward.

And it disappeared.

I didn't break the ward. I didn't hear the dull pop that told me I'd managed to shove my way through it with brute force. No, the ward disappeared as if it had never been there.

I'd managed to mimic Albert's power so closely, I'd *unlocked* his ward. And removed it.

My lungs seized, and I froze, staring at the door where the ward had been.

The pounding of footsteps ripped me from my shock. I glanced over my shoulder in time to see Blondie and Stubble hauling ass away from me.

I couldn't blame them.

I took a deep, steadying breath and attempted to pull myself together. I'd figure out exactly what had happened here later. For now, I needed to pretend like I'd meant for that to happen.

I smirked, rolled my shoulders, and swaggered into the warehouse.

It was incredibly quiet. Shockingly, the many pairs of eyes who'd been watching me were now gone. Either they'd seen what I'd managed to do to Albert's ward and skedaddled, or Albert himself had ordered them to leave.

I was betting on door number two. I knew enough about Albert to know he would be *pissed*.

The thought warmed my heart, and I wandered through the empty warehouse, toward the large area Albert had cordoned off for himself. The mages had computers set up on card tables, with folding chairs tucked beneath them. It was a long way from the high-tech, if utilitarian, facility they'd enjoyed.

My smile widened, and I lengthened my stride, ducking around the room dividers that Albert had used in place of walls. He sat at his cheap, rickety desk, and for a moment, I couldn't blame him for his hatred of my family.

Then he slowly got to his feet, his gray eyes burning with a mixture of wrath and rage.

My pity dried up. I couldn't forget what this man had done to my sister. And how, even now, he was taking advantage of Ellen Harrison's decision to target the werewolves.

"What did you do to my ward?"

"Removed it." I kept my voice bored, as if I'd meant to do whatever the hell I'd done. Never let your enemies see you sweat.

"Why are you here?"

"Come on, Bert. I was doing my best to ignore the fact that you're somehow still alive, when you decided to give Ellen Harrison a nice little quote. Did you really think I *wouldn't* come see what the fuck you thought you were doing?"

Albert slammed his hands down on his desk, and his power roared toward me. I wasn't dumb enough to walk into mage territory without a ward of my own, but I needed every ounce of my focus to hold that ward while he pummeled it with his power.

He finally pulled his power back, his chest heaving as he panted. It took everything I had to keep my own expression carefully neutral. In reality, I wanted to put my hands on my knees, lean over, and suck in a few deep breaths as my head spun from his attack.

But I could feel several other threads of my power, all of them lingering dangerously close to the surface. Something inside me had unlocked with whatever I'd done to Albert's ward, and I needed advice from someone who might know what was going on. That was a problem for later.

"Are you done?" I asked.

Albert just stared at me. "What sorcery is this?"

I bared my teeth in a feral smile. "Surprise."

His face slowly drained of color. He'd long called me a mutt, decrying the fact that I'd been created in a lab and no one truly knew what I was. But if there was one thing I knew about Albert, it was that he considered information to be power. He'd likely been keeping careful track of my power level, and I'd just surprised the shit out of him.

Seemed fair since I'd also surprised the shit out of myself.

"Careful," I said. "You wouldn't want me to demonstrate my *casual disregard for human life.*"

The color was slowly returning to Albert's face. In fact, it was turning a dull purple.

"I was unaware that I was speaking to a reporter when I made that comment," he gritted out.

I raised one eyebrow and waited him out.

"I was at a mage function. She arrived with one of the new recruits. I assumed she was a contractor. I had… consumed alcohol."

This little incident proved one thing. Hatred and bigotry could get the best of even the most controlled, powerful people. As far as I knew, Albert had never run his mouth like that before.

I wasn't exactly going to get an apology out of him. And from the sullen look on his face, he was already dealing with a healthy dose of self-loathing after his little tell-all to the reporter.

I shook my head at him and strolled out of the warehouse. It was time to deal with a displeased Alpha wolf.

EVIE

I rolled into wolf territory like a woman condemned.

Oh, I didn't think Nathaniel would kill me. That would start a war with my sister. But he certainly wasn't going to be happy.

There was no howl of welcome as I turned right onto Nathaniel's street. I slid out of my car, shoved my sunglasses up onto my head, and prepared to face the music.

Nathaniel opened his front door. Obviously waiting for me to arrive. He wore casual jeans, a black T-shirt, and a forbidding, you're-in-trouble scowl.

I hunched my shoulders and slunk toward him. If I'd been a wolf, I would've had my tail between my legs. A flicker of amusement crossed his face, and he regarded me with a lifted eyebrow.

"You look as meek as I've ever seen you."

"We need to talk."

"Yes. We do."

Tobias was nowhere to be seen today. I told myself it was because the submissive wolf didn't like confrontation and not because he was furious at me too.

I followed Nathaniel into the sitting room, where a copy of *Durham Denizens* was lying on the coffee table.

"Take a seat," Nathaniel said.

I sat.

"When I brought you into my territory, it was because I trusted you to adhere to a certain level of confidentiality."

My temper sparked. "What exactly do you believe happened, Nathaniel?"

He regarded me out of cool eyes. "Why don't you tell me what happened?"

"You think I waltzed up to this reporter and ran my mouth, don't you?" I laughed bitterly as I got to my feet.

He stood as well, and I was suddenly overly aware of just how much room his huge body took up. His eyes blazed, and his power filled the room.

Wolves didn't have magic—other than the magic that allowed them to shift. No, Nathaniel's power was that of a pissed-off Alpha wolf. And for the first time, I realized just how well he'd kept it hidden from me up until now. I'd seen him keep his wolves in line in the past, but I'd never truly felt that dominance licking at me, urging me to drop my eyes. To kneel.

I bared my teeth at him, letting my own power come out to play.

His power disappeared. Within a fraction of a second, it was as if he wasn't a werewolf at all. As if he was just a human man. I blinked, sure of what I'd felt. And yet he stood there with a mild expression of impatience on his face.

It made goose bumps break out on my arms. I was used to being able to tell exactly how much power people had—and what kind. Nathaniel kept his dominance locked down, tightly folded away, where you couldn't see it coming until it was too late.

I'd underestimated just how dangerous he was, and I didn't like it.

"Why don't you tell me what happened, Evelyn?"

I loathed it when he called me by my full name in that oh-so-formal tone. I had a feeling he knew it.

"I was having a private conversation in Meredith's

stock room. Kyla mentioned her new case, and I said I was coming out here to deal with the kids. At no point was I aware a group of humans had recently been slaughtered by werewolves. At no point was I aware that some journalist was using an eavesdropping charm to spy on us."

A muscle ticked in Nathaniel's jaw. Other than that, his face remained carefully blank.

"Mere banned her for life," I said. "And Gary won't sell her any more of those little charms. I shouldn't have talked about your business in the bar. In my defense, I thought Vas had raised a silence ward, like he usually does. But he was a little distracted."

Distracted by the thought of his pregnant bondmate getting caught up in our shenanigans.

"I apologize," Nathaniel said. "I shouldn't have assumed..."

"Apology accepted," I muttered. "I paid Albert a little visit too. The idiot didn't realize he was speaking to a reporter."

Nathaniel looked like he was close to rolling his eyes.

"What happened to those people in the paper, Nathaniel? Was it a feral wolf?"

Feral wolves lost their humanity. They saw humans as nothing but meat. There was no coming back once a wolf turned feral. The only option was to put them down.

A muscle tightened in his cheek. "I'm not at liberty

to say."

Because he thought I couldn't be trusted and I'd blab his business all over town. I took a deep, shaky breath and pushed the hurt down where he wouldn't smell it.

But I'd forgotten just how sensitive werewolves' senses were. Kyla had once told me emotions had a scent, and from the softening of Nathaniel's expression, he knew exactly how I felt.

Awesome.

"I need to get back to the office."

He studied me. "I still want you to investigate the kids."

"I don't think it's a good idea."

"This is interesting. I wasn't aware you knew the meaning of the word *quit*."

He might not know me well, but the Alpha *did* know just how to get under my skin. "I was doing you a favor, you jackass." I stiffened as soon as the words were out of my mouth. I probably shouldn't call the werewolf Alpha a jackass.

He just smiled at me. "I don't need you to do me any favors. Except the one you agreed to, which you're getting paid for."

"I'll return your deposit."

"No, you won't." He waited patiently–clearly certain I'd fall in line. Unfortunately, in this case he was right.

"Fine," I sighed. "I'll go talk to the kids."

I elbowed my way past the overgrown male and ignored his low snort as I stalked out of his house. If I'd thought the wolves were untrusting of me yesterday, today was much, much worse. Everywhere I went, they watched me out of cold eyes, silently judging me.

"Evie," a voice said, and I turned.

Kyla sauntered toward me, holding two cups in her hands. "I got you a latte."

"Thanks."

She glanced around, noting the group of human mates who'd gathered, keeping a close eye on me.

"Can we help you?"

They wandered away. Kyla gave me a sympathetic look. "I'm going to spread the word that the reporter targeted you."

"Thanks. I doubt it'll help, though. The pack doesn't seem to want much to do with me."

A strange look crossed Kyla's face, and then she shrugged. "They take a while to trust new people. It's nothing personal."

"Uh-huh. Well, I'm going to try to make friends with some of the kids. What's your plan for today?"

"Finvarra is right. Callula is gone. She must have been terrified of him." Kyla looked like she'd tasted something bitter. "I'm still interviewing people who were working the auction. There were at least a hundred people involved, so even with prioritizing those who had access to the artifacts, it's going to take a while."

"What's so special about this book?"

"No idea, and the fae are being cagey. Finvarra won't tell me what it does or why it was stolen."

"Let me know if you need help with the interviews."

"I will. Good luck here."

"Wait. One question. Why did Nathaniel hire me to do this and not you? You're a wolf."

She smiled. "It would be seen as cheating. Besides, after the whole kidnapping thing, Nathaniel doesn't want me to be ostracized from the pack in any way, even for a small thing like this."

I winced at the thought. It had taken Kyla months to come all the way back to human, and she would likely never again have the easy relationship she'd once had with her wolf.

"Okay, well, wish me luck." I heaved a dramatic sigh, and she grinned at me.

"You got this."

I took my latte back over to the swings. Only a few kids were playing in the playground this early, so I pondered exactly what could have killed so many humans in South Carolina.

If it was a werewolf—or worse, several wolves— the massacre was Nathaniel's problem. I didn't know exactly how large his pack's territory was. But Kyla had once mentioned that any wolf visitors to South Carolina, North Carolina, Virginia, Tennessee, or Kentucky had to get permission from him first.

By the time I'd finished my latte, more of the kids had arrived. A couple of teenagers leaned against a climbing wall, shooting me purposely disinterested looks every few minutes.

I smiled to myself and pulled three sparkly rubber balls out of my pockets. I threw the first into the air and held it there with my telekinesis, keeping my gaze focused on the pink orb as if I couldn't hear the shocked gasps of the littlest kids.

I was betting the pack children didn't get many chances to see magic, secluded as they were.

I threw another ball into the air—this one blue—and let it hover next to the first. More gasps. I pretended I didn't notice any attention and threw the final green ball up.

I lifted my hand. I didn't need to, but it looked more impressive. Rotating one finger in the air, I made the rubber balls spin in a circle.

Kids were approaching from every angle. I ignored them, spinning the balls faster and faster and faster.

Excited squeals broke out from some of the younger kids, and I grinned, enjoying myself now. The colors began to blur, until they were a dizzying rainbow circle.

I glanced away, using a tiny part of my attention to keep them in the air.

An older kid—twelve or so—caught my eye. She'd crept closer, but her expression turned bored when I glanced at her, so I moved on.

One of the younger children—a boy—was bouncing in place. I'd put him at six or seven, but I wasn't exactly an expert.

He grinned at me, and I couldn't help but grin back. He was missing his front teeth.

"Would you like to try?" I offered.

He nodded, racing toward me. I let the balls slow, plucking them from the air and handing them to him. He threw them up, and I froze them in place.

He made the same circling motion with his hand that I had, and I laughed, sending out a tendril of my power to make them rotate. He spun his hand faster, and I complied.

"I want a turn!"

I entertained the kids for an hour or so. The older kids refused to show much interest, but they stuck around. They were the ones I needed to get on my side, but there was a good chance one of their younger siblings knew what they were up to.

Besides, I was having fun.

"Charlie. It's time to go home."

I glanced away from the balls, and this time, my distraction made them fall to the ground. A group of human women were watching me, eyes hard, faces pale.

I knew that look.

Fear.

The kids weren't the only ones who weren't used

to seeing much magic. The human women's mates changed into huge, dangerous wolves, but seeing me use this tiny amount of my power had terrified them.

Charlie turned out to be the kid missing his two front teeth. He stuck out his lower lip. "But, Mom—"

"Now."

The other moms jumped in, dragging their kids away. One of them shot me a furious look, and I shrugged. I wasn't going to apologize for what I was. But my stomach twisted, and my eyes burned as I watched them leave.

Some of the teenagers stayed put, but they grouped together, ignoring me now.

"I see you're still making enemies wherever you go," an amused voice said.

I glanced over my shoulder. Liam strolled toward me on long legs, his green eyes gleaming. I scowled at him.

"You got any other suggestions?"

He leaned against the swing set, and we surveyed each other.

He'd filled out since I'd seen him last. His shoulders seemed wider. I sighed and kicked my own legs out. We swung next to each other in silence.

This was the first time I'd seen Liam since we'd broken up.

I glanced over at him. Liam had been my close friend—and crush—in high school. I'd been devastated when his parents relocated and he was suddenly gone.

It wasn't until I'd gone to Nathaniel's with Danica that we'd reunited.

It turned out that a feral wolf had broken in to his house and killed his parents. He'd survived and shifted, and the local pack in Florida had determined he was too dominant and untrained to stay. They'd sent him to Nathaniel.

"How are you doing, Evie?"

I shrugged. "Okay. I miss you."

He blew out a long breath. "I miss you too. I just need a little time."

Before Liam and I were a couple, we were friends. Part of me wished we'd never dated. But the moment I'd seen him again, I'd felt that spark.

Unfortunately, a spark meant nothing when one-half of a couple wanted commitment and the other half was desperate for freedom.

I slowed the swing and got to my feet. "I never meant to hurt you."

Liam's mouth twisted—an expression I'd never seen before on his face. He opened his mouth and then clamped it shut. "I know," he finally said.

He leaned over and wrapped me in a bear hug. "We'll be friends again," he promised. "I just need to wait until it doesn't hurt so bad."

"Okay." My voice was small, and I forced myself to suck it up. *I* was the one who'd broken up with him. Because I couldn't give him what he needed. We may not have worked romantically, but I was holding out hope that we'd be friends someday.

My phone buzzed, and Liam released me. I glanced at the screen. Detective Nelson.

"I'm sorry. I've got to take this."

Liam gave me a soft smile. "It's okay. Good luck with the kids—and the parents. I'll see you around."

I smiled back as I answered the call.

"We have a situation," Nelson said. "Crime scene just outside of Durham. When can you get here?" He rattled off the address, and I glanced at my watch.

"Twenty minutes if traffic isn't terrible. What is it?"

"You heard about that massacre in South Carolina?"

I rolled my eyes. "I know you saw the *Durham Denizens*, Nelson."

"Well, we've got another one. This time in my jurisdiction. You're on."

I received a small monthly retainer with Nelson's task force. For consulting. It was time for me to earn it.

"I'll be right there."

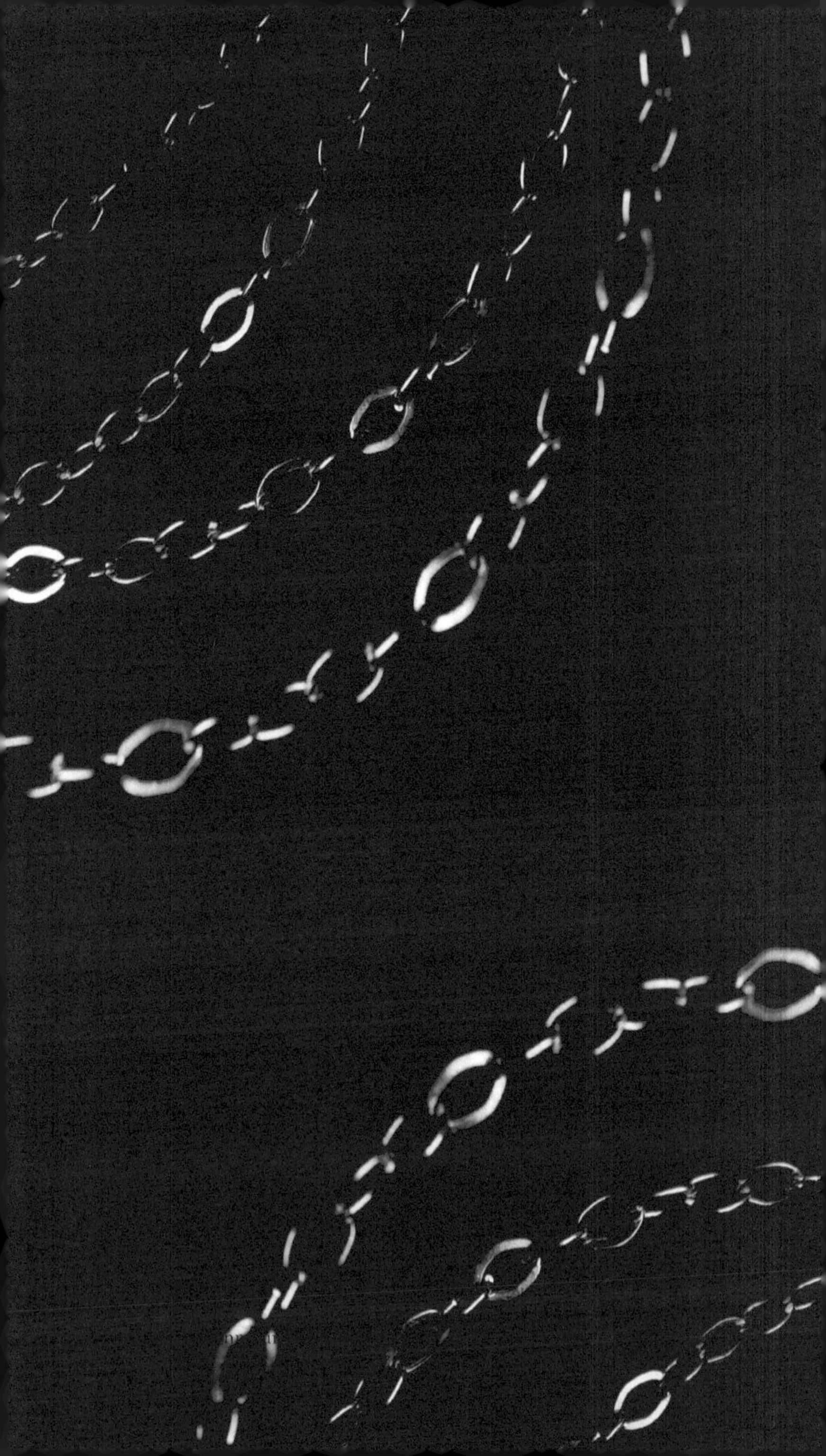

5

EVIE

I hauled ass toward my car. The crime scene was in Bethesda Park, not far from the warehouse where the mages had temporarily set up shop. My stomach roiled at the thought of walking into a scene like the one in *Durham Denizens*. That picture had been horrific enough to give me nightmares.

I distracted myself from the upcoming scene by replaying the look on Liam's face. I'd hurt him. Badly. I'd thought I was ready for a relationship, thought I could put myself back together while creating a life with him. I couldn't have been more wrong.

"Shit!" I bounced off something hard. Strong arms caught me, and I realized I'd slammed into Nathaniel's chest.

"Where are you going?"

"Crime scene."

His eyes turned an eerie icy blue. "Why?"

"I'm a consultant for Nelson's new task force. Paranormals and humans working together."

He watched me out of wolfy eyes. I didn't shiver, but it was close.

"I don't want you there."

So he knew which crime scene I was talking about. He'd obviously just been notified himself. As the werewolf Alpha, he had the right to check out anything paranormal-related.

And he thought I'd mess up the way I had with the reporter.

I needed to stay calm and assure him I could handle this. I needed to show him I was a mature, reasonable person.

"I don't give a fuck what you want."

I sighed. One day, my brain would fall in line with my good intentions.

A tiny hint of Nathaniel's power leaked out, giving me the urge to drop my gaze. I ignored all my instincts, which told me to submit.

Something furry pushed into my legs, making me stumble a few steps back. I glanced down at Virtus. Danica had found the griffin in the light fae realm. She'd been sent to kill him, and instead, he'd followed her home. The poor guy had been the runt of his pack, thanks to his twisted wings. Now, he was part of Nathaniel's pack, and he'd somehow slipped seamlessly into the role of peacekeeper.

He stared into my eyes. Conversations with Virtus

were weird, because he didn't talk. Instead, the things he wanted you to know simply appeared in your head.

And he wanted me to know that we shouldn't fight. Oh, and that he wanted to come with us.

"It's a crime scene," I reminded him. "There will be humans there. Curious humans with cameras."

He didn't care. He planned to stay in the car.

I lifted my gaze to Nathaniel's. His eyes had darkened back to their usual blue.

"I'm going to the crime scene," I informed him. "I understand you're not pleased, but it's not your call to make."

He watched me for a long moment. "I'm going to the same place," he said. "I'll drive."

I opened my mouth to tell him that didn't really make all that much sense since it would mean I'd have to come back here to get my car. But he was already stalking toward the black SUV in his driveway.

I ground my teeth but followed him. Interacting with dominant werewolves was all about picking your battles. And a werewolf as dominant as Nathaniel needed to be in control at all times. He didn't want me at the scene, and he'd conceded that much. If driving me helped him with his control, I'd deal with it.

I opened the back passenger door and pushed down the seats, then stalked around to the liftgate as Nathaniel opened it from inside the car. Virtus jumped into the back of the SUV, and Nathaniel opened the windows for him.

The griffin barely fit, but he seemed content, so I slipped into the front passenger seat. My lungs froze as my eyes met Nathaniel's once more.

His wolf was looking at me. His eyes were so pale they were almost white. And so bright they glowed.

In spite of my temper, I was no dummy. I dropped my eyes to my lap. My hands shook, and Nathaniel took a deep breath. I wasn't sure if he was breathing in my fear—and enjoying it—or if he was fighting for control.

Nope, nope, nope.

My hand scrambled for the door handle, and Nathaniel reached across and grabbed my wrist, so fast I hadn't seen him move. I went still.

I knew better than to run from predators. Especially the king of the predators. I could feel Virtus's attention behind me, but he seemed unconcerned. That helped bring my fear down a notch.

"Don't. Run. From. Me," Nathaniel gritted out.

I took a long, slow breath and lowered my gaze.

It took a few moments, but Nathaniel packed away the power that had prickled at my skin, until he was just a man in a car.

But I knew what I'd felt. The question was, why was I feeling it now?

Granted, the past few days were the most time I'd spent with Nathaniel alone. But I'd seen him enraged when Kyla was taken. This was different.

Two crime scenes in two days. Humans had likely

been killed by feral wolves. Was that why Nathaniel was so furious?

I shifted my gaze to him once more, ready to look away if I needed to. But his eyes were his usual color, and I relaxed some more as he started the car.

"You smell like Liam," he said mildly.

I frowned at him. "Yeah, I saw him in the playground."

"Any luck with the kids?"

He didn't want to talk about what had just happened. Fine with me.

"No. A group of human women saw me using my power and hauled most of them away."

Nathaniel winced. "They're not used to your kind of magic."

"I know. I'm not upset."

"Lie," he said softly, and I scowled. Kyla had given me a brief rundown on the Alpha wolf, but I hadn't known he could sense lies. That was a handy skill to have.

"Fine. I'm upset. It won't stop me. But Nelson's case takes priority."

"Of course."

His hands were light on the wheel as he drove, his shoulders relaxed. He looked like any other guy commuting to the office.

When the portals had opened, an unlucky minority began their first transformations into werewolves.

Werewolves didn't do well with fear or adrenaline.

They'd had no experience controlling their wolf halves, and they rampaged across the world.

At the same time, the fae and demons were entering our world and taking anything they wanted. There was a reason the ten years after the portals opened were called the Decade of Despair.

No one knew why some people turned into werewolves. Or why 99.99% of those turned were male. Nathaniel was one of the first to regain control. Not only did he harness his own wolf, but he managed to make every other wolf he came into contact with fall in line. And his self-control allowed *them* to help the others.

I peered at the Alpha from beneath my lashes. One day—when we weren't on the way to a crime scene—I'd ask him how he did it. How, against all odds, he managed to stop the wolves from destroying everyone left alive.

But right now, the flashing lights up ahead and a crowd of people told me we were pulling up to the crime scene. I steeled myself as Nathaniel parked the car.

This was going to suck.

"Make sure no one sees you," I warned Virtus. He nuzzled at my ear, his fur tickling my cheek. I got out of the car.

The police must have recognized Nathaniel, because they immediately began moving people out of the way, and we walked toward the hill in front of us. Someone jostled me, and Nathaniel took my arm, dropping it once we were led through the crime scene tape.

Nathaniel and Nelson did their man-nods, and Nelson gestured for us to follow him. The detective was in his early thirties, with shrewd green eyes and a can-do attitude that would likely turn to cynicism within the next few years on the job.

"I saw pictures of the scene in South Carolina," he said as he led us up the hill. "This looks similar. Either the same killers or a copycat," he said.

We cleared the top of the hill, and my breath caught in my throat.

Blood was splattered over the grass, over tree trunks, over branches. The sunlight filtered through gaps in the leaves above us, making some of the blood shine the color of cherries, while other spots appeared almost black.

Bodies—at least parts of them—lay in piles. I let my gaze drift up to where an arm hung, caught in one of the branches of the tree to our right. A slice of sunlight caught the sparkle of a ring on one finger.

The world spun around me. I managed to stumble deeper into the trees, away from the crime scene, as I vomited with enough force to make tears drip down my face.

I dropped to my knees and breathed through my mouth.

"Are you okay?"

My cheeks burned. I hadn't heard Nathaniel follow me. Although that wasn't surprising. Kyla was also capable of padding almost soundlessly through the forest, even in human form.

"Fine," I managed to get out, not yet ready to stand. "I'll be right there."

A few moments later, I slowly stood. The Alpha hadn't left, but I didn't even have it in me to scowl at him. I attempted to walk past him, and he grabbed my arm.

Nathaniel's hand was big and warm, and his chest looked like just the right place to rest my head. His arms would hold me tight...

I blinked. Where exactly had my mind just gone?

"Don't go back up there," he said.

"You know I have to."

"Goddamn it, Evelyn. You've proven you're a badass. But Danica's not here to applaud, and you need to stop comparing yourself to her."

I stared at him. "That's not it at all." I tugged on my arm. After a moment, he released me. I hated that I was free only because he *chose* to release me. Werewolves.

He frowned down at me, clearly unimpressed. "Why, then?"

"Because that day—when my friends, my family were slaughtered in our home—I should have been there. And I wasn't."

A strange, furious light entered his eyes. "You would have died."

"No. The house would have been stronger. The wards would have worked. My power could have saved them. And if I can do anything to make sure even one person doesn't go through that, I will. Nelson decided to consult with me because he knows I've had experience with all the different factions. He knows I've studied paranormals extensively, and he believes I may notice something that helps."

I turned and walked back to the crime scene. I couldn't hear Nathaniel, but the prickle of awareness on the back of my neck told me he was following me.

"Sorry," I muttered when I reached Nelson.

"Happens to the best of us. At least at the start." Another cop ambled toward us, his suit slightly rumpled.

"This is Detective Armstrong," Nelson said. I watched the cop warily. Nelson's last partner had been a bigot who'd resented having anything to do with paranormals.

"Armstrong requested this position," Nelson told me, reading my mind. "This is Evelyn Amana," he introduced me, and I shook hands with the detective.

"Tell me, what do you see here?" Armstrong asked.

I took a deep breath and forced myself to take the fresh gloves Nelson held out for me. Then I slipped the booties over my shoes.

Nathaniel had disappeared. I had a feeling he'd be back. He was pissed at me, but he was a professional. And I'd seen the rage in his eyes when he'd looked at what was left of these people.

"The ME would have to confirm, but whatever this was, I don't think it ate any of the…parts. It seems to me like this was either rage-driven or…play."

Nelson looked slightly sick at that. "Play?"

"Some creatures would enjoy this. You'll need to confirm with Nathaniel, but I believe feral wolves would have eaten at least a few of the…bodies."

"Yes," Nathaniel said, appearing back at my side, a bottle of water in his hand. "A feral wolf would see the first few people he killed as food. He would have become distracted—at least while he ate. There are enough bodies here that at least one of them would have managed to make it to the road—and found help. But there are no signs that anyone here managed to flee. That tells us that whatever did this killed them incredibly quickly."

Nathaniel handed the water to me, and our hands brushed, sending a jolt of awareness through my body.

"Uh, thanks."

Alpha wolves couldn't help but look after those they considered weaker than themselves. But something told me this was an apology as well. I rinsed out my mouth and pressed the cool bottle against the back of my neck.

"We found some black fur on one of the victims," Nelson said. "We assumed it was werewolf."

"You need to have it analyzed," I said.

"We have nothing to compare it to."

We both looked at Nathaniel while he deliberated. Obviously, he didn't want the humans having werewolf fur. But if this could help prove it wasn't a werewolf, it was likely worth it.

"I'll have someone bring you a sample for comparison," he finally said.

Surprise shot through Nelson's eyes. "Thank you."

"Why were these people here?" I asked Nelson.

"Company is called CertSure. This was some kind of corporate team building. Trust exercises or some shit." He shook his head. "As if spending extended amounts of time with your colleagues isn't bad enough."

"Do any of them have anything in common with the victims from the first scene? Or any ties?"

Nelson shrugged. "Uncertain as of now. We'll be looking into that."

So would I. And I'd probably be able to do it faster since I wouldn't have to rely on inconvenient things like warrants.

Armstrong glanced at Nathaniel. Someone had obviously given him a few tips for dealing with the wolves, because he kept his gaze away from Nathaniel's, staring at his chin.

"I know you said this was not the act of your wolves," he said carefully, "but can you expand upon why?"

Nathaniel nodded, taking in the scene once more.

"Wolves who are not feral will hunt deer, moose, even rabbits. You can see by the organs left in…piles—"

he shot me an apologetic look "—that this wasn't the work of a hungry predator."

"But wolves do eat humans," Armstrong said.

"Most wolves prefer deer. Humans have a salty aftertaste." Nathaniel smiled. It wasn't a very nice smile.

"Werewolves aren't monsters," I informed the detectives.

"Oh yes, we are," Nathaniel said softly. I gave him a look, which he ignored. "I'm not saying wolves didn't do this. But if they did, it was for a specific reason. To draw attention to themselves. Or to my pack."

"You think you're being set up?" Nelson asked.

Nathaniel shrugged but his eyes were shrewd. "I don't think anything yet. All I know is this wasn't an act of a feral wolf, and it wasn't anything *my* wolves did. It was either a well-thought-out attack by those who wanted it to look like rampaging wolves, or a creature completely unrelated to us. That's all I can tell you for now."

"Let us know if you think of anything else," Nelson said. "We'll have crime scene photos available. Whatever is doing this is moving quickly."

Nathaniel nodded, and we all walked back toward the yellow tape. I greedily inhaled the fresh air.

"Before I forget," Nelson said. "This is for you."

He handed me a badge. I stared down at the teeny picture of my face.

"It won't get you in everywhere. This task force is still brand-new, and there are plenty of people who don't think it should exist. But it'll cut through some of the red tape."

"Thanks."

"Ms. Amana," a familiar voice called, and I stiffened.

Ellen Harrison smiled at me like we were best buddies. Next to me, Nathaniel let out a growl so low, it was almost soundless.

That's right. The Alpha had read the little article Ellen wrote. And he'd clearly memorized her face.

Nelson flicked him a startled look.

Nathaniel slid his sunglasses over eyes that had lightened several shades.

Cameras clicked as we walked back toward Nathaniel's car. I stiffened, feeling hunted, and Nathaniel placed his hand on my lower back. Usually, I'd shrug it off, but today, I allowed it. His silent support helped while my mind screamed *danger, danger, danger.*

HFE knew where I was. They'd known since they burned down my home and killed many of the witches I called family. There were things I did to compensate for that knowledge—for the feeling that they were just waiting for their chance at me.

My apartment was heavily warded. I was always aware of my surroundings. I practiced spells to improve my personal wards. And I *never* drew public, human attention to myself.

I scanned the reporters who were still taking pictures. My ward appeared before I was aware I'd created it. One of the reporters got too close and bounced off my ward with a curse. Nathaniel glanced at me, and I caught the humor in his eyes.

"Ms. Amana?" Harrison tried again. "A comment?"

I wasn't wearing sunglasses. And I turned, giving her a look that let her know silently, but in no uncertain terms, exactly what I thought of her.

Her face tightened, her gaze falling to my back, where Nathaniel was still steadying me. Another reporter glanced off my ward, and Nathaniel went still. He raised his head, surveying the crowd of humans.

Every single one of them dropped their eyes and went silent.

"Move. Back."

His voice was quiet, but that didn't seem to matter. The reporters almost fell over each other, clearing a path so we could get to the car.

There were benefits to walking beside an Alpha wolf.

NATHANIEL

"The reporters are going to make you pay for that," Evie murmured.

I glanced at her. I wasn't concerned about anything the reporters felt like printing about me. It was my pack that needed protection. Besides, my wolf had made it abundantly clear that he wouldn't tolerate the reporters stepping close enough to hit Evie's ward. Not while she was still so pale, her eyes haunted by the scene.

I tightened my hands around the steering wheel, and something cracked. Evie slid me a wary glance, and I eased up my grip.

"Sorry."

"It must be difficult for you," she said softly. "All the blood and death and..." Her voice trailed off, and I knew she was picturing the scene once more. Knew she'd likely have nightmares from it. I tightened my hands once more.

She took a deep, shaky breath. "Do you want me to drive?"

"No." And the most difficult part of being there was seeing the blood drain from Evie's face. I'd seen much, much worse than that scene. When the portals opened...

"Nathaniel?"

"Sorry." I glanced at Evie. She thought I was struggling with my control because of what we'd just been looking at. I'd done things that had come close to the pain and carnage before. No, I was wrestling with my wolf because he was *displeased* that I'd taken Evie to such a place.

Virtus laid one huge paw on my shoulder, and I turned my head.

He stared into my eyes, and I couldn't help but smile. "So that's why you wanted to come with us." I glanced at Evie. "Virtus would like us to drop him at Meredith's. He misses her and Vas."

Some of the tension left Evie's face. "Ah." She turned and scratched beneath the griffin's jaw. He let out a loud purr, one of his wings smacking against the right side of my car.

"If you smash through the window, it'll hurt your wing," I advised him, turning toward Main Street.

"You still haven't told us whether you'd like us to try to find someone who can heal your wing," Evie said softly, still scratching the griffin beneath his huge chin.

He looked at her, and she smiled. "Of course we'd be there. Is that a yes?"

Virtus chuffed, and Evie's smile widened. "Awesome. We're not going to rush this. We'll find someone who knows what they're doing. Someone who can cause you the least amount of pain."

His gold eyes gleamed with something like amusement, and some of the tension drained from my body. The griffin wasn't afraid of pain. He'd been wounded protecting his own pack, saving his leader's life. The pack moved on, leaving him to crawl after them when he finally regained enough strength. That had continued for years as they flew between the best hunting grounds, leaving the griffin with the twisted wing to sprint after them on foot.

When Danica had saved his life, he'd followed

her home. And I'd invited him to stay in my pack. I understood the griffins—they were operating for the good of the whole. But my own pack was only as strong as its weakest member.

I glanced at Evie.

"I'm sorry for what I said about Danica."

I knew Evie better than she could ever have imagined. To her, I was just the Alpha of the local pack. But I'd been keeping a close eye on her since the moment we'd met. And I'd learned plenty about her, including the way she stiffened whenever she was compared to her sister.

Evie gave me a cool look, and I almost smiled. She wasn't a doormat. She gave anyone who wronged her the opportunity to apologize. If they didn't, she made them pay.

Her wrath made me hard.

Whatever she saw in my eyes made her own heat. She swallowed and glanced away.

"Theories about the scene?" she asked.

"Either there's some connection between people from each scene—and they're being targeted—or the attacks are completely random, perhaps a message from someone. Or a threat."

She took a shaky breath. I restrained myself from reaching for her hand.

"You don't think it's feral wolves?"

"No. I've seen feral wolves attack in packs. Even they wouldn't have been capable of that level of destruction so quickly, wiping out the entire group.”

We were silent for a while. Then she cleared her throat.

“There’s something I need to talk to you about.”

I flicked a glance at her as we pulled up outside Meredith’s bar. I opened the trunk for Virtus, who gave us both a nuzzle before slowly backing out of the car. We both watched as he meandered into the bar, and I smiled as I heard Meredith’s excited squeal.

“What is it?”

“Meredith spotted him. He’s about to be doted on.”

She gave me a look. “As if you don’t do the same.”

“Tell me what you wanted me to know.”

She peered at her nails. Since she was obviously feeling awkward, I backed out of the parking spot and headed toward my territory.

“I’ve been having…issues with my power.”

She’d started picking at her cuticles now. I couldn’t remember a time I’d seen her look so awkward. She’d likely attempt to hit me if I told her it was cute as hell.

“What kinds of issues?”

She sighed. “I’ve always been able to do things other witches couldn’t really do. I thought I was just lucky. Now, we know it’s likely because of my freak-show genetics.”

“Don’t talk about yourself that way,” I said mildly.

She shot me a look. “It’s the truth.”

“Don’t make me pull this car over.”

The ghost of a smile lit up her face. She bit down on her lower lip, and I forced myself to ignore the urge to replace her teeth with my own.

"During the battle in the underworld, my power began to spike. For the first time, I could feel different... threads. Each of them seems to have a different type of power, and if I pull them, I don't *know* what will happen. When I went to see Albert, I made his ward disappear."

I frowned. "Those with power can break wards. That just means you have more power than the mage." My wolf preened at that, proud that she would never be on the back foot when it came to that slimy son of a bitch.

"No, you don't understand. My power mimicked his well enough that the ward allowed me to undo it. It was as if the ward had never been there."

I raised one eyebrow. "Impressive."

"You're not hearing what I'm saying."

I pulled the car over so I could look at her. She frowned at me. "Drive."

"No. What is it you're trying to say, Evelyn?"

Her eyes fired, and I barely hid my smile. "I'm trying to say, maybe I shouldn't be around the kids. I can't control my power, and I'm worried that I'll pull on the wrong thread and they'll get hurt."

I shook my head at her and started the car. "It won't happen."

"You don't know that!"

"This isn't like you. Why are you questioning yourself now?"

Evie was bold, brash, and overconfident. She jumped into everything feetfirst.

"Because there are kids involved, you bossy jackass."

Case in point. I gave her a look, and she huffed, crossing her arms.

"You would never hurt the kids. Conversation over."

I knew that would piss her off, and I was right. I parked my car, and she immediately unbuckled, threw open her door, and stalked toward her own car.

I smiled. She wouldn't worry about losing control of her power today. No, she'd be too busy cursing me out.

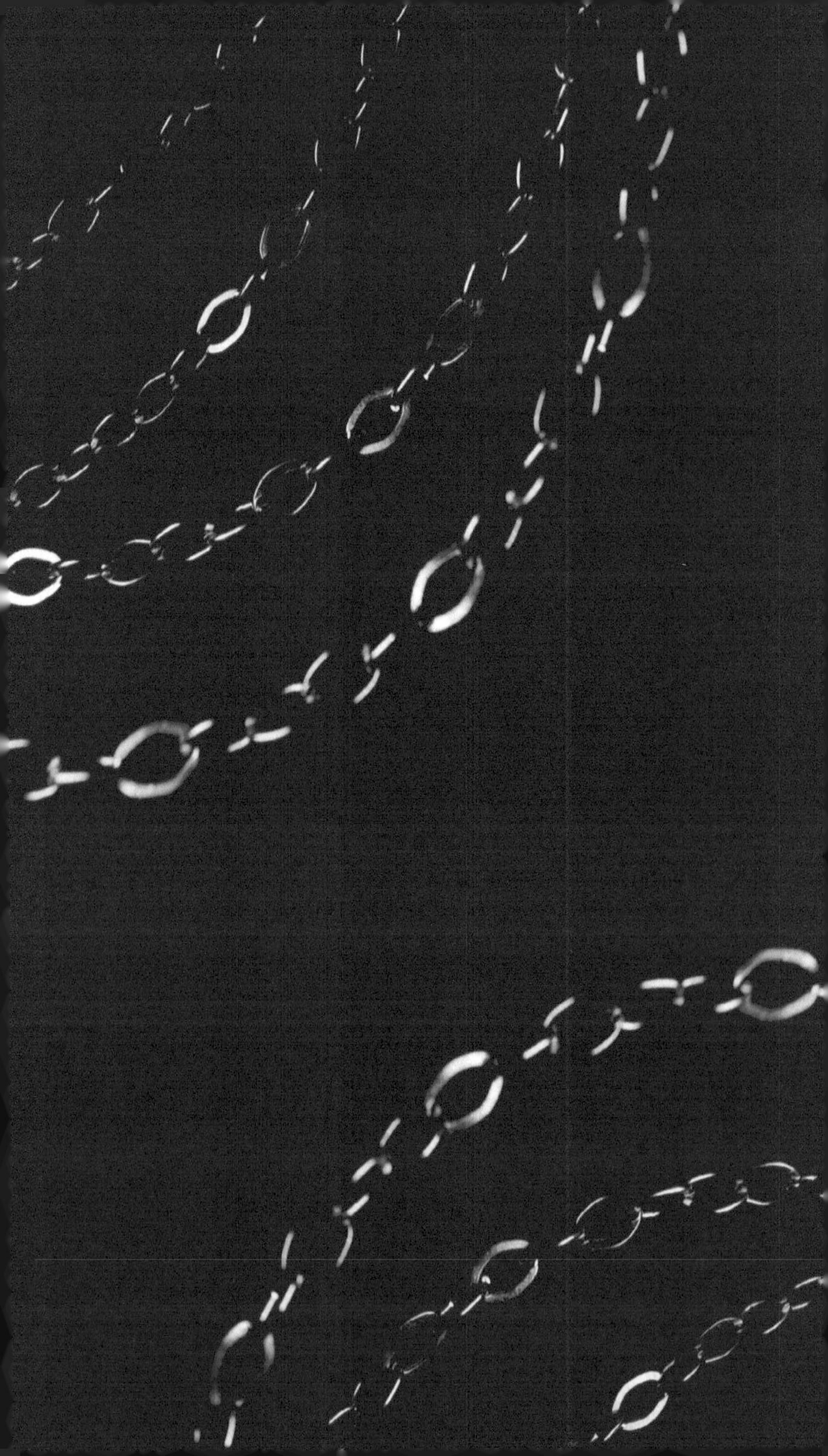

6

EVIE

Smack.

"Ow," I whined, although Vas hadn't hit me hard. He just smirked at me.

"And that's why you keep your guard up."

I narrowed my eyes. On the other side of the empty gym, Meredith snorted.

I waved my gloved fist at her. "Bael will be here soon. And he's not going to baby you like Vas will."

"Vas doesn't baby me."

Vas winced, and I gave him a toothy grin. "Uh-huh."

I tried to train with the demons most mornings, but I'd skipped a few sessions this week. Now, Vas was making me pay for it. I didn't mind. While I'd recently gone to stay with Edward Sutton, the intense training with Danica's instructor on all things deadly had only lasted a few months. I had a lot more to learn if I was going to stay alive.

Sweat dripped down my back as Bael walked in. He ran his gaze over my stance. "Still dropping that right hand," he said.

"Oh, I know."

Vas grinned at me. "Twenty more minutes and you're done."

"Good." This morning, I'd sprinted, weaved, and jumped through the obstacle course the demons liked to change each week. Then I'd done a quick strength training session before meeting Vas on the mat.

Vas swung again. He was probably at half his usual speed. Demons were lightning-fast. But every week, he increased his speed a little more.

I shifted to the side, darted behind him, and slammed my hand into the back of his neck.

Edward had made it clear that I'd never fight as well as my sister, so he'd taught me every dirty trick he knew.

Vas slapped his hand over his neck and laughed. "Nice hit. Needs to be harder, though."

I sniffed. "That would have been my knife, not my hand."

He reached out one hand and ruffled my hair. I shoved his hand away. The teeny ward I usually used to protect my hair from his annoying hands wasn't allowed in sparring. The demons wanted me to be able to protect myself *without* my power.

Vas grinned at me. "You look like a pissed-off poodle."

Mere walked past us both, toward Bael, who was waiting on the mat for her. "One day," she said to Vas, "she's going to kick your ass."

I grinned at her. "Damn right. I need to get going."

"I left something for you. By the door," Bael said.

I wandered over and picked up today's copy of *Durham Denizens.*

I'd made the front page. Again. This time, it was a black-and-white picture of Nathaniel helping me to my feet after I'd vomited. We were standing close enough that it looked almost intimate. But it was the headline that did the damage.

Werewolf Alpha and Local Witch Canoodle at Crime Scene.

How the fuck had Harrison gotten this picture? I ran my mind back to where I'd been standing. Long-range lens, good angle from the road. It was possible. Although I was betting she'd used some kind of charm—likely bought before I talked to Gary. For a woman who seemed to have it in for paranormals, she sure seemed to enjoy playing with our toys.

Vas wandered toward me and let out a low hiss when he caught the headline. Then he continued reading over my shoulder.

"While Ms. Amana and Mr. Savage are 'investigating' these horrifying murders, their insistence on mixing business with pleasure proves that paranormals are willing to allow each other to prey on defenseless humans."

I closed my eyes. When I opened them, the words were still there. In print.

"I don't get it," I said. "This is the only newspaper most paranormals read. Harrison has just made herself a target."

"Maybe she thinks it's worth it if she can take you down with her."

"This is insane." I frowned. "It can't just be about me."

I needed to talk to Nathaniel. But first, I'd head into my office. I wanted to see if the victims of the two massacres had anything—or anyone—in common.

"I've got to go."

I stuffed the newspaper into my duffel and took advantage of the demons' water pressure in their changing rooms.

Half an hour later, I'd pulled on a pair of cropped jeans and a tank top, before shoving my wet curls into a messy bun. I took the elevator down to the lobby, nodding at the demons I recognized, although they were few and far between.

Most of them were in the underworld now, helping Samael and Danica set up their court.

My office and the tower were only a few blocks apart. Since I'd need my car later, I'd driven to the tower, which meant I had to fight my way down Main Street through commuter traffic.

Kyla was waiting when I arrived, her gaze on her phone. From the cold lines of her face, she was reading the article.

I dumped my purse on my desk and took out the list of victims Nelson had sent me.

"You got time to take half of these?"

Kyla leaned back in her chair. "We're not going to talk about this?" She stabbed her finger toward her phone.

"Nope."

"Fine. I've got about an hour before I have more interviews from the auction house. I'll take as many names as I can."

I emailed her through some of the names and started making my lists.

The first massacre was the Foster family's reunion. I pulled up pictures of the crime scene and attempted to locate some professional distance.

I didn't find it.

Madeline Foster had been celebrating her ninetieth birthday. Since it was a big deal, members of the family had flown in from various states, mostly on the East Coast.

Fifty-six people in total. All of them dead.

I went through the adults who were still of

working age. One of them, a guy named Thomas, worked for NASA. I put him aside to investigate later and shifted my attention to the group of employees from CertSure—the insurance company.

"Knock knock."

I glanced at the door as Rose strolled in. The mercenary had once been one of my sister's enemies. Then she'd saved her life.

It was complicated.

Now, she was staying in Danica's old apartment since the Mage Council would happily kill Rose for her "betrayal."

"I heard you were back," Rose said. "I need answers. Please."

I sighed. I either needed a coffee the size of my head or a strong drink, and it was barely ten a.m.

Rose narrowed her eyes at me. "All of you disappeared. And Danica never returned. For a while, I thought most of you were dead. Please, just tell me what happened."

I glanced at Kyla, who shrugged. At this point, everyone else seemed to know exactly what had happened. The only reason Rose didn't was because she'd been mostly hunkered down and hiding from the mages.

"How much do you know?" I asked.

Rose leaned against a wall. "I know Samael's grandfather ruled the underworld before Lucifer staged a coup and killed his family when Samael was still a kid. Samael made it to our realm once the portals opened and ruled most of the demons on Earth. But he'd always vowed to take back his throne. Once Lucifer learned Danica was his granddaughter, he had her kidnapped."

She knew a lot. And she'd saved my sister's life once, when a group of mages had attempted to deliver her to Lucifer.

I sighed. "Yes, Danica was his granddaughter. A granddaughter who would never have been born if he'd had his way. She was prophesied to kill him. One of the light fae king's advisers kidnapped her, and then the light fae allied with Lucifer during Samael's battle to take the throne. That's why we're now all at war with the seelie."

Rose nodded. "But Danica was gone for a long time. What happened?"

"Lucifer stole her memories. Kyla here was kidnapped with Danica, and she spent her time stuck in wolf form in the dungeons with Keigan."

Rose's eyes widened. "Keigan was there?"

I'd forgotten. Rose and Keigan had worked together. This was going to be tough. "Yes. Danica saw him as a father figure, but while she was in the underworld, she learned… She learned…" My voice broke.

Kyla stepped forward and squeezed my shoulder. "Evie and Danica's mom was lured by an organization called Humans for Equality

when Danica was a toddler. They were doing...
experiments. Evie was created in that lab. And
Keigan worked for them."

I hated the look of pity on Rose's face. But that
look shifted to sorrow as she thought about what
Kyla had said.

"Keigan's dead, isn't he?"

I nodded. "I'm sorry. Someone should've told
you before now."

"It sounds like it has been a crazy few months.
I knew Danica was in the underworld, but I didn't
know where you guys were."

"I was in Texas. Training."

And Kyla had been stuck to Nathaniel's side,
desperately holding on to her humanity.

Rose flicked a glance at Kyla and clearly realized
we weren't going to tell her more than that.

"I was wondering...if you need any help."

I raised my eyebrow. "What kind of help?"

"Anything," she said quickly. "I'm going crazy
not working. Danica said she'd hire me eventually,
but she's not here..."

I glanced at Kyla. She gave me a nod so small, I
barely caught it.

"It just so happens, we both have cases right
now. If you're willing to do grunt work and
research—"

"Done. Hand it over."

I couldn't help but grin. I pointed her toward

the sofa, filled her in about the massacres, and gave her some of the CertSure employees to investigate.

"Once we've researched them for any links to paranormals, or anything else that could make them targets, we'll cross-reference the two groups against each other and see if we can find any connections."

Two hours later, my brain was fried. Kyla had left to get cracking with her own investigation, and my stomach was rumbling.

I got to my feet. "I'm going to go out to the wolves. I'll be back in a couple of hours."

Rose nodded. "I'll text you if I find anything."

"Thanks."

I hadn't forgotten about my other case. Obviously, it was low priority compared to the massacres. But I'd be heading to the morgue this afternoon to talk to the ME. I may as well attempt to clear my head with a visit to the wolves.

Wolf territory stretched from the edge of Duke Forest and encompassed the Hollow Rock Nature Park, Johnston Mill Nature Preserve, Brumley Forest Nature Preserve, and the edge of Hillsborough, where I'd tricked the roc into going through the portal. It also included neighborhoods that had once been called Colony Park and Pickran Estates. When the humans had realized how close they were to what had become wolf territory, they'd moved out. The wolves had happily demolished the houses and allowed the forest to spread.

No one would think to approach wolf territory any other way than through the sign-posted route leading to Nathaniel's, however. Rumor had it, the wolves controlled more forested territory than most people could imagine, and the deeper you traveled into that territory, the more likely you were to come across a half-wild wolf who hadn't yet gone truly feral but wasn't trusted to be around the kids.

I left the windows down as I drove. My stomach rumbled again. I'd forgotten to grab something to eat. Oh well.

I parked outside Nathaniel's. After a moment of deliberation, I stalked to his door and gave several solid knocks.

Naomi opened the door. We'd met before. She was one of Nathaniel's dominants. I didn't know exactly what she did for him, but I'd definitely noted her ability to get shit done. The fact that he had a female human in his upper echelon proved Nathaniel didn't discriminate.

"Hey."

She gave me a cool nod. Obviously, she believed I'd been blabbing wolf business all over town. Or perhaps she truly thought I'd been flirting with Nathaniel at a crime scene.

"He's in a meeting," she said. "He'll be done in the next ten minutes or so."

My stomach let out another howl, and the

ghost of a smile crossed her face. "That'll piss him off. Go through to the kitchen. Tobias just made sandwiches."

"Thanks."

Tobias gave me a pleased grin as I poked my head into his domain.

"Sit, sit."

I did as I was told. It was my first time in Nathaniel's kitchen, and I took it in. Most of the space was dominated by a huge island, which held six chairs. I got the feeling the wolves ate in here more often than in the formal dining room. The island held a huge vase of purple and blue flowers.

The refrigerator was the largest I'd ever seen, Tobias was standing in front of *three* ovens, and the double sinks took up a slice of the large counter.

In spite of how ridiculously oversized everything was—likely due to the number of people Tobias regularly cooked for—the kitchen had a homey feel. The soft, neutral colors toned down the steel appliances, and the air was redolent with the scent of some kind of soup simmering on the stove.

The chilly air conditioning was welcome after the oppressive heat outside. Werewolves tended to run hot.

Tobias bustled around, handing me another glass of orange juice. I angled my head, and he shook his finger at me.

"I know you're not eating well. Drink your vitamins."

I obeyed. Tobias's orange juice was freshly squeezed.

"I wanted to thank you," I said as Tobias reached up into a cupboard.

"Whatever for?"

When Kyla and Danica were kidnapped, the wolves had worked with the demons, all of us staying in Samael's tower. Seeing so many predators forced to tamp down their natural instincts and tolerate each other had been an eye-opening experience, to say the least.

Tobias had insisted on coming with the other wolves—all of them dominant. He'd always seemed to know when the tension was about to snap, and he'd had an uncanny way of bustling into the room with a plate of food at the exact right moment.

"When Dani and Kyla were taken...you not only kept the peace, but you lightened the mood. You also kept me from losing my mind a few times."

His expression softened. "It was my privilege."

Tobias put a plate in front of me, and I stared at the huge sub. "Uh..."

"Eat. If you can't finish it, you can take the rest with you."

Chicken salad on freshly baked bread. I dug in with a muffled moan.

"You know the demons want to steal you," I said

around my next bite. Bael had made it clear he was eyeing the butler slash housekeeper for the tower. I was pretty sure the thought of going to war with the werewolves over their butler had given Samael a migraine.

Tobias threw back his head and laughed. "They'd find me an uncooperative prisoner. And I don't cook when I'm mad."

"He's not lying," Nathaniel said from behind me. "The only times I've ever ordered takeout are the times I pissed him off."

The kitchen immediately seemed to shrink down to half the size when he walked in. I glanced at him, but he was grinning at Tobias, who shook his head at Nathaniel.

Before I'd seen their relationship, I'd assumed submissive wolves were treated like garbage. But it was clear Nathaniel considered Tobias family. My chest clenched at the thought.

Tobias gave him a smug smile. "We submissives must use the tools we have."

Nathaniel took the plate Tobias handed him and sat next to me. He was so large, I was surprised the stool beneath him didn't groan in protest.

I took the newspaper out of my purse and slid it across the counter to him. He leaned over and glanced at it. Then he went very still.

Tobias busied himself with placing more sandwiches on plates.

"I thought it was something I'd done to piss her off," I said carefully. "But this isn't just about catching her eavesdropping or having her kicked out of Meredith's. I don't think I'm the target here."

Nathaniel raised one eyebrow. "And you think I am?"

I shrugged. "She writes for the *Durham Denizens.*" I pointed to her comment about paranormals not having respect for human life. "She's making enemies of her own with that shit. And if she was close enough to take that picture, she knew you were helping me after..."

The crime scene flashed through my mind, and I placed my sandwich back on my plate.

This wasn't about me. I was certain of it. But it *was* personal. I glanced at Nathaniel, who was plowing through his sandwich.

"Is she an ex?" I asked carefully.

Good god. Was that a tendril of...jealousy winding its way through my gut?

No. I'd just eaten too fast.

Nathaniel placed his own sandwich on his plate.

"No."

My hands unfisted, and I let out the breath I'd been holding. It definitely shouldn't matter to me if the reporter was Nathaniel's ex. So where was this overwhelming sense of relief coming from?

Nathaniel gave me a look I couldn't decipher,

but his eyes darkened back to their usual hue. Of course, he could smell just how relieved I was by that information. Shit.

"Are you positive you've never met her before?" I pressed.

"I saw her at the crime scene. At the first one in South Carolina. Other than that, I don't know her," Nathaniel said, and this time, some of his annoyance leaked through.

Ryker strolled in. "Hey, boss. Evie."

Tobias poked his head out from the pantry. "Eat," he ordered, and Ryker grinned at him.

"Thanks."

Ryker, Hunter, and Xander were Nathaniel's most-trusted—and most dominant—wolves. I wasn't entirely sure where Naomi fit in, but I was determined to figure it out.

Ryker took his own sandwich and wandered around the counter, leaning over my shoulder to read the newspaper.

Nathaniel let out a low growl, and I stared at him. Ryker grabbed the newspaper, took one large step away from me, and scanned it.

"That bitch," he muttered.

Nathaniel gave him a look, and he shrugged. "Sorry, boss, but it's the truth. I knew she was going to be bad news."

Nathaniel stiffened, and I craned my head around him.

"What?"

Had Nathaniel...lied to me?

I surveyed him, and he stared back at me, a hint of his wolf in his eyes. I dropped my gaze back to my plate until he shifted his attention to Ryker, who'd plonked himself down on Nathaniel's other side.

"What are you talking about?"

Ryker took a huge bite of his sub, his black hair falling over his forehead. "Few months ago," he said around his sub. "She wanted a comment on something..." He frowned and swallowed, taking a sip of water. "Maybe our alliance with the demons? Anyway, I gave her a comment, but she wanted to talk to you. I asked you about it, remember?"

Nathaniel's expression was ice-cold. "No."

He shrugged. "Not surprising. Dealing with reporters is my job," he sneered and took another bite. "Anyway, she got pissy about it. Made a few vague threats. I put them in an email." He raised an eyebrow at his Alpha. Then he dropped his own gaze with a swallow.

Nathaniel was not pleased. By any of it.

"You're telling me this *reporter* is fabricating these lies because I wouldn't speak to her?"

He sounded genuinely shocked, and I couldn't help the snort that escaped me. He looked at me, and I attempted to hide my smirk. It didn't work.

"I'm sorry," I said. "But you have to admit, it's

kind of funny. This human woman is out for blood, and you don't even know who she is. Which is probably why she's so pissed. It's kind of ironic."

Naomi strolled into the kitchen, taking the plate Tobias held out.

"You want me to take care of her?" she asked Nathaniel.

He slowly shook his head.

"Are you sure?" Ryker asked. "She's only going to get worse."

"We can stand up to anything she prints. So can Evie."

I attempted to ignore the warmth that spread through my chest at that.

"We can at least warn her off," Naomi argued.

"No. You don't give a misbehaving child what they want. And she wants my attention."

Fair point. I got to my feet, and Tobias took my plate, slid the rest of my sub into a paper sandwich bag, and handed it back.

"Thank you. I need to get moving," I said. Naomi ignored me. Ryker nodded. Nathaniel...

He gave me a look that suddenly made me feel like *I* was his prey.

I backed out of the room. But not before I heard Naomi say something that sounded a lot like "scared little rabbit."

NATHANIEL

Lunch turned into an unofficial meeting with my dominants. I'd finished my meal an hour ago, but it wasn't uncommon for us to get more done in these random get-togethers than in our formal weekly meetings.

I hadn't missed the stiffening of Evie's shoulders when she heard Naomi's "rabbit" comment. Naomi had sneered when Evie kept walking, while Ryker just shook his head at her.

"Playing with fire," he'd muttered.

I narrowed my eyes at him. "Explain."

"Evie doesn't get mad. She gets even." I watched him, and he sighed. "I pissed her off when we were at the tower. The demons were following her around on Samael's orders. He'd figured she was impulsive and crazy enough to try to get her sister back on her own." He scratched at his jaw. "They're probably not wrong," he admitted. "Anyway, she was arguing with them one day, and I backed them up. Told her if she could be trusted not to fly off the handle, maybe we wouldn't have to split our resources."

I shook my head at that. Ryker nodded at me.

"She waited until I was in the changing rooms after a workout. While I was showering, she took all the towels, my clothes, and anything else I could've used to keep this glorious body covered. Then she set them on fire and left the ashes in a neat little pile near the shower. And that was nothing compared to some of the shit she did to the demons."

I was torn between annoyance that Evie had been that close to a naked Ryker and pride that she'd proven she wasn't to be messed with.

Across the kitchen, Naomi snorted. I watched her, and she dropped her gaze.

"Evie didn't have anything to do with the article," I said softly.

She shrugged, and I left it alone. Evie wouldn't thank me for defending her to my wolves. In fact, it would probably just annoy her.

Xander stepped into the room. Naomi had messaged him when we began talking.

"Any news from Harry?" I asked him. The Alpha's territory encompassed all of California and Nevada.

Xander shook his head. "No mass attacks on humans in his territory. He said, if anything, it's been quiet."

"Could this be the light fae king?" Ryker asked.

"It could be anyone." Naomi scowled. "That's the problem."

I thought about it. "Taraghlan has been quiet.

Too quiet. But he's got problems of his own. Now that he's officially at war with almost every paranormal faction, he has to plan something big if he's going to hold on to his throne. I don't see how targeting groups of humans would benefit him."

"Bad optics for us," Hunter said. He'd mostly stayed quiet during this meeting. He wasn't one for talking unless he had something to say. "We're the only monsters the humans know for sure could create that kind of carnage."

We were all quiet for a moment. Finally, Xander pulled out his phone. "Trevor Brunt wants to set up a meeting. He wants to discuss a corporate contract with our security firm."

I raised one eyebrow. Brunt was notoriously anti-paranormals.

"Why?"

He smirked. "Brunt began getting threats after a particularly bad business deal. Bad for the other party. His business was targeted, and the human security company dropped the ball. He made it clear that any contract with us would include a strict NDA. After donating so much to all those paranormal hate groups, he doesn't want it known that he's now considering hiring us."

"Deny him the meeting." There were few things I hated worse than hypocrites. Bigoted hypocrites were one of them.

"Have our spies check on the seelie king," I said,

my mind returning to the massacres. Taraghlan kidnapped one of my wolves when he took Danica. Kyla almost died. Our healers had given her a twenty percent chance of retaining her humanity even after she'd managed to shift back to human. And that had been generous. They hadn't known just how stubborn Kyla was, but that didn't mean the pack hadn't been sent into a deep mourning.

I owed Taraghlan some pain. And he knew it. Perhaps this was a way to distract us so he could take us out in one move.

"Look into any other group attacks that have been attributed to wolves in the past six months. Check the entire country. It could be that there have been more attacks that have been missed."

Humans in other territories might have assumed the attacks were by werewolves, making it an open-and-shut case. If that was the case, we were in even deeper trouble than we could've imagined.

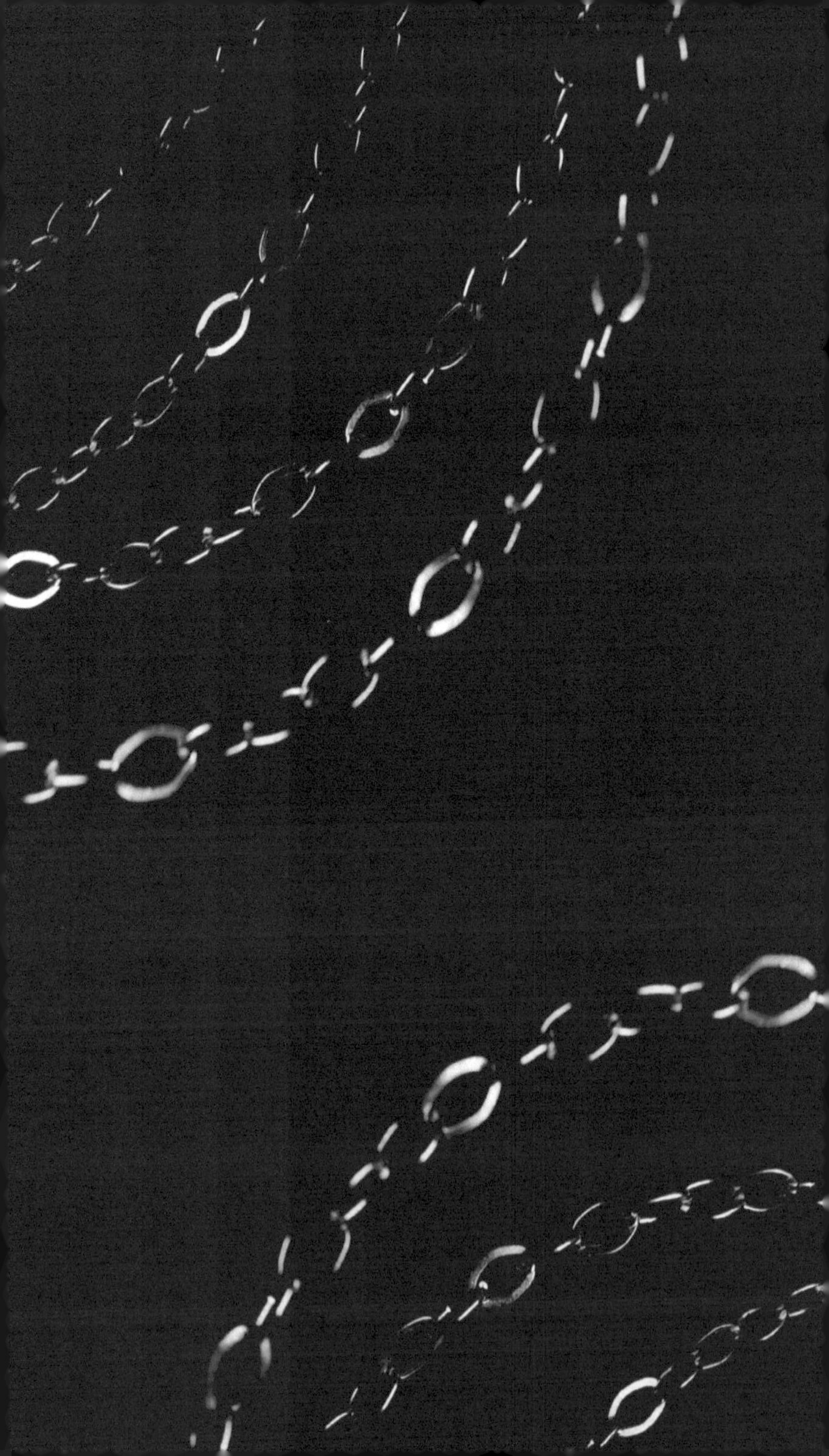

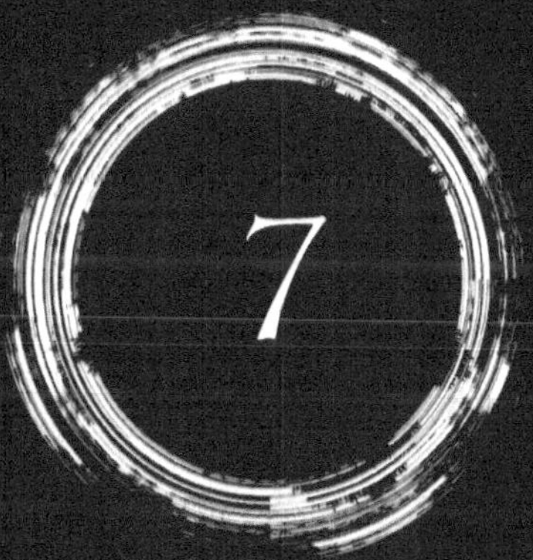

EVIE

eat lay like a heavy hand on the back of my neck as I walked toward the playground. Now that I was away from the wolves, my appetite had returned, and I took a seat on my usual swing and took a massive bite of my chicken sandwich.

I had another half hour to kill before I was due to meet Kyla at the morgue.

"How'd you learn to do magic?" a squeaky voice asked, and I glanced over at the boy as he approached.

"Does your mom know you're here?"

Charlie gave me a cheeky, gap-toothed smile. "She said I'm allowed to play in the playground this morning. Did you bring your magic with you?"

I couldn't help but smile. "Yeah. My magic always comes with me."

"How did you get it?"

"I was born with it."

Charlie frowned at that. "The big kids have magic, but we're not allowed to use it."

I went still. "What kind of magic?"

He shrugged, and I chewed on my lower lip. Was *that* how the kids were disappearing? Some kind of magic?

Most magic didn't work on werewolves, but the kids were only half wolf. As far as I knew, they'd never be able to shift—unless they suffered some kind of attack from a wolf and it didn't kill them.

"Listen, buddy," I said softly. "If the big kids are using magic to disappear—"

"Charlie," a sharp voice said, and I glanced at the climbing wall. Several of the preteens were hanging out together.

A boy I didn't recognize took a few steps toward us. "Go home. Now."

Charlie stuck out his lower lip, and I glanced between them, noting the similar features. This was obviously Charlie's big brother. Which meant he was one of the kids I needed to talk to.

"You're not the boss of me, Levi. Mom said I could play!"

Levi took a threatening step closer. Since Charlie didn't flinch or cower, I didn't think Levi was the kind of kid who'd hit his little brother, but he was definitely annoyed.

And it wasn't just annoyance in his eyes. It was fear and fury. He knew Charlie could tell me something that would help me figure out what they were up to.

"Go home," Levi ordered again.

Charlie shook his head. Levi stepped closer.

"You're so fucking stupid," he spat.

That was quite enough.

I waved my hand, and Levi rose several inches off the ground. This kind of power was tricky to use, which was why I didn't take him higher. Also, I was pretty sure his parents would lose their minds if they glanced out the window and saw him hovering six feet above my head.

The blood drained from Levi's face. Oops.

I hopped off the swing and strolled toward him. "It's okay. I won't hurt you."

He gave me a suspicious look. And then he swung his feet with the beginning of a smile on his face. His friends were gaping at us, several of them wide-eyed. One of them reached for his phone, and I shook my head at him. I was going to be in enough trouble for this. I didn't need video evidence floating around.

"Can you take me higher?"

"Maybe another day." When he told me exactly what he was up to.

He stuck out his lower lip, and I laughed. For a moment, he looked just like Charlie.

I took him another few inches higher, and he did a little boogie in the air.

"I want a turn," one of his friends said. He looked sixteen or so, and he flushed as his voice cracked.

Obviously, the colorful balls flying through the air just hadn't been cool enough for these kids. Flying? That was another story.

I grinned at him and waved my hand, sending him up a few inches as well. He high-fived Levi, and Charlie ran toward us.

"Me, me, me!"

I opened my mouth, but my phone buzzed. Since I didn't want my inattention to risk dropping the kids—even if they were less than a foot from the ground—I slowly brought them down.

"Hello?"

"I'm at the morgue. Where are you?"

"Oops. My bad. I'll be right there."

"No worries. I'll go grab lunch while I wait."

I ended the call. "Gotta go, guys," I said.

Several "awwws" broke out, and I hid my grin.

Always leave them wanting more.

I turned, and my eyes collided with one of the wolves. He slowly prowled toward me.

"Dad's here!"

Charlie launched himself at the wolf, and I tensed. Even knowing his dad wouldn't hurt him, it worried me to watch Charlie climb up on him as if he were a horse.

The wolf gave me one last look and turned, slowly padding toward the forest.

"It's okay," Levi said, clearly reading my mind. "Most wolves don't like that kind of thing, but my dad is the best."

I grinned at that. "See you soon."

"When are you coming back?" one of the older girls asked casually. I was pretty sure her name was Alyssa.

"Tomorrow morning." I decided on the spot. If the wolves hadn't had me barred from even talking to the kids.

She smiled at me. "Cool."

I made my way back toward my car, finally allowing myself to consider just how dangerous Ellen Harrison could be to the wolves.

Thanks to growing up in the coven, I knew my history. When the portals opened, almost a billion humans died. They hated the witches, who'd been responsible for waking a demigod and opening the portals. They hated the light fae, and that hatred only grew for the dark fae. They even hated the mages, who'd come into their power accidentally, and used it to protect humans.

But the werewolves? Humans *loathed* the werewolves.

Even though they'd spent the past seventy-plus years sticking to their own territory and even helping the humans occasionally. Even though there were far worse things from realms like the middleground— many of them sneaking through into our world.

It didn't matter. Werewolves had once been human themselves. And humans had a particular hatred for those who turned on each other.

My gut twisted. Ellen thought she'd get Nathaniel's attention. In the process, she was risking the wolves. If she wasn't careful, she was going to get his attention, all right. And she wouldn't like it.

My car had been sitting in the heat for long enough that I switched on the air conditioning as I drove out of wolf territory. By the time I pulled into the morgue's parking lot on Elizabeth Street, I'd mentally turned my attention from the wolves to whatever was killing large groups of humans.

The morgue was a sprawling concrete building situated right behind the Durham Police Department Headquarters on East Main Street. I caught sight of Kyla leaning against her car and parked near her.

I slid out of the car and shoved my sunglasses on top of my head.

"About time." Kyla smiled at me. "You smell like pack."

"I had lunch with Nathaniel and Ryker. Naomi stopped by to sneer at me for a bit. Oh, and I showed Nathaniel the article. He wasn't pleased."

"Did he know the reporter?"

"He said no. And then Ryker mentioned she'd tried to get him to comment on something a few months ago. Couldn't take no for an answer. I guess now she's pissed."

"And clearly loony tunes. I'm sorry you got caught up in it, Evie."

I shrugged. "The good news is I managed to get

Charlie to talk to me about the 'magic' the older kids are using."

The smile disappeared from Kyla's face, and she frowned. We walked toward the morgue's entrance, and I filled her in. "Magic. Shit. No wonder they're disappearing. This is not good, Evie."

"I know. But it could be Charlie's talking about some kind of charm one of the older kids got from Gary's. Let's not panic until I know more. Any luck with the interviews?"

"Not really. One of the security guards from the auction was just found dead in his car. Another security guard hasn't been seen for three days." She slid me a look. "You up for a little breaking and entering after this?"

"Always."

She grinned and took out her phone. "I'm sending you the address."

We stepped inside the morgue, and Kyla seemed to perk up at the cooler air. A guard sat at a long marble counter on the left.

"We're here to see Wilson," I said.

"IDs," the guard said, and we handed them to him. He examined them, then picked up the phone.

"Take a seat," he said when he was done. We took our licenses and sat on the red plastic chairs against the wall.

A few minutes later, the ME appeared. She nodded at Kyla. "Nice to see you again."

I held out my hand. "Evie Amana."

"Amy Wilson. I sent my report to Detective Nelson."

"I know. He'll send it over to me at some point. I just wanted to stop in and get your overall impression."

She raised one eyebrow, and I sighed. "Whatever is killing these people…it's doing it fast. I think we're going to have another crime scene on our hands and soon. Is there anything you can tell us, any impression you got that could help?"

"Looks like a rampaging werewolf attacked," she said, and Kyla stiffened. "But…I've seen the results of those kinds of attacks before. There isn't much the bodies can tell us, but I think whatever killed them…I believe the claws were much, much larger than the average werewolf. That's just speculation, I'm sorry. We still don't know much about werewolves themselves." She flicked a glance at Kyla, who just smiled. The wolves weren't exactly the type to train law enforcement on how to spot their kills.

"I put everything else in the report," Wilson said.

I made a mental note to ask Nelson to have the report sent to me. It had been a long shot, but I'd hoped Wilson would have some kind of instinct about the beast. Something she wouldn't have put in a report.

"Thanks for your help. Let me know if you think of anything else."

Wilson nodded at us and scanned her way back through the double doors. I glanced at Kyla.

"What's bigger than a werewolf, kills faster than anything we've ever seen, and doesn't bother eating the best parts?"

Her shoulders slumped as she leaned back in the plastic chair. "I don't know."

"Me neither. But all signs are pointing to this not being a werewolf. That's good news."

I glanced at my phone as it vibrated. "Rose messaged. So far, the only connection she's found between the two massacres is that one of the family members from the first group was planning to do some business with CertSure. Oh, and there were low-level mages among the victims in both groups."

"Did the mages know each other?"

I passed the question on to Rose.

"Rose says she's not sure. She's going to see what she can find from the South Carolina attack and figure out if there were any connections there, too."

Thanks. I messaged Rose. *Keep me updated.*

We got to our feet and headed out into the heat. "What's the security guard's address?" I asked. "I'll follow you to the house, but then I need to get back to the office."

Kyla pulled out her phone, and my own phone buzzed with the address. Then she froze.

Kyla stared past me, the color draining from her eyes. I shivered.

"Ms. Amana," a voice said.

I recognized that voice. I whirled, stepping in front

of Kyla. It wouldn't help much, but I'd at least slow her down.

Ellen Harrison had her long red hair braided back from her face. She wore a tight pencil skirt, a tank top that looked like silk, and strappy sandals.

She also held out a recording device. Kyla let out a low growl, and Ellen gave her a patronizing look. Her gaze automatically dropped, though, proving that either she wasn't a complete idiot, or her human instincts had overridden her ego.

I could feel other eyes on us. Malevolent eyes. I glanced at Kyla, and she jerked her head to the left, but I couldn't see anything there.

Ellen swallowed and managed to raise her head, keeping her gaze on me.

"What is it you want, Harrison?" I asked.

I caught the hint of a sneer before she turned it into a smile. "A comment. Word is you're dating the Alpha."

I stared at her. "Over sixty humans dead so far, and you want to know about my love life?"

She didn't even have the grace to blush. Instead, she stared at me as if she was waiting me out. She would be waiting an eternity.

Kyla took a single step closer, and I held up one hand.

"You're the one who created the rumor about us *canoodling*," I said softly. "Now, I suggest you leave me alone."

"I saw how he looked at you."

Oh shit. She'd obviously pulled on her crazy pants when she got dressed this morning.

Ellen stalked closer, and Kyla was done. She shoved me behind her, and a vicious snarl ripped from her throat. Her claws popped out, and I wished desperately for Nathaniel. If Kyla snapped…

She'd never forgive herself.

Ellen had gone stark white. "You fucking *animal*," she hissed.

"You just don't know when to shut up," I said casually, hoping Kyla would take it down a notch.

I held up my hand, and a ball of red light appeared. It was just that—light—but it sure looked impressive.

"You can't have it both ways, Ellen. Either we're a threat to humans, or we're not. Since you've made it clear we can't be trusted, I suggest you fuck off."

Ellen finally got the message. Her lips rolled tight and disappeared into her mouth—suppressing the words she clearly wanted to say. But it was too late. One moment, Kyla was a human, and the next, she was a wolf.

Oh shit.

Ellen turned and sprinted toward her car. For all the reporter's obsession with the wolves—or at least one in particular—she was still stupid enough to run from them.

"Kyla, stop," I snapped. She turned and snarled at me.

I bared my own teeth back. But I also popped my ward into place.

We stared at each other for a long moment. Distantly, I was aware of someone on the other side of the parking lot, their voice high and thready as they spoke on the phone—likely calling the police.

Finally, Kyla heaved a sigh. She dropped her head. I leaned over and ran my hand over her silky ears. When she didn't rip my hand off, I figured she'd managed to regain control.

She let out a soft whine. "It's okay," I said. "You'll figure it out. You want to drive with me? I can drop you back here afterward."

She nodded. Then she jerked her head toward her car. I picked up her clothes, which had torn to pieces when she shifted. Tucking her shoes under my arm, I used her key to unlock her trunk, shoved the ripped remnants of her clothes in the corner, and opened one of the plastic containers she kept in her trunk for just this purpose.

I pulled out a T-shirt, underwear, and a pair of jeans, locked the car, then carried the shoes and clothes toward my own car.

Kyla followed me like a puppy who'd been kicked one too many times.

"You need to relax," I told her. "The reporter was *trying* to piss us off. There's something seriously not right about her. But if you rip her head off her shoulders, you're the one Nathaniel will have to put down."

Nausea swept through me at the thought. I didn't know the Alpha all that well, but I knew he had a special place in his heart for Kyla. Female wolves were one-in-a-million rare, but that wasn't just it. He loved her like a sister, and I'd seen how frantic he'd been when she was kidnapped.

Hurting Kyla would kill a piece of him.

Not that Danica or I would allow that to happen. The demons would go to war with the wolves…

Kyla stepped on my foot with her paw and gazed up at me. I was still standing in the middle of the parking lot.

"Sorry."

I opened the back door of my car for her, and she jumped in, keeping her claws tucked away.

I pulled my phone out of my pocket and noted the address Kyla had sent me. Beau Stewart lived in Croasdaile, which had once been a retirement village. I started the car and headed toward his neighborhood, my mind racing. I was worried about Kyla. She'd made a ton of progress after the battle. When I'd gone to Austin to train, she'd been pretty much glued to Nathaniel's side. But if she snapped and killed a human, it was game over for her.

Dull fury twisted my stomach, and I clenched my hands on the wheel. Kyla whined at me, and I forced myself to let out a long breath.

"Sorry." My emotions wouldn't help her keep her control.

I pulled up to Beau's house—a tribute to modernity made of cement and glass. The tasteless McMansion also boasted a sterile front yard with regulation-length grass.

I counted windows and frowned at the sheer size of the house.

"How does a guy who works security afford this place? Does he have a wife or partner?"

Kyla shook her head. We got out of the car, and I surveyed the house as we walked up the drive.

Kyla suddenly went stiff, her lips peeling back from her teeth.

"What is it, girl? Did Timmy fall down the well?"

She shot me an unamused look, then returned her attention to the house.

I knocked again, and she pressed against my leg, shaking her head at me.

"Uh-oh." I had a pretty good idea of what we were about to find in the house. I glanced over my shoulder, then slid my trusty lock-picking tools out of my purse.

"Keep an eye out for me."

It didn't take long. My skills were new, but thanks to Edward, they were finely honed. The lock clicked, and I opened the door.

"Fuck."

Beau Stewart lay on his stomach, one hand stretched out toward the door, as if he'd been running for his life. He hadn't made it.

NATHANIEL

I shifted, my wolf form allowing me to pick up fainter scents than I could in my human form. My vision narrowed, and I lowered my head, inhaling deeply.

Several of my wolves were spaced out, ten feet apart, all of them doing the same.

Something had come into my territory.

Something that smelled *different*.

I couldn't tell if it was seelie or unseelie. It didn't smell like demon. My whole body grew hot with frustration.

I shifted back to human as Hunter approached.

"What do we know?"

"Nothing on the cameras leading into this part of our territory. It's as if it appeared out of nowhere."

Not *uncommon* with paranormal creatures, but that made it more powerful than anything I'd gone up against recently.

"Do we need to evacuate the kids?" he asked.

"No. But anyone going for a run needs to stick to the monitored areas for now."

"They're not going to like it."

"I don't like it either. We don't know what this thing is, and it could be simple luck that no one was attacked. Put the word out."

Doug lifted his head, and I made my way over to him. He nosed near the trunk of a tree, and I leaned down, taking the scent into my own lungs. I still didn't know what it was, but if I came up against it, I would recognize it.

And I would kill it for invading my territory.

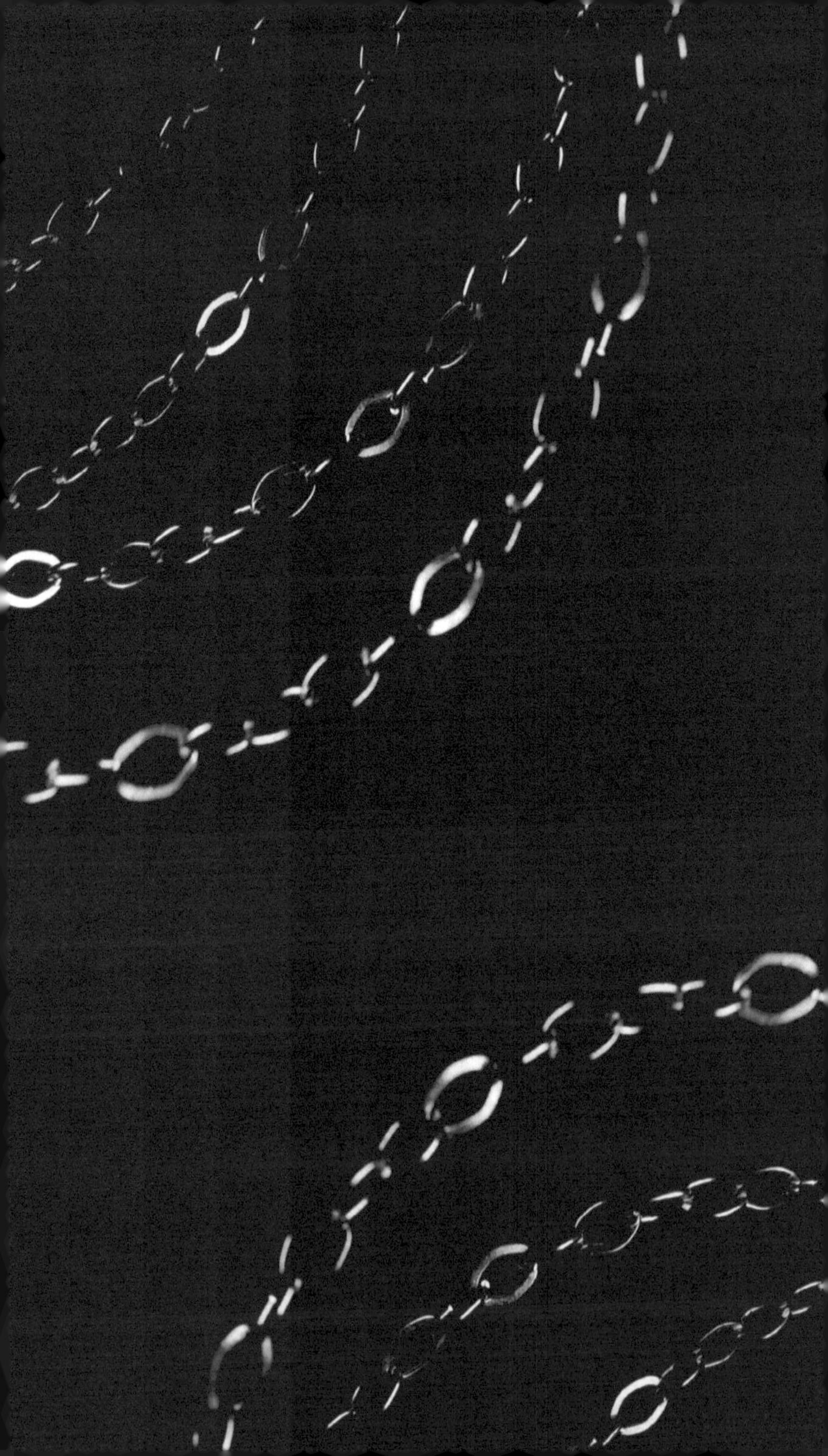

8

EVIE

I took a single step closer, while Kyla lowered her nose to the ground and walked around the scene, careful to stay away from the body.

Beau had died from a gunshot to the head. And the blood splatter... I took a deep breath.

"Let's go wait outside," I said. "I need to call it in." I had no authority to poke around an active crime scene. At least not when the body was human.

Kyla followed me outside, but she kept walking.

"Where are you going?"

She jerked her head toward the closest house, and I raised one eyebrow.

She was right. Maybe they'd heard something. I opened my mouth to suggest the werewolf stay behind. It was likely she'd scare the shit out of the homeowners, who were probably human.

She glanced at me, her eyes cool, and I shrugged.

We wandered up their driveway, and Kyla raised one foot, hitting the doorbell.

A Black guy opened the door. I put him in his early fifties. Deep smile lines had been carved around his eyes, which sharpened in surprise as he took in Kyla. His gaze immediately dropped down and away, proving he'd had experience with werewolves.

His gaze flicked up and met mine instead. "Can I help you?"

I introduced us both and explained about the dead guy next door. The neighbor's name was Kelvin, and his face fell when I told him Beau Stewart was no longer breathing.

"Did you notice anything unusual going on at his house?"

Kelvin shook his head. "I'm usually at the office. Come on in, and you can ask the brownie."

My eyebrows shot up before I could control them. Stupid eyebrows. Kelvin smiled at me. "My grandfather did a favor for one of the fae, and he was given the brownie when the portals first opened. I'm not sure how that worked since typically brownies choose their own positions, but we kind of inherited the little guy."

He led us through the entranceway and into a formal living room. Above our heads, a crystal chandelier sparkled. The whole room smelled like lemon cleaner and wood polish.

Kyla sneezed, and Kelvin sent her an apologetic look, careful not to make eye contact, although she likely wouldn't mind, now that she'd established her dominance.

"Sorry about that. The brownie has been at it all day."

It had always weirded me out that brownies were nameless. At least, to other people. I wasn't sure if they had their own names, but if you were dumb enough to give them a name, the magic tying them to your home would disappear, and so would the brownie.

He was currently dusting the marble fireplace, although his bat-like ears had twitched when we walked in, making it clear he was paying attention.

Kelvin strode over to the brownie and crouched down until they were at eye level. "Our next-door neighbor has passed away," he said. "I would appreciate if you would tell us if you heard or saw anything suspicious recently."

Since brownies were tied to a house, it would be easy to treat them as if they were invisible robots. Cleaning was, after all, a compulsion they couldn't ignore. But it was obvious from Kelvin's gentle tone that he treated the brownie well. From the smile that crossed the brownie's face, he clearly had at least a little fondness for his master.

The brownie turned to me. "Three humans walked into Mr. Stewart's home at approximately 2:39 p.m. yesterday. They stayed for close to ten minutes and then left. I did not hear any suspicious noises."

"Can you describe the humans?"

"Three males. They walked quickly, with purpose. Two white, one Hispanic. They all had dark hair. That was all I managed to see."

"Did you hear anything from the house when they went in?"

"No."

They could've used a silencer.

"Can you describe their car?"

"Of course. The car was a silver Nissan. I memorized the license plate number as I hadn't seen the car on this street before."

I smiled. Most people had no idea just how territorial brownies could be over the house they considered theirs.

I pulled out my phone and noted the license plate number. "That's extremely helpful. Thank you."

"You're welcome."

"Let us know if there's anything else you need," Kelvin said. "I didn't know Beau well, but he always had a friendly wave and a smile." He shifted uncomfortably on his feet. "This is usually a quiet neighborhood. Do I need to be worried?"

"I don't think so. Stay alert and keep your doors locked. If I learn otherwise, I'll let you know."

He escorted us to the door, and I noted the bowl of what looked like milk or cream on the floor in one corner. Next to it, a plate held a cupcake. Kelvin may have inherited his brownie, but he clearly knew how to keep him happy.

I pulled out my phone and messaged my tech-wizard friend, Steve, with the license plate and a few details about the case. He liked to collect favors, and I'd definitely owe him one for this.

By the time we got to the end of the drive, a patrol car was parked outside, and two uniforms were walking toward the security guard's house. One of them caught sight of us and tensed. Kyla opened her mouth in a wolfy smile, clearly enjoying his terror.

"Not nice," I told her, and she blinked both eyes at me. She was determined to learn how to wink in wolf form. While she'd been trying for weeks, she hadn't figured it out.

"You still just look like a befuddled puppy when you do that," I said.

Some people got scared and listened to their instincts. Other people got scared and channeled it into rage. From the way the cop was stalking toward us, he belonged to the second category.

Kyla wandered off, and I knew it was so she wouldn't be tempted to rip out his throat. I waited for the cop to approach, keeping my hands out by my sides so he could see I was unarmed. No use tempting him into anything stupid.

"Officer Franks," he introduced himself. "And you are?"

"Evie Amana."

"And the wolf?"

"Kyla Hill."

He gave Kyla a suspicious look, but she was busy ignoring him as she sidled up closer to the house.

"What were you two doing here?"

"We're investigating a theft. Beau Stewart was on duty the night in question and hadn't shown up to work. We were hoping to talk to him."

"And how did you get into the house?"

This was where it got tricky. "My friend smelled the body. At the time, we didn't know if there was anyone else in there who could be hurt. We thought it would be best if we checked it out."

He gave me a look that said I was full of shit and he knew it. "Wait here."

I didn't like being told what to do. I especially didn't like being told what to do by bigoted men who were blinded by their own self-importance.

But I also didn't want to get on the bad side of the local cops. Especially now that I was consulting for them and all. I leaned against my car, watching as Franks gave Kyla a wide berth and stalked into the house.

This wasn't Franks's crime scene, as much as he'd like it to be. He'd be securing the scene until the detectives assigned the case arrived.

They showed up twenty minutes later. Detective Marlow was a thin, wiry guy with glasses and sharp gray eyes that seemed to note everything—and everyone. Those eyes lingered on Kyla, but it was curiosity, not hate, that gleamed in them. He nodded at me and walked inside to examine the body.

Detective Lopez was a huge man who walked with a swagger. He gave me a wide smile, flashing white teeth as he wandered toward me. Obviously, he was on witness duty.

"You found the body?" he asked me.

"That's right." I filled him in. Then, since *he* wasn't a dickbag, I shared what the brownie had told me.

"You got that license plate number?"

I nodded and handed it over. I'd already made a note of it in my phone. He gave me a long stare.

"I don't need to tell you that since the security guard is human, this makes it a police case."

I gazed back steadily. "Of course you don't."

He wasn't buying it. "That means leaving the police work to us, Ms. Amana."

I had two options here. I could pull out my shiny new ID and attempt to muscle my way into this investigation, or I could go about my business. Since I'd already seen everything I'd needed to see here—and I'd already messaged Steve—I went for door number two.

"Of course." I smiled at him. "Well, now that we've handed this over, we can get on with our day. Let's go, Kyla."

His eyes narrowed, but he didn't call me out. I felt his gaze on me as we got in the car, and I did a nine-point turn. The street was narrow, and I was distracted. After I reversed for the sixth time, Kyla hunkered down and placed one paw over her eyes.

Rude.

I dropped Kyla back at the morgue parking lot, so she could shift and get her car. Then I hit the drive-thru, picking up five extra burgers. Kyla would be hungry.

We met back at the office, and I handed Rose her combo.

"You didn't need to do that." Surprise flashed across her face. The kind of surprise that told me she wasn't used to anyone thinking about her.

"Eat up," I smiled. "We've got some serious work to do."

I ate as I got back into the massacre case, continuing to make notes about the victims. I'd shared my notes with Nelson, and he'd helpfully shared his own. Technically, I was only supposed to be consulting on this case, but he'd obviously decided I could be of some use when it came to boring legwork. Kind of him.

Kyla strolled in as we were finishing stuffing our faces. "Thanks," she said when I gestured toward the burgers. Rose watched in awe as she began to make her way through them.

"Wow," she said. "I wish I could eat like that."

"No, you don't," Kyla said. "My body burns through calories like a fire burns through a forest after a drought. Eating this much, this often? Inconvenient as hell."

Kyla shoved the last of her burger into her mouth and got to her feet.

Someone knocked on the door.

I glanced at Kyla. "You expecting anyone?"

She shook her head slowly, turning her attention to the door.

"Come in," I said.

A large guy stepped through the door. He had green eyes, a weathered face, and pointed ears.

His gaze scanned the room before landing on me.

"Evelyn," he said. "I'm your uncle Eachann."

I slowly got to my feet. It took a lot to make someone like me speechless. I'd been searching for him for months, and after all this time, he just walked through my front door.

Rose grabbed her bag and beelined for the door. "I think I'll work from home."

I shot her a grateful look before returning my attention to Eachann. "Um, hi."

To his credit, he seemed to realize how awkward this was, and his expression softened. "You've been looking for me."

"Yeah. I, um, I met your ex, Ainfean. A while ago now. I was looking for my father. She told me about you. About how you'd gone looking for him."

Ainfean was unseelie, just like my father and uncle. Eachann had abandoned her with no warning, and I'd turned up out of the blue. But she'd been kind to me.

Something that looked like regret flickered across Eachann's face. "She was the one to get in touch. I knew there was a baby, but I'd hoped… I'd hoped you were happy."

"I won't be happy until HFE are nothing but ash."

He shook his head. And then suddenly, without warning, his mouth curved into a blinding smile. "You're just like him. Gods, if he could see you now."

The lump in my throat burned. I picked up the glass of water on my desk in an effort to get rid of it.

Eachann gave me a moment to compose myself, turning away to study my whiteboard. And the timeline I'd started.

"Where have you been?" I asked him. "Ainfean told me when my father first disappeared, you thought he was…frolicking. Then, when you realized he was gone for good, you blamed yourself for not paying attention."

"That's correct." He kept his eyes on my whiteboard. Obviously, I came across my inability to share my feelings naturally. "I went to the middleground. Lorcan had gotten involved with some bad people over the years. He'd worked off and on as a merc, much to our king's displeasure. But Lorcan could charm even Finvarra. The amount of whiskey those two consumed together…" He rolled his eyes and turned to face me.

It was a little strange picturing my father drinking with the unseelie king.

"Anyway, it wasn't until he'd been gone for a while that I realized I hadn't heard from him. I put the word out, and no one had seen him for over a year, your time. That's when I knew something was wrong. I left Ainfean and went searching. It wasn't until I returned, briefly, that she told me she'd met your mother. She told me they'd both been captured. Lorcan had been tortured and Charlotte impregnated. He'd learned from a guard that most of your genetics were his. Lorcan fell in love with Charlotte, and, even at his worst, when he was losing his sanity, he managed to get her out."

I knew most of this. But hearing it from my uncle, seeing the tears he attempted to blink away, made tears of my own spill from my eyes.

"My father sent Mom to Ainfean."

"That's right. Your mother told her that Lorcan had stayed behind in an attempt to save the rest of them. And none of us ever heard from him again."

"You think he's dead."

He sighed, rubbing his hand across his face. "I never gave up on him. I searched for any hint of that human hate group. I heard rumors some of them had formed an alliance with other paranormals, and I moved my search to the other realms. I shut down a few satellite labs. Just as you did." He gave me a nod, and pride unfurled in my chest. "But no matter how many times I cut the head off the snake, another regrows."

"So we need to blow the whole fucking snake up," I said, in my best "duh" voice.

He stared at me. And then he laughed. "I should have known you'd be like this. Young and enthusiastic, and so fucking powerful."

I widened my eyes, and he angled his head. "You think I can't feel it? Your power is just under the surface."

I'd unpack that later. "Will you help me?"

He nodded. "I'll help you. Your father may be gone, but we'll cut the head off this snake. I promise."

NATHANIEL

I woke up with a low whine. The kind of whine that would have made Ryker roar with laughter if he had heard.

My wolf wanted to see Evie.

After everything that had happened in the past few days, the monster inside me wasn't happy that she was out of our sight.

Since I felt the same, I pulled on my clothes, brushed my teeth, and avoided Tobias as I stalked out my front door. The submissive wolf saw too much.

I glanced at my phone. A little after five p.m. I'd taken a late-afternoon nap after spending most of the night working. Hunter gave me a knowing look as he walked past me, likely about to hound Tobias for some food. I ignored him and slid into my car.

My mind was occupied as I drove to Evie's. I didn't like the neighborhood surrounding her apartment. I didn't like that she lived alone here. And I certainly didn't like that she was being hunted by HFE. I had no doubt they were just waiting for their chance to take her.

I pulled up outside of her apartment building and opened my car door. I froze, catching sight of her beautiful, curly hair. My eyes narrowed. She was walking out of her apartment building, eyes on her phone as she turned right.

What was she doing?

Evie strode toward a pickup truck. She lifted her head and scanned the street, but I'd parked far enough away that she didn't notice me.

She opened the passenger side door and leaned in, clearly speaking to someone. I wrote down the license plate of the pickup truck. A few moments later, she closed the door and sauntered back toward her building, a package in her hand.

I opened my door and intercepted her.

Her eyes fired as I stepped in front of her, then softened slightly as she recognized me.

"Nathaniel? What are you doing here?"

"What's in the package?"

"None of your business." She held it tighter and

gave me a dark scowl.

Now my wolf was even more curious. I inhaled, but I couldn't catch a scent that would tip me off. It wasn't food...

"Stop trying to smell it," she snapped at me.

I couldn't help but grin. This woman made me... laugh. For the first time in a long time. I could already scent almost every ingredient. What I couldn't figure out was what it was used for.

"What are you thinking?" she asked me, the frown disappearing.

"Just wondering what you're doing."

"My business." She eyed me. "Your eyes just lightened."

The truth was, I'd missed her. It was embarrassing, given I'd seen her yesterday, and yet, I'd woken in my bed alone and wanted to hear her voice more than any other sound in the world.

"Nathaniel?"

"We need to talk."

She gave me a solemn look. "About the case?"

I nodded. "Something was in my territory last night. The sentries smelled a strange creature and alerted me. By the time we got close to the scent, it was gone."

"You think it was whatever's attacking the humans?"

I shrugged. "I don't know. But I do know that you need to be careful, even in my territory."

My wolf let out a silent howl at that. My people should be more than safe when they were in a territory we had claimed as ours.

She watched me, and for a moment, it seemed as if she could see too much. "Anything else?"

I raised one eyebrow. Was she trying to get rid of me? My gaze dropped to the package she was holding, and she tightened her hands around it with a scowl. I suppressed a smile.

"Nathaniel?"

"A couple other things, actually. My people have been looking into similar attacks across the country. So far, none of them look like they could be from the same creature."

Relief flickered over her face. "Thank God."

"One more thing. Three of Frederik's wolves were spotted near the CertSure massacre."

"Who is Frederik?"

"An enemy. He wants my territory."

"You think he's responsible for the massacre?"

"I don't know. But my people have reached out to him, asking for an explanation. He hasn't responded."

And that lack of response meant Frederik was either guilty or stupid. Either way, I would find out.

I couldn't help it. I brushed a curl off her face. She allowed it, and I barely restrained myself from letting out a contented rumble. "His wolves were in my territory without permission. Deep in my territory. Any other Alpha would take that as an automatic declaration of war. I'm willing to allow him to explain himself."

Evie frowned, and I could practically see her attempting to figure out how she could resolve the situation. I just shook my head at her. "How was your day?"

She smiled, and my breath caught. Sometimes, this woman was so fucking beautiful it was hard not to bury my hand in her hair and kiss her until all of her breaths were *mine*.

"I met my uncle today."

I angled my head. She looked so pleased, I chose not to tell her that any man who'd shown up, claiming to be her uncle, was destined to be investigated until I knew everything—from where he went to college to the brand of toothpaste he preferred.

"What's his name?"

"Eachann."

I made a mental note. She scowled at me, obviously immediately regretting letting me know. I didn't tell her I would've found out his name the moment I learned about him. "No, you may not look into him," she said.

I just smiled at her. "I work security. Anyone in your circle is now in the pack's outer circle."

She sighed but didn't argue, proving that, despite what most people thought about her willingness to fight, Evie knew how to pick her battles.

"I'll leave you to whatever it is you're doing," I

said.

"Wait... Uh, do you want coffee or something?"

Something in my chest clenched. Even while annoyed, Evie didn't want to hurt my feelings.

"No. I have a meeting with Nelson. I'm allowing several of his cops to take a look at Hunter in wolf form. Hopefully that'll help next time something like this happens."

Her eyes widened. "Wow. I thought you guys didn't like humans knowing about you."

"We don't. But the fear of the unknown is proving more difficult to deal with than the monster they could know. Be careful today."

I couldn't help myself. I watched as Evie wrestled with the urge to tell me to fuck off. Finally, she rolled her eyes.

"I will."

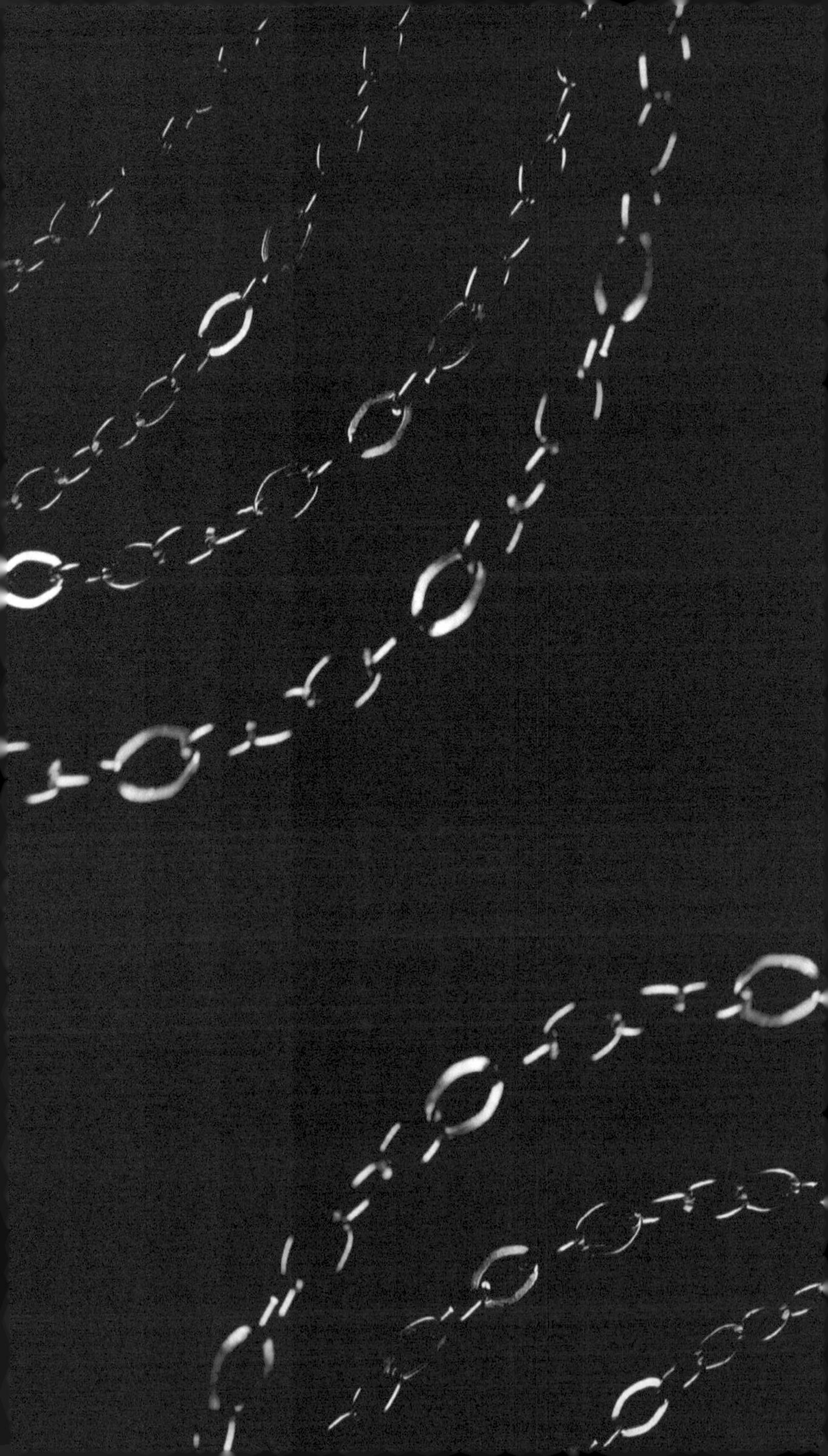

9

EVIE

The next morning, I woke to more of Ellen's shenanigans. Only this time, it was much worse.

Because this time, she hadn't come after me. This time, she'd come after Kyla.

I shot out of bed so fast, little dots filled my vision.

"Motherfucker."

Werewolf Alpha Protects Feral Wolf. Allows Her to Threaten Human Citizens.

Oh, hell no.

It was one thing to fuck with me. It was quite another to fuck with my friends.

I called Kyla. She didn't answer. Shit.

I threw on my clothes, brushed my teeth, and stalked out the door. I was hoping Kyla would shake this off, but she'd had a rough few months. What if this tipped her over the edge and she killed the reporter?

Or worse, what if it sent her into a deep depression and she regressed back into her half-feral self?

I slowed as I hit the turnoff for Nathaniel's territory, the blue-and-red flashing lights thankfully pulling someone else over. By the time I pulled up outside Nathaniel's house, my jaw hurt from clenching my teeth.

This had to be libel or slander or something, right?

I knew better. Giving in to Ellen's shit would just make it worse.

I stalked down the path and toward the playground. I still hadn't actually been inside Kyla's house, but she'd pointed it out to me the last time I was here.

"Evelyn."

I whirled, teeth bared. Nathaniel stared at me, and his lips twitched.

"Don't laugh at me."

"Are you okay?"

"No. Have you seen this shit?" I waved my phone at him.

"If that's the article about Kyla, then yes, I have." His expression turned cold, remote, and a little feral, and I wondered what his little stalker would think of him if she could see him now.

I opened my mouth, but he glanced around and took my hand, pulling me down a side path and away from curious eyes.

"Your rage isn't going to help her stay in control,"

he said, and I made myself take a deep, shaky breath. His hand was still on mine, and I forced myself to ignore just how good it felt.

"I'm *pissed*," I stated the obvious. "Aren't you?"

"Of course." A muscle ticked in his jaw. "One of my wolves had their car graffitied last night. Thanks to the speculation that we're responsible for the massacres, the humans are already turning on us. Small things now, but these kinds of things tend to escalate. And when humans escalate, werewolves struggle to suppress their natural instincts."

"What are you going to do about it?"

Annoyance gleamed in his eyes. "What would you suggest?"

I opened my mouth, but I came up blank. There wasn't much he could do. Sure, he could throw his weight around, but that would just piss people off more.

"Exactly," he said softly. "Kyla's tough. She'll bounce back from this."

I leaned my head against the rough tree trunk and sighed. "I guess I kind of lost it."

He smiled. "You were on a rampage. It was kind of cute."

I narrowed my eyes at him. He threw his head back and laughed.

Then his mouth was on mine.

I hadn't expected it. But I was learning that Nathaniel was a tricky wolf. His mouth sent a jolt of awareness from my lips down, through my body, until my toes curled in my shoes. He brushed his thumb along my throat, and my heart began to beat double time in my chest.

His lips were a warm, slow caress, teasing instead of dominating until I was the one pressing against him, my own mouth needy, desperate, insatiable.

Nathaniel let out a rough growl. It was a sound of such *want* that my skin suddenly seemed two sizes too small. My body went hot, languid, and breathing became secondary to keeping his mouth on mine.

He dragged that mouth away, and I let out a whimper that would likely mortify me when I thought about it later. His lips caressed my neck, then he was kissing his way up my cheek to nuzzle at my ear.

"Nate," I sighed.

"You make me lose control," he rumbled, and my hands clawed at his shirt, pulling him closer.

"Ahem."

I froze.

Nathaniel buried his head in my neck with a put-upon sigh.

My gaze met Kyla's. She stood behind Nathaniel, her lips curved in a cat-that-ate-the-canary grin.

"Kyla," Nathaniel rumbled warningly against my neck, his lips brushing my skin.

She ignored him and made a lewd humping motion with her hips. "Hubba-hubba," she mouthed at me.

"Kyla," Nathaniel said again.

The feel of his mouth against my neck made it difficult for me to focus.

"Uh," I started, but I had nothing.

Kyla shook her head at me, as if I was hopeless. She wasn't wrong.

"A little birdie told me you were looking for me," Kyla said. "But I can come back later if you're...busy with my Alpha."

"*Kyla.*" Nathaniel pulled away from me, and I instantly mourned the feel of his body against my own.

His eyes met mine, and they held a dark promise. Those eyes told me it was only a matter of time before I was naked beneath him. Or above him.

I swallowed, taking a single, large step away from temptation. This seemed to amuse Nathaniel, but he nodded at both of us, turning to prowl back through the forest.

Kyla gave me a wide grin. "How long has this been happening for?"

"It kind of just happened."

She studied my face. "You don't look happy about it."

"I'm a little confused," I admitted.

"What's there to be confused about?"

I turned, heading back toward my car. "I came here to find *you*," I said. "I was worried..."

"About my reaction to that reporter's little article?" Kyla shrugged, falling into step beside me.

"I'm not worried."

I gave her a look, and she angled her head. "I'm serious. Nathaniel is pissed enough for both of us."

"He didn't seem pissed."

"He keeps his feelings on the down-low, but I know him well enough to see it. Either way, I'm not afraid of anything Harrison decides to print."

I chewed on that. "I hate that she can say whatever she wants."

"Life isn't fair. Besides, we've got more than enough to worry about between your case, my case, whatever is killing groups of humans, your mom's murder, and Operation Steal-a-Sword."

Well, when she listed it all off like that...

"You're right." I blew out a breath. My phone buzzed, and I glanced down at it.

Steve.

"We've got the address for the car," I told Kyla. "Steve says it was registered to the guy's cousin, so it took a while."

I flicked it through to her and then attempted to figure out what I was doing with my day. Turned out, I wasn't the best at planning when I was half crazed with fury.

"Okay, I'm going to go hang out with the kids for an hour or so, and then I need to head into the office. I want to keep checking out the victims of the massacre. Maybe they were targeted for a reason."

"Sounds good. I'm going to take Rose to that

address with me. She's a merc, so she can be another pair of hands if the humans get rowdy. Then I'm heading to the morgue. Whoever killed Beau decided he knew too much."

"Good luck."

I headed back to my usual swing. The playground was quiet. Too quiet. As much as Levi had enjoyed being levitated, I had a feeling he'd put the word out that the other kids were not to talk to me. It was disappointing but not surprising. He was clearly the leader around here.

With nothing else to focus on, my mind strayed to the Alpha. I'd imagined kissing him. Of course I had. What I hadn't imagined was how I'd lose all track of time and space when he put his hands on me. And when his mouth had crashed down on mine…

I took a deep breath, pushing off the ground and letting my swing rock. I tried not to lie to myself. I'd been lied to enough in my life. And when Nathaniel kissed me, I'd wanted nothing more than for him to keep kissing me. For him to take me into his arms and—

I cut that thought off. There were plenty of wolves around. Wolves who could scent if I was getting hot and bothered. And with the way they all gossiped, they'd likely soon know I'd been kissing their Alpha. My cheeks heated.

I hadn't expected his kiss. Hadn't seen it coming, or I would've dodged it. Not because I didn't want to kiss him…

It seemed ludicrous that the werewolf Alpha would be interested in me—not because I wasn't smart, funny, and criminally cute. But because we were so different.

He was a dominant control freak.

I loathed authority and adored my freedom.

It would never work between us.

But…maybe we could have some fun. A little lighthearted flirtation.

"Evie?"

I blinked. "Oh hey, Charlie." I glanced around. "Where's everyone else?"

"They're not allowed to come out this morning."

I sighed. "Who said?"

"My brother."

"How'd you get past him?"

"I snuck out the window."

"That sounds dangerous." I frowned at him, and he shrugged.

"My room is on the first floor. Besides, *Mom* didn't say I couldn't come."

He smiled at me, and I couldn't help but grin back.

His gaze narrowed on me. "Will you make me fly?"

I raised one hand, and he slowly lifted into the air. Levi was worried about the kids filling me in, which meant whatever they were involved in was dangerous. If they wouldn't come to me, it was time to go to them. Nathaniel had asked their parents to cooperate with me, so I would soon be going door-to-door and interviewing the kids without Levi being there.

"Woo-hoo," Charlie shrieked, "I'm a bird!"

I laughed and took him a little higher. With a flick of my wrist, I rotated him through the air until he was horizontal, and then I gently guided him through the playground, a couple of feet off the ground.

A few minutes later, I had to stop. My telekinesis didn't come naturally, and it drained quickly.

"More," Charlie laughed, and I shook my head.

"Can't, buddy. I need to get going. And I bet your mom is looking for you."

He pouted, but it didn't last long.

I gave him my hard stare. "Is there anything you'd like to tell me?"

He gave me a hard stare of his own. It was pretty good, considering his age. "No."

I watched him, and he looked at the ground. "Just tell me one thing, Charlie. Could whatever the older kids are doing get them hurt?"

He opened his mouth.

"Charlie!"

"Uh-oh. That's Mom."

He turned and ran in the direction of his home. I sighed. Time to bring out the big guns. But first, I needed to speak to a well-connected witch.

EVIE

"I want to put the word out," I said.

Mere leaned on the table between us. Across the bar, Vas winked at me. Orin was busy serving regulars. I'd managed to get here before it got too busy.

"You don't need to put the word out."

"I don't want anyone talking to Ellen Harrison. I want her blacklisted, Mere. It was one thing to come after me, but targeting Kyla…"

"Everyone else feels the same way."

"Huh?"

"Look, Evie, people *like* Kyla. She's funny and wild, and she's been through some shit. They like you too. And those who don't like you, well, they know all about your ties to both the demons and the werewolves. No one is going to talk to the reporter."

I contemplated that for a moment. Then I shrugged. "Good."

Mere had cooled the worst of my wrath. Unfortunately, I wasn't sleeping all that well. I was so tired and mentally wrung out, I needed that wrath to function.

My phone buzzed, and I pulled it from my pocket. Kyla. "I need to take this."

I stepped outside, leaning against the concrete wall of the bar.

"I found the humans who were at Beau Stewart's. They're all dead." Her voice was mournful with a touch of rage.

"We were too late."

"We were too late, even when we found Beau Stewart's body. They must have been killed straight after him."

"How were they killed?"

"Gunshots to the head. The last one tried to run. It's...bad."

We were constantly two steps behind with this case. And it was pissing me off.

"See if you can scent anything and then call it in. Anonymously. We don't need the detectives who were at Beau's to know we were poking around."

"Good plan. I just heard from Finvarra's people. They've told Callula's family to cooperate with us. You down for a trip to the unseelie realm?"

"Now?"

"You got something else you need to be doing?"

"I need to do more cross-checking of the victims. I'll come with you, but I'll need you to help me with some of that when we get back."

"Deal."

"I'm at Mere's."

"Good. I'm around the corner. I'll be there in five."

"Evie."

I ended the call and turned. Marie stood in front of me, a tentative smile on her face. I would've smiled back, except I knew she'd been a vocal supporter of throwing me out of the coven.

"Hi."

"Um, we haven't seen you around much."

I gave her an incredulous look. Then I forced my expression into one of blank disinterest. When someone thrusts a dagger into your back, never let them see you bleed out. I didn't let the coven know how much they'd hurt me, because my pain was private.

I stayed silent. I wasn't going to make this any easier for her.

She swallowed. "I'm sorry for how it all went down."

"I'm not."

She stared at me, and I shrugged. "I'm sorry to have learned that the people I considered family weren't really my family after all. But I'm glad I left. It was the right decision. For all of us."

Kyla prowled up the path, and Marie watched her warily. After a long moment, she turned back to me. "You could come one day. For dinner."

"Maybe." I kept my tone noncommittal. Marie seemed to get the hint because her lips thinned.

"We need to get going," Kyla said.

I nodded. It was going to be a long night, but according to Kyla, it was still the middle of the day in the unseelie realm.

"Goodbye, Marie."

"Bye, Evie."

Marie turned and walked away. Kyla let out a low whistle. "That was awkward. Did she think you wouldn't remember how she was campaigning for you to be kicked out of the coven?"

"I guess not." My heart gave a single pang in my chest, but I ignored it. "What's the deal with this little trip?"

"Finvarra gave some kind of royal declaration, which means anyone we choose has to answer our questions. They won't be pleased, but they'll do it. Thanks for coming with me. If we need to, we can divide and conquer."

The fae couldn't lie. But they'd had so many centuries of dancing around the truth, their inability to tell an outright lie wasn't exactly the benefit you'd think it would be.

Finvarra had ordered them to cooperate, but who knew how loyal they'd be to Callula?

"I'm curious. I've never visited the unseelie realm."

She sneered. "It's nothing to write home about."

Something in Kyla's voice made me pay attention. "Is that right?"

"Yes. Okay, fine," she huffed when I just stared at her. "It's beautiful in a scary, dangerous kind of way. Unlike the seelie realm, at least in the dark fae realm, you know what you're getting into, right?"

I shivered. "Right." The last time I'd visited the

seelie realm, Mere and I were chased by a fluffle of killer bunnies. The seelie realm was pretty enough to make you let down your guard, until the forest attempted to murder you.

Kyla parked her car outside the Duke Gardens. We strolled inside, and I took in the high fence, which sectioned off the portal from the rest of the gardens. This was the closest portal to the dark fae realm.

Kyla unhooked a hidden latch, and the fence opened just wide enough for us to each slip through. The portal was crimson at the edges, lightening to the palest of pink in the center.

"You ready?" Kyla asked.

I nodded, and we both stepped through.

I sucked in a breath as pain scraped along my nerve endings. But a second later, it was over, and we both stood on a cobblestone path.

The temperature was much cooler here.

My teeth didn't chatter, but it was close. I watched as a weight seemed to disappear from Kyla's shoulders. She rolled her neck with a sigh.

"Nice break from the Durham heat, huh?" Werewolves liked the cold.

"First relief I've felt in weeks." Kyla scowled. "I hate that I'm finding that relief in Finvarra's realm, but what can you do? The king lives that way." She waved dismissively.

I just stared at her, and she sighed. "Fine."

I followed her down the path as it curved to the

left. I took one look at the huge structure in front of us and let out a low whistle.

"No wonder no one wants to mess with him," I said.

The keep had been positioned strategically against the mountain behind it. In fact, if I wasn't wrong, some fae magic had allowed them to build *into* the mountain. The stone was the color of thick, dark smoke, sucking in the light around it and reflecting it back in a dull gleam.

Guards were positioned at regular intervals around the keep. The closest group watched us intently, more than prepared if we decided to start some shit.

"Are you thinking what I'm thinking?" Kyla asked.

We both surveyed the guards.

"Yeah. I'm thinking we need to go back to Selina and check if her vision still applies." The witch had been the one to tell us that Kyla's theft of the sword wouldn't end with the seelie king.

But that was a problem for another day.

"Callula lives with her siblings in an estate nearby," Kyla said. "It's a town called Smolten, mostly made up of those who are either close to the throne or those who work for them. The nearest big city is half a day by horseback. We can jog to Smolten and walk through, or we can take those stairs down to where most of the people related to the royals live. It'll mean we can skip walking through the town and save us some time."

Typical fae realm shit. The royal court's ancestors had obviously decided to make it difficult for visitors to access them, and time and space had adjusted accordingly.

We strolled past the entrance to Finvarra's keep and stopped at the edge of the hill. A set of stairs had been carved into the hill, leading down to the town entrance.

Morbid curiosity made me count the stairs as we walked down them. Some 503 steps later, I was already dreading the walk back up.

The staircase opened up onto a cobblestone street. It was trippy, suddenly being on the opposite side of town. Even though we'd come down the stairs, I could also see the mountain in the distance in front of me, Finvarra's keep at the top.

Several horses and carts were waiting, and from the looks of things, they were the dark fae version of Uber.

Most technology didn't work all that well in the fae realms. Hence why they were so obsessed with it in our realm.

"Ride, ladies?" A grizzled gnome nodded toward his cart as we crossed the street. At that moment, the wind changed, and the horse got a whiff of werewolf.

The gnome cursed as the horse sidestepped, gazing warily at Kyla, who ignored the horse so completely, my heart broke a little for her.

Kyla used to ride. In fact, she'd exchanged time

mucking out stalls for time in the ring. Unfortunately, horses didn't trust werewolves. They knew when they were in the presence of a predator.

I glanced at her. "Have you considered—"

"Leave it, Evie."

I snapped my mouth shut. I hadn't even known what I was going to say. I just wanted to do something about this small hurt that Kyla faced so often.

She sighed. "I bought a spell," she admitted. "It was supposed to change my scent so the horses would tolerate me. It just made things worse."

Worse, because it had given her hope, and then it hadn't worked. Oh, Kyla.

"I'm sorry."

She shrugged. "We've all lost things. I'll get over it."

But Kyla had lost more than most.

"We don't need a ride. We're close enough. This way," she said, and I followed her down a side street. It was quiet down here. Baskets of black flowers hung from balconies, and the cobblestones were spotlessly clean. Pixies darted here and there, while high fae wandered, wearing boots and cloaks, shopping baskets in their arms.

"I bet sunset is gorgeous here," Kyla said.

"I'm surprised you're even entertaining the idea that this realm could be at all interesting," I said.

She snorted. "I can hate their king and still admire how eerily beautiful his realm is. This is it."

We both surveyed the estate. It was set back from the street, but the gates were open. Kyla had likely told them we were on the way.

We moseyed up the front path, and Kyla reached for the knocker. I smacked her hand away.

"They've hidden a ward in there. It's so well created, I almost missed it."

Kyla studied the knocker. "Where?"

I pointed at what looked like a clump of chipped paint. She gaped at me.

"How the hell is it so small?"

"Someone knows what they're doing. And they've got power. It would've knocked both of us on our asses."

I lowered my shields and let my own power out to play, curious to see exactly how the ward functioned. If I figured out how it was created, I could replicate it.

I'd call it the Stealth Ward, and I'd amp it up to a ten.

The door opened, and I sighed. Looked like I'd have to study it later.

A handsome unseelie stood in front of us, a glimmer of surprise in his eyes. Realization replaced the surprise, and he stepped aside.

"His Majesty sent you," he said. Dimples appeared when he smiled, and his green eyes gleamed. "Come in."

We stepped inside, and I inhaled the scent of some kind of spicy, pungent incense.

"I'm Terence," the fae said. "I'm Callula's brother. Come into the sitting room, and I'll get our sister."

He seemed relaxed—casual, even. We followed him into a large sitting room, and Kyla sneezed.

Every surface held a vase filled with flowers. The floral scent combined with the incense was headache-inducing. If I spent too much time here, I was practically guaranteed to get a migraine.

Terence excused himself to find his sister. I glanced at Kyla, and she nodded. Someone in this house was relatively sure that werewolves could sniff out lies. And they'd done everything they could to dull Kyla's senses.

Their information was wrong. I'm sure some of it was scent, but most werewolves could determine if you were lying simply by the speed of your breathing, the number of times you swallowed, the microexpressions a human wouldn't catch. Not to mention, wolves were experts in body language.

I stifled my grin. Let them think Kyla was incapable of figuring out they were playing with us. It would be entertaining at least.

All this had done was pique my curiosity. Someone in this house knew something, and while the fae couldn't lie, they'd figured they could deaden Kyla's nose and dance around the truth.

Amateurs.

Terence returned with a beautiful dark fae woman wearing a long, crimson dress. Unlike most of the unseelie, she had light-blond hair that looked more suited for the seelie court. She strolled into the room and took in our casual clothes with a sneer.

Something told me I wasn't about to make a new friend.

Terence chose the armchair across from us, while the woman leaned against the arm of the chair, still studying us with disdain.

"This is my sister Parila," Terence said.

Kyla nodded. "We also have a cousin to speak with. Wimbar?"

"Wim isn't here," Parila said, as if we were idiots. "He's traveling right now."

Because *that* wasn't suspicious. I made a note to figure out where he was.

"What did you know about Callula's plans?" Kyla asked.

Terence folded his hands in front of him. "I'm not close with Callula," he said. "We never really clicked—even as children—and I haven't had a decent conversation with her for centuries. I'll cooperate with you, of course, but I'm unsure how helpful I'll actually be."

"Any information you have about the artifacts could help," I said.

"Well, the first I heard of the artifact was when His Majesty told me it was missing. I have to admit, I was intrigued. But I've never seen it before."

"And, Parila?"

She gave me a look that made me want to slap her upside her head.

"I knew about the book."

Terence's eyebrows shot up, and she waved one elegant hand through the air.

"*Knew* about it. I'm not stupid enough to steal from the king. I'm also not desperate. *My* finances are in pristine order."

I glanced at Kyla. She nodded at me. Parila may not have directly stolen the book, but she knew more than that. Unfortunately, I couldn't prove it.

Someone walked past the door, and I turned my gaze back to Terence while paying attention to my peripheral vision. It was the servants that we needed to talk to. They would know exactly what was going on in this house.

And if any of them liked Parila, I'd run up and down those stairs a hundred times.

I glanced at Kyla. This wasn't helping. It was time to wrap this shit up and try another tactic.

She got to her feet. "Thank you for your time," she said. "Do you mind if we get back in touch if we have any questions?"

Parila gave an aggrieved sigh, but Terence nodded. "Of course."

We strolled out of the house, not talking until we were huffing and puffing our way back up the steps toward the portal. Well, *I* was huffing and puffing. Kyla looked like she was out for a stroll. Werewolves, man.

"I asked around," Kyla said, keeping her voice low. "There's a high fae woman named Adione who used to work for Parila. She fled a few years ago and ended up in our realm. Apparently, Parila attempted to make her return. Sent a few threats and then finally appealed to Finvarra."

"What did he do?"

She shrugged. "Told her the fae had a little thing called free will." Kyla sneered. "Must've been something in it for him."

I elbowed her, and she rolled her eyes. "I hear myself. You'd hate him too if there was a chance you'd end up *chained to his throne*."

"I hate him with you. That's called friendship."

She gave me a reluctant smile. "Anyway, I left Adione a message. Hopefully, she'll get back to me. I'll let you know what she says."

The trip through the portal was uneventful, but we came across a group of humans approaching the portal when we returned to our side. They seemed to be egging each other on as they got closer.

"Dumb way to die," I advised one of them. He looked like he was in his midtwenties. Far too old to be contemplating suicide.

"You got through."

I rolled my eyes and did my red-light trick. He took a large step back.

"Not our responsibility," Kyla said loudly. "If they want to die, who are we to stop them? Darwinism at its finest. Sometimes we just have to clean out the gene pool."

One of them gave her a stubborn look and took another step closer to the portal. Kyla shrugged. "Survival of the fittest. Bad way to go. I've heard it feels like having every cell in your body pulled apart, but who are we to stop you? Go on."

The guys dispersed.

I glanced at Kyla. "Feeling pissy?"

She showed me her teeth. "Idiots."

NATHANIEL

I watched Eachann from across the table. He watched me back. The fae had enough power to counter my dominance. Of course, I wasn't trying to make him bend. He smiled at me, and my wolf perked up. We could have a good fight with this fae. It would be fun.

I sighed. Eachann smiled like he could sense my inner struggle. "I always imagined it would be difficult to have a beast within," he murmured.

"I've lived with it so long, I can barely remember any other way."

I forgive you.

I shut down the memory before it could get a

good hold on me.

Eachann sipped at his wine. "You came here to meet me because you're sniffing around my niece."

He wasn't entitled to *that*. I gave him a look, allowing a hint of my wolf out, and he smiled.

"I came here because I want to know your intentions. Many people have left Evelyn over the years. I want to know if you're planning to do the same."

He leaned back, a pleased smile on his face. "I've just met Evie, and you're warning me not to abandon her. You must care a great deal for her."

I just watched him.

Evie had been wounded by her sister. Betrayed. Separated as children, she'd expected Danica to come back for her as she'd promised. Now she knew Danica had stayed away to keep her safe. But when she found out what else Danica was keeping from her...

She'd never forgive either of us.

I just wanted her to have this one thing. This one person who would be her family.

Eachann's face turned serious. "Relax, wolf. I never imagined my brother's baby had survived. Once I learned of her, I made a vow to protect her in my brother's name. And the moment I met her, I loved her like a daughter. You have no threat from me."

Someone pounded on the door, and I raised an eyebrow at the familiar scent that drifted toward me. "Expecting someone?"

He merely smiled and waved a hand. "Go ahead."

I stalked to the door and opened it. Evie stood on the doorstep. Surprise flickered across her face, turning into a glower.

"Alpha," she said, and I scowled down at her. I knew what she was doing, and I wanted her to look up at me and purr "Nate." The way she had when I kissed her.

"Evelyn."

I also knew she hated it when I called her that. It was our own little battle of wills.

If she was annoyed with me, she was thinking about me.

"What exactly are you doing here?" she gritted out.

"Meeting your uncle."

"And why would you think that's appropriate?"

Truthfully, I had nothing. I'd overstepped, and Evie was pissed. She'd use this as another opportunity to push me away.

"High-ranking fae are expected to notify the werewolf Alpha when they enter their territory," her uncle said from behind me.

I kept my face carefully blank, although it wanted to crease in a smile. This was why he'd asked to meet today when I contacted him. He knew Evie was dropping by, and he wanted her to find me here so he could cover for me.

Now, I'd owe him a favor. Tricky fae.

Our eyes met, and he smiled at me.

"I should be going," I murmured.

"I don't need your paws padding over every inch of my life," Evie muttered to me as Eachann made some excuse and left the room.

"Alpha wolf, sweetheart. My paws belong wherever I say they do."

She sneered at me, and I couldn't help but grin, wanting nothing more than to take her mouth and turn that sneer into a moan.

"Don't even think about it," she hissed, glancing over her shoulder in the direction of her uncle.

"Believe me, I'm thinking about it."

I leaned close and nipped her ear, pleased at her tiny shiver before she pushed me away. "And so are you."

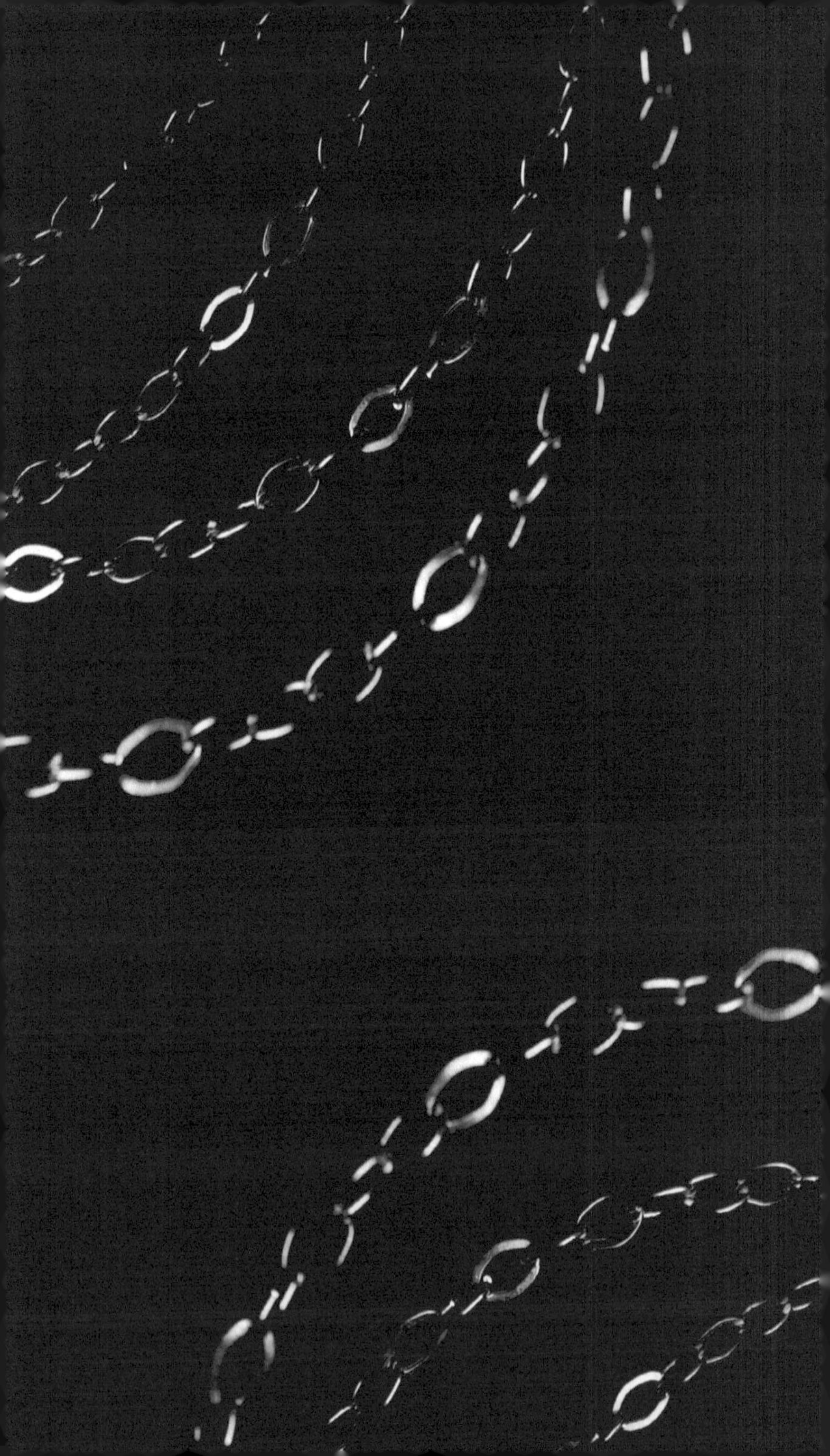

10

EVIE

Someone was at my door.

I knew it before my ward alerted me. According to that ward, whoever had arrived in the middle of the night didn't wish me any harm.

I grabbed my gun anyway. My footsteps were light as I padded toward the door. I may not have lived here for long, but I knew the location of every squeaky floorboard.

I leaned against the door and peered through the peephole. What the hell was the werewolf Alpha doing here at one in the morning?

"I can hear you breathing, Evelyn. Open the door."

God, he was annoying. I opened the door and turned my fiercest scowl on him.

His gaze dropped to my feet, traveled up my bare legs, and slid along the short nightgown I wore. His eyes met mine, and his wolf stared back at me. I froze.

Then his gaze shifted up, and his eyes were human once more.

Human and endlessly amused.

"What exactly are you wearing on your head?"

My cheeks heated. *Fuck. Fuck. Fuck.* "A silk bonnet. Otherwise, I wake up to hair anarchy." I attempted nonchalance, but I knew he saw through it.

My bonnet was a pale pink, with a large, flirty bow above my forehead. Bows were pretty, and I wasn't expecting anyone to see it.

I sighed. Why was I always on the back foot with the Alpha? My tough, competent act was continually taking a hit.

He opened his mouth, and I cut him off. "Why are you here, Nathaniel?"

"Another massacre. I thought you might like a ride."

I frowned. "Nelson hasn't called."

"One of my wolves found it. We've notified the police, but I need to get there now." He smiled. "You may want to get dressed."

I nodded. My bow fluttered against my forehead with the movement. Nathaniel's lips twitched.

I gave him squinty eyes. "You're not going to tell anyone about this, are you?"

"Oh no. This image will live in my head and my head only," he purred.

I swallowed, my mouth suddenly dry. "And why is that?"

His teeth flashed in a predatory, your-ass-is-mine smile. "Because I'm picturing you wearing your little bonnet…and nothing else."

I sucked in a sharp breath, and my toes curled. He dropped his gaze to my feet, and I turned, stalking into my room.

My nightgown had shrunk slightly the last time I washed it, and Nathaniel's low groan told me I'd given him a nice view of my ass cheeks.

Awesome.

I yanked the bonnet off my head, pulled on jeans and a long-sleeved T-shirt, and strapped on my weapons. After brushing my teeth and grabbing my phone, I was back in my living room within three minutes, where I found Nathaniel gazing at the pictures on my wall.

"This was your coven."

"Yes."

My chest ached at the past tense, but it was the truth. Most of those witches—my family—were dead now. Because I'd been targeted by HFE.

"I'm sorry. I didn't mean to make you sad."

I glanced at the wolf. "It's okay. I think I'll always be sad."

Truthfully, I thought I *should* always be sad. After the way I'd gotten them killed, the least I could do was drown myself in guilt for the rest of my life.

He shifted his gaze back to a picture of Brooke and me, holding up tequila shots and wearing devious grins. "I don't think they'd want that for you. Do you?"

I shrugged. I couldn't talk about this now. Not if I wanted to face whatever horror the crime scene would bring.

Nathaniel obviously understood, because he stepped aside and opened my apartment door for me without another word.

I grabbed my keys from the coffee table and followed him out.

"Where is it?" I asked him as we got into the elevator. I focused on the numbers slowly going down so I could avoid looking at him.

Unfortunately, his warm scent engulfed me. He smelled of the forest, with an underlying hint of amber. I breathed through my mouth and attempted to ignore it.

"I can scent your desire," he said, his voice rough. I jolted, my eyes meeting his.

"You—I—we—"

"Yes," he agreed, grinning at my stuttering. "All of those things."

The elevator doors opened, and I darted out into the lobby like my hair was on fire.

"I don't like you living in this building," he said when he caught up to me with his long stride.

I shot him a look. "It's not fancy, but I needed my own place."

"This area isn't safe."

And just like that, I dried up like the Sahara. There

was no bigger turn-off than someone attempting to tell me what to do.

If Nathaniel could scent my annoyance, it clearly didn't bother him, because he wrapped one hand around my arm and escorted me to his car.

"What's with the manhandling?" I snapped, pulling away from him once he'd opened the passenger door for me.

Surprise flashed through his eyes, along with something like...embarrassment.

"I apologize. There is a scent here that my wolf does not like. I was operating on instinct." I didn't have to be a werewolf to sense his shame, although his expression had turned carefully blank.

"It's okay," I said. "I just wasn't expecting it."

He nodded and closed my door, loping around the car to the driver's side.

"The massacre is closer to Raleigh than Durham. Near the airport," he said, his tone suddenly all-business.

"You've changed your tune. I thought you didn't want me at these scenes."

"I don't. But my wolf has decided that if you're going to be there anyway, he will keep you where he can see you."

I turned and watched him. He kept his eyes on the road.

"You talk about your wolf as if you're two different...beings."

He shrugged. "Werewolves have various relationships with the creature inside them. Mine has always been able to communicate exactly what he wants. It allows me to make snap decisions based on potential threats."

We were both quiet as he drove to the scene. "What was it?" I asked him as we pulled up outside a huge, sprawling home.

"Birthday party," Nathaniel said, his voice tight.

The muscles around my heart began to ache. Forcing myself to get out of the car was one of the hardest things I'd ever done. Nathaniel held out his arm, and I took it, suddenly grateful for the feel of it, so strong and warm beneath my hand.

Nelson was already waiting for us, his face blank. But his eyes burned with fury. Cops were moving in and out of the house, along with people dressed in white jumpsuits, a few of them taking photos of the scene.

Behind Nelson, two balloons welcomed visitors into the entranceway. A giant 3 next to a 0. Someone had turned thirty today.

"We haven't analyzed the scene," Nelson said. "Most people were in the backyard where the party was."

We followed him into the house, through the open-plan living room and onto a huge deck. For a moment, my brain struggled to make sense of what I was looking at.

I must've made some sound, because Nathaniel reached out and squeezed my shoulder. I took a deep breath and forced myself to look.

Whatever had attacked these people had come from the state park behind the house. It had left a trail of death and destruction in its wake.

Bodies littered the scene, most of them in small groups, the way people tended to congregate at parties. The pool was a deep red, and I forced my gaze away from the things floating inside it.

"We have a witness," Nelson said suddenly, and I stared at him.

"Someone survived?"

He nodded. "She was upstairs in a guest bathroom. She's...shocky."

Nelson led us back through the house and up the stairs, where a tiny blonde sat in a sparkly blue dress. A medic was taking her blood pressure, and he gave us a fierce look.

"Now is not the time," he snapped.

His eyes must have met Nathaniel's, because his face drained of color, and his gaze slid away.

"We're not going to hound her," I said. "We're trying to stop this from happening to anyone else." I stepped closer to the girl.

Shocky was putting it mildly.

She was whispering something I couldn't catch. I crouched in front of her, looking up into her deathly pale face.

"Dead," she was whispering. "They're all dead."

"I'm so sorry," I said softly.

"Dead."

I got to my feet. I wasn't going to make her relive the horror she'd just gone through.

I backed away, but Nathaniel took my place, his gaze gentle.

"What's your name, little one?"

He'd managed to get through some of her shock. She stared at him, then automatically dropped her gaze. But he held out his hand, and after a moment, she slid her own hand into his.

"Hayley."

"Hayley, we want to find out what did this to your friends. Did you see it?"

She began to shake. The medic opened his mouth, but Nathaniel sent him a look before turning back to Hayley.

"I wanted some privacy," she whispered. "They were setting off fireworks."

That explained why everyone else was outside.

"Brent turned up with his new girlfriend, so I thought I'd cry a little and get it out of my system."

"Did you hear anything?"

"Bangs, pops. Laughing, cheering. And then screaming."

Had the beast been smart enough to know the sound of fireworks would help cover the sound of the slaughter, or had that been a coincidence?

"What did you do?"

"I climbed into the bathroom closet. There was a space at the bottom. And I hid."

Her gaze slid away from Nathaniel's and met mine. "I hid."

"It was a smart move," I told her. "You didn't know if it would come inside."

"They're all dead."

Nathaniel reached out and stroked her hair, giving her what comfort he could. Then he stepped away, and the medic moved back in.

We walked out of the bedroom and back downstairs.

"Lucky girl," Nelson said.

"She won't feel lucky," I muttered. "She'll wish she died with them. She'll see this every time she closes her eyes before she goes to sleep. If she manages to sleep at all."

Nathaniel sent me a sharp, searching look, and I shut my mouth.

We were all quiet for a moment. Nathaniel placed his hand on my lower back, and I allowed it. "How many people have been on the scene?" he asked Nelson.

"Three. We knew you were coming, so we wanted to wait and see if you could get a…scent."

Nathaniel nodded. "This scene is still fresh and undisturbed enough that I may be able to pick one up. My wolf will have a greater chance. I'll change."

Nelson nodded, and Nathaniel stepped into the

bathroom downstairs.

A few moments later, he thumped against the door. I opened it and let him out. I'd never seen Nathaniel in his wolf form. His wolf was silver, darkening to black on his face, ears, and along his back. His mouth dropped open as he watched me taking him in. He was glorious and likely knew it.

Gasps sounded at the sight of his huge wolf. He ignored them and padded out onto the deck, nose down, as he began quartering the scene.

I turned to Nelson. "All the scenes have a few things in common. Large groups of humans. Most of them in some kind of remote location, which means no one saw what attacked."

"Maximum impact, without the chance of getting caught." He cleared his throat. "I have to tell you, the higher-ups are convinced a werewolf is behind this."

I watched Nathaniel as he made his way down to the pool area, near the grill. He ignored us, but I knew he'd heard Nelson.

I took in the body parts strewn around the scene, as if a giant monster had rampaged through the party. Once again, no one who'd been outside had gotten the chance to run. "Werewolves don't—"

"Attack like this. I know. But people want to focus on the monster they know. It's easier to believe this is due to some kind of pack politics than a terrifying, rampaging beast no one has seen before."

I fisted my hands. I was pretty sure Ellen's article

had helped that theory along.

I watched Nathaniel as he went still. He glanced at me, and I strode down the steps, thankful for the plastic booties I'd slipped on before stepping outside. I crouched next to Nathaniel and glanced at Nelson, who'd followed me over.

"Here's your proof," I said.

The tooth was huge—longer than my middle finger and just as thick. And it was also a dark, obsidian black. I gestured toward Nathaniel's open mouth. He helpfully widened it, showing off his gleaming white fangs.

"Spot the difference," I said.

The teeth were a similar shape. Only, the black tooth was three or four times larger than Nathaniel's front fangs.

Nelson picked up the tooth with his gloved hand. "What kind of creature does this belong to?"

"I don't know. But if you let me take it, I can ask around."

He gave me a look. "I know you like to play fast and loose with chain of custody for evidence, but I can't have you strolling off with the most valuable piece of the puzzle."

Nathaniel snapped his mouth shut, clicking his teeth. Nelson gave him a look, carefully avoiding his eyes.

"What's your plan?" I gestured impatiently to the tooth in Nelson's hand. "Give it to the lab for analysis?

They'll tell you what you already know. It's from some kind of creature they've never encountered before. If *I* take it, I can ask paranormals. I can also take it to Danica and see if she's got any thoughts."

He was thinking about it.

I forced my voice to remain level. "What's the point in setting up this task force if you're not going to use the access to paranormals? The old rules are no longer working."

Nelson heaved a sigh. "Seventy-two hours. You get it for seventy-two hours, and if you haven't found what did this, I want it back."

"Deal."

He pulled out a tiny plastic bag and placed the tooth inside. I took it, and Nathaniel strolled back toward the bathroom, presumably so he could shift and change.

"I hope you're being careful."

I glanced at Nelson. "What are you talking about?"

"I've seen how he looks at you. Remember what he is."

I stiffened. "And what is he?" Nelson had never struck me as prejudiced before.

He raised one eyebrow, his dark green eyes sharp. "He's an Alpha werewolf, Evie. And the only thing he cares about is the survival of his wolves. You should remember that."

"That's not the *only* thing I care about."

I jumped about a foot in the air as Nathaniel's

hand landed on my shoulder. I glanced at him, but he was giving the detective a wide smile.

"Did you notice any scents?" I asked.

Nathaniel nodded. "Over on the west side of the property near the fence."

"What was it?"

A muscle ticked in Nathaniel's cheek. "Mage."

Nelson nodded. "Two of the guests are low-level mages."

I thought about that. Typically, the mages kept to themselves. They sure as hell weren't chummy with paranormals, but they didn't interact with humans much, unless they were responding to some kind of callout. So what were the mages doing at this human birthday party?

"I'll talk to Albert," I said.

Nathaniel gave me a look. "Maybe I should talk to him."

"I left him alive last time."

Nelson winced. "I didn't hear that." Someone gestured for him. "If you don't have anything else for me, you can go. Let me know what happens with that tooth." He beelined for the evidence tech.

"Are you okay?" Nathaniel asked.

I shrugged, and Nathaniel pushed a curl off my face, the movement strangely intimate. He must've seen how close I was to breaking down, because he took my arm, leading me back through the house.

We were both quiet as he drove back toward

Durham. The streets were almost empty at this time of the early morning, shadows flowing from buildings like spilled ink.

I turned my attention to the huge black tooth in the plastic bag, holding it up to the light. I had no idea what kind of creature this belonged to.

"You think Danica will know what that is?" Nathaniel asked.

I shrugged. "She's pretty good at that kind of thing. Edward taught her well."

We slowed for a red light. I could feel Nathaniel's gaze on me. "Weren't you trained by the same guy?"

I snorted. "For a few months. Sure, when I wasn't getting my ass handed to me, I was cramming, but Danica trained under Edward for *years*."

"What happened between you and your sister?" Nathaniel asked gently.

I took a deep breath.

My mom, my sister, and I had lived with most of the coven. It was a happy childhood, until soon after I turned ten.

I clutched at Danica, my nails digging into her shirt.

"No, no, no! Let me go!" I screamed.

The coven was surrounding us, but they weren't helping. They just looked sad and accepting. Mom was crying, tears running silently down her face as she lifted her hands and her power forced Dani away from me. Gemma waved her hand, and I was stuck in place as Mom's power dragged Dani away.

"I don't want to go!" she was howling now, desperate. *"Let me stay here!"*

"It's for the best," Mom sobbed, and Dani reached for me, her hand outstretched.

"I'll come back for you," she screamed. *"I promise!"*

"She didn't keep that promise," I said. "I forgave her for it, not long ago, but I'll never forget how it felt to be abandoned. To wait. For *years*. By the time I was fourteen, Mom was dead. When Danica arrived, I told her to leave."

I swallowed around the lump in my throat. Nathaniel shook his head at me. "She shouldn't have. She let her own guilt get to her, but she should've stayed. She should've kept trying."

I studied the Alpha as he turned his attention back to the road. He would never have stopped trying. I didn't think he knew the meaning of the word "quit."

"Well, Danica went on and continued her training. When she learned it wasn't an accident and Mom had been murdered, she returned to Durham to hunt the killers."

That hunt had led Danica to Samael's club, where a demon ended up dead. Samael gave my sister two weeks to find out who was killing his demons. That little task hadn't exactly worked out the way Danica had thought it would since she and Samael were both now disgustingly happy and ruling the underworld together.

"Then your coven kicked you out."

Every now and then, the grief seemed to swallow me whole. All I could see when I closed my eyes were the faces of those I'd lost.

"I deserved it," I said hoarsely.

A strong hand wrapped around mine. I glanced down at it, so large compared to my own. Nathaniel didn't say anything else. He didn't need to. He just held my hand, providing silent support.

When we arrived at my apartment building, Nathaniel walked me to the elevator. I didn't protest.

"You're being very cooperative," Nathaniel said, and I pressed the elevator button. The doors opened, and I wasn't entirely surprised when he stepped in with me.

"I've seen how difficult it can be for Kyla to deal with her wolf when she's stressed or pissed."

"And you figured it was the same for me."

I shrugged, waving my hand in between us. "Clearly, your wolf is going through some shit."

Nathaniel let out a rough laugh, raking a hand through his hair. My own hand twitched, as if wishing it could do the same thing.

The elevator doors opened, and he walked me to my door.

"The situations are very different," he murmured.

"How so?"

Nathaniel stepped closer, and I instinctively backed up until I was leaning against my door.

I blinked up at him like a stunned rabbit as he

slowly lifted his hand, pushing one of my curls off my face. He cupped my cheek with that hand, and my breath caught in my throat.

He leaned close, bending down until his warm breath caressed the side of my neck.

"Figure it out," he growled.

With a wink, he turned and stepped back into the elevator.

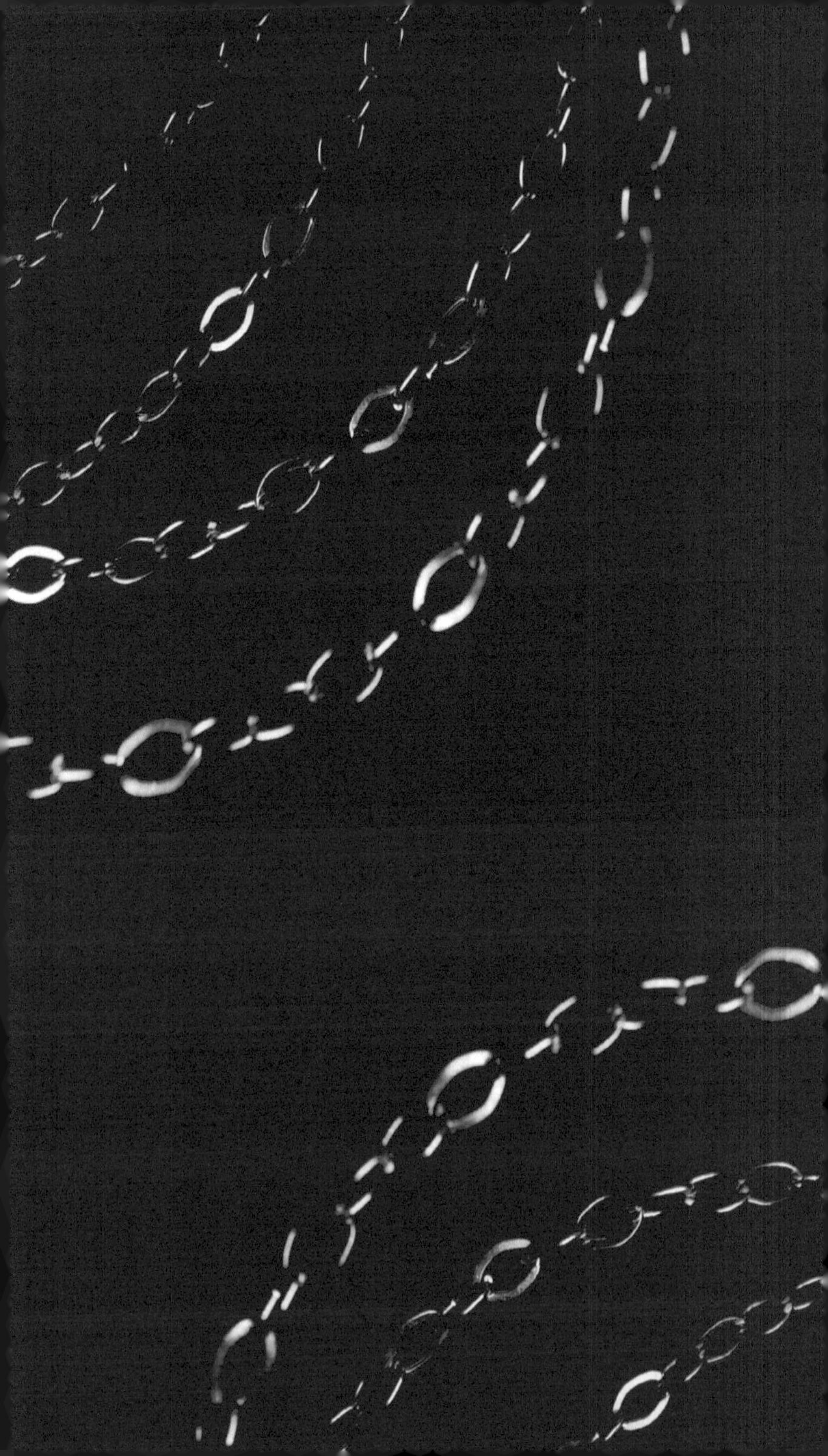

EVIE

The building was a large stone block. It radiated doom and desperation.

I stepped inside, my stomach clenching as I fought to hold on to my breakfast. I didn't want to go in there. I would do almost anything I could not to go in there.

But my legs moved anyway, carrying me forward without my permission.

It was quiet. Too quiet. My heart slammed in my chest, and my hand trembled as I lifted it to the door, pushing it open.

Stray papers floated around my feet—evidence that whoever had been here had tried to cover their tracks.

I leaned down and picked one up.

It was in a language I couldn't read. But I could see my name multiple times in the document. Frustration roared through me, and I stalked through the entrance and into the first corridor.

To the left, an empty concrete cell waited, chains dangling. One of them was covered in rust-colored stains.

I wanted to stop. But my body kept moving. I was suddenly in a medical room, with beds spaced six feet apart, restraints hanging from them. This time, I wanted to move faster, to ignore the reality in front of me. But my feet slowed, forcing me to take in every detail.

Then, I was walking downstairs. This was a prison, with each cell showing remnants of the people—or creatures—who'd been here.

"Evie?"

My heart stopped.

"Mom?"

She was in one of the cells at the end of the corridor. I pumped my legs, thighs straining, breath sawing in and out of my lungs. But the faster I ran, the longer the corridor stretched out in front of me.

I stopped with a frustrated sob. I'd find a different way. I'd—

"Evie."

I turned. And there she was. Chained in a cell. Her belly swollen and round. She was pregnant. With me.

"Evie, you shouldn't be here. You need to leave."

"I'm getting you out of here."

"You know that's not how it works."

Mom gave me a shaky smile. Behind me, something roared. I jumped.

"Don't worry, dear. That's just your father."

I stared at her, and her smile widened. "He's coming

for me, you know. It's time for you to leave. If you get stuck here, you can't help them."

"Mom..." There was so much I wanted to say. So many things on the tip of my tongue. But when I opened my mouth, the only thing that came out was a strangled sob.

"I know, darling. Mothers always know. Now, go!"

I didn't want to leave her here.

"Go, Evie. You have to save the babies."

I jolted. Babies?

"They're upstairs. Go."

I sobbed as I ran. As I left my mother in that cell. But I hauled myself up the next staircase and through the next room, which was packed with examining tables. Restraints gave the indication that none of the women who were supposed to climb onto those tables were there of their own free will. The stirrups also made it clear that this was where the women were examined.

Cries sounded. A symphony of screams. I pushed open the next door and saw them.

Bassinets, each of them holding a tiny newborn. I had to get them out. How was I going to get them out?

I reached for the first baby. I'd carry them out one by one if I had to.

My gaze flicked to the name tag on the bassinet. Where the name should be, there were only numbers.

But scrawled lovingly beneath that was...Evie Amana.

I jolted back from the baby, my knees turning to rubber.

"How are you going to save the others if you won't even

save yourself?" a deep voice asked.

I whirled. The unseelie was huge. Covered in scars. He emanated power.

"Who are you?"

He just smiled at me and gestured to the baby. "Go on, then. Take her."

I flicked my glance back at the innocent little newborn. The name tag had changed.

Now, it read "Monster #4503292."

"Ah," said the man behind me. "So that's what this is about. Interesting."

I sent him an infuriated glare, but he wasn't looking at me. He was staring at the baby, who chose that moment to let out a desperate wail. His finger slid into her palm, and her tiny fingers wrapped around it.

"My love for her was so all-encompassing, I was almost paralyzed by it." He looked at me then, and I swallowed around the lump in my throat.

"You're my father." I glanced around at the lab. "Well, one of them anyway."

His gaze burned into me. "They may have added some extra DNA here and there, but make no mistake. You have only one father. And only one mother."

Tears trickled down my cheeks. He gave me a sympathetic look. Then his face hardened. "Take her. Take her, and then find the others."

I took a deep breath. Then I reached for the baby again. Reached for myself, so small and alone.

The moment she was in my arms, my father smiled.

And it was my smile.

I jolted awake, my face wet. Then I turned and sobbed into my pillow.

I knew it was a dream. But it had been so real. My father... The photo I'd seen of him was before the scars. Was that even what he would look like now? Or was that just another example of my subconscious filling in the gaps?

When I'd cried myself out, I sat up again, wiping my cheeks. I slid out of bed and padded to the bathroom, where I splashed cold water on my face.

My eyes were puffy and bloodshot. My cheeks were pale, and I'd bitten into my lower lip in my dream.

Cool.

I flicked on the shower and turned the temperature up as high as I could stand, cursing the fact that I'd have to wash my hair—a long, laborious process.

It was only in the last few years that I'd learned to tolerate my curls. Growing up, I'd spent hours each week with a straighter in my hand, paying careful attention to the weather so I could avoid any hint of rain.

When I was finally done, I wrapped a cotton T-shirt around my hair and made my way to the coffee machine. I sipped the first cup while leaning against the counter and reading *Durham Denizens*.

Ellen was quiet today. The front page was about a merger between Finvarra and a human tech company.

I'd like to think the reporter had chosen to focus her attention elsewhere, but I wasn't that naïve.

I didn't *think* I'd be seeing any bad guys today. I combed my secret weapon through my hair and pulled on a pretty summer dress. After the carnage I'd seen last night, followed by the nightmare, I needed something cheerful in my life this morning. My dress was white, with giant pink lilies stamped all over it. Did I look like an ass-kicker? No. Did I give a flying fuck? Also no.

I did pull on a pair of bike shorts beneath the skirt. At least if I ended up wrestling with a bad guy, I wouldn't be flashing innocent bystanders half my ass.

My gun went into my thigh holster. I was still trying out a few different types of firearms as I attempted to figure out which would make the cut for my day-to-day gun. Right now, I was using the Beretta 92 9mm, which was reliable, accurate, and, most importantly, easy to shoot. My biggest issue was its size, and my hands were just a little too small for it to be comfortable.

Danica had suggested I try the Glock 17, but the Beretta had a larger magazine capacity.

I slid my A-F into its sheath, which I strapped onto my other thigh. The dress was accessible enough that I could reach all my weapons by pulling it up. Yes, it would look ridiculous, but it wouldn't slow me down.

I grabbed my purse and took the stairs down to the parking lot. Old Mr. Dwight wolf-whistled as I walked past him, and I flipped my hair with a wink.

I picked up donuts for breakfast, because I had a tendency to eat my feelings.

"Well, well, well," Kyla said when I strolled in. "Carbs, sugar, and fashion. What happened last night?"

I took a deep breath and told her all about the massacre, handing her the tooth. She took it with a wince. "I wouldn't want to go up against whatever this belongs to."

I nodded. "If I hadn't seen a hellhound with my own two eyes, I would've thought that's what we had here. But their teeth are white."

I took a donut and sat at my desk. Kyla studied me. "You've been crying."

I scowled at her. "Do you know how long I spent trying to cover that shit up?"

She rolled her eyes. "Spill."

"I had a nightmare. That's all."

She gave me her hard stare until I rolled my eyes and filled her in.

"Wow, so you were a baby, but in your dream, it literally said *Monster*? And you didn't want to pick up the baby version of you?" She shook her head at me. "A therapist would have a field day with you."

"Thanks. That really means a lot."

She grinned at me. "But seriously, we could analyze that shit all morning. Tell me about your dad."

"I know nothing about him. After we found the lab, and I realized what had happened, I went looking for him. I found a woman called Ainfean, who was my uncle Eachann's lover. Lorcan—my father—disappeared, and they thought he'd found a woman. In reality, he was in the same lab as my mother. They fell in love, but he was brutally tortured until he was barely sane. He still managed to help Mom escape."

"What happened to him?"

"He stayed behind to try to help the others. Mom never saw him again. Neither did his brother."

He was likely dead.

"I'm sorry."

"Thanks."

I looked up at the timeline on the whiteboard.

Getting to my feet, I stuffed the rest of my donut into my mouth and grabbed a marker.

Lab discovered, empty. I added, *HFE on the run. New location??*

"They must have regrouped," I muttered. "They would've had a backup plan. And dream-dad was right—I've been so focused on myself and Mom, I haven't even thought about the other victims."

"We know they killed a lot of them before they left the lab," Kyla said gently.

"They did. But they wouldn't have killed all of them. Sure, I need to find HFE to make them pay for what they did to Mom, but we also need to find their prisoners. What if they have more babies, Kyla?"

"We'll find them."

Panic was fluttering like a trapped bird in my

chest. My current case needed to take priority. People were dying. In groups. And yet...

"Put Rose on it," Kyla said.

I turned to face her. Of course, she'd scented my panic. Werewolves.

"Basic grunt work," Kyla said. "Get her to work with Steve. We're looking for any shell companies connected with HFE. Any real estate purchases they could have made within the past thirty years."

I took a deep, steadying breath.

"You're right. Thanks for talking me off the ledge." I needed to feel like I was making *some* progress.

"Anytime. What's your plan for today?"

"I'm going to visit Albert. I want to hear what he has to say about his mages being victims. Usually, he would be the first to condemn the violence. He'd be all over the media, using this as another example of why paranormals should all be put down. So why isn't he doing that now?"

"Good point."

"I thought so. Then I thought we could go see Aubrey. I want him to take a look at the tooth. Plus, I think we should talk to him about Operation Steal-a-Sword. Now that he has officially split with his court, maybe he'll help us."

Kyla's eyes sharpened at that, and she smiled. She liked Aubrey. In fact, I didn't know anyone who didn't like the light fae. Other than his king, of course.

The seelie was one of our friends, and he had

turned on his king after Taraghlan betrayed us to Lucifer. Aubrey had fought on our side, and plenty of seelie were backing him over Taraghlan.

"What's your plan?" I asked Kyla.

"I'm looking into Elizabeth from the auction house. I don't trust anyone that wimpy and naïve."

I grinned at that.

"On that note..." I hauled my purse up, grabbed another donut for the road, and strolled out the door. I had training with the demons tomorrow morning, so I should probably be carb-loading anyway, right?

The same two mages who'd been on the door at Albert's last time were standing guard again today. I gave them my best beady-eyed stare, and they parted to let me through. Nice.

I surveyed the ward.

It flickered, temporarily allowing me access. I raised one eyebrow as I stepped through, finding Albert waiting for me. This was too easy.

"I don't have time for your power games today," he said coolly. "Why are you here?"

"Ouch. And I thought we were finally becoming friends. I'm here to talk to you about the massacres."

His eyes narrowed, and I angled my head. "There were mages at both the birthday party last night and the family reunion. I'm not sure about the corporate gathering yet, but we're looking into it. What's going on, Albert? Are your people being targeted?"

He shook his head. "There are far more low-level

mages in the general population than paranormals such as yourself would like to admit. Unsurprisingly, seeing the threat that creatures like your sister represent, and the way she tore down our building without any repercussions..." He gave me a sharp smile. "Let's just say it has been good for recruitment."

"You don't think there's any chance your mages are being targeted?"

"No. If they were, whatever is attacking the humans would have focused on mages with actual power."

"Mages like yourself."

"Yes. And the Discipulus Mages beneath me."

I eyed him. "You've been very quiet about these attacks."

"I am capable of being circumspect when grieving families are dealing with unimaginable loss," he said. "That doesn't mean I won't use this as another demonstration of why paranormals are a blight on our realm."

There was the Albert I knew and hated.

"Fine."

I turned to go.

Another mage stood by the door.

"You don't want to mess with me today," I advised him. "Just ask your friends."

He took in my dress, my purse, and my hair. Then he sneered.

I sighed. Of course I'd end up fighting more often

when dressed nicely than I would if I were wearing leather with my knives in full visibility.

The mage looked at Albert. I glanced over my shoulder and watched their silent discussion. Albert gave the mage one nod, and he smiled.

I strolled toward the door. The mage stepped out of my way. Then he shoved his body into me, slamming me into the wall. He wrapped his hand around the back of my neck and pulled me toward him, his fist raised.

One hand on me and one hand raised meant no hands protecting his goods. Moron.

I kneed him in the balls. He folded, and I punched him straight in the throat. I pushed my ward into existence, and he bounced off it with a snarl.

"Control your people," I advised Albert, before turning back to the mage in front of me. His face was turning a dull purple, and I memorized his features.

"Come at me again, and I'll hurt you," I told him matter-of-factly.

He sneered. "You're going to pay, mutt."

I rolled my eyes and set his shirt on fire.

Holy shit.

He screamed and ripped his shirt off his body. My pulse pounded in my throat, but I managed to keep my face blank.

"Come at me again, and it'll be your jeans I burn," I advised, dropping my gaze to what was likely a teeny weeny. "We wouldn't want you to lose your best friend."

He snarled at me but backed away. I nodded at Albert. A vein was pounding in his temple.

I strutted out of Albert's building, blew a kiss to the mages on the door, and slid into my car.

I managed to make it to the next block before I began trembling.

I could've killed that man because he pushed me. Talk about an overreaction. I could feel that thread of my power, burning bright and practically begging me to use it.

If I couldn't trust myself to use my magic without consequences, I was going to need to get *really* good with my weapons.

I pulled over and flicked Kyla a message, letting her know I was on the way to Aubrey's. If she was done with Elizabeth, she could meet me there.

I headed toward Hope Valley. Without my permission, my thoughts returned to the werewolf Alpha.

Before I'd been sucked into unrelenting nightmares last night, I'd struggled to fall asleep, Nathaniel's words replayed in my head over and over again.

Figure it out.

I'd fought hard for my independence. I broke up with Liam because I knew I wasn't ready for a relationship. I was still discovering who exactly I was—away from the coven, without the chip in my body, and without the spell on the house influencing me.

The Alpha would steamroll over me if I let him. I was always up for a good power struggle, but not with him.

He'd been alive for longer than I had. He had the power of the pack behind him, and when it came down to it, he was much more patient than most people gave him credit for.

I pulled up behind Kyla's car. She got out, her long-legged stride graceful as always. She crossed in front of the large marble fountain in the middle of Aubrey's driveway. Like most seelie in our realm, he'd built incredible wealth.

A group of pixies fluttered out of Aubrey's front door. I got out of my car and winced, their high-pitched voices straining my ears as they swooped past on incandescent wings.

"Evie, Kyla. I feel as if I haven't seen either of you for months." Aubrey smiled at us both. He was beautiful in a way that few men could achieve without dancing across the line into femininity. His features were more delicate than most, and yet his jaw looked like it could take a punch. His eyes were a light lavender, yet they were shrewd, often sharp.

"I hope we're not interrupting."

"No, of course not. I was just meeting with some of the pixie queen's representatives. She can't be seen meeting with me herself just yet. Not if she doesn't want to face repercussions from Taraghlan." His expression hardened briefly before smoothing out once more. "Come have some coffee," he said.

We followed him into his home.

The fae had an affinity for greenery, but it was a key part of Aubrey's power. Plants and flowers covered every inch of his home—most of them varieties I'd never seen before. A long vine crawled toward us as we stepped through the front door, and Aubrey shot it a sharp look. It froze and then slowly slid away, as if contrite.

Kyla sneezed three times, rubbed at her nose, and sighed. Her nose would adjust, but Aubrey's home always irritated her sensitive senses.

Aubrey let us into his kitchen and gestured for us to take a seat. He took great pleasure in operating his own coffee machine. "Latte? Cappuccino?" he offered, and I grinned.

"Cappuccino."

Kyla asked for the same, and Aubrey got to work. Seeing a fae so close to the throne doing menial tasks like this—and taking pleasure from them—gave me hope. He would be an incredible ruler, if only we could remove Taraghlan's ass from the seelie throne.

"I'm guessing you didn't come over for a coffee break. As much as I would love for that to be the case."

I smiled. "No. We have a couple of things to talk to you about, actually."

"I'm intrigued." Aubrey placed our cappuccinos on the kitchen island in front of us, and we all took our seats.

"Have you ever seen a creature with teeth like this before?" I handed Aubrey the tooth. He held it up to the light and examined it from the cracked end to the sharp point.

"The jaw that this must have come from..." he marveled.

"Yeah."

His gaze moved from the tooth to my face. "You're investigating the human murders."

"Yes. This was found at one of the scenes."

One silver eyebrow shot up. "I thought they were werewolf attacks."

Beside me, Kyla let out a low growl. Aubrey gave her an amused look. "My apologies."

She sipped at her coffee. I nodded at the tooth. "So? Anything about it jog your memory?"

"No. I'm sorry. I haven't had the pleasure of meeting whatever beast lost that tooth. But I will ask around." Aubrey slid his phone from his pocket and took a picture. Then he sat back in his chair and surveyed us both.

"You also want to ask me about the sword."

"Yup."

"Last time, you couldn't give us much information, as you were still loyal to Taraghlan," Kyla said. "I'm guessing that's changed."

Aubrey sighed. "Yes. It has. His decisions have not been worthy of the throne. I could overlook some of them, but joining with Lucifer, betraying his alliances, allowing Danica to be taken by his adviser... I fear for the future of our race if these are his decisions."

I didn't know what to say to that. "Sorry about your fuckwit ruler" didn't seem quite right.

"Wellll," Kyla drawled. "We need to get into that castle. Do you know anyone who can help us?"

"I'm not the only one who is unhappy with the decisions Taraghlan has been making. I believe I know someone who can help you."

"Our biggest problem is going to be getting over that moat."

Aubrey merely smiled. "You don't need to get over it. You need to get under it."

I almost choked. It was so obvious. The seelie king used to have an adviser who could make his own portals from anywhere. That adviser was now dead. *Of course* Taraghlan would have a hidden way out of his castle. Which we could use to get *in*.

"Who is it that will help us?" Kyla asked.

Aubrey held up a hand. "I'm not guaranteeing anything. I'll need to explain exactly why you need to steal the sword and the repercussions if you can't get it to Finvarra. But...I'm hoping my contact will listen."

"When can we talk to them?"

"Soon. I have spies in the castle. I'll get in touch with them."

Kyla's phone buzzed, and she swiped it from the counter. "Excuse me a minute." She loped outside.

I studied Aubrey. "So, you really don't want to be

king, huh?"

He threw back his head with a laugh. "No."

"What if you're the only choice?"

He sighed. "I will, of course, do what is best for my kingdom. But I enjoy my life here. I have no desire to rule our people."

"Neither did Danica."

Kyla stepped back inside. "We need to go."

"Sorry," I told Aubrey. "When this is all over, we'll come over for a proper coffee break."

He smiled at me. "Sounds good."

I followed Kyla outside. "That was Adione," she said. "She says we should be looking at Wimbar."

"Not surprising since he was mysteriously absent during our little visit."

"Yeah. She also said she has friends in that house still. It's not good, Evie. One of the lesser fae servants told her that Wim has been using Callula as his lackey for years. *He's* the one who made her travel to Finvarra's estate to find the book. He told her that since it would be stolen from the auction house, she'd be paid out the insurance money. When they sold the stolen artifacts, they'd split the money they got from the sale."

I sighed. "She's dead, isn't she?"

"I don't know. It's likely, though." Kyla was silent for a moment. "If she is, I'm going to make Wim pay. He probably figured he'd tie up any loose ends. He probably killed the humans who stole the artifacts *and* the security guards."

"He must've had buyers lined up for everything. It could be that he's holding Callula somewhere." I frowned as I got out of the car, the summer heat punching me in the face. "Here's what I don't understand. Wim's not having any issues with money, right? When you looked into his finances, you didn't find anything that stuck out?"

"Nothing so far. And Finvarra's people sent everything I needed for the financial part of the investigation."

"Maybe he wants one of the artifacts for himself."

"Or maybe he just wants to fuck with Finvarra. Maybe he's a thrill-seeker. I dunno. But since we can't find him, I've been having his little friends investigated."

"Finvarra gave you that much power?"

"Oh yeah. Finny boy wants that book back."

"I dare you to call him that to his face."

She grinned.

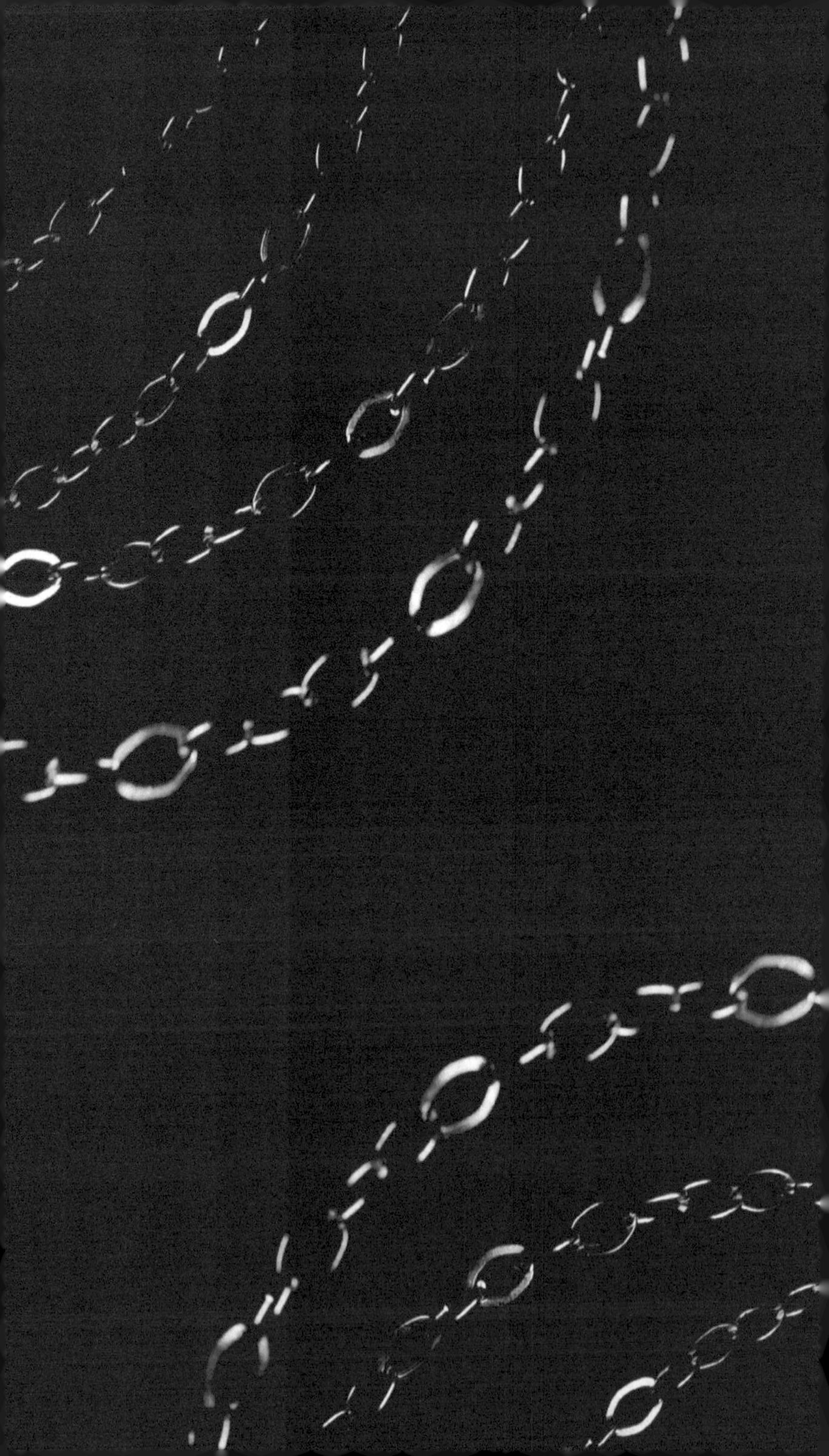

12

EVIE

The next morning, I hauled myself out of bed with a groan. It was six a.m., and I'd worked until two a.m., comparing pictures of various paranormal creatures, searching for one that could match the black tooth.

I had nothing.

After less sleep than I needed, the last thing I wanted to do was work out with the demons. But keeping in shape would keep me alive.

I started the coffee, pulled on clothes and weapons, then took the elevator down to the lobby.

I heard the screams before the elevator doors fully opened.

Picking up my pace, I sprinted through the lobby and pushed open the door.

Carnage greeted me.

It took me several seconds to reconcile what I was

seeing.

A...body.

And blood. So much blood.

Splattered across the parking lot, close to my car.

My car, which was covered in black paint.

WHORE.

Red liquid splattered the car, but it had dried to the rusty color that told me it wasn't paint.

I couldn't put it together in my head. Wasn't entirely sure what had happened.

Someone was still screaming.

I managed to turn. A crowd was forming, drawn by the screams. I fumbled for my phone.

"Evelyn."

"Can you come? Please?"

"I'm on my way."

Maybe later, I'd contemplate why my first call had been to the werewolf Alpha and not to the demons.

My next call was to Nelson.

"I'll be right there," he told me. "Secure the scene as much as you can."

I could already see bloody footprints, where some unsuspecting resident, likely phone in hand, had walked out of the building before they realized exactly what they were walking through. The pool of vomit close to those footprints told me they'd figured it out.

"You guys need to move back. The police are on the way."

Everyone ignored me. I couldn't blame them. The

woman was still screaming.

And then Nathaniel was striding across the parking lot toward me.

I had no idea how he'd gotten here so fast, but my hands shook at the sight of him.

Don't fall apart, dammit.

He reached me a few seconds later, his hand sliding around to cup the back of my neck. The movement was possessive, and any other time, I would've snarled at him. Right now, I was barely resisting the urge to burrow against his chest.

"Are you okay?"

I nodded. His gaze searched my face. Finally, he glanced in the direction of the woman who was *still* screaming.

The screams cut off.

Werewolf dominance for the win.

My lips were numb. It took me a few moments to get the words I needed out. "The body. It's Ellen Harrison. The reporter."

"The reporter who's been harassing you?" Nelson's voice came from behind me.

I turned, finding him standing with his thumbs hooked into his pockets as he surveyed the scene. More cops were rolling out the yellow crime scene tape.

"Yeah. Although she's been harassing a few people."

"From the state of your car, it looks like she was doing more than just harassing," Nelson said.

"Yeah," I frowned. "I don't know why she suddenly escalated like this."

"Maybe it had something to do with this." Nelson gestured to a cop who bought him a newspaper. He handed it to me.

Today's *Durham Denizens*. There was a picture of me, standing outside my apartment, scowling up at Nathaniel. The expression on his face was hopelessly amused, with a hint of tenderness. He had his hand raised to tuck a curl behind my ear. Nelson gave the newspaper back to the cop before I could catch the headline.

"You think this made her graffiti my car?"

Nelson shrugged, his gaze on my face. "Where were you last night?"

The world slowed to a crawl. "You think I did this?"

Nathaniel tensed, and I caught his wolf in his eyes before he glanced away. He was letting me deal with this.

"You know I have to ask," Nelson said softly.

I took a deep, shuddering breath. Yeah, I knew that. "I was here. Upstairs. I, uh, got in a little after eight p.m. Ate some toast, worked until around two a.m."

"Toast?" Nathaniel asked, his voice disapproving. "Two a.m.?" For some reason, his coddling Alpha instincts made the vise squeezing my chest loosen slightly.

"Dinner of champions," I informed him. I turned back to Nelson. "My apartment is on the other side of the building. I didn't hear anything."

Nathaniel was carefully watching the scene. I touched his arm, and he shifted his gaze to me, his eyes so light I almost shivered.

"What is it?" I asked.

He waited until Nelson had stepped away. "I scent the same creature who invaded my territory the other night. Wait here for a moment."

I nodded, watching as he stepped closer to the scene. No one protested as he leaned closer to... Harrison's head. I took another steadying breath as he stood there for a few seconds, clearly sorting through the scents. Then he stepped closer to my car, carefully avoiding the blood and...other things strewn across the scene.

I hadn't liked Ellen. In fact, I'd hated her. But this was a grisly, miserable way to die.

Nathaniel returned, took my hand, and led me back toward my apartment. Vas dropped out of the sky, landing in front of us.

Nathaniel gave a vicious snarl, pushing me behind him, and I gaped at him. I'd thought the Alpha had kept his cool, but obviously not.

"You know me," Vas said mildly. "You know I'm not a threat to Evie."

"You should know better than to sneak up on a werewolf."

Vas gave a languid shrug, and I shook my head at him. "I'm fine."

"Do you know who did it?"

Nathaniel took my arm. From the shit-eating grin on Vas's face, he didn't miss the possessiveness in that gesture. "No."

The grin disappeared as if it had never been there. Vas looked at the body, pondered it for a while, and then cursed. "You think it's hunting Evie?"

"I don't know."

"Whoa, whoa, whoa," I said. "Look at the... body." Bile climbed up my throat, and I had to take several deep breaths before I could continue. "This is gruesome, sure, but it's not on the same level as the massacres. Besides, it only killed one person. Not twenty or thirty."

"Witnesses described it as a huge, brown beast. Some of them glimpsed it before they fled," Nathaniel said.

I shouldn't be surprised that he'd collected that information already.

"You're moving in to the tower," Vas declared.

I bared my teeth at him. "Oh no, I'm not."

Nathaniel had gone very still. When I looked at him, all I saw was wolf. His hand slowly released my arm, and his claws slid out.

"She's not yours to give orders to, demon."

I elbowed him in the ribs. That little declaration would be sweet if I wasn't sure Nathaniel felt *he* could give me orders.

Vas's expression went cold. Then he glanced between us. I wasn't sure what he'd seen, but I caught a flicker of amusement.

"Ah," he said. "So it's like that."

I gave him a dark scowl. "Are you here to help or what?"

"Of course." He took a step back. "I still don't think you should stay here."

"Um…"

"Whoever did this knows where you live," Nathaniel said. "You'll come stay with me," he continued when I didn't reply.

I eyed him. "I don't know if that's a good idea."

"You visit every day anyway. You'll have your own space."

I shifted my gaze past him to the parking lot. Did I want to leave my apartment? No. But I also wanted to stay alive. And for whatever reason, something deadly was killing people in my parking lot. Or Harrison could have simply been in the wrong place at the wrong time. Either way, it was definitely dangerous.

Nathaniel was right—I *was* spending most of my time out there anyway.

"Fine," I said. "I'll pack a few things. But this is just for a couple of days."

EVIE

We were both quiet as Nathaniel drove me to his house. Vas had given me a long look as I left.

I had no doubt he'd be filling Danica in about this little situation.

Nathaniel parked his car, and I slid out. He grabbed my suitcase—I'd never learned to pack light—and carried it toward his house.

Tobias opened the door and beamed at me. He seemed to realize why I was there, because his smile dropped by half the wattage. "Evie," he said. "I'm sorry about what happened, but I'm glad you're visiting. Let me show you to your room."

"Thanks." I smiled at him. He took my suitcase from Nathaniel.

"I'll leave you to get settled in," Nathaniel said. "I have a few meetings, but you can message me if you need anything."

I nodded. "Thanks. I, uh, appreciate this."

He smiled. "You resent the hell out of the need for it."

"That too."

I followed Tobias up the stairs. He turned left on the second floor and opened the door at the end of the hall, stepping inside and placing my suitcase next to the door.

I scanned the room. The hardwood floors continued here—I would've judged Nathaniel if he'd covered them in carpet. But several blue-and-white rugs were positioned in a way that told me someone had put some thought into guests who'd be walking barefoot in cooler temperatures.

The walls were painted a pale blue, while the bed was a romantic, white-canopied affair, heaped with almost as many pillows as my own bed. The side tables were some kind of polished, pale wood, each holding a gold lamp and a vase of flowers. I didn't need to ask if they were real flowers. I knew Tobias well enough to know he'd be appalled at the suggestion of fake ones.

"This is beautiful," I said, still taking in the thick white drapes tied back with gold curtain holders, each formed into a wolf's paw. On the opposite side of the room, a small desk sat next to a chest of drawers.

Tobias opened a door next to the drawers. "Closet," he said. "Let me know if you need any help unpacking. That door leads to your bathroom." He pointed at the door next to it.

"Thank you." I eyed him, suddenly curious. "Can I ask you something?"

"Of course."

"What's it like, being a submissive wolf?"

He smiled. "I had a feeling you'd ask something like that."

"You don't have to answer," I said quickly, hoping I hadn't offended him.

He waved that off. "A healthy Alpha is driven to protect his submissives. Of course, all wolves are under the Alpha's protection, but submissives have a special status in the pack. It's to the pack's benefit that we're happy and healthy."

"How come?"

"Too many dominant wolves and not enough submissives, and a pack will turn into a continual power struggle as they fight for dominance. We... lighten the load."

"Nathaniel's a good Alpha?"

He nodded. "Nathaniel is an excellent Alpha. He doesn't truly need me to manage his home, but it brings me joy, so he hired me full time. He didn't need to hire you to figure out what the juveniles are doing, but he wanted to show them he respects them. He would've moved heaven and earth to get Kyla back when she was taken. He's always focused on how he can make life a little better for every single person in this pack, which is much more than I can say for some Alphas." His expression turned bleak for a second, but he seemed to shake it off.

"Nathaniel understands that submissive doesn't mean weak. All of us are creatures capable of killing hundreds of humans within minutes, whether we're submissive or dominant," he said matter-of-factly.

Someone called his name, and he smiled at me.

"Help yourself to anything you need. If you're hungry, I keep snack bags in the fridge and pantry."

I unpacked my toiletries, then spent the day at the desk. I'd grabbed my notes and laptop when I left my apartment, so I was able to work without needing to go into the office.

Someone knocked on the door at one point, jolting me from my thoughts.

"Come in."

Kyla poked her head in. She was carrying a tray, and my stomach let out a howl.

"Tobias thought you might be hungry. It's after lunch."

"I lost track of time."

"Nathaniel told me to check on you. He got caught up in some contract dispute with one of his clients, and he had to go out of town."

"I don't need him to check up on me."

Kyla placed the tray on one of the bedside tables. "Tobias added lunch for me too."

The soup smelled glorious and tasted better. The sandwiches were comforting, the bread freshly baked. Kyla made her way through four of them before she started on the chocolate cake Tobias had added.

"Any luck with your case?" Kyla asked when we were lying on the bed, almost in a food coma. I was going to need coffee to get through the afternoon.

I sighed. "Luck would be the wrong word. I want to look into Ellen Harrison's finances. It's just a hunch, but I want to see if anyone was paying her off."

"You think someone was paying her to write bad shit about the wolves?"

"I think it's strange that she was at every crime scene—including the one in South Carolina. Don't you?"

"Well, yeah, when you put it like that. What you really need to do is get into her email."

"You're not wrong." I sat up. "You reckon Steve could get me in?"

"That man could get into anything. It's kind of scary."

I sent Steve a message as Kyla got to her feet. "Thanks."

"Don't mention it. I'll be out in the field. Good luck at dinner tonight."

My eyes widened. "Why would I need luck? Dammit, Kyla." She'd waltzed out.

A few hours later, I got my reply from Steve. He hadn't had a chance to go through Harrison's emails yet, but he'd sent me her financials. And there were several transactions, each of them just under ten thousand dollars. All perfectly corresponding with the articles she'd printed which made the wolves look bad.

"I knew it," I muttered.

"Dinner," someone knocked on my door. Where the hell had the afternoon gone?

"Coming," I called, sending Steve a thank-you message. He'd said the transactions were difficult to trace, and it might take him a couple of days.

I filled Nathaniel in the moment I got downstairs. He gestured for me to sit next to him before loading my plate with fried chicken, mashed potatoes, and broccoli. Dinner was a quiet affair, with only the dominants joining us tonight.

"We're on a rotating schedule," Hunter explained when I asked him about it. "One night a week, we like to have a smaller dinner so we can talk business."

I chewed on my lower lip. "I can eat upstairs if you guys have stuff to discuss."

Nathaniel shot Hunter a look. "No. Eat your food."

I narrowed my eyes at him and carefully placed my fork down. He stared back at me. Tobias stepped into the room, lowering himself into his own chair. He'd insisted we get started without him.

"I know you're not wasting my delicious food, Evie," he said.

I grinned at him and picked my fork back up, ignoring the satisfaction radiating off the Alpha next to me.

Conversation turned to lighter topics. After dinner, I helped Tobias with the dishes before he shooed me away, insisting I sit and have a glass of wine at the table.

This seemed to be an informal catch-up time for the pack. A few of them trickled in, and I smiled at Jo from the coffee shop as she sat next to me.

"How are you?"

"Busy," I said. "Still working on the kids, but I've had a few other things taking up some time."

She nodded. "I heard about the attacks. I hope you guys catch whatever it is."

"We will."

We both watched as one of the human women wandered in, a newborn baby in her arms. She smiled at Nathaniel and handed over the tiny bundle.

I couldn't help but stare, every ounce of my attention on the way Nathaniel took the baby, his movements so natural and relaxed. She let out a squawk, and he grinned, lifted her closer to his chest, and gently patted her butt. Beneath his T-shirt, muscles rolled, drawing my attention. I forced my body under control before the wolves could figure out just how badly I was lusting after their Alpha.

The baby looked absurdly small in Nathaniel's arms, but she quieted, her tiny hand fisting in his shirt as he murmured to her mom. The Alpha raised his pinky, and the baby wrapped her little fingers around it instead.

"There's just something about a dangerous man holding a baby, isn't there?" Jo asked cheerfully.

I glanced at her, well aware that Nathaniel could hear every word I said.

"She's so small."

"Cindy and Dan tried for a while. Werewolves can only have babies with their mates, but it sometimes still takes some time."

"Their mates?" I knew werewolves mated for life, but they kept most of the information about how it all worked on the down-low.

Her eyes widened. "Uh—"

"Jo," Nathaniel said. "Come meet our newest pack member."

His eyes met mine, and a sharp pain shot through my gut. So, he didn't trust me with information about pack mates. No fucking worries.

Jo sent me an apologetic look and got to her feet, ambling over to her Alpha, where she bent and cooed at the baby.

I took one last look at the newborn in Nathaniel's arms, and my heart gave a weird little flutter. With a nod and a smile to Cindy, I got to my feet and wandered down into the basement.

Several wolves were sprawled out in front of the TV, watching sitcom reruns. Virtus lay on the ground, eyes closed as he snoozed. He opened one gold eye in a silent greeting as I walked in. Hunter shifted over and gestured for me to take a seat next to him.

"How's it going?"

"Fine," I said, keeping my gaze on the TV, where a middle-aged, bumbling fool was married to a beautiful woman who only put up with his bullshit because she had to read her scripted lines.

"Fine?"

I glanced at Hunter. Okay, maybe I *was* in a mood. Problem was, I couldn't figure out why. Now that I wasn't continually enspelled by the coven, it was as if I suddenly had all these new emotions I'd never contended with before. And it was exhausting trying to figure them all out.

"It's been a long day."

"And you're pissed at Nathaniel?"

I narrowed my gaze at him. "What makes you think that?"

He merely grinned, affable as ever. "I know when a woman is pissed off at a man. It just so happens I see that expression more than a little often myself."

I couldn't help but grin back. "I'm not pissed off. I'm just...trying to understand him."

"He's preparing for war," Naomi said from across the room, her gaze on the TV. "Excuse the guy if he doesn't have time for your drama."

"Naomi," Hunter said warningly, and all good humor had fled from his expression. She glanced at him, and her gaze dropped, making it clear who was the dominant wolf.

"War?" I asked, my mouth dry.

Hunter sighed. "I know Nathaniel's told you about Frederik."

"He's not responsible for the attacks, Hunter. I know it."

Naomi sneered at me. "Just because it's not wolves doing the attacking doesn't mean Frederik isn't somehow behind it. And if he's not going to account for his people in our territory, he deserves what's coming to him.”

Hunter shot her a look, and she turned away dismissively.

“I think I’ll get some rest,” I murmured. “Goodnight, everyone.”

The other wolves chorused their goodnights, and I slipped out of the basement and up the stairs, sliding around the next set of stairs and making my way up to my room.

I sat on my bed and stared out the window. I hadn’t yet processed everything that had happened today.

Ellen Harrison had been a pain in the ass. She’d had zero professional ethics, and she’d made life harder for paranormals—many of them already hated by humans. But I hadn’t wanted her dead. She hadn’t deserved to lose her life, even if she’d been branding me a whore and graffitiing my car. She’d needed help, and instead, she’d wound up dead.

It should have been me.

I didn’t feel guilt over it. I didn’t deserve to die either. But whatever had followed me home had clearly meant to kill me. Either it had mistaken Ellen for me, or she’d simply been in the wrong place at the wrong time—close enough to my car to draw the beast’s attention.

But there was something about her body—

“Evelyn?”

I raised my eyebrow as Nathaniel knocked.

“Come in.”

I didn't bother asking why he called me Evelyn most of the time. He did it to place distance between us. The same way I attempted to avoid him whenever we got too close. It was a defense mechanism I understood well.

"Are you okay?"

I attempted a smile. "Yeah. Just tired. And... thinking."

He leaned against the wall and watched me, those incredible blue eyes glued to my face.

"Thinking about what?"

"Ellen Harrison, mostly. And the fact that whatever killed her had managed to follow me home. We're lucky she was the only one in that parking lot, Nathaniel. There could have been kids there."

"Hey. Don't do that."

I wiped at my eyes. He stepped toward me.

"Tell me what was in the package," he said.

I frowned. "What package?"

"The package you took from whoever was in that pickup truck."

My mouth dropped open. "You're still thinking about that?"

Nathaniel shifted, and if I didn't know him, I might've thought he was uncomfortable.

"My wolf is fixated on it."

"And the man is curious."

He didn't deny it. Heaving a sigh, I got to my feet and headed into the bathroom. When I came back out,

Nathaniel had sat on the edge of my bed.

I opened the package and handed him the small bottle. It was expensive as hell and the one real concession I made to my vanity.

Nathaniel opened the bottle, taking a deep inhale. His eyes turned a shade lighter. "It smells like you. Like your hair."

"Yeah. There's an ingredient in it from the middleground. I use it to tame my curls," I admitted. "If I didn't, I'd likely end up shaving my head."

He smiled. "That would be a tragedy."

My heart fluttered at the way his gaze lingered on my curls. He handed me back the bottle, and I eyed him.

"So, why exactly were you following me that day?"

"I told you. My wolf was curious."

"No, before that."

"I wasn't following you. I was visiting you."

"Uh-huh. Why?"

"Because I wanted to see you."

He said it simply, unembarrassed, and it was *my* face that heated.

I shifted on my feet. "You wanted to see me, huh?"

"Yes." He took a single step closer. "I always want to see you."

I took a deep, shaky breath. When Nathaniel looked at me like that, it was all I could do not to jump into his arms and…

"What are you thinking?" He smiled at me, as if

he knew just what I was thinking, and his nose flared enough to tell me he could *smell* what I was thinking.

My cheeks burned, and I covered my face with my hands.

Nathaniel was instantly there, his body shaking against mine as he chuckled. He removed my hands, pressing a gentle kiss to each palm. He tightened his hands around mine as he leaned down.

My breath caught in my throat, and my eyes fluttered shut.

He placed an achingly gentle kiss against my forehead, and I felt his lips curve as he smiled. My eyes shot open, and I glowered at him as he headed toward the door.

"Goodnight, Evelyn."

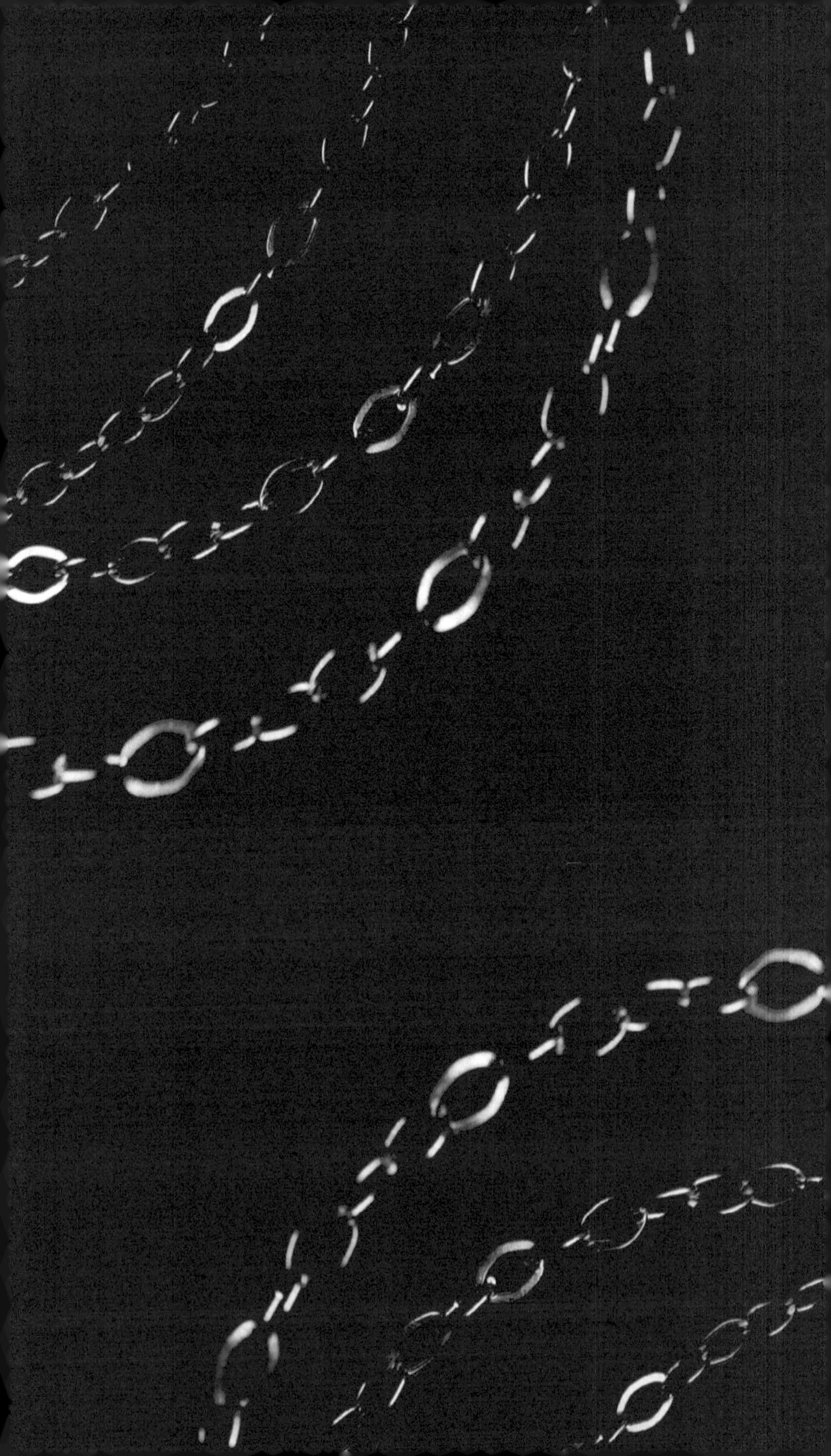

13

EVIE

I slept like a baby in Nathaniel's guest room. No nightmares, no tossing and turning.

When I woke up, I lifted the corner of one sheet and took a picture of the mattress tag. Although I had a sneaking suspicion it wasn't just the mattress that had given me the best night's sleep I'd had in months.

Scowling, I flipped open my suitcase and reached for leggings and a tank top. I also pulled on a zip-up hoodie, which would make me sweat, but would also hide my Beretta and my A-F. As I pulled on a pair of sneakers, the buzzing of my phone jolted me from my thoughts. Kyla.

"What's up?" I asked.

"Wimbar's on the run, but Finvarra gave us permission to search his house," Kyla crowed. "Want to come poke through all his shit?"

I glanced at my watch. "I have a couple of hours, and then I want to go see Selina. She knows all kinds of things about all kinds of creatures, so I'm going to take the tooth to her. I also want to stop by the morgue and see if they'll tell me anything about Ellen Harrison."

"Deal. I'll meet you by the playground."

I strode down the stairs. The morning light slid through the trees and made patterns on Nathaniel's hardwood floors. I gave a single sigh at the beauty and then forced myself to keep walking. If I sat down on that long, comfy-looking sofa, I'd likely never leave.

"Evie," Tobias called, and I poked my head into the kitchen. "You haven't eaten," he said disapprovingly, and I laughed. While the werewolves had to make sure they kept themselves fed, skipping breakfast wouldn't do me any harm.

"I need to go meet Kyla," I said.

"Good, you can give her one of these as well."

He handed me two wrapped breakfast burritos, and I gave a lustful sigh. "Marry me," I said seriously.

"I don't think so," a low voice said, and an arm came around my shoulders, pulling me into Nathaniel's hard body. "Mine," he told Tobias with a mock scowl. But beneath the humor was a dark promise.

I swallowed, and he leaned close. "You look like a deer caught in headlights."

"Or a deer caught in a full moon." Tobias grinned at us both.

The thought of Bambi was enough to make me shake off whatever had me staring stupidly at the Alpha wolf. I frowned at him, but even I couldn't prevent my lips from twitching at the humor in his eyes.

"I'm not talking to you," I said. I was still pissed about the *forehead kiss* from last night. I knew why he'd done it too. He wanted me frustrated. Wanted me focused on him. Wanted me thinking about his damn mouth all day.

He was playing me like a violin.

"I need to go meet Kyla," I said. Why was my voice so low and husky?

"Where are you going?"

I hesitated, and he hit me with his Alpha stare. Keeping my eyes locked with his, I took a large step back. Tobias tutted and turned away to deal with the dishes.

"The dark fae realm," I said, waiting for his reaction.

Nathaniel just smiled. "Be careful."

I stared at him. He reached out and played with a curl that had fallen free from my bun. "You don't need to look so surprised," he murmured. "I'm a reasonable man."

"Uh-huh." I squinted at him, but he didn't seem to be playing with me. Across the kitchen, Tobias's shoulders shook. I had a feeling *I* was the butt of the joke. I hadn't had nearly enough coffee to deal with this.

"M'kay. In that case, I'll see you guys later."

I stepped around the Alpha and strode out of the kitchen. Was Nathaniel *trying* to keep me guessing?

Shaking it off, I strolled down the path leading deeper into wolf territory. I munched on my breakfast burrito, attempting to keep my moans to myself.

I nodded at Jo as I walked past the coffee shop, and she sent me a cheery wave.

A wolf streaked past me, at least eight kids hot on her heels. I stopped and stared as Kyla weaved in and out of the playground, her mouth open in a wolfy grin as the kids attempted to tackle her.

"Get her!" A little girl about Charlie's age was attempting to cut her off. Kyla jumped over her, and I couldn't help but laugh as the kids split up, one of them climbing up a rope wall and turning to lean against it, as if he was about to launch himself down at the wolf. He had to be close to twenty feet high. Jesus, these kids had no fear.

My heart pounded, and I was standing next to him before I knew I'd moved.

"That's a nope," I said. I used my magic to guide him off the rope ladder and onto the ground, where he scowled at me. I gave him a wide grin. "I'll help you catch her."

"Really? You're not a wolf. You're not fast."

I laughed, leaning down to whisper in his ear. His eyes widened, and he turned, sprinting behind a climbing wall, where he crouched and hid.

A few moments later, Kyla darted past the climbing wall. I lifted one hand, and she tripped over her own two feet. Not enough to hurt, but enough to slow her down.

She lost her natural grace as she rolled. The little boy jumped at her, and the other kids all piled on. Kyla let out a mournful howl, and the kids laughed as she lay beneath them as if dead.

"It's good to see her like this," a voice said from behind me. I turned. Hunter was watching the scene with soft eyes. "Not many werewolves tolerate the kids climbing all over them the way Kyla always has. When she first came back from the underworld, Nathaniel had to warn the kids to leave her alone."

His eyes glimmered as Kyla let out another howl. Her tongue darted out and licked one of the kids' cheeks, making her squeal with laughter. Kyla's claws were tucked carefully away.

"She's still half wild," Hunter said. "We're all keeping an eye on her. But this gives me hope." He gestured at the group of adults who'd gathered outside the coffee shop, all of them watching on. A few wolves melted out of the forest around us. "It gives us all hope."

Kyla wiggled out from the pile of kids and trotted toward me.

"I have breakfast," I told her.

She blinked both eyes at me.

Hunter frowned. "What is she doing?"

I sighed. "She's attempting to wink."

He shook his head sadly. "I'd stop that if I were you. You look like a drugged puppy." He wandered away, and Kyla strolled toward the forest.

She returned a few minutes later in her human form. I handed her the burrito, and she took a giant bite. "Good," she declared, waving goodbye to the kids as they called out to her.

"I'll drive," she said.

"No car, remember?"

"Oh yeah, that sucks. I'll message Nathaniel. The pack has a few spares."

"You don't need to do that."

"If he hasn't already organized it, it's only because it's slipped his mind."

I shrugged and followed her to where she'd parked outside Nathaniel's. Kyla tended to be a speed demon, but she also had werewolf reflexes, which meant she spotted issues much quicker than I did.

"I saw you talking to Hunter," she said once we were driving out of wolf territory.

"Yeah. Unlike Naomi, he actually gives me the time of day."

Kyla grinned, one hand on the steering wheel, while the other held her breakfast burrito. "Naomi has always been like that. She'll just take some time."

I shrugged. "I don't need to be liked."

Kyla shot me a disbelieving look, and I frowned. "I *don't*."

"Uh-huh."

I ground my teeth. "I hate when you do that," I muttered.

"I know. That's why I do it. So, Elizabeth was a bust. I was hoping for some kind of dark side, but it turns out she really is that boring. I went through her finances, and unless she's a magician, she has no extra income coming in."

"Hidden accounts?"

"I used Steve." She frowned. "Is no one worried about how many favors we're all going to end up owing that human?"

"He'll probably use those favors to take over the world."

We finished our burritos before we arrived at the portal, and I studied the dark fae who were walking through. I'd always wondered why people didn't crash into each other when they stepped through from opposite realms.

By the time we got to Wimbar's, my thighs were burning from walking down all those steps. I may not have trained with the demons this morning, but Vas couldn't say I wasn't working out. Planting my hands on my hips, I surveyed Wim's house.

"How close is he to the throne exactly?"

"I haven't had a chance to figure it out. He's a

distant relative, though."

"Hmmm. Something tells me our good friend Wim doesn't see it that way."

The gates in front of us were an ostentatious display, made entirely of gold. The tops of the gates were delicately ornamental, curving around various jeweled flowers and birds. At the highest point, where the two gates met, the filigree spiraled up to hold a gold crown in place.

A servant strode toward us, his back so straight, it was as if he'd had metal poles inserted in his shirt.

"We've been given permission—"

"By the king. Yes. I need to see some identification."

We handed over our IDs, and he glanced at them before holding his hand up to the gate in front of us. The two halves of the crown opened, and the gates slid apart.

In front of the house, a paved path wound through a thick lawn. On the left stood a white marble fountain, and on the right, a dozen statues of various gods lined the walkway.

"My name is Bylous," the unseelie said. "His Majesty has instructed everyone here to cooperate with you."

I surveyed him as Kyla strolled down the path, stopping to sneer at one of the statues, which bore a startling resemblance to the picture we had of Wimbar.

"Here's the thing, Bylous. We could probably poke around in this house for weeks and we'd never find anything that could lead us to Wimbar. You and I both know he has some secret stash in this place. Maybe a few floorboards he's lifted up, a hidden compartment somewhere. He's dangerous and he's sneaky, and his cousin's life is in danger, so how about you help us out?"

Bylous raised one eyebrow.

"You misunderstand, Ms. Amana. While everyone in this house has been instructed to help you, we never required such orders from our king. All of us will give you anything you ask, simply because we loathe Wimbar with such incredible fury that, if our fury were power, he would have been dead a thousand times over."

I blinked. "Uh..."

"Sweet," Kyla called from the front door, her hearing as excellent as ever. "Glad we're all on the same page. Let's get started."

EVIE

Wimbar's marble floors had been polished to a mirrorlike gleam. My gaze immediately flicked to the staircase in front of us, which wound from both the left and the right to meet up at the top where a mezzanine jutted out, overlooking the lower level. I could just see Wimbar standing up there, gazing down at whomever he'd deigned to invite to his home.

"Bylous?" a high-pitched feminine voice asked, and we all turned.

The fae was stunningly beautiful. A long red scar the only flaw in an otherwise perfect face. It trailed down from her right temple, across her cheek, and disappeared beneath the collar of her dress.

"These are the people His Majesty sent," Bylous said, his voice gentle.

"We-we can't help them. Wimbar will... He'll—" Her voice cut off in a choked sob. Kyla was across the floor in an instant, taking the woman's hands in her own.

"Hey," she said. "You don't need to worry. Wimbar will never touch you again."

The woman shook her head. "You don't understand. He'll come back. He'll be so angry."

Fury burned through my stomach, radiated up to my chest, and burned down into the deep well where I'd stuffed the threads of my power. I clenched my teeth, taking long, slow breaths. Wimbar wasn't here for me to hurt him, and displaying my power would only terrify this poor woman.

"What's your name?" Kyla asked gently.

"Sudall."

Tears spilled over. And then Bylous was there, wrapping one arm around her shoulders. "The king has said we are all to go work for him. I didn't get a chance to tell you."

Kyla smiled. "If there's one thing I know about your king, other than the fact that he's obnoxiously arrogant, it's that he protects those he considers his. You'll be safe with him. If you'd like, you can leave now. I'm sure Bylous can show us everything we need to see."

"We're...we're going to work for the king?"

"Yes." Bylous grinned down at her. "If you pack your things, you can go now."

"No." Sudall straightened her spine, her gaze flicking to me. "I know who you are."

I waited to hear "the underqueen's sister," but she angled her head. "You fought Lucifer. You helped kill him."

"I was one among many."

"Don't listen to her," Kyla said. "She's stupidly powerful."

Sudall nodded. "I'll help you. And then I'll go."

Bylous released her and gestured for us to follow him. "Come, I'll show you to his rooms."

"No," Sudall said. "He doesn't keep anything there. I'll show you to his secrets."

I glanced at Bylous, who shrugged, his gaze on Sudall.

"Lead on," Kyla said. We followed her upstairs.

"These are his rooms," Sudall said. "But as I said, he's too paranoid to keep anything in them."

She led us down the hall to an area she called the east wing. "This is where the servants sleep," she said. "He didn't think anyone would come here."

We walked down the long hall. Unsurprisingly, the comfort that was so apparent in every inch of the rest of the house was nowhere to be found in the servant's quarters.

We passed servant after servant, all of them carrying their things. A few of them glanced at us curiously, but most of them walked with their heads down, shoulders hunched.

"Through here," Sudall said. She opened a storage closet, and we all piled in, although there wasn't much room.

"I don't understand," Kyla said.

"I have to remember how to..." Sudall closed her eyes and placed one hand on the wall. Then she said a word in a language I'd never heard before.

The wall disappeared.

I jolted. Kyla went still. Bylous reached for Sudall and thrust her behind him.

"It's okay," Sudall said. "This is where Wimbar keeps his secrets."

"How did you know?" Bylous asked.

"He used to bring me here. When he would...do things to me. Before he ruined me." Her hand darted up to her scar before fisting and falling to her side.

Kyla let out a low growl. I knew her, and my heart still tripped. "He did that to you?"

Sudall pressed back into the door behind us. Bylous turned, and their eyes met.

"You said you were being careless in the kitchen. Why did you lie to me?"

"I knew you'd be angry. You don't have enough power to risk Wimbar's rage."

"I wouldn't have cared!"

He was desperately in love with her. My heart ached.

Sudall gazed at him wonderingly, as if she'd just realized the same herself. "It only happened for a few months. It was right before you began working here. One day, I got so mad. I threw something at him, and he cut me. Slowly. He said he'd ruined me, and no one would ever want me again."

The room began to tremble. Everyone looked at me.

Shit. "Sorry. I promise, Wimbar will pay for everything he did to you."

Sudall stared at me. "I believe you."

"Good," Kyla said. "Because his life is over."

I knew she meant it too. But I hoped Finvarra found Wimbar before Kyla did. It wouldn't take much to turn her feral again.

Sudall darted past us and through the space where the wall had once been. We trailed after her, and I stared at the room.

It was a trophy room. There was no other way to describe it. Old books, jewels, weapons, and strange artifacts I'd never seen before were placed on shelves.

I took a step closer to one of the combs. Then I froze.

"No one move. He's warded everything in here. Individually."

I didn't bother trying to recreate whatever I'd done to Albert's ward. Instead, I smashed my hand into his ward, pouring every inch of my rage and power into it.

Wimbar was powerful. But I had him beat. Still, little dots danced in front of my eyes at the sudden use of so much power.

"Are you okay?" Kyla asked.

"Yeah. Bet that hurt like a son of a bitch. Poor Wimmy. He'll know we're in here."

"He's got enough friends in high places," Bylous said. "He'll already know you're hunting him. And he'll definitely know His Majesty has instructed him to be brought in."

I pointed at a comb that was sitting up on a shelf at eye height.

"Anyone know what that is?"

"I do," Sudall said. "I'm not sure where he got it or even who created it. But I know if the owner convinces someone to run it through their hair, they'll lose the ability to speak until the owner uses the comb on them again."

We went through more of the artifacts. All of them were similar, all with the ability to cause death, heartache, and destruction—most of them from afar.

Kyla was ticking things off the list. "That's one of the artifacts that was stolen." She showed us a picture on her phone, and we compared it to the bronze goblet in front of us.

"So, Wimbar either decided not to sell all of them, or he figured he'd wait until enough time had passed that the search wasn't quite so hot," I mused.

Kyla nodded, using a canvas bag Sudall had found to collect the various artifacts that had been stolen from the auction. "About a third of them," she said. "And no book."

When we were done, Bylous called a final meeting. All staff members sat in the huge entranceway, their bags next to them.

He explained what had happened and who we were. Then Kyla stepped forward.

"We're looking for Callula. I'm not sure if any of you have met her, but she was desperate and Wimbar preyed on that desperation. I think she's in big trouble, and anything you can tell us about their relationship might help, no matter how small."

"I think she's dead," a woman piped up.

"Why?" I asked. "Did Wimbar threaten her?"

She gave me a look like I was too stupid to live. "Every word Wimbar said was a silent threat. I overheard their conversation the day before she disappeared. I was cleaning in the formal living room, and they walked in."

Her gaze dropped, and some of the bravado disappeared. "I hid."

Another woman reached out and grabbed her hand. "I would have, too."

I was going to make Wimbar swallow his teeth when I finally found him. From the look of retribution on Kyla's face, she was thinking the same.

"What did Wimbar say?" Kyla asked.

The woman hesitated. The brunette who'd grabbed her hand leaned closer. "He can't hurt you. He's finally going to get what's coming for him."

"He told us if we ever cooperated with anyone asking questions, he'd made us disappear. He said not even the best scryer in the world would be able to find us. He said it was a slow, miserable death."

"We'll protect you," I said. "I promise."

"And so will Finvarra," Kyla said. Gasps sounded, and she rolled her eyes. "I mean His Majesty. Tell us everything you heard."

"Callula was...distraught. I'd never heard her like that. She said she hadn't known what the book did, and His Majesty would kill them both when he found out. She told Wimbar he had to return the book and beg forgiveness. He...laughed. He said His Majesty didn't know the meaning of forgiveness, and if she thought she could betray him and beg the king for her life, he'd make sure she disappeared."

Kyla asked a few more questions, while I considered everything we'd learned. Wimbar hadn't been threatening to kill people. He'd been threatening to make them disappear. Did he have some kind of spell that would make them lose their corporeal form? Did he know someone who would kidnap them and take them to another realm?

"Thank you for your help," Kyla said. "All of you. Here are my details. If you think of anything else, please don't hesitate to get in touch. If you can't call me, your king will get a message to me."

The servants began to file out. I glanced outside, where several horses and carriages were pulling up, ready to take them to their new lives.

"You guys saved us a lot of work," I told Sudall and Bylous. "You may have also saved Callula's life. If you need anything, let us know."

"Just find him," Sudall said. "Please, just find him and make him stop."

"We will," Kyla said. "I promise."

Bylous escorted Sudall out of the house. We followed them, continuing past the gold gates and making our way back toward the stairs.

"What are you thinking?" I asked Kyla.

"I'm thinking Finvarra is a self-involved asshole for not seeing how evil his cousin was."

"Distant cousin."

She gave me a look.

I threw up my hands. "Look, you know I'll talk

some serious shit about him any day of the week, but you've gotta give the man *some* credit. The moment he learned what was going on here, he shut it down. All of those servants are going to have a cushy job at the palace."

"He only shut it down because it directly affected him. Sudall could've been killed, and no one would ever have known what had happened to her."

"He's a king, Kyla. You think those servants could get word to him that they were being abused? You think most of them would even consider going to him? Wimbar had them terrified. Finvarra is many things, but last time I checked, he's not omnipotent."

"He acts like he is," she muttered.

I elbowed her in the ribs as we started up the stairs.

"You're right," she said finally, when we were halfway up.

"Can't talk," I puffed. "Too busy dying."

She grinned at me. "Vas would have you running stairs if he could see you right now."

"Tell him about this, and I'll get my revenge."

Her grin widened as I bent over, sucking in a breath. I hated these stairs. *Hated* them.

"Hey!"

We both turned. I slid my hand to my knife and tried to appear like I wasn't close to cardiac arrest.

I surveyed the man. Or should I say, the giant. He took the steps five at a time, and I felt Kyla get into a better position beside me, preparing to shift and leap at him.

The giant seemed to realize we were about to start some shit. He froze, and confusion slid over his face.

"My friends said you were asking about Wimbar."

I relaxed. A little. Kyla smiled at him. He smiled back. It was a surprisingly sweet smile.

"I'm Hertarr. Wimbar's head groom."

"I guess you'd have no issues making his horses behave, given you're a giant," Kyla said.

"Half giant," he said. "But yes, Wimbar has a fondness for horses. He buys them mostly wild. Anyway, I was getting the horses transported when you visited. My friends said I should come to you if I had any information."

"What do you know?"

"One of the last times I saw Wimbar, he told me to drive him to his friend's. His friend lives on the other side of the city. I took him there and waited outside. While I was waiting outside, I heard screaming. It sounded like Callula."

I froze. "How do you know it sounded like Callula?"

"I used to work for her brother. Before Wimbar decided he wanted me to work for him. I know the sound of her voice."

"What did you do?"

Hertarr flushed. "I wrote a letter to her family,

asking if they had seen her recently. The next time I had to take Wimbar to his friend's, he gave me the letter back. He'd found it and read it. He said I should remember my manners. He'd given me a promotion. He also said Callula was fine and I'd been hearing things. That's when I knew."

"Knew what?"

"That she's dead, of course." His voice turned rough, as if he was struggling to get the words out.

"Take us to his friend," Kyla said.

A sharp nod. "I thought you might say that. I brought the horses around."

Kyla sighed. "That's not going to work. Give us the address, and we'll meet you there."

I looked mournfully at the stairs we'd just climbed. "What a waste."

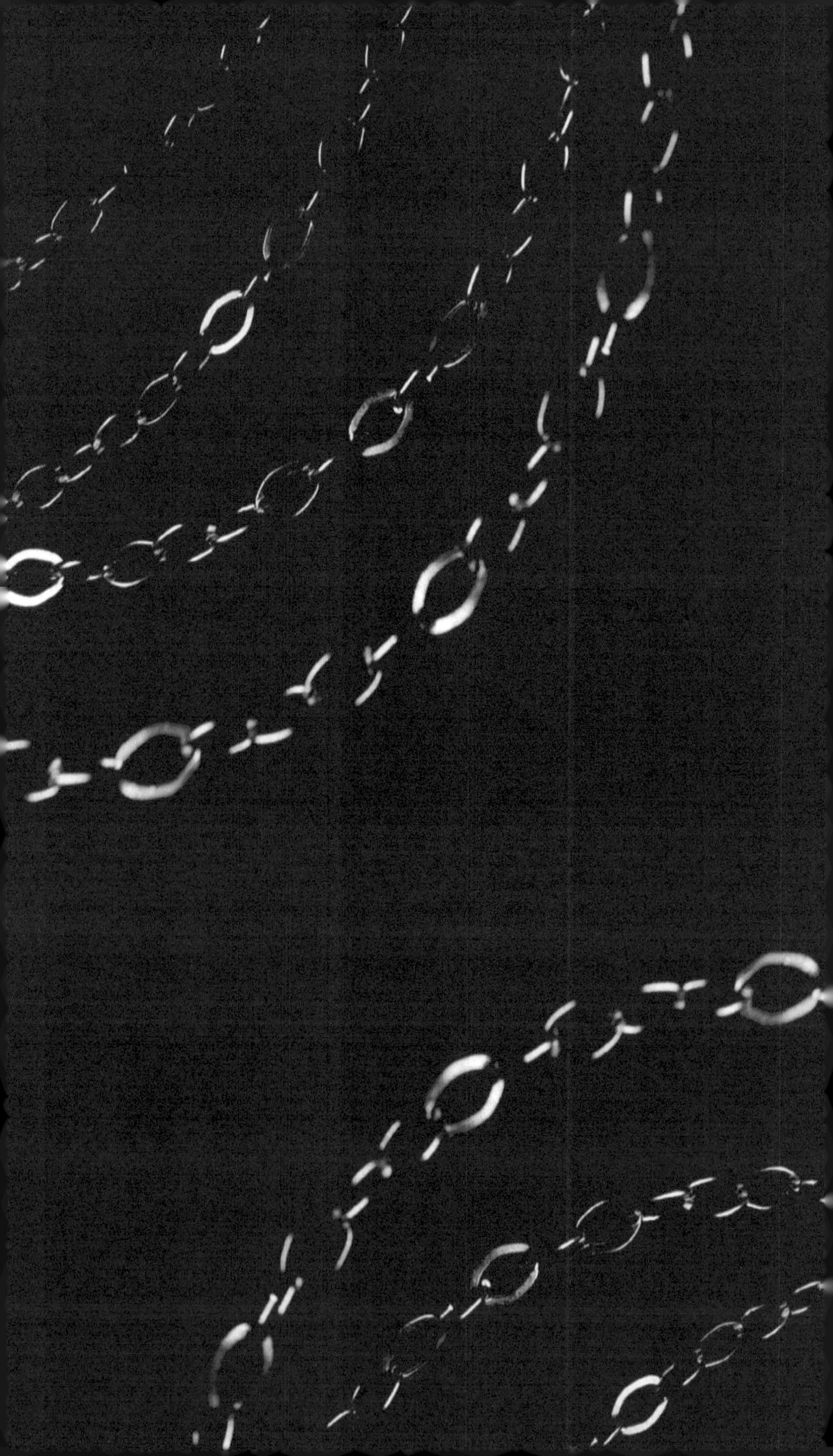

14

EVIE

Hertarr watched wide-eyed as the horses freaked out when Kyla approached. "Never seen them do that."

"What can I say?" Kyla muttered. "I'm special."

"It's okay." Hertarr smiled good-naturedly. "It's not a far walk."

He led us along the outskirts of the city until we came to a large estate. It wasn't quite as big as Wim's house, but it was obvious his friend had both wealth and power.

"I'll wait out here if you don't mind," Hertarr said. "Orasil isn't the violent type, so you don't need to be afraid."

I almost snorted. He greatly underestimated both Kyla's and my ability to drive even the most laid-back person to violence.

Unlike Wimbar, Orasil didn't have guards on the

door. In fact, he opened it himself when we arrived.

"I had a feeling this would happen," he sighed when we introduced ourselves. "Come in."

I narrowed my eyes, allowing my power to peek out and scan for traps. Next to me, Kyla prowled inside as if she didn't have a care in the world. But I could tell from the way she flared her nostrils that she was checking for any other scents.

Orasil led us past a staircase and into a living room. He waved at the sofa, gesturing for us to take a seat before he wandered around the room, closing the curtains.

He paused, obviously watching Hertarr, who was still waiting outside.

"I always knew Wim's servants would be his downfall one day."

"What do you mean?"

"Wim had many blind spots, but the largest was the way he treated those he considered less than him. If he had only inspired loyalty, you might not have found anything in your search of his property. His people might have lied, giving him a few days longer to go about his business and disappear. Instead, they likely lined up to tell you as much as they could."

"They *were* unusually cooperative. Probably because they were sick and tired of being treated like shit," I said.

Orasil nodded. "I told Wimbar to take his frustrations out on those who didn't hold his secrets.

Once again, he didn't listen."

I shook my head. Orasil may not be the kind of monster Wimbar was—may treat his servants better—but it wasn't because he thought they deserved to be treated as people. It was because he was smart enough to attempt to inspire loyalty.

He pulled the last curtain closed and then took a seat across from us. "What is it that you'd like to know?"

I didn't like this guy. He was pretending he ran the show, but we all knew differently. I bared my teeth in a sharp smile and leaned back against the sofa.

He watched me out of cool blue eyes. They really were the most stunning shade. A girl could get lost in those eyes. Surely no one who had eyes that color could be responsible for doing harm to anyone?

Kyla let out a feral snarl, and I tensed.

"It's rude to use your power on visitors without their permission, Orasil," I said quietly. Kyla was getting to her feet, and I shot her a warning look. "Now you've gone and pissed off the werewolf."

"Werewolf?" His mouth dropped open, and Kyla gave him a wicked grin.

"I'm sorry," he stammered out. "It's nerves, that's all. My power leaks when I'm feeling threatened."

I didn't buy it. This guy had centuries on us. But I nodded at Kyla, and she sat back down, leaning forward as if itching to tear Orasil's throat out.

The color slowly drained from his face. He was

getting it now.

"Your king gave us permission to use whatever means necessary to get the information we need," Kyla said. "If you choose not to cooperate, we also have permission to transport you directly to Finvarra for questioning."

"Okay." He shoved his long, dark hair behind one pointed ear. "Okay."

We waited.

"Wimbar's mother was my mother's closest friend," he said. "We grew up together. Wim was always... envious. Instead of appreciating his connection to the throne, he'd complain bitterly about the fact that a luck of genetics had given his cousin power, while he would never rule."

"And when did you realize he was undermining Finvarra?"

He swallowed, his hand fluttering as he pushed his hair back once more. "From a young age," he admitted. "But you have to understand... Wimbar couldn't be convinced to see reason. And most people close to him saw it as a harmless obsession."

"Harmless?"

"Well...yes. Our king has the kind of power Wim could only dream of. There are rumors..."

"What kinds of rumors?" Kyla asked, gathering information on her enemy.

"There are rumors he is the most powerful unseelie king to ever live."

Kyla ground her teeth. I suppressed a smile and turned my attention back to Orasil. "When did you know Wimbar was stealing from Finvarra?"

"I didn't. I swear. It wasn't until he came to me a few weeks ago."

I watched Orasil, analyzing his every word as he continued speaking.

"He was *furious*. He said everything had gone perfectly, and somehow the humans had lost the one artifact he needed. He said he wished he didn't need to kill them quickly. I'd never seen him like that before."

Wim was smart. He'd known we wouldn't expect a high fae to use a gun. "And what did you do?"

Orasil took a shaky breath. "I told him I couldn't help him. Our king… Let's just say I have no desire to end up in his dungeon."

"I'm guessing Wimbar wasn't used to being told no," Kyla said.

Orasil ran one hand over his face. "No. He told me he'd laid the groundwork, connecting me to all his plans. Even if I didn't help him, there was enough proof to make it look like whatever he was up to was *my* idea. So I may as well help him and make sure we both lived to see another day."

"Tell us about Callula."

"By now, you know Wim had her take the book from one of Finvarra's estates. He would never have been trusted to visit without the king's express permission. He could have taken it then, but he wanted the auction."

"Why? It makes no sense. He had everything he wanted."

He shook his head. "No, Wim will *never* be satisfied. It's part of what makes him…Wim. He learned about the auction and began telling his contacts that it was an opportunity to off-load any dusty artifacts, jewelry, or books they had lying around. Word spread, and he talked Callula into placing the book in the auction. He didn't want to be connected to it in any way. He arranged for everything. The security guards were his idea. He already had a group of human criminals who would steal the artifacts he'd picked out."

"Callula didn't know that part," Kyla said.

"No. When Wimbar found out she'd hired you, he lost his mind."

"I'm guessing Callula was a good target for his tantrum."

"Yes. Callula was many things, but she has always been pliable. She was the last born after her siblings, both of whom came out of the womb scheming."

"So Wim had her brought here."

He sighed, pinching the bridge of his nose. "Yes. Callula realized what he'd done. And she said she was going to the king. Stupid move to warn him. But Callula was never particularly bright."

"Where is her body?"

He immediately shook his head. "I didn't kill her."

"Then what happened, Orasil? Tell us, and we'll

ask Finvarra for leniency."

He got to his feet. Kyla went still, angling her head as she watched him. He moved slowly, clearly not wanting to antagonize the werewolf. He walked to the antique desk and opened the drawer. I created a ward around Kyla and myself, and from the way Orasil tensed, he'd felt the draw on my power.

He turned and held up a rock. The kind of rock found in any dirt in any garden around the world. It was about the size of a tennis ball, smooth on one side, craggy on the other.

"Explain," Kyla growled.

"This is a...portal."

My eyes narrowed. I'd seen these before. Pocket realms could be connected to artifacts and used for many nefarious things. Although I'd never seen one attached to a grimy rock before.

"Callula's in a pocket realm?"

Orasil slowly shook his head. His eyes were so beautiful. So beautiful and calming.

I shot to my feet and took a single step closer to him.

"I'm sorry. I swear I'm not doing it on purpose."

I watched him. I would bet every dollar I had that Wim had used Orasil's power to his benefit over the years.

"It's not a pocket realm. This is a portal to a tiny area within the middleground."

Finvarra had said Callula was in the middleground.

Was that a rumor Wim had started?

"Why hasn't Callula found a portal and returned home?"

Orasil fished a handkerchief out of his pocket and began to blot his forehead. "There's no way to return. The portal leads to a cave so large, it spans for miles. If you manage to make it out of the cave, you'll be trapped on the bank of a lake."

"I'm sure Callula can swim."

"A lava lake. According to legends, one of our king's ancestors loved a mortal woman. He gave her immortality, but over time, she fell out of love with him. He placed her in the caves and turned the water to lava, as a way to make her stay put."

The amount of power it would require to turn water to lava… And Finvarra was rumored to be *more* powerful than his ancestors?

"He eventually retrieved his mortal love," Orasil assured us. "And she had a change of heart. They ruled in peace for many centuries."

I shook my head at that. A change of heart. Sure. More like she just wanted to keep breathing. Even immortals could starve to death.

"So Callula has been trapped in these caves with no food or water?"

Orasil hesitated. Then he finally nodded. I closed my eyes.

"I had to," he said. "I had to help him, or he would've killed me too."

This was why Wim kept talking about making his enemies disappear. He left them to a slow, brutal death. Alone in the middleground.

"Give us the rock."

He hesitated, and I took another step closer to him. I was *done* playing nice. I reached for the closest thread of power, and this time, the red light I held in my hand turned to fire.

The air disappeared from my lungs, but I managed to keep my face expressionless.

Kyla stared at me. "How'd you do that?"

"I don't know."

I'd created fire before, of course, but only with the help of a spell. This? This had jumped into my hand as if it had always been there. And it gave me the heebie-jeebies.

I shifted my attention to Orasil. "Did you hear that, friend? I have no idea what's going on with my power right now, so if I were you, I'd cooperate."

He looked at the fire, looked at my face, then held out his hand and floated the rock to Kyla, who plucked it out of the air.

"Will you... Will you tell Finvarra it wasn't my fault?"

I watched him. Disgust roared through me. "When Callula was screaming and begging not to go into that portal, what did you do?"

He slammed his mouth shut. Suddenly, he wasn't feeling all that chatty. I could picture Callula in this room, fighting for her life as her cousin and his friend dragged her toward that rock.

From the way his blue eyes suddenly glowed, I had a feeling he was using his power for all he was worth. Unfortunately for him, I'd shored up my ward.

We backed out of the room, keeping a close eye on the distraught unseelie. I had no sympathy.

"Did you get what you needed?" Hertarr asked when we stepped outside.

"Yes."

"Is Callula okay?"

"No."

His face fell. I didn't have it in me to feel any pity for him either. He would have to live with his silence.

"We'll be in touch if we need anything else," I said. He nodded, and we left the estate, both of us quiet.

We trudged up the stairs and back through the portal. Both of us had hoped we'd find Callula alive.

"Let's take the rock to Selina's," I said finally. "I need to see her anyway. I was hoping to ask her about the tooth. Maybe she'll be able to examine the rock and tell us if Callula is still alive. Maybe…maybe Callula managed to find some water."

Kyla nodded as we got in her car. "Maybe."

We both knew it wasn't likely, and we were lost in our own thoughts as she drove us to Selina's.

We pulled up outside the light-blue, two-story home in North Trinity Park, and I was zero percent surprised when Selina immediately opened the door, as if she'd been expecting us.

She waved at us, the stack of gold bangles on her arm flashing in the sunlight and providing a brilliant contrast to her dark skin. She wore a tailored white sundress and flat gold sandals that matched her bangles.

We climbed the steps to her porch, and she kissed us each on the cheek, opening her front door. "It's been far too long. Come inside where it's cool."

My sister had met Selina when she was investigating a case, and they'd become friends. I wasn't entirely certain she was only a white witch—she had far too much power for that—but she certainly didn't stink of black magic the way most of her less discerning sisters would have. Her magic was interesting and mysterious, and she knew I wasn't all witch. She'd felt my own power, and she'd never once treated me like a freak.

"I was just making some iced tea," she said. "And your sister had one of her demons drop off some cookies. We were hoping to catch up this week, but she had to travel to a different region in the underworld."

Guilt pricked at the back of my neck. I should probably know that. I needed to visit Danica, but with the massacres...

She'd understand.

We followed Selina into her kitchen, which had been done in gray and white, with gold accents. She gestured toward the long wooden table near the French doors, and we took a seat while she stacked cookies onto a plate and carried a pitcher of iced tea to the table.

Three cups already sat waiting. I squinted at her.

"How did you know we were coming?"

She gave me a serene smile. "Just a feeling." She laughed at me. "You likely have the same feelings and instincts, only you're not as in touch with them. Spending time with the wolves will be good for you."

Kyla smirked at that, and Selina filled her cup.

We each took a cookie, munched for a moment, and I figured the small talk was done.

I pulled out the rock and placed it on the table. Then I filled Selina in. Her eyes welled up as she took the rock.

"I can feel its power," she said. "I don't know if I'll be able to see within it. I've never done this before."

She held the rock in both hands and closed her eyes. Five minutes later, she was still focusing, and a small line had appeared between her eyebrows. Finally, she shook her head and placed the rock back on the table. "I can't sense any life. *But,*" she added, when both of our faces fell, "that doesn't mean anything. You need to take this rock to Finvarra. He will likely be able to sense his subject and whether she is alive. If she is, he may be able to find her."

"Okay." Kyla nodded. "I'll take it to him as soon as we're done here."

I reached into my other pocket and pulled out the black tooth, handing it to her.

Selina's brows rose. "This is from the creature that is responsible for so many human deaths?"

"Yeah. I have a few theories, but I was wondering if you can pick up anything."

She held it in her hand. This time, she didn't need to close her eyes. Instead, they widened as if she'd gotten something she wasn't prepared for.

"It's not a seelie creature. It's not unseelie. And it's not from the underworld."

I stared at her. "Then what the hell is it?"

"I'm not sure. But I do know that it's a kind of power I haven't seen before. Be careful, Evie."

Nodding absently, I pulled out my phone and removed several creatures from my list of possibilities.

Selina waited until I was done. "How else can I help you?"

Guilt stabbed into my stomach and buried deep. I hoped Selina didn't just think we wanted to use her for her abilities. But why wouldn't she, when every time we visited, we had questions about cases or our own futures?

She shook her head at me. "Don't be silly. I consider you two my friends. And I know you feel the same."

"It's fucking creepy when you do that." I took a deep breath. "Danica and Kyla told me about the vision you had when they gave you the sword, before they handed it over to the seelie king."

Selina nodded. "You want to know if I can pick

anything else up."

"Yeah."

She glanced at Kyla. "Do you remember what I said last time?"

Kyla swallowed around a huge bite. "The sword is a linchpin. Of *vital importance*," she said. "My fate is tied to the sword."

Kyla looked unhappy at that, but Selina simply nodded again. "You must steal the sword to complete your bargain with Finvarra. But that's not where your part in this ends."

I could quote the rest of what Selina had told Kyla. I'd picked it apart enough times.

You will trust someone who will betray their word. But you will find allies in the places you will least expect. You must return the sword to its rightful owner.

Danica had pointed out that Finvarra wasn't the rightful owner. He was, after all, making Kyla steal it from the light fae king.

The bargain has been struck. But you must return the sword to its true sheath or the realms will burn. You will have a choice to make. Choose wrongly, and you will be chained to a throne. Choose correctly, and you will sit on one.

I angled my head as I watched Selina. "You told Kyla that your visions aren't always literal. They can be interpreted in various ways, and sometimes the meanings only become clear closer to the time."

"That's right. Ah, you'd like to know if I've

managed to interpret this vision differently."

Kyla nodded. "Here's the thing. Stealing the sword from Taraghlan will be difficult enough. Stealing it again from Finvarra? Flirting with death. But I can't figure out what the sword's 'true sheath' is. You said Finvarra can't hold the sword for more than a few months or the worlds burn. But I've combed through the history of the sword, and I've got nothing."

If that worried Selina, it was impossible to tell. She reminded me of a sphinx. Or maybe a duck, skimming along the top of a pond, its legs working furiously out of sight.

"Do you know more than you're saying?" I asked, and Selina raised an eyebrow.

"I would tell you anything I thought could help you on your mission," she said.

"That's not a no."

She sighed, pushing her iced tea away. "I didn't always have glimpses of the future. I came across this gift later in life, and so I made many mistakes."

I opened my mouth, but she waved her hand through the air. "That's a story for another time. My point is, I've learned that just because I see a potential thread in the future, doesn't mean I should always disclose it." Her eyes darkened, and she pushed several braids away from her face impatiently.

"Because…they'll try to make a different decision," Kyla said softly. "And the outcome could be worse."

Some of the color drained from Selina's face, and

she suddenly looked exhausted. "Yes."

"Am I going to die?" Kyla asked, and sweat broke out on the back of my neck. I watched Selina carefully, but her expression stayed blank.

"I can't tell you that."

Kyla snorted. I couldn't blame her. That sounded a lot like a yes.

Selina scowled at us both, and it was the first time I'd ever seen her irritated. "I can't tell you that because I don't *know*. Do you truly believe I would foresee your death and not search for a way to change it?"

"No," Kyla said. "But I believe you'd allow me to go to my death to save me from a fate worse than death. Or to prevent me from suffering another, much worse death."

Selina closed her eyes. Kyla reached out and grabbed her hand, giving it a squeeze. "It's okay," she said. "I'm sorry, we shouldn't have come here."

Selina's eyes flew open. "You should always come here." She managed a smile as she glanced between us. "But trust that if I see anything else related to the sword, I will let you know."

"If you can," I said.

She nodded. "If I can."

It must be excruciatingly difficult to see glimpses of the future and to have to decide what to disclose. To try to shape that future, even when it was your friends who would potentially suffer.

Selina held out the plate of cookies. I took one,

and then it was my turn to question her.

"I...did something the other day."

Selina was nothing if not patient. She merely sat back and watched me.

"When I was trying to get into Albert's ward... I thought my power was being sucked into it. I panicked. But then I realized my power was becoming similar. It was as if it was mimicking the mage power he used to set his ward. I attempted to break it, but instead, I pulled on that thread of power and his ward... disappeared, as if it had never been there. And then today, I conjured a ball of fire like a demon."

Selina's eyes widened a fraction before narrowing in thought. "It's difficult to theorize without knowing exactly what they did in that lab," she said. "But we know you have many different types of power, hidden below the surface. You've only ever used your witch magic because that was what was expected of you, and it never would have occurred to you to use the other 'threads,' as you call them. Likely, any other powers you have were bolstering your witch power anyway."

"I've never heard of anyone being able to mimic another's power signature before. I took down that ward as if it had never existed. What does that mean?"

Selina was silent for a long moment. It was the first time I'd ever stumped her, and I didn't like it.

Finally, Kyla sat back in her chair and took a large bite of her third cookie. Werewolf metabolism.

"It means," Kyla said around the cookie in her

mouth, "that we have a much better chance at being able to steal that sword."

We left half an hour later. Selina hugged us both. She waited until Kyla was halfway down the path before leaning close to me.

"That thing you're thinking about doing? Tomorrow would be a good day for it," she said.

I pulled back, wide-eyed, but she was already pushing me out the door.

"Good luck," she smiled cheerfully and closed the door in my face.

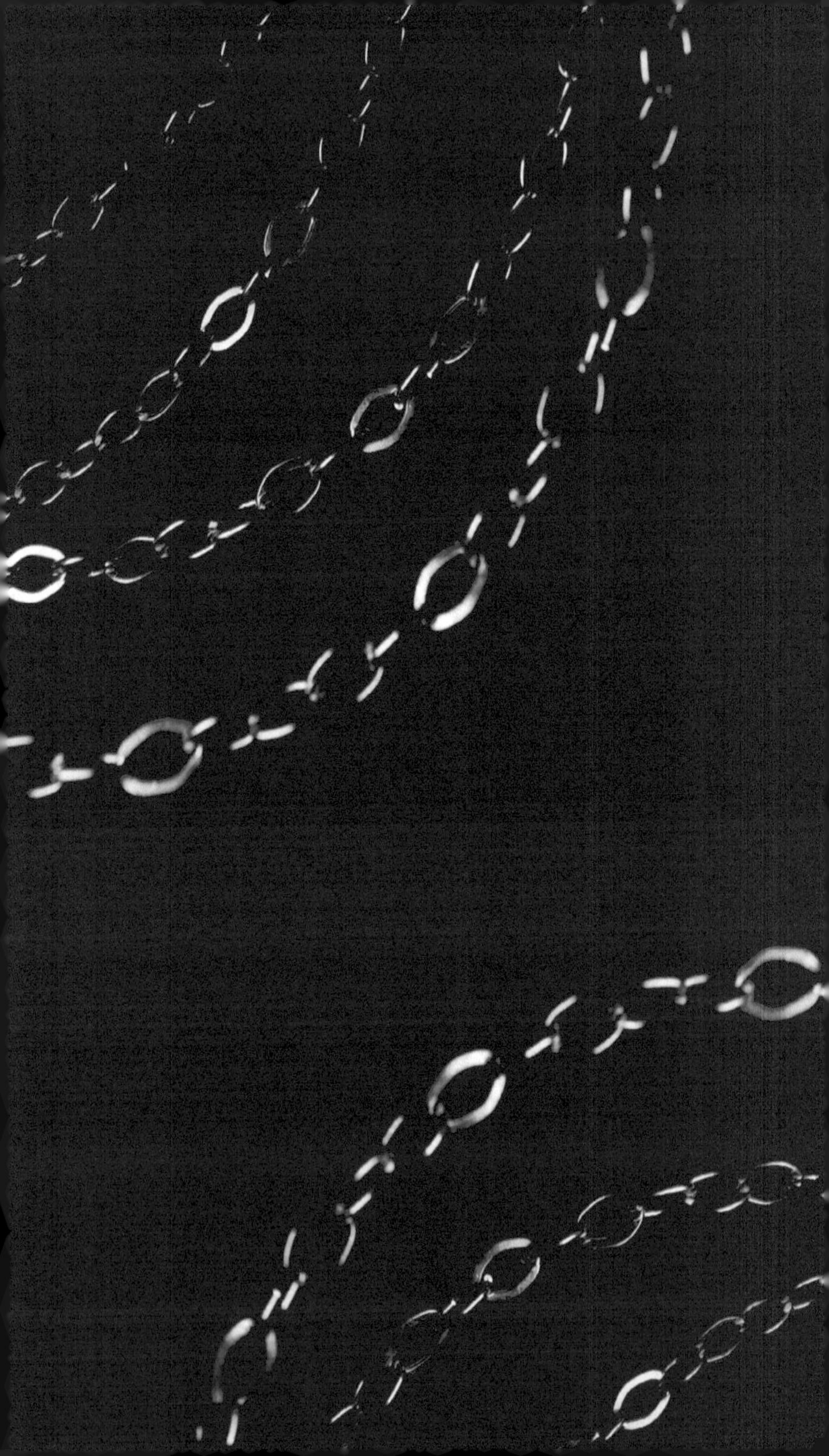

15

EVIE

K yla raised one eyebrow as we stared at the door. "You want to tell me what that was about?"

"Not particularly." I rolled my eyes as hers lightened in wolfy curiosity. "I'll fill you in when I get a chance. I'm assuming you're going straight to Finvarra."

"Yeah. I should've thought of it when we were there."

"Quit beating yourself up. If Selina had found evidence of life, we could have Callula back by now."

I glanced at my phone with a scowl.

"What is it?" Kyla asked.

"Gemma wants to see me."

"What does that poisonous old witch want?"

I raised one eyebrow, and she shrugged. "*I* wasn't raised by her. And I know exactly how awful she was to you."

I searched for a response. After a long moment,

Then I'll hit up the morgue. Let me know how it goes with Finvarra." I paused. "Shit, I keep forgetting I don't have my car."

"Take mine. I'll get one of the wolves to pick me up. Someone will be in town."

"Thanks."

I drove toward my apartment, then continued driving until I was deep in Trinity Park. I turned onto Watts Street, then took a right, slowing down until I was almost crawling along the road. I couldn't help it. I stopped.

The burned-out husk that had once been my home was no longer standing. At some point, it had been demolished, leaving only an overgrown yard and a few blackened pieces of wood.

I'd spent my childhood playing on the wide porch here. I'd explored every inch of this house with Danica before she was taken away. I'd had sleepovers here. I'd told my friends about my first crush here.

My best friend had died here.

The lump in my throat was so large, I could barely breathe around it.

A car horn sounded from behind me, and I jolted, putting my foot down. I continued driving to the coven's new house, parked, and took it in.

It was much, much smaller than the house I'd grown up in. Because so many members of the coven were dead. And so many no longer lived in the coven house, unwilling to risk their lives if the coven was ever targeted again as a whole.

I couldn't do this.

The door opened. Gemma stood there, one brow cocked, as if waiting for me to find my spine.

I got out of the car.

Gemma was twelve when the portals opened. She saw some of the chaos in the city before her parents took her away, but she returned when she was seventeen. She began forming her own coven, focused on witches who were not only powerful, but could be trusted not to stab each other in the back. As black witches turned to nasty methods like human sacrifice and power theft, white witches were forced to band together if they wanted to survive.

Gemma looked smaller and older than I'd ever seen her. Sharp eyes glared at me as if reading my mind, and I walked up the front path. Her hand tightened around her cane.

The coven leader was dying. Even if I hadn't learned the truth a few months ago, I would've seen it now. With the help of good healers, she could've lived at least another thirty years. But the attack on our coven, losing so many friends and family members... it had done what nothing else had been able to. It had broken her.

She silently stepped back, gesturing for me to walk inside. It was quiet, the remaining witches either out for the day or choosing to stay in their rooms where they wouldn't have to see me.

And yet, when Danica had been taken, they'd joined our war. The witches had helped move the needle when we marched on Lucifer's castle.

"Come, sit," Gemma ordered. I followed her into the living room. She'd pulled the blinds, and it was dim, the air stale.

I didn't bother with pleasantries. She hated them. Instead, I waited.

Gemma stretched her legs out in front of her and squinted at me.

"You've put on weight."

I shrugged. I'd always been curvy, but all my training had added muscle. That just meant more force behind my punch if I needed to hit someone in the face.

"You're upset with me."

"No. I understand why you did what you did."

It had hurt like hell, but you couldn't force people to trust you. After the number of years I'd been a coven member, the way I'd grown up believing they were my family, I would've thought I was deserving of more trust. But what the fuck did I know?

Gemma's gaze missed nothing. "It wasn't just the outspoken witches who chose not to trust you that impacted my decision. You may have gotten rid of that chip, but those who hunt you know we were your coven. If you'd stayed, they would have killed those who remained."

And yet, all this time and they hadn't tried again.

Was it because they knew the demons were keeping an eye on me? Or did they know I was beginning to access some of the very power they'd had bred into me? Did that make me more of a threat to them, or were they simply biding their time?

"I understand why you made your decision," I said finally.

Gemma frowned, clearly unhappy with my response. I sat back on the sofa and watched her.

The wolves would never kick someone out for drawing danger closer. No, they'd close ranks and fight to the death to keep the entire pack safe. Nathaniel would never push a wolf out simply because that wolf was targeted.

I'd thought I'd accepted what my coven had done. The way they'd kicked me out, banishing me from the only family I'd ever known.

Turned out, I'd just shoved that shit down where it had slowly festered.

"I want you to come back," she said.

I stared at her.

"Excuse me?"

A faint smile crossed her face. "You heard me."

"You just explained, in detail, exactly how much the others would have been in danger if I'd stayed."

"It was the correct decision at the time. However, that doesn't mean it's the correct decision now." Gemma heaved a sigh, and she suddenly looked even older than she truly was. "The coven misses you. You may bring danger with you, but you also bring light. And connection. And joy."

I swallowed around the bitter lump in my throat.

"You kicked me out."

"I know."

"And it was the best thing you could have done for me."

Her expression went blank, and I sighed. "I was fading away in that house, Gemma. You knew it. Leaving the coven was awful in so many ways, but I'm free now. I'm learning how to live in the world alone."

"You're not alone, girl. From what I hear, you've fallen in with the wolves."

I shook my head at her. "That's temporary. I've had to learn how to fend for myself. To pay my own bills. To run a business. To figure out why my air conditioner wasn't working. It was the stupid filter, by the way. Turns out you have to actually clean that shit."

Was that a faint smile dancing around her lips? No, I must be imagining it.

"I'd like to visit. One day," I said. "I'd like to be a friend to the coven. But I'll never again be a member. I need you to be okay with that."

"Suit yourself." She shrugged.

I watched her. She'd never let me see if that saddened her or not. Stubborn until the end. And she wondered where I got it from.

I left Gemma sitting in her chair, gazing out the window, and stopped by the morgue.

When Wilson finally met me in the reception area, she gave me a hard stare. "You know I have an actual job to do, right?"

I sighed. "Yeah. Can you just tell me...was Harrison killed by the same creature that's been killing groups of humans?"

"In my *preliminary* opinion...no. However, I haven't finished. If I find anything that I think will help you with your case, I'll let you know."

With that, she turned and strode back toward the door.

I'd missed dinner by now, so I stopped at a drive-thru, amusing myself at the thought of Tobias's aghast expression if he found out. I didn't cook, and I was so tired, I didn't have it in me to go searching for leftovers.

I munched on fries as I drove on autopilot. When I walked in the door, Nathaniel was sitting in the sitting room, alone for the first time in days. He had a glass of what looked like whiskey in his hand, and his eyes lightened as they met mine.

He scanned me, as if checking for damage. I let it go and took a seat beside him. Then I reached for his whiskey and took a sip, wrinkling my nose before handing it back to him.

"How'd it go?" he asked.

I filled him in about our day. His eyes turned hard when I told him about Wimbar and what he'd done to Callula.

"Finvarra will make him hurt," I told his wolf.

"That's true."

"I also stopped by the morgue. And they confirmed my theory. Two different monsters."

Nathaniel cursed. "Because one rampaging monster wasn't bad enough."

"Better to know, though. I also went to see Gemma."

I'd thought I could sneak that in, but Nathaniel was silent for a long moment. Finally, he pushed a curl off my forehead. "Why would you do that to yourself?"

I shrugged. "I had to go." But I still felt raw, as if my skin had been ripped off, all my nerve endings exposed.

From the way Nathaniel was looking at me, he could tell. He'd always been able to see too much.

"She failed you, Evie."

I shook my head. "She had to look out for the other witches."

He slid his hand around to the back of my neck until I gazed up at him.

"She had a responsibility to *every* member of her coven. If you'd been part of my pack, I would never have let you go."

Warmth spread outward from my chest, along each of my limbs. "I know." I took a deep breath. "She asked me to rejoin the coven."

Nathaniel stiffened, placing his drink on the table next to the sofa. "And what did you say?"

"I said no. I told her leaving the coven was good for me. Better than I could've imagined. But that's not the only reason why."

"What are the other reasons?"

I sighed. "She lied to me. For my whole life. So did other people, but Gemma… She'll never admit it was the wrong thing to do. She'll never apologize."

"Perhaps she was trying to protect you."

It was my turn to stiffen. "Don't stick up for her, Nathaniel. You don't know what it's like. There's nothing I hate worse than being lied to."

He merely nodded. We were both quiet as he stroked my back until my eyelids grew heavy. I needed to go to bed soon. When I forced my eyes open to look at him again, his expression was tormented, his gaze focused on the wall behind me.

Nathaniel's eyes met mine. "You smell like fast food."

I scowled, raising one hand and lifting it to my nose. "Are you serious right now?"

"You need to look after yourself. I would've made you something."

I gaped. "You cook?"

"Occasionally."

My mind helpfully provided me with a vision of Nathaniel standing in the kitchen wearing an apron… and nothing else.

Nathaniel's eyes darkened, and he gave me a slow smile. "Well, well, well. I had no idea *cooking* would get you so hot and bothered," he purred.

My heart stuttered, and I leaned back. No one could

make me feel like prey like this man. Unfortunately, I was the kind of prey that wanted to get caught.

"It's not the cooking," I said, forcing myself to get to my feet.

"Well, then. What is it?"

"I pictured you in an apron, that's all," I muttered.

"An apron, hmm? Kinky."

I groaned.

Nathaniel laughed, and before I could blink, he was standing in front of me. "You are so adorable," he said.

I scowled up at him. "I think you mean sexy and mysterious."

He twirled his finger around a curl that had escaped my bun. "That too."

I opened my mouth, but the door flew open. We both turned.

Kyla stalked in, her face wet with tears.

I could count on one finger how many times I'd seen her cry.

"Hey." I wiggled away from Nathaniel and headed for her. "What's going on?"

"She's dead, Evie. Callula is dead, and it's all my fault."

"Oh, Kyla." I threw my arms around her, and her whole body shook against me with her silent sobs. "You did everything right. She was centuries old. She knew her cousin. She could have gone to Finvarra at any time."

She snorted, pulling away to wipe at her face. "That's what *he* said. Why he would think anyone would go to him for anything, I'll never understand."

Nathaniel held out his arms, and I lifted my eyebrows as Kyla walked into them. She wasn't exactly known for taking comfort from others. She must be feeling terrible.

"You're staying here tonight," Nathaniel declared.

She pushed at his chest, and he held on. I rolled my eyes. Kyla wasn't going to win that battle.

"Finvarra tried to pull the same crap," Kyla muttered. "Said some shit about me being too distraught to be alone. *Me!*"

I hid a smile. Nathaniel merely let out a growl. "As much as I would like the unseelie dead, he's right. You need to be surrounded by pack tonight."

"Fine," she growled. Then she smirked up at him, still wiping at her eyes. "I'll stay in Evie's room."

Nathaniel simply nodded and released her.

"Goodnight," I murmured to him. His eyes met mine, still heated from our earlier discussion. My mouth went dry, and Kyla grabbed my arm, almost dragging me upstairs.

"What was that about?" I asked her, clomping up the stairs. "There are a ton of spare rooms here. Not that you're not welcome to hang in mine if you want to talk or whatever..."

She snorted. "Whenever a bossy male makes you do something you otherwise wouldn't do, you have to make them pay, even if it's just in a small way. Otherwise, they think they can walk all over you." She rolled her eyes at me. "As if I need to explain that to *you*, Queen of Revenge."

I gaped at her. She shook her head and linked arms with me. "That's what the demons are calling you."

"Why?"

"Something about the way you took out your frustration on them when Danica was taken."

I scowled. "Samael had them following me around. He was scared I'd go after Danica. I couldn't even *pee* without someone like Lilith trailing after me! But we're getting off topic. Why would you sleeping in my room annoy Nathaniel?"

"Because I'm cockblocking him, duh."

My cheeks burned. I knew Nathaniel could hear every word I said. "It's not—we don't—"

"Uh-huh. Don't worry about having to share your bed, you cover hog. I'll go wolf."

I opened my bedroom door and sat on the bed. Kyla had gone from sobbing to laughing incredibly quickly. I knew that tactic. It was called "shove your feelings down and pretend they don't exist." I was kind of an expert at that method.

I narrowed my eyes at her, and she just shook her head.

"I'll deal with it, Evie. But not until I've made Wim pay."

She watched me. "Sooo, what's going on with you

and Nathaniel?"

I gaped at her. She just shook her head. "Every room in this house is soundproofed for werewolf ears. You can tell me the goss."

"There is no…goss."

"Well, that's disappointing."

"I don't know what's happening. *Something* is, but… He's the Alpha, Kyla. Whatever is happening isn't exactly smart on my part."

"Nathaniel never wanted to be Alpha. If he could, I think he'd be a normal guy." She smirked. "Of course, he'd be either an old man or dead by now, so you never would've met him."

My gut twisted at the thought. Kyla gave me a knowing look.

I flopped back on the bed and stared at the ceiling. Next to me, Kyla did the same.

"I'm really enjoying my life. For the first time, I know I'm entirely free. Nothing and no one are influencing me in any way."

"And you think Nathaniel will put an end to that."

"Well…yeah."

My phone buzzed, and I fished it out from beneath my back. I glanced at the screen and frowned. "It's Aubrey."

"Taraghlan is planning to move the sword," Aubrey said as soon as I answered.

I cursed.

Kyla echoed me, her sensitive ears picking up

every word Aubrey said.

"Did something tip him off?"

"I don't know. Taraghlan's relocating to another area of our realm. It could just be that he's moving his court for a period of time. All I know is that he's taking the sword with him."

I glanced at Kyla. "We need to move up our plans."

Her mouth thinned into a grim line, but she gave me one sharp nod.

"We still don't know everything you'll face in that castle," Aubrey said cautiously. "We may be able to get you in, but—"

"We do this, or Kyla ends up chained to Finvarra's throne," I cut him off. I had no doubt the unseelie menace would do it too. "Not to mention, we need that sword or the worlds burn. I don't know about you, but I don't want to become barbecue."

Aubrey sighed. I echoed it. He knew I was right.

"When is he due to move?"

"Within the month."

He wasn't leaving us much time. Nerves fluttered in my stomach. The only thing worse than breaking in to the seelie king's castle was breaking in unprepared.

No. I steeled my shoulders. We could do this.

"We need to talk to your spies."

"I know. They've agreed to talk to you. When can you meet them?"

"Let me get back to you. It might have to be a couple of days from now. I have plans for tomorrow."

The kinds of plans that would make Kyla kick my ass if she found out about them.

EVIE

The next morning, I borrowed one of Nathaniel's cars. After fighting rush-hour traffic, I walked into Nelson's office before nine a.m.

"I said seventy-two hours," he muttered without looking up from his paperwork.

"That's what I wanted to talk to you about. I need a little longer."

Nelson raised his head, a deep crease between his eyes. "Have you got something?"

"No. That's why I need longer. I have some theories, Nelson. And I'm going to take the tooth to Danica."

My sister's name was just what he needed to hear. He rolled his eyes but leaned back in his chair, folding his hands on his desk in front of him. "You're a pain in my ass."

"I've heard that before."

"I bet."

"Can I take a look at the crime scene photos from all the scenes? I have some of them, but I need to see everything together."

"Yeah." He picked up a phone and mumbled to one of his cops.

Office Tarron appeared a few moments later.

"Take Evie to Rob's desk. He's out this morning. Give her whatever she needs. And bring me coffee."

"Yes, sir."

Officer Tarron was a sweet young man whose voice kept breaking. He couldn't seem to look at me without blushing. I did the polite thing and pretended not to notice.

"You can sit here, ma'am." He gestured to an empty desk.

I gave an internal wince. "Please, call me Evie."

"Evie," he said, and his voice cracked again. I suppressed a grin.

Tarron loaded the desk with a couple of boxes, and I got to work.

An hour later, I was sipping on a cup of coffee Tarron had kindly brought me. I was also focused on the list of items found at the scenes.

Across all the scenes so far, we had five guns, sixteen daggers, six low-level charms—and I'd be checking if they really were for fighting nausea, finding luck, and building confidence—and a diary. The diary had broken my heart a little. It was clearly written by a teenager and had no relevance to the case. Mariah Campbell had wanted to be a teacher. She'd had a crush on a boy from her gym class. And she'd never get to realize any of her dreams.

It was depressing as hell.

I ran my gaze over the items found near the mages at the birthday party. Two burner phones, two guns, a retainer, a notebook written entirely in code, two ancient coins—likely from another realm—a set of tarot cards, and a forget-me spell.

I ground my teeth. A forget-me spell was highly illegal for civilians. Human therapists occasionally used it for their clients with disabling PTSD, but they had to jump through many, many hoops before they were approved. But before it was banned, the spell had been responsible for some of the worst actions against humans in history. And many of them had been by humans themselves.

I glanced at the name on my list. The forget-me spell was found on what was left of a mage called Craig Hipple. If he'd survived, he'd likely be in a cell right about now. I made a mental note to look into his background. I wondered if Albert knew his mages were showing up at parties with magical roofies in their pockets.

I waved goodbye to Tarron and slipped my notes back into my purse. I was wearing jeans and a T-shirt today. No pretty sundresses for my plans this afternoon.

My mind was whirling as I drove back toward my office. I needed access to the books I'd brought back from Austin.

The insurance guy entered the parking lot from the opposite entrance. I shot toward my spot and slid into it with a victorious grin. He scowled at me.

I had to take my wins where I could find them.

Rose had messaged that she was planning to work from home, so I had the office to myself. I kicked off my shoes and beelined for the coffee maker. While the coffee did its thing, I started up my computer and stacked the textbooks I needed on my desk. Edward had given me some of them with a gruff instruction to "study like your life depends on it, because one day it will."

I spent the next couple of hours flipping through textbooks, hunting down obscure references, and analyzing the crime scene photos.

My stomach clenched as I made extensive notes that did nothing to help me feel better about this situation.

In fact, with every piece of evidence I found supporting my theory, I felt worse and worse.

The claws would have to be huge to do so much damage so quickly. The black tooth was definitely from something no one I knew had ever encountered. And… the piece of fur everyone had assumed belonged to a werewolf? The analysis had come back, and it most definitely did not. At least that proved beyond all doubt that the wolves weren't responsible.

I needed to leave soon if I was going to make my meeting. But first, I needed to talk to Selina. She was one of the few people in this realm who could likely confirm if I was on the right track.

"I need you to do me a favor," I said when she answered. "I need you to tell me everything you know about Gleipnir."

"Gleipnir? I don't know much. You may need to talk to the seelie."

"The seelie? Why?"

"Some say it wasn't the gods who created Gleipnir. It's theorized that the seelie had already developed it and the gods stole it from them."

"Shit. Tell me everything you've got."

My heart tripped as Selina filled me in about the magical chain. I told her my own theories, and she went quiet for a few moments.

"Most of the accounts were written before the portals opened," she said finally. "When humans had a limited understanding of our world and the realms connected to it."

By noon, I had to get going. Keeping my next little plan on the down-low from Nathaniel hadn't been a big deal. He was busy with his own shit, like running his pack.

Thankfully, Kyla was still out and busy with her own case.

I'd gotten Frederik's details by calling Meredith, who'd asked around for me. Yes, I was cashing in on the fact that my sister was the underqueen. Sue me.

I'd messaged the Alpha wolf after visiting Selina. As far as I was concerned, her encouragement when we'd hugged before I left yesterday had given me the green light. If there was one thing I knew, it was that Selina had *everyone's* best interests at heart.

A few hours later, I pulled my car to the side of the road and stepped out, my skin turning clammy. I was officially outside of Nathaniel's territory. I bolstered my own wards and leaned against my car, waiting for the representative who was supposed to meet me.

Five minutes later, a car pulled up behind me.

The guy who stepped out of the car was huge, with light-brown skin and muscles that told me he spent every spare moment in the gym. We surveyed each other silently, and he began walking toward me.

The threads of my power seemed to tickle me, desperate to be used.

He held out his hand. "Name's Brick," he said.

I shook his hand. "Evie."

"I'll drive you to Frederik," he said.

"I'll follow you, if it's all the same."

He angled his head like he was wondering if he should be offended. If he was, that was on him. I listened to true crime podcasts, and I wasn't getting murdered.

"Call me paranoid, but I don't get into enclosed spaces with huge men I've just met. Especially not when they put as much effort into pumping iron as you do, and most definitely not when they're a werewolf who could kill me with one hit."

Surprise flashed across his face. My honesty had shocked him a little. Good.

"Seems like a good policy," he finally said. "Frederik

won't like it, but he didn't specifically say I had to drive you."

"Perfect."

I followed Brick down the road. When we pulled into a long drive, I reached for my phone and sent the coordinates to Mere. If I didn't come back, she'd alert Vas, who would ensure every demon in the vicinity came looking.

I really hoped that didn't happen.

Brick parked outside a rambling, ranch-style house. It was quiet out here. Creepily quiet. I got out of the car, and the wolves appeared in front of me.

I tried not to jump, but they could definitely hear the way my heart rate had sped up.

"I told you to drive her here," a low, furious voice said.

"Sorry, boss. I misunderstood," Brick replied.

I didn't smirk, but it was close. Nathaniel's dominants didn't need to *misunderstand* anything. I'd seen them question Nathaniel's orders to his face. As he'd once told me, he didn't want to rule a pack of slaves.

I surveyed the Alpha wolf. A few inches taller than me, Frederik had pale skin and cropped dark hair. The deep frown lines between his brows told me he was prone to scowling.

My research had told me Frederik was lower on the power scale than Nathaniel. And yet, his power spread out, climbing toward me, until I felt as if I would choke on it.

I managed to keep my feet. Barely. This little show of power was more than just a demonstration of how dominant he was. Frederik was pissed.

I'd been around paranormals for long enough to know that true power wasn't about how much magic or dominance someone had at their disposal. It was about how much control that person had over themselves—and their power.

I'd seen Nathaniel frustrated. Heartbroken. Furious. But he'd never shoved his power down my throat like this before. He didn't have to.

The one time he'd let a hint of his power out, he'd shut it down so viciously, it was as if it had disappeared.

This was a perfect example of why Nathaniel was so feared. And why so many werewolves would follow him to the ends of the earth. He was always ruthlessly controlled.

Frederik watched me out of dark eyes. "So the underqueen's sister came here. To my territory. For what?"

I indulged in one moment of resentment that I would forever be known as the underqueen's sister, and then I tucked that thought away to examine later.

"I'm not here in that capacity."

"Then what capacity *are* you here in? As Nathaniel's plaything?"

Most of the wolves chortled. Brick didn't. I knew I liked Brick.

Frederik gave them one look, and they went silent.

I let a hint of my own power peek out. Ever since the spell tying me to the coven's house disappeared, my magic had become increasingly...strange. Frederik's eyes widened as he likely attempted to figure out just what I was.

Good luck with that. Let me know what you come up with.

"You're aware of the massacres," I said.

Frederik shrugged. "Humans. Why would I care?"

I stared at him. Werewolves had to mate with humans to survive. The fact that he was so dismissive of their deaths made me wonder just how well the humans in his pack were treated.

"Because the authorities believe werewolves are responsible," I said in my best "you're a fucking idiot" voice.

"So Nathaniel sent you here to warn me?"

"Nathaniel didn't send me here. I'm investigating the massacres myself."

He gave me a look that told me he wasn't buying whatever I was selling. I sighed.

"Three of your wolves were seen near the CertSure massacre." I tried again. "And yet you refuse to cooperate with Nathaniel—"

It was the wrong thing to say. Frederik let out a low, vicious snarl, and every single one of his wolves took a step closer to me.

NATHANIEL

I rubbed at the bridge of my nose as Keith droned on about pack finances. The accountant meant well, but he kept forgetting that we didn't need a rundown of every cent.

"Sum it up, mate," Corey said. The young wolf was from South Africa and had never been known for his patience. I shot him a look, and he sighed.

Keith flushed. He wasn't quite as submissive as Tobias, but he tended to get flustered easily.

"That's about it," he said. "Our investments are all performing above projections."

"Thank you." I gave him a nod, and he smiled back, finding his seat. Weekly pack meetings were important for the overall health of the pack. Wolves could petition for anything they felt was important, and the humans could come to me with any problems or concerns.

"Are we boring you, Hunter?" I raised one eyebrow at my dominant. He was usually the one sending dirty looks to anyone chatting during these meetings.

He glanced up from his phone and swallowed. "Evie went to Frederik."

Every muscle in my body tensed. My gut twisted, and it took me a moment to recognize the emotion.

Fear.

Hunter's gaze skittered away, his head angling submissively to show me his throat.

Rage slowly crept at my vision. The kind of rage that led to the people around me dying.

I closed my eyes until all I could see were pale blue eyes in a face lined with age.

It's okay, child. I forgive you.

"Nathaniel?" Xander was sitting next to me.

I opened my eyes and took a deep breath. At some point, he'd cleared the room. Only my dominants remained.

I held up a hand while I attempted to bargain with my wolf.

"We do not know that she is hurt...yet. Evie is smart and powerful. But if Frederik has touched her, we will kill him slowly."

My wolf accepted that. I got to my feet and stalked toward the window, staring out at the forest. "What the hell was she thinking?"

It was a rhetorical question, but Hunter answered it anyway.

"Naomi told her you were readying for war. I believe Evie thought she could fix it. I assume she is attempting to negotiate with Frederik."

Frustration warred with an odd...tenderness.

She was terrified of ever experiencing a repeat of the attack on the coven. Of ever losing anyone that mattered. So Evie was putting herself in danger in an attempt to protect my wolves.

I wanted to spank her ass and press gentle kisses across her cheeks. I wanted to fuck her raw and make love to her gently. The two urges battled inside me until all I could do was heave a sigh.

"We give her two hours to return to my territory," I said. "If she hasn't returned by then, I'll pay Frederik a visit of my own. He wants to play games with me, then that's fine. I won't allow him to play those games with Evie."

"Sounds like *she's* the one playing games with *him*," Naomi muttered.

I glanced at her, and she hunched her shoulders. "I'm just saying. She's the one who chose to go into enemy territory."

"She's one of the few people who would make Frederik curious enough to talk to her, without causing him to immediately declare war because one of our people dared to visit his territory without an invitation," Hunter explained. "It's a smart plan if it works. She may be able to determine if he's up to no good."

"If he doesn't decide to keep her," I growled out. It would be just like Frederik to push *me* into declaring war.

"She's too powerful for that," Xander said.

I fisted my hand at my side. If Frederik touched one curl on her head, I'd make him wish he'd never been born.

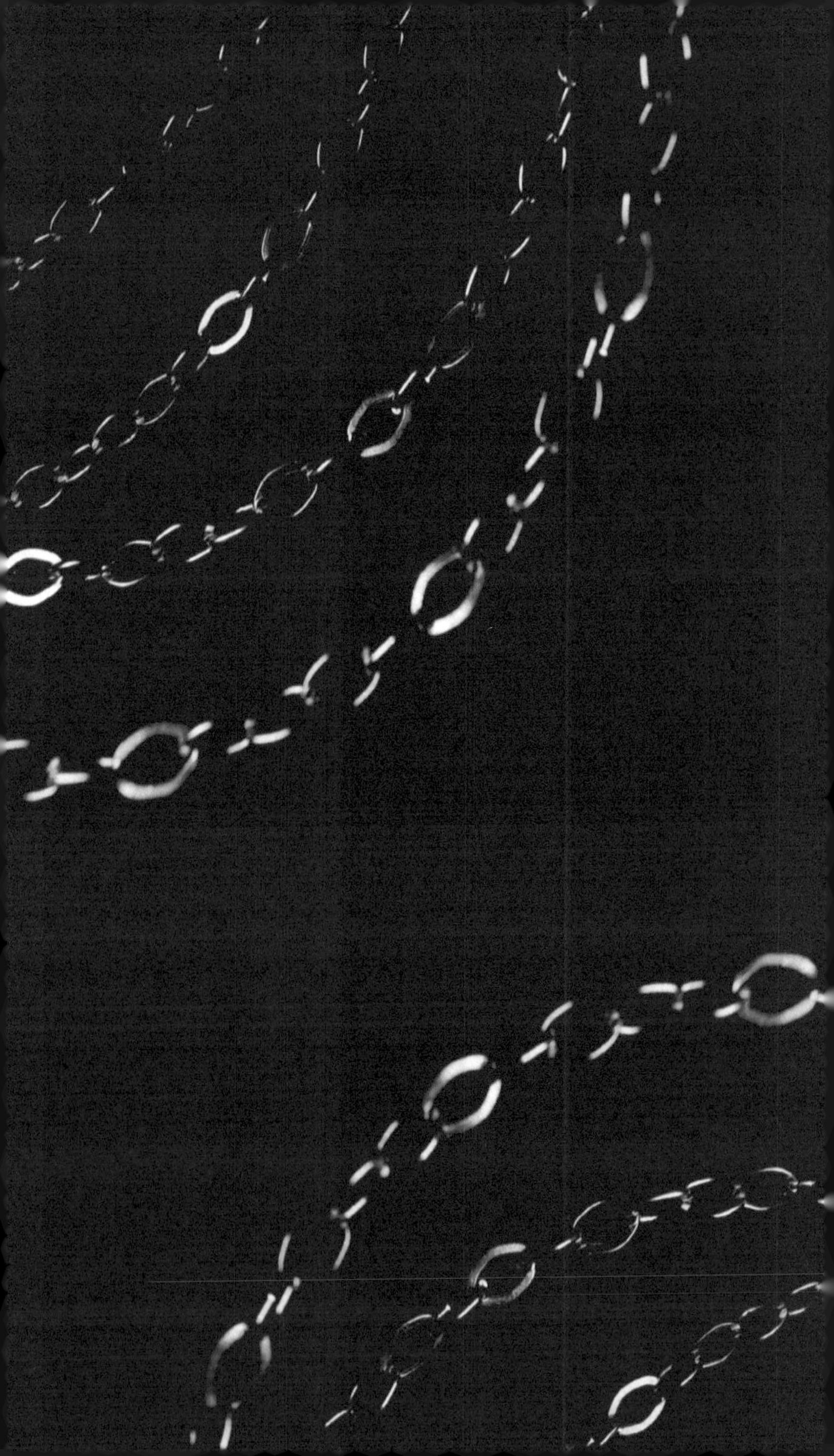

16

EVIE

Iraised a ward. It might not last for long if they all attacked at once, but it would buy me some time.

"Nathaniel is not my Alpha," Frederik bit out. "He is nothing but a self-righteous, overly moralistic, naïve Boy Scout."

"Wow," I mused. "You're really afraid of him, huh?"

I wasn't getting anywhere with honey. Maybe pissing him off would help.

He went still, and his dominance lashed out at me again. It felt like needles on my skin, but this time, my ward kept most of it at bay.

"Ah," he said, as all of his wolves dropped to the ground, but I stayed standing. "I see why Nathaniel is intrigued by you." His voice changed to a low purr. "When you tire of his holier-than-thou rule, let me know."

I considered a few answers to that. *Hell would freeze over first* was one of them. Finally, I settled on, "Thanks for the offer, but I'm more interested in avoiding this war."

He gave a languid shrug of his shoulder. "War comes for all of us, eventually."

I stared at him. He was bored. And he wanted to go up against Nathaniel. There was nothing I could do or say to make him see reason.

Nothing I could say except…

"You want to meet Nathaniel on the battlefield? Fine. But be prepared for all of Nathaniel's allies to be standing next to him."

Frederik's eyes sharpened. "The underqueen is allied with *all of* the wolves."

"No. Danica is allied with *Nathaniel's* wolves. Neither she nor Samael will tolerate a war that involves humans. And we both know a werewolf war would decimate this country. You may wish to die, but I'm sure the rest of your pack does not."

"Be very careful," he breathed.

I shrugged. "As you mentioned, I have no authority here. I'm not negotiating on behalf of Nathaniel or Danica. I'm just telling you the consequences of choosing war instead of an alliance."

He watched me for a long moment, and I saw him consider my death. Finally, he laughed.

"Ah, you will lead my enemy by his tail. I find myself intrigued enough to want to see it."

I had no idea what he was talking about, but the idea that anyone could lead Nathaniel by his tail was ludicrous. Frederik pulled back his power, and his wolves were able to get to their feet.

"Mark, Jonas, Weston," he said.

Three wolves stepped forward. Frederik waved his hand at me. "Tell her why you were seen in Nathaniel's territory. And why you were stupid enough to be caught on human cameras." His voice had dropped to a threatening growl by the end of the sentence, and one of his wolves shuddered, ducking his head.

This was a submissive. I thought of Tobias and the other submissives I'd seen in Nathaniel's pack, all of whom were protected. Tobias had told me that the pack was driven to keep their submissives happy. They were the foundation of a healthy pack.

Obviously, Frederik didn't feel the same way.

"We had been scouting near Nathaniel's territory," Jonas said. He was dominant enough that he'd kept his head raised when Frederik growled.

"Why?" I asked.

"That's privileged," Frederik purred.

I almost rolled my eyes. Clearly, they were planning to start some shit with Nathaniel.

"What happened?"

"We were still outside of Nathaniel's territory when Weston got a call." Jonas gestured toward the submissive wolf. "It was a human who said she had information about Nathaniel's defenses."

"So you entered Nathaniel's territory. Not just entered it, but drove all the way into Durham to meet the human."

Weston nodded, his gaze dropping to the ground.

"What was the human's name?"

"Ellen Harrison." Weston kept his gaze down. I took a second to come to terms with that. Harrison was just showing up fucking everywhere, wasn't she?

"They should have known better than to be lured by a human," Frederik said softly. "And they will be punished accordingly."

Weston flinched, and I had the strangest urge to grab his hand and squeeze. That likely wouldn't do him any favors, though.

"What exactly was Harrison going to show you?"

Mark placed one hand on Jonas's shoulder. At least *he* seemed to be protective of the submissive wolf. "We don't know. We thought we would be in and out of Nathaniel's territory before he realized we'd crossed over. She never showed."

"Is there anything else I need to know?"

All three wolves glanced at Frederik. He didn't move. They didn't say a word. I barely suppressed a sigh.

"Thank you for your cooperation," I said.

Frederik watched me. "We could use someone as powerful as you in our pack."

"No thank you."

His gaze burned into mine. "Why?"

"You're a bully. And if there's one thing I've always loathed, it's people who pick on those weaker than them."

His face flushed, his eyes glittered, and I took that as my sign to leave. With a nod, I shored up my ward and stalked toward my car.

EVIE

By the time I got back to Duke Forest, night had fallen. I was more than ready for a shower and an early night. But the moment I opened the door, I went very still.

A strange kind of silence hit me. I let a tendril of my power out, but I couldn't sense anything dangerous.

Well, anything except the seething dominant in the next room.

"I know you're here, Evelyn." Nathaniel's voice was quiet, but it still carried to me.

His tone made the hair on the back of my neck stand up. But I refused to be scared of him. I slowly took off my shoes, buying myself time as I thought about my approach.

I walked into the large, informal living room and froze. A vise clamped around my lungs.

Nathaniel sat in an armchair, with ten or twelve

of his wolves either sitting on the massive sofa or hugging the wall. Tobias flicked me a quick glance from his spot near the coffee table, but I couldn't read his expression.

"You smell like my enemy," Nathaniel breathed. When his gaze met mine, I could see his wolf.

And he wasn't happy.

Nathaniel slowly got to his feet, and I took a deep breath. "Frederik's wolves were lured by Harrison. He had nothing to do with the attacks. He *is* a giant dick, though."

"You could have been killed!"

Every wolf in the room dropped to their knees, head bowed. My own head swam dizzily, and I realized I'd dropped too. I hadn't been truly scared in Frederik's territory, but I was scared now.

And that little realization pissed me off.

I shoved out with my own power, giving myself some breathing room. That allowed me to meet Nathaniel's eyes, which had gone so light it was difficult to see his irises in the whites of his eyes.

Surprise flared in those eyes as I managed to meet his gaze, quickly followed by something that seemed to be...pride.

I dropped my eyes once more. It seemed like the smart thing to do.

Nathaniel stalked closer to me. He shot out his hand and stroked my face. Then he cupped my chin and leaned close, until his warm breath caressed the shell of my ear.

"You're in so much trouble."

I tensed, but he was already stalking away. I watched as he took a slow, deep breath, packing away the power that had infiltrated the entire house. It took a few minutes, but the invisible hand clamped around the back of my neck disappeared, and I was able to get to my feet.

So was everyone else.

"Out," Nathaniel said softly.

I turned to go, and his eyes met mine, still feral. "Not you."

Everyone else filed out. Naomi gave me a look I couldn't read and strolled out the door. Liam widened his eyes at me, and I shrugged at him, suddenly exhausted.

Nathaniel waited until everyone had left, and then he was in front of me. I took an automatic step back. He'd moved so fast, I hadn't seen it.

"Are you frightened of me?"

I shook my head, mute, but he just smiled. Werewolves could sense lies.

I wasn't truly frightened of him. I was more… perturbed.

I yelped as I was suddenly over his shoulder, and he stalked upstairs.

"What the hell are you doing?"

"What I should have done the moment I saw you."

That could be a lot of things. I struggled, and

he slapped my ass with his huge hand. I let out an indignant shriek.

His shoulders shook.

The fucking audacity. "Are you *laughing* at me?"

Nathaniel pushed open his door, and I couldn't help but lift my head as curiosity spun through me. I'd never seen his bedroom before.

Then I was flying through the air. I landed on his bed, but I didn't bother taking in my surroundings. No, it was smarter to keep my gaze on the predator in front of me.

We stared at each other for an endless moment. Then Nathaniel smiled. He was leaning over me in the next moment, with one of those too-fast-to-see movements.

I jolted, and he let out a soothing sound as he nibbled on my lower lip.

"When I learned you'd gone to Frederik, I thought you were dead," he told me. He tensed, and I met his eyes.

"Hi," I told his wolf.

His eyes darkened once more, and it was Nathaniel who brushed my hair back from my face. "I haven't truly disagreed with my wolf since the day I was turned," he said. "We negotiate, but never do we have such competing thoughts about the correct choice to make."

"What choice is that?" My voice was shaky, and he smiled at me.

"My wolf wants to spank your ass and tie you to my bed, where no one could ever harm you again."

I gaped at him. "And the man?"

He gave me a slow smile. "The man wants to devour your pussy until you admit you are mine."

I ignored the little voice that wanted me to ask him to do all of those things. That little voice was a hussy.

"It's a good thing you're so disciplined," I said, and he let out a rough laugh.

"In every aspect of my life, I am disciplined. Until you."

He leaned down and took my mouth with his. There was no doubt that this was a claiming. My hands were trapped between us, and I dug my nails into his chest in warning. He let out a sound like a purr, and I shuddered in pure want.

My tank top disappeared, and I was barely aware of the cooler air caressing my skin. He unbuttoned my jeans, and I stared up at him as he stripped them from me.

Nathaniel crawled back up my body, moving with a predatory grace that made my heart trip.

He nuzzled at my hair, playing with one curl that had fallen over my eyebrow.

"There was a little girl," he whispered, "who had a little curl..."

I glowered at him, but he replaced the curl with his lips, brushing them over my skin. "Right in the middle of her forehead."

I attempted to push the stupid curl off my head, but Nathaniel caught my hand in his.

"When she was good, she was very, very good," he crooned.

I swallowed. I'd heard this rhyme before, but never in *this* tone.

Nathaniel tightened his other hand around my waist. "But when she was bad…" His lips crashed down on mine, and I gasped at the sudden intrusion of his tongue, sweeping over mine. He pulled back enough to murmur against my lips. "She was horrid."

I scowled at him—even as a laugh trickled from my throat. "This probably isn't a good idea," I said.

He just gave me a slow smile. "You decided to play with me, sweetheart. Now open those pretty thighs so I can show you why you shouldn't have risked your life on my behalf."

I was so wet, I was pretty sure I'd soaked through my underwear. Nathaniel inhaled, a long, slow breath through his nose, and my face burned as I covered my eyes with one arm, suddenly unable to look at him.

He let out a sound somewhere between an amused laugh and a satisfied purr.

Then my underwear was gone. I opened my eyes to see him tucking his claws away.

"I want to see you," he told me.

I couldn't help but grin. "I think you are."

He gestured to my bra. "All of you."

There was no point pretending I wasn't all in at this point. Later, I'd likely berate myself for giving in to the werewolf Alpha. But right now...

I would go crazy if I didn't feel his hands on me soon.

I flicked open my bra and pulled it off. He watched, his hands buried in the fluffy comforter beneath me.

I was pretty sure his claws had sliced into that comforter as well. A hint of trepidation made me bite my lower lip, and Nathaniel's gaze dropped to my mouth.

"You never need to be afraid of me," he said.

His mouth lowered to mine, teasing and stroking, and I gasped against his lips, my hands sliding to his shirt as I attempted to pull it over his head.

He let out a tight laugh. "I don't think so." He pulled back, and I frowned at him, but he was already moving down, until he was staring at me, drinking me in.

I opened my mouth, but he pushed my thighs apart and gave me one slow lick.

My breath escaped my lungs, and I held perfectly still, desperate for him to do it again.

"Ah," he said. "So this is how I make you obey me."

I snarled at that, and he lowered his head once more, licking and playing. His hands on my thighs held me in place for him as I arched in a desperate bid to get closer. His tongue circled my clit, and I let out a whine that made him curse against me.

Then he stopped.

I opened my eyes, and I swear I almost came at the sight of him between my legs, his cheeks flushed, a muscle twitching in his jaw as he retained his famous self-control.

"Tell me you will not see Frederik again unless I give you permission."

"Permission?" My voice was so high it cracked. He merely waited me out.

I attempted to wiggle away, but he slowly shook his head at me. Then his mouth returned to my pussy, and I moaned.

He stopped.

"You motherfucking sadist."

He laughed, but it was tight.

"Swear to me, Evie."

It wasn't often that he called me by my nickname, and my breath caught in my throat.

"I'll never ask permission to do my job," I told him. "You know I'm part of this investigation."

"If you had told me your plans, I would have sent one of my wolves with you."

"Frederik would have lost his shit."

"And that proves you should never have gone," he said.

I let out a low growl, and a hint of humor appeared in his eyes. Then he licked me once more.

Every muscle in my body tightened. I fought his hands, writhing in an attempt to get closer as I balanced on the precipice…

"I don't think so."

I let out a string of curses that made him laugh, but I could see this was costing him too.

"If you're waiting for me to ask permission from you to do my job, you're going to be waiting for the rest of your long life. Now, make me come."

"Silly woman. I give the orders here."

In spite of my frustration, I couldn't help the giggle that escaped me. I clamped my hand over my mouth, but his gaze met mine.

Reluctant humor gleamed at me. He nuzzled me once more, his tongue laving me in the exact right spot. Then he stopped.

"Let's compromise," I gasped out.

He raised one eyebrow at me, and I wished I could take a picture of him just like this. There was something…oddly powerful about seeing Nathaniel unraveled. The king of self-control didn't look like he had much control right now.

"Compromise?" He licked me again, and a frustrated whine escaped my throat.

"Please…"

"I enjoy hearing you beg. My wolf enjoys it too."

"I won't ask permission," I snapped. "But…I'll let you know before I do anything I consider dangerous."

He let out a low growl, then rested his chin on my hip, pausing to nuzzle at the sensitive skin near my belly button.

"You will let me know before you do anything *I* would consider dangerous," he said.

"How am I supposed to figure out what *you* consider dangerous?"

"Whenever you're in the vicinity of anyone who could harm a hair on your head."

I stared at him. "Um, you're joking, right?"

Nathaniel sighed. "I am. My wolf isn't."

"Well, you can tell your wolf I'm perfectly capable of looking after myself."

He just gave me a look. I shifted beneath him, still desperate to feel his mouth on me again. But he easily held me in place while we negotiated.

If not for the bulge I'd spotted when he moved, and the way he held me so carefully, I would've thought he was cold and unaffected.

But I didn't have to be a wolf to sense *his* desire.

"I'll let you know if I'm doing anything *you* might consider dangerous. But only if it involves werewolves. And not to ask *permission*. To give you the opportunity to send Kyla with me."

He watched me. "Not just if it involves werewolves."

I sighed, and some of the lust that had clouded my mind disappeared. "What exactly are we doing here, Nathaniel?"

He raised his head off my hip, licked my lower belly, and blew cool air across it. Just like that, I was desperate for him once more.

It had been a while since I'd had sex. A small part of me had thought maybe I could have a brief, lighthearted affair with the werewolf king, but this was proving he didn't do lighthearted affairs.

It was a shame, because I sure didn't do commitment.

"We're negotiating," he purred, and his mouth dropped once more, his tongue exploring the wet heat of me.

He stopped.

"You son of a bitch. This is not the way to get what you want."

He laughed. "Are you sure?"

Evil werewolf. I glowered at him.

"Promise me," he said. "That you will call me before risking your life."

"Fine," I snarled.

He gave me a warm, pleased look, and I ignored the tiny part of me that wanted to see that look every day. That must be some kind of Alpha werewolf magic right there.

His hands gentled on my thighs, one of them moving beneath my butt so he could angle me for him. I sucked in a sharp breath as he spread me open with his other hand, allowing him access as his tongue explored every inch of me.

One finger slipped inside me, immediately followed by another. He sucked my clit, and I went still.

"Nate," I gasped out, and he let out a rough curse.

"Come for me," he ordered.

I did. God, I did. My entire body clenched, my vision turned white, and pleasure roared through me from my core, through each limb, until I felt as if I was floating through the air.

Nathaniel continued to lick and tease until I was boneless beneath him, so sensitive I had to push his head away. He kissed his way up my body, stopping to lick one nipple, and then his gaze met mine.

No one had ever looked at me like that before. I reached for him, desperate to feel him inside me.

Someone pounded on the door, and he let out a vicious snarl. "What?"

"We're under attack," Hunter said.

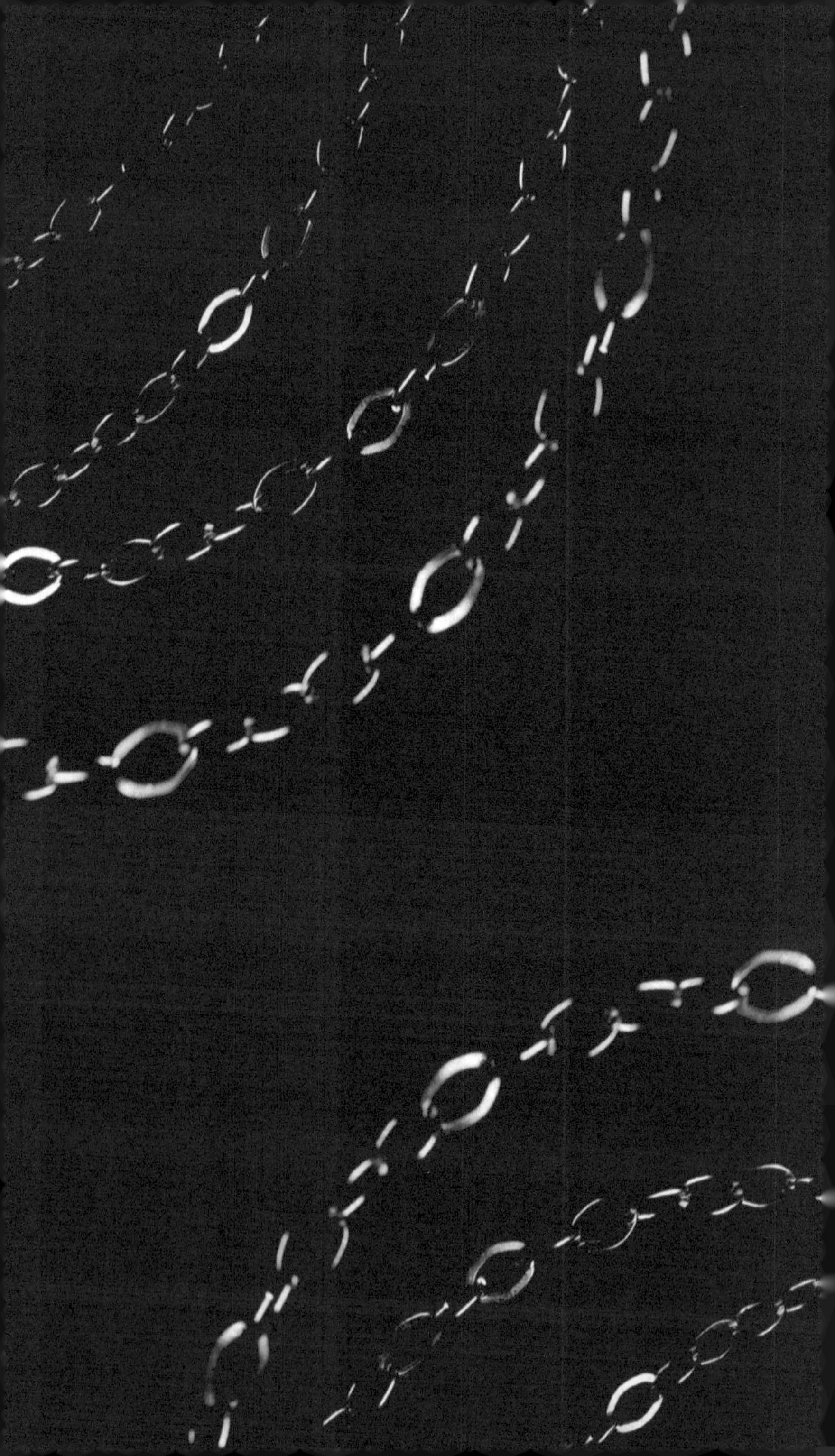

17

EVIE

Nathaniel shot to his feet.

"Stay here," he told me.

I ignored that. While he insisted on seeing me as a weak, underpowered woman in need of his protection, I knew my worth.

And there were kids here.

Nathaniel strode out the door, closing it behind him. Clearly, he didn't doubt I would follow his orders. That was cute.

I got dressed, strapped on my weapons, and opened the sliding doors. My heart thumped as I stepped onto Nathaniel's balcony. Below me, wolves were sprinting from the forest, toward the road, ready to fight.

I climbed over the balcony, thankful that I'd been working on my upper body strength. I let myself hang for a long moment, softening my knees, and then I let go.

"What the hell are you doing?" Naomi snarled.

I jolted, whirling to face her. "Jesus, give a girl some warning. I'm going to go protect the kids."

"Nathaniel's going to whip your hide," she said, but she didn't argue. "Don't let him see you."

I nodded and turned, weaving in and out of the werewolves who were running toward the road. Half of them had shifted. Most of them shot me dirty looks.

But I was getting used to that now.

By the time I got to the playground, the area was silent. I caught a glimpse of someone furry in the meeting hall window, followed by the sound of a baby wailing. They'd obviously packed all the kids into the hall, so it was more easily defensible. Good strategy.

I lowered my shields and reached out with my power.

A malevolent presence greeted me. It was radiating from across the small, man-made lake, deeper in wolf territory. In the opposite direction from where the wolves were going.

"It can cloak itself," I screamed, but no one was around to pay attention. Shit.

I sprinted down the forest path, lifting my feet higher than usual so I wouldn't trip. It was dark, and while the wolves had set up softly glowing lights among the trees, I still stumbled.

"Evie. Where do you think you're going?"

"Ryker. Thank God. The wolves are heading the wrong way. Whatever it is, it's smart enough to hide.

To trick you."

He brought his hands out to steady me, and he frowned. "Are you sure? I can feel it. Wolves aren't prone to being tricked by magic."

Was *I* the one being tricked? Possibly. Either way, I had to check.

"If they don't find it on that side of the forest, it's by the lake."

He nodded. "I need to help guard the kids. Be careful."

I jogged down the path, my instincts insisting I was right. But it took serious power to cloak, and even more power for that cloaking to work on werewolves.

The lake came into view, and a chill slid over every inch of my skin. I went still, wishing I had the night vision of a wolf.

Just like that, my vision sharpened.

I sucked in a breath as the gray blobs in the distance became trees and bushes. My senses screamed at me, and I reached down, pulling my Beretta.

Something hit me with the force of a rampaging elephant. I flew through the air, landing close to the lake.

My mouth opened, and I stared up at the night sky as I attempted to suck in a breath. Winded. My ankle howled at me. If it was broken, I was dead.

I fought panic as I managed to flip myself onto all fours, finally taking in the creature that had hit me.

Fuck.

It was huge. Larger than any werewolf I'd ever seen. It stared at me through baleful yellow eyes, its brown fur in matted clumps. Its fangs were longer than my middle fingers, but they weren't black like the tooth I'd collected. They were blindingly white.

What the hell was it?

I finally sucked in a deep breath and managed to haul myself to my feet. Well, one foot. I gingerly placed my other foot on the ground, the sharp pain warning me not to run on it. It wasn't broken, but it hurt like a motherfucker.

My only real hope was to get to my gun. I wasn't sure how fast it was, but I was about to find out. The gun was several feet away. Closer to the beast than to me.

I raised my hand and created a ward. The beast snarled at me, and I went still. It could feel the magic I'd used?

Tucking that away to think about later, I softened my knees, ready to launch myself forward. The beast showed me its teeth in warning, and an odd intelligence gleamed in its eyes. What the hell was it?

I ran through everything I knew about the creatures from other realms and came up empty.

I dropped my gaze to my Beretta. It lay close enough to taunt me, but far enough away that lunging at it might be the last move I ever made. The beast trembled, letting out an ominous growl. It was far too smart.

Something itched at my ward. I focused, and my skin turned clammy, my fingertips tingling at what I found approaching from the left. The ground trembled slightly, and I knew, deep in my gut, that something worse was on the way. Something much worse than the creature in front of me, and if I fought it alone, I would die.

The beast was slowly walking to the left. I turned with it until it stood in front of me, guarding its prey from another predator. The creature in the distance let out a snarl, and the hair on my arms stood at attention.

My only hope was to wait until both beasts were distracted and run like hell.

A werewolf melted out of the forest, silent and deadly. Nathaniel pinned his ears back and showed me his teeth.

Yeah, he was pissed.

The malevolent presence was still approaching from across the lake, but slower now.

More werewolves appeared.

Nathaniel prowled toward me. The beast slowly turned its head and snarled at him. Nathaniel snarled right back. The beast stepped closer to me, turning to face Nathaniel. Nathaniel lowered his head.

He roared.

It was the kind of sound I'd never heard a wolf make. His wolves howled in response.

The beast snarled, clearly enraged by Nathaniel daring to challenge it. I crouched and pulled my A-F from my ankle sheath. This was my chance.

I raced toward the beast and slashed along one of its back legs. Blood spurted, and it turned toward me, bellowing its rage.

The look in its eyes...betrayal. It thought I had double-crossed it. I didn't know how I knew that, but as it stared at me, I felt a recognition I'd never felt before.

"I'm sorry," I blurted out. It roared again.

Nathaniel let out a low growl, and the beast turned to face him once more.

The presence across the lake began to retreat.

The beast took a single step away from me...

And disappeared.

Nathaniel growled his fury. Then he was directly in front of me, showing me his sharp, white teeth.

I swallowed and swiped my gun from the forest floor. "Impressive fangs."

He snapped his teeth an inch from my face. Then he lowered his head and sniffed at my ankle.

"I'm fine," I told him. "I'm pretty sure it's just a sprain."

He let out another low growl, and I sighed. Then I leaned down and wrapped my arms around his neck.

He went still. His tongue darted out and swiped along my cheek, and I laughed.

"Gross."

One moment, I was cuddling the wolf, and the next, I was clutching the man.

Fur became skin, and Nathaniel was suddenly human again. I squeaked and let him go, but his arms came around me, and he stood, lifting me like I was weightless.

"Put me down," I hissed. His wolves were ignoring us for the most part, but one of them chuffed in obvious amusement. Was that Hunter?

Nathaniel strode a few feet away and gestured to a plant that was covered in blood. I swallowed against the bile that wanted to rise and glanced at Nathaniel. "What is it?"

He gave me a steady look. "The blood smells similar to yours."

"What do you mean?"

His gaze was still on my face, as if he wanted to memorize my reaction. "Your blood smells different. We know it's because your genetics are different. Because HFE somehow managed to combine many different types of DNA from multiple factions."

"And you think whoever this blood belongs to is…the same as me?"

He shrugged. "I think it's a theory. It could have been one of the mages. Or it could've been someone here who was posing as human. Perhaps they didn't even know they had access to power."

"How could they not know?"

He gave me a look. "For the same reason that you refuse to attempt to access the deep well of power I can sense in you."

I glanced away. Nathaniel began strolling back through the forest, still naked as the day he was born.

Wolves had fewer hang-ups about nudity, as Kyla had proven many times. But my face still burned as Nathaniel carried me away from the lake, back toward his house.

Naomi met us on the way. "There's food," she said, her expression missing some of its usual annoyance when she looked at me. "Come eat."

She turned and walked away. I glanced up at Nathaniel.

"Since when does she care if I'm hungry?"

He gave a soft laugh. "You put yourself at risk to protect the pack. By distracting that monster, you prevented it from making its way toward the kids before we could arrive to back you up. Naomi values loyalty and bravery higher than most."

He nuzzled my ear, and I shivered. "That doesn't mean I'm not pissed at you for disobeying my order."

I stiffened, glancing up at his face. He was focused on the path ahead of us, the skin around his eyes tight. I forced myself to relax. Now was not the time for *that* discussion. "Order? I thought that was a suggestion."

He laughed again, but it was humorless. "Of course you did."

"Put me down."

"No."

I ground my teeth, but I should've known better. Nathaniel carried me toward the meeting hall, waiting while Ryker opened the door. The wolf nodded at me, then gestured at a seat on the left side of the room.

Long tables had been set up, and Tobias presided over a group of humans who were bringing steaming platters of food out from a connected kitchen. My stomach rumbled, and Nathaniel laughed at me.

All eyes turned toward us, and I sighed. Being carried into the meeting hall like a wounded maiden was not the kind of impression I was going for.

I'd only been staying with the wolves for a few days, but I'd already seen how much they valued eating together. Still, I couldn't help but marvel at how quickly they'd put together this impromptu meal.

Chicken, pork, potatoes, salad, mac and cheese… My mouth watered, and Nathaniel sat me at a table, taking the seat next to me. His dominants filed in, taking the seats around us as the table filled with food.

The atmosphere turned almost celebratory. Kids fell asleep in their parents' arms, and someone broke out wine and beer. Trust the wolves to turn a death threat into a party.

"I want your ankle looked at," Nathaniel murmured in my ear as I shoved chicken into my mouth.

"It's fine, Mommy."

"Be careful." He sank his teeth into the side of my neck. Not enough to hurt, but enough to warn.

I held up my hand and showed him my new trick. Fire burned, and the wolves at our table sucked in a breath. I kept my gaze on Nathaniel, and his eyes flared with pride.

"And why exactly didn't you use that little power on the creature who wanted to eat you?"

"Well, first, I kind of froze a little. I figured I could shoot it. And then…I didn't want to hurt it, Nathaniel. Not until you guys showed up and it looked like it would attack you." I let my mind return to the forest, when it had stood in front of me, snarling at Nathaniel. That moment of recognition…

"We were right, and there are two creatures. The one that attacked tonight…it had white teeth. It sounds weird, but I could feel another creature approaching. I think *that's* the creature that's doing the slaughtering. Think about it. I'm powerful, sure. But those humans didn't have a chance when they were attacked. There were mages at the birthday party, and they couldn't do shit. I think if whatever is responsible for the massacres had found me, I'd be dead."

"You're choosing to forget one thing."

"What?"

"That creature you didn't want to kill? It killed the reporter in your parking lot. And they could very well be working together."

I couldn't explain it, but I knew it wouldn't kill me.

I took a bite of some salad. "I have a theory about what the second creature is. The one responsible for the massacres. I'm going to take that theory to Danica tomorrow."

A muscle ticked in Nathaniel's jaw. "You go nowhere alone."

The wolves went quiet around us. Then, conversation immediately picked up, as if they were attempting to give us privacy. But I was damn sure they could hear every word.

"Excuse me?" I kept my voice calm, level-headed. One of us had to be.

"You heard me."

I clenched my teeth until it felt like my jaw would crack. I couldn't even accuse him of *not* being calm. He was talking like he was commenting on the weather.

"This is not how you get what you want from me," I gritted out.

"Is that so? Why don't you tell me how I *do* get what I want from you, then?" Nathaniel purred. He shifted his hand from my chin to the back of my neck, and just like that, I wanted nothing more than to pull him into the nearest closet and have my way with him. He smiled at me.

"I'll be careful," I said finally. "But I'm not walking around with a guard. That's nonnegotiable, Nathaniel."

He watched me, his eyes hard. I watched him back as he obviously debated the wisdom of forcing the issue.

"*My* definition of careful," he said.

I didn't make any remarks about how his definition of careful likely involved me staying firmly within wolf territory.

"I've got this," I told him instead. "I promise."

He released me. "Fine."

I instantly craved the feel of his hands on me again, and I leaned back.

"You know Frederik had nothing to do with this, right?"

He gave me a dark look, obviously reliving his rage from when I'd walked in earlier. "Yes."

Some of the tension left my shoulders. This was why Selina had told me to go to Frederik today. So I could assure Nathaniel he had nothing to do with the beasts attacking people. I hadn't sensed any magic around him, no wards other than the basic warding around his home, which he would have paid a witch to create.

Nathaniel was watching me. "We need to talk."

Well, those words had never boded well for anyone in the history of relationships.

I angled my head, a ball of anxiety forming in my chest. He reached out and played with one of my curls, straightening it, and then watching it boing back into place.

"It'll be okay," he told me.

I concentrated on my food, shaking my head when a woman named Lily offered me a glass of wine.

Nathaniel squeezed my hand and then got to his feet, moving to another table so he could comfort his pack members. I watched as he wandered from table to table, answering questions, playing with the kids, and reassuring the human women of their safety.

Kyla slid into Nathaniel's empty chair and helped herself to the remains of his meal.

"Where were you?" I asked.

"I went wolf and went for a run. By the time I felt what was happening, I was miles away."

I nodded absently, still watching the Alpha as he threw Charlie into the air.

"Nathaniel's been smothering you, huh?" Kyla sounded exceedingly amused.

"He's been doing his Alpha thing. Someone needs to remind him that I'm not a member of his pack."

Kyla cleared her throat. "Alphas," she said after a strange, awkward moment. "What can you do?"

"Sorry. I know it must be weird for you to hear me whine about your Alpha."

She snorted. "Believe me, it's nice to have someone who gets it around here. Are you going to eat that?"

I handed her my plate. "You know, you could just go get your own."

"Waste not, want not."

The other dominants were finishing up. They nodded at us and did their own rounds, making sure everyone who was in the meeting hall felt secure.

I watched as Naomi said something to Hunter, giving him a wicked grin as he rolled his eyes.

"What's up with Naomi?" I asked.

Kyla raised one eyebrow. "What do you mean?"

I gave her a look. She knew what I meant.

Kyla smirked. "Oh, you mean how she's a human but also one of Nathaniel's dominants? Naomi's father was a dominant back in the day. He was killed in a skirmish near Nathaniel's territory when she was a baby. She grew up in the pack, and Nathaniel kept an eye on her. Eventually, she got in trouble for fighting with the other kids—and picking fights with the younger wolves.

"Then she started kicking the asses of the wolves who'd recently been turned. The way Nathaniel tells it, he figured if she was going to shoot off her mouth, he needed to teach her to shoot with a gun. When she petitioned to be a dominant, most wolves laughed at her. But she was willing to do the hard work."

"I thought a dominant wolf was based on some kind of built-in power level."

"Yes and no. Nathaniel's male dominants happen to be the most dominant, mostly because that's what is required of them to keep the pack in line when he's not around. Some other packs see it more as a position to be interviewed for." She shrugged. "This works for Nathaniel."

The Alpha wandered over, clearly listening to every word we said. He gave me a slow smile.

"Time for bed."

NATHANIEL

If my wolf could have purred, my chest would have rumbled with contentment. I'd somehow convinced Evie to lie with me, and I was currently wrapped around her on one of the sofas in the basement, a fluffy blanket pulled over both of us.

My wolves were giving us some space, and Evie's eyelids were heavy as she curled up like a kitten against me.

"Something happened to my eyes today," she mumbled. Her whole body tensed, as if she was waiting for me to lash out at her.

"What kind of something?" I kept my voice calm and played with one of her curls.

"I couldn't see properly, and I wished my eyes would cooperate. My vision…changed. I imagine it's close to what you see when you're in wolf form."

I went still but continued stroking her hair. "Now that's a handy power to have."

She took a deep breath. "You're not freaked out?"

"Why would I be? I want you safe. Any extra powers you have are a good thing, as far as I'm concerned."

She was quiet some more. I let her think it over.

When it didn't seem like she was going to speak again, I pressed a kiss to her forehead. "You already know some of your DNA is from different paranormal factions. Tonight, you learned that one of those factions is likely werewolf. It's not a big deal."

She snorted. "Not a big deal, huh?"

"Nope." I let my voice drop lower. "It's kind of a turn-on, to be honest. The idea that you've had a hint of wolf inside you this whole time, and it's only just come out now, on *my* territory..." I attempted not to sound too smug, but from the smirk on Evie's face, I wasn't succeeding.

"Your wolf is beautiful," she murmured, an obvious change of subject. I allowed it. Mostly because my wolf was preening, pleased that she found him attractive.

But I needed to make sure she was under no illusions as to how safe she—or anyone else—was if I ever lost control.

"If I ever turn, and you meet my wolf for real, you need to kill me, Evie."

"I could never kill you."

I tilted her chin up until our eyes met. "If it meant protecting everyone you loved, you could. If you ever look into my eyes and see nothing but wolf, you need to do the world a favor and put me down."

She didn't reply. If there was one thing this woman had in spades, it was stubbornness. Of course, she would likely say the same about me.

"How did you get hold of your wolf, Nathaniel?

When the portals opened."

I took a deep breath. Evie stroked her fingers across the side of my neck, and something in me loosened.

"You don't need to talk about it if you don't want to," she murmured.

No. I wanted to tell her. Wanted to share everything with her, and have her do the same with me. I wanted to own her past, her present, her future. I wanted no secrets between us. Ever.

"I grew up with a drunk for a mother and an abusive narcissist for a father. Neither of them should have ever been parents. I had a little sister…"

My voice trailed off as my heart cracked, even after all these years. "Her name was Emma. You would've liked her." I attempted a smile, playing with one of Evie's curls. "In fact, I can't even imagine the kind of trouble you would've gotten into together."

Of course, if she'd lived, Emma would be an old woman now. I would still be watching her die, but she could have married, had children, explored the world. She might've had a high-powered career or maybe moved out of the city for a slower kind of life. She could've done anything.

"Little sisters don't demand perfection, not even brilliance. They don't care if you're the strongest or the smartest or the funniest. All they want is love and protection. I loved Emma from the moment she was placed in my arms. It was the last part I failed."

"You don't need to talk about it if you don't want to," Evie whispered. I fisted my hand in her hair and tipped her head back. Her beautiful blue-green eyes had filled with tears. I pressed a kiss to her small nose.

"Emma was born when I was eleven. Mom hadn't known she was pregnant, and there were worries that Emma might've been impacted by all the alcohol. But she thrived. My father wanted nothing to do with her. He was convinced she wasn't his, and the way he would look at her... Even as a dumb kid, I knew I needed to keep her close.

"I was in charge of her from the time she was born. I heated her bottles, changed her diapers. She slept in my room. When she went to school, I'd get her ready each morning and pack her lunch. By that time, I was sixteen. I'd dropped out of school, and I had a crappy part-time job. I was saving for us to leave."

"You were an awesome big brother," Evie said.

I just shook my head. "After school, Emma would go to this kids' club thing run by the local church. I hated religion, thought it was all bullshit for people too stupid to think for themselves. But they looked after Emma every day so I could work. When I picked her up, the priest would tell me he'd given her a snack. He helped her with her homework. One day, he told me I was doing a good job. His name was Father Phillips."

Evie shifted until our faces were closer. "He sounds like an incredible man."

"He was. He never preached at us. He knew I

would've taken Emma and never returned. We were two kids just trying to survive our parents—God had proven he didn't give a shit about us. But Father Phillips cared. Not because his God had said he needed to, but because he was a human who cared, and he could see we were trying our best just to survive.

"I could've left when I was eighteen—I wanted to take Emma and move us out, but my father had said he'd report me for kidnapping. He didn't want Emma, but he charged me rent for our rooms each week. By the time I was twenty, Emma was the smartest kid in her class. She loved books and wanted to be a librarian when she grew up." I grinned. "Either a librarian or an astronaut."

Evie let out a wet laugh. She'd been stroking my cheek, gently giving me what little comfort she could, and I dropped another kiss to her nose.

"One weekend, I picked up an extra shift. Our father was out for the afternoon, and I figured Emma would be okay. Mom was nowhere to be seen, and Emma knew to stay away from him if he did come around."

I sat up. "You don't need to hear the rest."

Evie pushed me back down. "If you don't want to talk about it, you don't have to, Nathaniel. But don't think you need to protect me. From anything."

Yeah, Evie and Emma would've been fast friends, even with their age difference.

I took a deep breath. "I got home at the end of

my shift, and it was so quiet. I think I knew before I even walked inside. Emma was lying on the sofa. Her neck was broken. My father was sitting beside her, tears rolling down his face. He said he didn't mean to. He'd caught her searching through the cupboards for a snack, and he'd lost control." My voice broke, and I buried my head in my hands. "She was eleven years old, and she was hungry because I was late coming home. All she wanted was a snack. And that was the moment the portals opened."

"And you turned into a werewolf."

"Yes. I remember tearing out his throat. I'm pretty sure I ate parts of him. Then I rampaged through my neighborhood. I wasn't conscious of turning into a wolf. All I knew was rage. My vision had narrowed, and people weren't *people* to me anymore. They were nothing but prey."

"I'm so sorry, Nathaniel."

I shifted until Evie was lying closer, almost sprawled out on top of me. "Thank you. Everyone wants to know how I managed to regain control. I've never talked about it before now."

"You don't have to."

"I want to."

Even my wolf wanted her to know. I could feel him, paying careful attention to Evie's every move. To the smallest inflection in her tone when she spoke. He wanted to know if she would hate us like I hated myself. The *wolf* didn't hate himself. He was far too coolly logical for that. But he cared what Evie thought of us. We both did.

"I made my way to the church. I hadn't realized it at the time, but I'd shifted into a kind of half form. It usually takes years before a werewolf can master that form. I killed everyone in the church. And when I stood in front of Father Phillips, he told me he forgave me. I was confused. I thought maybe we'd been having some kind of discussion and I'd yelled at him. For a moment, I thought I was dreaming..."

My stomach sank. Nathaniel took a deep breath.

"Then his eyes went blank, and I looked down. My claws were shoved into his stomach. I turned, and all I could see was blood and death. Blood and death that *I'd* caused. I walked outside, and I could see other wolves doing the same thing. They were slaughtering everything that moved. Some part of me knew I needed to be in the same form, and then I suddenly *was*. And when I howled, the wolves listened. Little by little, they began to turn back into their human selves."

"And that's how you became the pack leader."

"Yes." He pressed a kiss to the tip of my nose. "Now get some sleep."

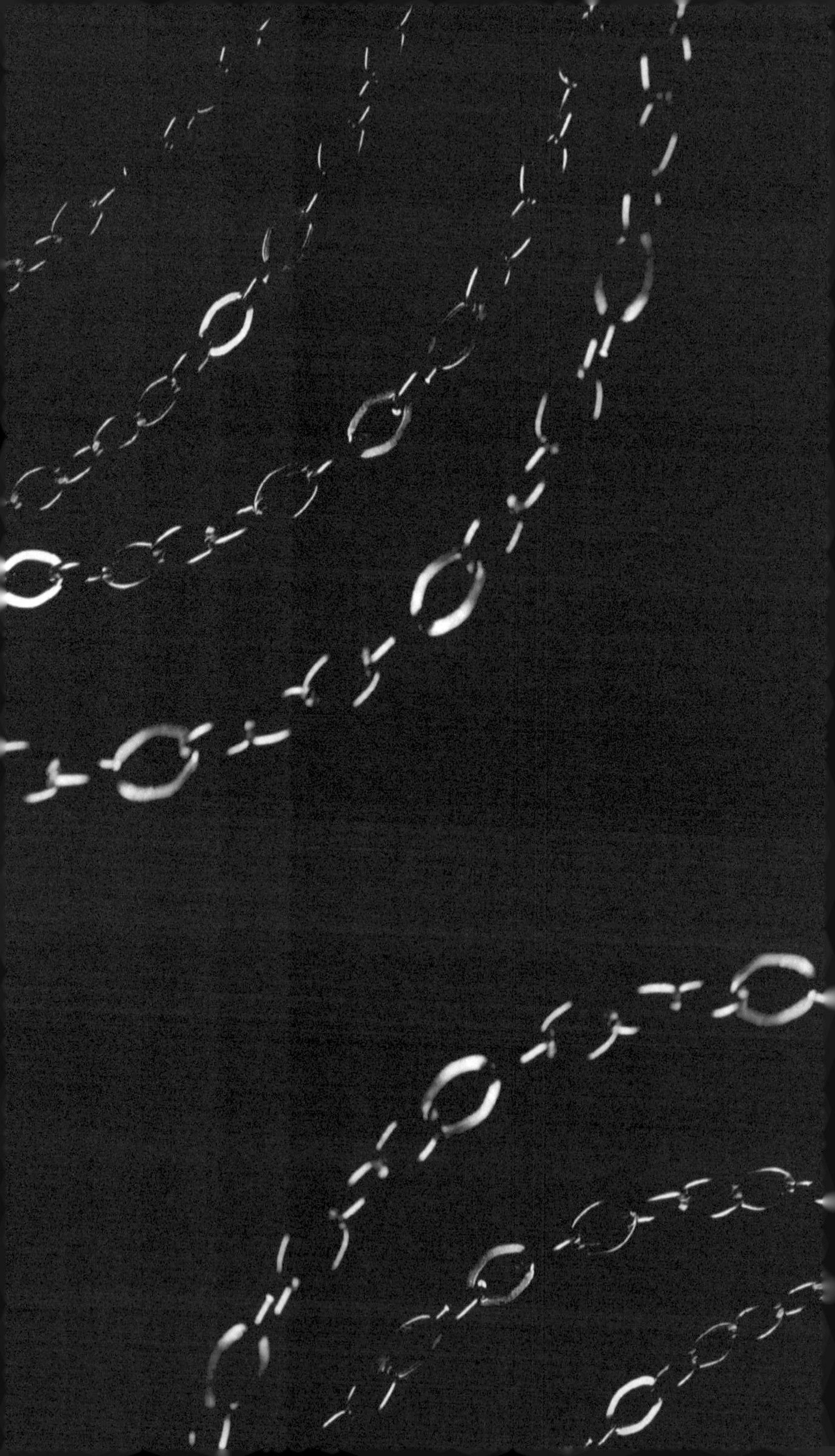

18

EVIE

The next morning, I woke to an empty bed. I stared up at the ceiling for a few moments, completely befuddled.

I'd fallen asleep in the basement on the sofa next to Nathaniel.

Okay, wrapped around Nathaniel. He must've carried me up here. And I felt more rested than I should have.

I fumbled for my phone and growled.

Ten a.m. Why the hell had I slept so long?

Pulling up my alarm app, I cursed up a storm. Nathaniel had turned off my fucking alarm, that's why.

I shouldn't even be surprised at this point. I hadn't gotten to sleep until three a.m.

Still, someone needed to teach the Alpha that he needed to *ask* before turning off people's alarms.

I hauled myself out of bed, pummeled myself

awake with Nathaniel's amazing water pressure, and pulled on jeans and a tank.

Tobias passed me on the landing as I beelined for the stairs.

"There's French toast and berries waiting downstairs."

My stomach grumbled, and he grinned at me. I shook my head. "Can't. Need to get to the underworld.

His grin disappeared. "Nathaniel said you should eat."

Enough was enough. I needed to calmly let these wolves know that, while I appreciated Nathaniel caring, I could make my own decisions.

"Nathaniel isn't the boss of me."

Tobias's mouth trembled, and I silently cursed. Nice one, Evie. Way to sound mature.

I turned and stalked down the stairs, ignoring Tobias's low chuckle. Since I had a weakness for French toast, which I was sure Nathaniel somehow *knew,* I grabbed a piece, smothered it in syrup, added some berries, and plopped it on a paper plate that had been left out for me.

The closest portal to the underworld was located in Southeast Raleigh, next to Lake Wheeler. I ate my French toast on the way and mused about the Alpha.

We need to talk.

I took a deep breath. That was never good. As soon as we killed the creature responsible for the massacres, I'd move back in to my own apartment. I'd have my freedom back.

The problem? I wanted to feel Nathaniel's mouth on me again. Wanted to finally know what he felt like inside me. And wanted to sleep with him wrapped around me every night.

This was *not* the time to think about how right it had felt to curl up in his arms.

When I finally reached the portal, I recognized one of the demons guarding it on my side. I grinned at him.

"Long time no see," Azazyel grinned back.

"Yeah. I've been busy doing hot-girl summer shit like investigating murders and fighting random, unknown creatures."

His grin widened. "You're overdue for one of Samael's dinners."

"Soon."

I stepped through the portal, ignoring the way it felt like my skin was going to burst into flames. A second later, I was in the underworld, smiling at Sitri—one of Samael's closest friends.

"Danica is in the garden," he told me.

"Thanks."

I took a moment to survey my sister's new home.

Lesser demons were perched on almost every turret, wings folded in. They reminded me of gargoyles.

I wandered inside the gate, where the garthia plant had kept so many witches busy during the battle for the underworld thrones. A lot had changed since I was here last. A path veered off from the gate, toward my sister's favorite garden, and I followed it slowly, meandering among plants and flowers I didn't recognize.

"Evie!"

Danica launched herself at me. She was in her usual queenly uniform of jeans and a T-shirt. The T-shirt had a pair of black wings on the back.

"Hey," I laughed when she finally loosened the iron grip she had on me. "It's good to see you, too."

"I wasn't sure if you'd make it."

I winced, and Dani elbowed me. "I'm not being salty, I just know you've been busy."

"Yeah. It's been a lot. That's actually what I wanted to talk to you about."

"Come sit over here in the shade. I was just having a drink."

She led me to one of her favorite nooks, where an outdoor sofa had been positioned in the shade, next to a low table. A high demon appeared with a tray of drinks, and I wasn't even surprised when he offered me my favorite juice.

"Thank you."

"So," Dani said, tucking her feet up beneath her. "We have half an hour or so before lunch. You can stay for lunch, right?"

I nodded. It would have to be a quick lunch, but I'd stay.

Danica grinned. "Awesome. Fill me in."

I told her everything. She paled when I described the massacres, and I handed her the huge black tooth, which she examined silently.

"I have a few thoughts," she said. "But I want to hear all the other details first."

"Nathaniel was sure it wasn't the wolves, even from the beginning. But he thinks his pack is being set up by his enemies."

Danica frowned. "Interesting."

I watched her, and she shrugged. "The Triangle was always a melting pot for paranormals. No one really knows why there are so many portals in the area, but with multiple factions competing for territory—and power—we were always poised on a knife's edge, one misunderstanding away from war. Now that Samael has left, it makes sense that those factions are planning to expand."

"But you guys have left plenty of demons in the tower."

"Yeah, but people will choose to believe the absence of Samael himself is an opportunity." She frowned. "Maybe we need to pay Durham a visit."

She glanced around, as if wondering about her next move, and I reached for her hand. "What's going on, Dani?"

My sister seemed…stressed.

"Nothing. Nothing really," she assured me. "We have rumblings of war in the south, and there was recently an attack on one of Samael's patrols to the east. Plenty of demons are still loyal to Lucifer—even though that bastard is dead."

"I'm sorry. I shouldn't have—"

"Don't, Evie. I always want you to come to me. No matter what." A flicker of what looked like sadness crossed her face, and I frowned at her.

"You're not telling me everything."

Surprisingly, she nodded. "There are some things I can't tell you right now. But…I want you to know that anything I've done—anything I've kept from you—has been because I truly believed it was necessary. Because I love you, and I have your best interests at heart."

A knot of anxiety formed in my stomach. "Dani…"

"It will be okay." She attempted a smile. "Now, let's get back to this tooth. What kills like a werewolf, with fangs three times the size, and can slaughter up to fifty people before disappearing without a trace?" Her gaze sharpened. "You think you know what it is. Why don't you trust yourself?"

"Because if I'm wrong, we'll be wasting time. If I'm right, we're in deep shit."

"Tell me what you're thinking. I'll give you my opinion."

I took a deep breath. "I think it's Fenrir."

Her gaze stayed steady, but I saw the flash of surprise. "Why?"

"I don't know." I got to my feet, turning to pace. "It makes no sense. All I have to go on is the fact that it kills similarly to a werewolf—if the werewolf wasn't hungry and was instead determined to create as much death and destruction as possible. When I saw that tooth—saw how much larger it was than Nathaniel's—all I could imagine was a wolf three or four times larger. And then I got to thinking…what if it is? What if Fenrir is in our realm?"

"First rule of investigating is to trust your instincts," Dani said. "If you have a feeling, you need to pay attention to it. If it's not Fenrir, it could be something similar. I really, really hope it's not Fenrir. I can't remember much about him, other than the fact that even the gods found him too dangerous to be allowed his freedom."

"I did some research." I took a deep breath as I turned, pacing toward the castle. I felt as if all my muscles were tight with dread. "It's bad, Dani. Real bad. Fenrir is a giant wolf. Son of Loki. From everything I read, he was the gods' loyal pet until they betrayed him." A tiny tendril of pity grew from my chest, and I killed it. If I was right, and Fenrir was responsible for the carnage I'd seen, for the families dealing with their grief right now, I couldn't afford to feel any pity.

"Evie?"

"Sorry. Anyway, he was raised by the gods but began to grow alarmingly large. Since he was prophesied to kill Odin, the gods decided to bind him. Each time, he broke the bonds, until Odin finally got his hands on a chain called Gleipnir. We know this chain is superpowerful, because it's made of six elements which are described as the sinews of a bear, the sound of a cat's footsteps, the breath of a fish, the roots of a mountain, the spittle of a bird, and a woman's beard."

"I'm assuming that chain worked? What, with the bird spit and all."

In spite of the situation, I couldn't help but smirk. Dani grinned back. Likely, what really had happened was six gods had combined their powers to form the chains.

"Yeah. They tricked Fenrir into allowing them to put the chain on him to see if he could break it like the others." I swallowed. "This is where it gets…bad. The more Fenrir struggled, the tighter Gleipnir became. The gods laughed at him as he howled, and then they shoved a sword through his jaw, pinning it shut to keep him quiet. His sons tried to free him, but Odin caught them."

"Sit, Evie. You're making me dizzy."

I plopped onto the sofa. "I looked into every description I could find of him, and I found a few sentences that mentioned 'teeth black as night.' I called Selina today. She said I should talk to the seelie, but she agreed with my theory. She also said that while many accounts state that both Odin and Fenrir are dead, they were written before the portals opened."

Since a coven of witches had woken a demigod more than seventy years ago, we knew there was much more out there than our grandparents had ever imagined. Whether Fenrir really was the son of Loki didn't matter as much as the fact that if he *had* been chained up for so long, he was likely batshit crazy by now.

"So, Fenrir might have really spent thousands of years chained to that rock," I continued. "But Selina also said there are theories that it wasn't the gods who made Gleipnir. Some say the seelie created it, and the gods stole it when they realized Fenrir was going to be a threat to them."

"You're thinking it was the seelie king who freed him."

I shrugged. "If the seelie created Gleipnir, they'd know how to free Fenrir. We all know Taraghlan likes to create chaos."

"Why kill humans? And why these contained attacks?"

"I don't know. It's still just a working theory."

"I think you're on the right track."

"Really?"

Danica gave me a long-suffering look. "You've done the legwork, Evie. You did everything right. And in this case, we need to hope for the best but prepare for the worst. Maybe it's some other creature and we'll be able to easily kill it. But if it really is Fenrir, we're going to need help." Her eyes turned cold. "And if the seelie king freed him, he's going to learn why he shouldn't have involved humans in our war."

A throat cleared behind us. A high demon stood at attention. "Lunch is ready, Your Majesty."

"Perfect."

Danica got to her feet and offered me her hand, hauling me off the sofa. "Someone has been packing on the muscle."

I grinned, but my mind was stuck on the implications of what I'd learned. I needed to talk to Nathaniel. I needed—

"Just put it away for a few hours, Evie."

I sighed. "You're right."

The high demon had melted away into the garden.

"So. When were you going to tell me about the reporter?" Danica asked, her voice exceedingly casual.

I should've known the demons watching me would've reported back to my sister.

"I didn't want you to worry."

She merely raised one eyebrow at me. I scowled. "I *was* planning to tell you. You know how I feel about lying."

My sister looked uncomfortable, but she nodded. "I know. So, you're staying with the wolves?"

"Temporarily."

"In one of the cabins?"

I blinked. It hadn't even occurred to me to question why I *wasn't* in one of the guest cabins. Why hadn't Nathaniel offered me one of those instead of a room in his house?

"Uh, no. I'm staying at Nathaniel's."

Dani's eyes lit up as we walked down the hall toward the large dining room she used for family dinners. Likely, several of Samael's closest friends would end up joining us.

"So, you and Nathaniel?"

I shrugged. I didn't know *what* was happening between us. I'd thought it would just be sex, but hearing him open up to me, learning more about who he was as a person… If I weren't careful, my heart would be making the kinds of decisions that my head should be making instead.

Dani opened her mouth—likely to question me further—but we stepped into the room, and her face lit up.

Samael stood next to one of the wide windows, a glass in his hand. He turned and gave Danica a wickedly sensual grin. I didn't fan my face, but I came close.

They stared at each other until I cleared my throat. Samael rearranged his expression until it was carefully neutral and then gave me a polite smile.

"Evie."

I'd once seen him with his wings out, sparks dripping from them as he ordered his demons into action. I'd been mesmerized—and more than a little terrified. Now, I knew I was one of the only people safe from Samael. He'd never harm a hair on my head since that would upset Danica. And everything he did, every single action he took, was always with the intention of keeping her happy.

"Samael."

"Drink?"

I shook my head. As much as I'd love a boozy brunch, I needed to get back to work as soon as we'd eaten. Demons filed in, their hair almost glowing beneath the warm light of the chandeliers above us. I greeted Bael, Asmodeus, and Sathanas, giving Bael a dark look as he poured himself a drink. I knew damn well he was the one who was keeping Danica and Samael updated on my every move before I could talk to them myself.

"Where's Vas?" I asked Sitri as he wandered in.

"Busy with his witch. She has a private function at her bar this afternoon, and Vassago stayed to help." He frowned, likely confused by the thought. The demons were so powerful, so wealthy, Vas could have hired the best bartenders and managers in the country to lighten the load for Mere. But he knew she would hate that. Knew she wanted to grow her business on her own terms. So he stayed and helped her whenever he could.

Samael flicked a throwing knife in his hand. I glanced at Danica. "What's with the knife?" I murmured as everyone took their seats.

A blush. It wasn't often that my sister blushed, and I stared. "I threw it at him. A long time ago. He kept it."

"Aw. A symbol of your affection and intent to murder. Adorable."

She gave me squinty eyes. "It got stuck in his calf. Jeez."

We sat. Danica insisted I sit next to her. She also insisted on serving herself, waving the servants away.

It was good to see becoming queen of the underworld hadn't changed her.

She offered me a plate of green beans, and I took it. The ring on her finger glinted at me, and I chewed on my lower lip as I passed the plate to Bael. When placed in a person's mouth, Angelica's ring could turn them invisible, along with anyone they touched. I needed to convince Danica to let Kyla and me borrow it for Operation Steal-a-Sword. The problem? The moment Danica knew we were going after the sword, she would want to be involved.

And if we were caught, it would be a political nightmare. The seelie king would have a hostage he could use to make Samael do anything he liked.

How would I get that ring off my sister's finger without alerting her to our plans?

"Evie?"

"Sorry." I took the roast beef and passed it down the table.

"What else has been going on?" she asked.

I forced myself to quit staring at the ring. Danica wasn't stupid, and I needed to come up with a game plan before I asked her for it.

I filled her in about the kids, because it was something a little lighter. She burst out laughing when I told her how they were managing to hide from Nathaniel.

"I bet he loves that."

"It's kind of cute. He could make them all fall in

line with a single word, but he's giving them a long leash."

"Cute, huh." She winked at me. "And how's Kyla's case going?"

I told her about the artifacts, about Callula, Wimbar, and everyone else involved. Her expression darkened.

"Where do you think Wimbar is?"

"He'll want to get rid of the artifacts as fast as possible. Some of them, he had buyers lined up for. The others, he'll need to negotiate before word spreads that the unseelie king is looking for him."

"I have a contact who may be able to help." Danica reached into her pocket and pulled out a pen. I handed her a receipt from my purse.

"This guy helped me with a case right before I met Samael," she said. The demon leaned close, all of his attention suddenly on our conversation. Danica gave him a look, and he simply smiled.

"I find myself *very* interested in any men you dealt with before you met me, little witch."

I rolled my eyes. Across the table, Lilith made a gagging sound. I knew I liked her.

"He's unseelie, but for whatever reason, he prefers the seelie realm. It can't have made him many friends, as most people would consider him a spy for Finvarra. But he lives close to the portal in the seelie realm."

I could do that. I'd stop by on my way back to Nathaniel's. Kyla wouldn't be pleased that I'd gone without her, but she had enough on her plate right now. Besides, *this* time, I'd stay away from that fucking forest.

"You don't think the king will have guards on the portal?"

Danica smiled. "Of course he will. But they're not going to attempt to take you in. They will, however, be watching you closely. Talk to the guy and get out."

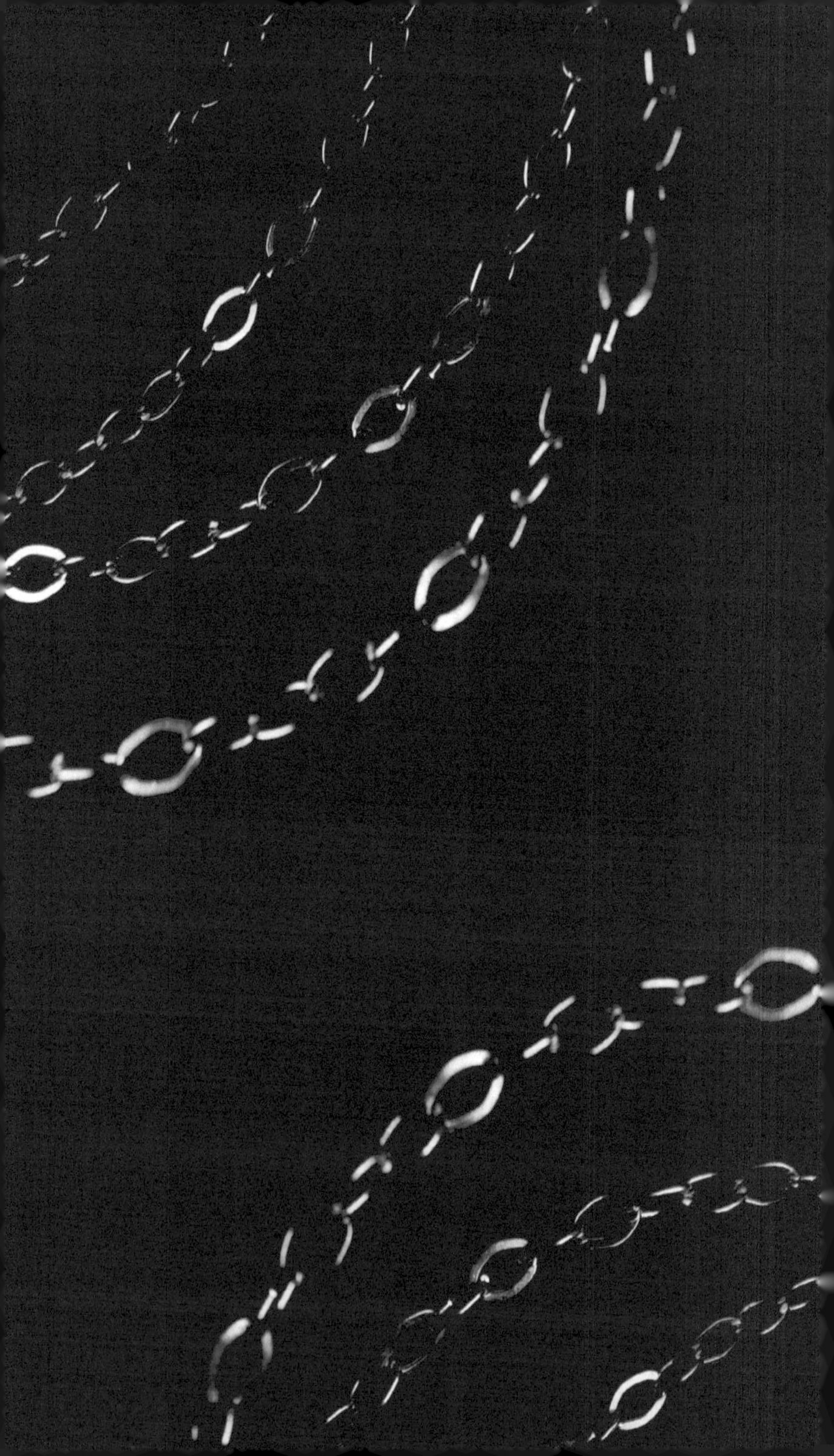

19

EVIE

Chewed over what Danica had said as I made my way to Aubrey's. I was meeting Kyla there since the light fae had somehow arranged for his contacts to slip out from beneath their king's nose. But we wouldn't have long.

I pulled up outside Aubrey's. Kyla was still on her way, so I leaned against my car, pondering exactly how I was going to convince Danica to hand over her ring. Maybe I could persuade one of the demons to steal it. I just needed to get my hands on some blackmail material.

"Yo."

Jolting, I scowled. I hadn't even noticed Kyla pulling up behind me. She gave me a long look. "That kind of shit is how you get dead."

"Yeah, yeah."

Her gaze stayed steady, and I rolled my eyes. "My

power would've let me know if you were a threat."

"Why were you so deep in thought?"

I filled her in, and she sighed. "Stealing it won't work. Those demons are way too loyal to Danica. And even if they weren't, Samael would kill anyone who stole from her, even if it's with good intentions. No, we're going to have to convince her to hand it over."

"And how do you suggest we do that?"

"Let me think on it."

"If you two are finished with this scintillating conversation, perhaps we could get to work?"

My gaze met Aubrey's, and I hunched my shoulders. He just raised an eyebrow and turned, strolling back into his house. We followed him inside.

Two seelie were sitting on the sofa in Aubrey's living room.

"Evie and Kyla, this is Tilella and Entaris."

Both of the seelie surveyed us as we walked in. We did the same back. Entaris had cut his hair shorter than most seelie. It was almost a buzz cut. He gave us a businesslike nod. Tilella was small, delicate-looking, but something about the hard set of her jaw warned me that she was far more dangerous than she looked.

We both took our seats. One of Aubrey's maids wheeled in a cart that held coffee, tea, and various cakes. I was too nervous to eat, but I would for sure be taking whatever that chocolate thing was to go.

"Tell us why we should help you," Entaris said.

I glanced at Aubrey uncertainly. I'd thought these

guys knew the deal.

Entaris shook his head. "I want to hear it from you."

I told them everything. Including the prophecy from Selina. "So it's not like we're just stealing the sword so Finvarra can use it to kill your king. We're directly preventing the worlds from burning."

Kyla nodded. "I'm not saying we're heroes, but I'm not, *not* saying it, if you know what I mean."

The corner of Tilella's mouth twitched.

"We want to be clear." Entaris took a sip of his coffee and then placed it on the table. "Helping you will be treason. If our king finds out, our lives are forfeit."

My heart pounded harder at the thought. "I understand. And we wouldn't even ask if we had a better way. All we can say is that we'll never let anyone know you were the ones to help us."

Tilella cleared her throat delicately. "We are both concerned. Not just about this prophecy you say you heard, but by the recent actions of our king. Attacking the unseelie king without provocation would mean war. Even if Finvarra were to die, the unseelie would fight in his name. I believe it is best if our king does not have access to the sword. If, as you have promised, Finvarra will not have access to it either."

"We give you our word," I said. Kyla nodded.

And Tilella told us how to get in.

"Any disruption in power levels will draw the attention of all kinds of creatures," Entaris warned when Tilella was done. "You need to be incredibly careful when using magic. Only use it when you absolutely have to. And be prepared to deal with the consequences."

My stomach clenched at the thought. "Does that apply to magical items we bring with us?"

He glanced at Tilella, who shook her head. "It shouldn't, but I would still have a care," she said. "Most of the lower level is unguarded by the seelie themselves, as the wards and spells put in place have lasted for centuries. The creatures the seelie king has at his beck and call are much, much worse than any of his guards."

Cool.

"One more thing," Entaris said. He held out a metal key. "This has the ability to get through any door."

"Entaris," Tilella said softly, fear sparking in her eyes.

"You're one of the only people with a key like this, aren't you?" Kyla asked. "If we use it, Taraghlan will have a much smaller pool of suspects."

"I am hoping my record will speak for itself," Entaris said stiffly. "There are others closer to the king, whom he already suspects of treason. He will look there first. If it becomes likely that he will discover us, we will flee to this realm."

They were ready to lose their home to help us. All their friends would turn on them, and their king would likely send his assassins, even here.

I opened my mouth to refuse it, but he leaned forward and pressed the key into my hand. "I have seen what happens when a king's lust for power outweighs his care for his subjects. Taraghlan needs to be stopped before thousands of my people die in his wars."

"We won't use it unless we absolutely have to."

By the time we were finished talking to Tilella and Entaris, my head was reeling. Aubrey had stayed inside to talk to his friends, but Kyla and I had said our goodbyes, wandering outside.

"Am I the only one freaking out about this?" Kyla asked.

I took a bite of the chocolate tart I'd taken with me. "No. I'm worried we're going to fuck up and Entaris and Tilella will end up dead." We were both quiet as we thought about that. "At least we know we can get in. That's the hardest part. Without the sword, he'll no longer be a threat to Finvarra. Hopefully, he'll be so focused on getting it back, he won't get close to learning who helped us out."

Kyla nodded. "We'll deal with the traps once we're in there." She glanced at her phone. "I need to get going."

"Where are you off to?"

"I meant to tell you. I got a lead on our good friend Wim. I'm heading to Atlanta."

"Atlanta? What would he be doing there?"

"Negotiating with buyers for a few of the other

stolen items," she said grimly.

"Be careful, Kyla. We don't know how powerful he is."

"I know. I just want to see if he's there. If he is, I'll notify Finvarra."

I smirked. She said *Finvarra* like the very word was poison.

I got back into the car I was borrowing and started the engine, flicking on the air conditioner. I was going to need to arrange a replacement for my own car just as soon as I had the time. For now, I was heading to the seelie realm to talk to Danica's contact.

My phone buzzed, and I glanced at it. Rose.

Research has paid off. I've got a few different options for HFE's headquarters. Call me when you get a chance.

Surprise flashed through me, but I messaged her back.

I've been searching for months. How'd you find these options?

My pulse increased as I waited for her to reply.

I have someone who owes me a favor. We'll talk about it on the phone.

I felt like a wolf who'd just gotten the scent of a hunt. I'd have to make sure Eachann met Rose. I didn't want to get my hopes up, but at this point, I felt like I couldn't help it.

I headed toward the seelie portal, my chest feeling lighter than it had in days.

That light feeling disappeared the moment I turned

onto the street holding the portal in Hillsborough.

Wolf kids. Scattering.

Son of a bitch.

I threw open my door and stood, forming a ward surrounding all of the kids. Nothing could touch them, but they weren't going anywhere either. One of the youngest touched it, a look of wonder on her face.

"Rainbow," she said.

The kids realized they were locked into the bubble of my ward. I stood and waited until they eventually wandered close.

"What are you guys doing near the portal? You know it's dangerous."

The kids were stubbornly silent. Charlie opened his mouth, and his brother shot him a furious look. I raised my eyebrow at Levi, who stuck out his chin.

Charlie was the weak link here. We all knew it.

"You guys weren't going to try to travel through the portal, were you?" My heart tripped in my chest at the thought.

Levi rolled his eyes at me. "Of course not. We're not suicidal."

You had to have power to travel through the portals. Some werewolves could, but much of their power was tied to their dominance. Kyla was dominant enough to make the trip, but powerless humans who attempted to travel from our realm to another were always killed.

"Then what were you doing? There are dangerous

people traveling between realms. You know that."

Charlie's lower lip trembled, and Levi sent him another warning look. But that look also held resignation. He knew it was only a matter of time before Charlie spilled.

Levi heaved a sigh. "A few weeks ago, some of the kids were at Central Park."

I raised one eyebrow. "That's outside wolf territory."

He shrugged. "We're allowed. Well, not right now, since Nathaniel put us in lockdown." His bitter tone told me exactly what he thought about that. "My friend Sam drove us in, and we dropped the younger kids off. We were going to meet some friends for ice cream, and then we'd pick up the kids on our way back. They like to play on the playground."

And wolves didn't believe in helicoptering.

"Okay. So, what happened?"

"One of the local kids had been bullying Charlie. He hadn't told me. He was at Central Park that day."

Charlie's eyes filled with tears, and he hung his head.

I wrapped an arm around him. "I'm sorry."

He sniffed. "My mom said we're not allowed to fight. But Colton said I was a f-freak. He said wolves are disgusting and dangerous. I pushed him, and he told his big brother." Charlie shivered. "Kayden is *mean*. So I ran away. I play with dad in the forest, and I'm fast."

Levi nodded. "When we went to pick the kids up, Charlie wasn't there. We split up and started looking for him, but we had to get the little kids back. I stayed, and Sam drove back to our territory. I wasn't worried at first. Dad would've come if I told him, and he could track Charlie anywhere. But I thought he'd be close by."

"Where did you go, Charlie?"

"I ran for a long time. And then I hid behind a big building. I was tired, and I could hear Colton and Kayden yelling at me. I crawled under a car and covered my ears."

Poor kid must have been terrified. I was going to have a word with this Colton. *And* his brother.

"Then what happened?" I prodded gently.

"Some people came out of the building and told them to leave. They were *scary*. I think they were paranormals. Colton and Kayden ran away, but I knew they would be waiting for me. So I stayed hiding when the sun went down."

"Dad was away on pack business," Levi told me. "I got a group together, and we went out looking for Charlie. I didn't want the adults to know unless we had to tell them."

Because he was supposed to look after his little brother. I opened my mouth to tell him how badly this could have gone if Charlie had been kidnapped, but from the self-loathing in Levi's eyes, he already knew.

"You must've been scared," I said to Charlie instead.

He nodded. "Yeah, but I stayed put. A patient wolf is a smart wolf. I'm a smart wolf."

I laughed at that. "Okay, so then what happened?"

"There were lots of people in the building. They came in and out, and they used bad words. Then a truck came. It pulled up right next to where I was hiding. Some people ran out of the building. They were putting things in the back of the truck. But they had a fight. They used magic, and they were k-killing each other."

Shit.

"One of them dropped a book," Charlie said. "It was so pretty and shiny. I just wanted to see."

I closed my eyes as bile crawled up my throat. When I opened them, Levi was running his hand through his hair, devastation written all over his face.

If the thieves had seen Charlie, he'd be dead. They wouldn't have looked at him and seen a tie to the wolves. They would've seen a small human boy who was in the wrong place at the wrong time.

"They were coming closer," Charlie said. His little face turned pale, his freckles standing out in stark contrast. "I held on to the book really tight and wished I was invisible."

He flashed a sudden grin at me. "And it worked!"

I stared at him. And just like that, it all made sense.

"So I stayed quiet like a mouse, and they picked up the other things they had dropped. Then they left. I waited for a long time, but I was tired and I missed my mom. I held on to the book and walked back toward the park. And then I found Levi."

"Except I couldn't see him," Levi told me. "I could hear him, though. He dropped the book, and I realized he'd found something with magic. We're half werewolf. We don't shift, but we still have werewolf blood. That means magic doesn't always work on us. But the book does."

I sighed. "The book you found belongs to the unseelie king."

Charlie's mouth dropped open. Even Levi looked perturbed by that, but then he firmed his jaw. "Finders keepers."

I gave him the look that deserved. "That's not how the world works. You're old enough to know that. Finvarra hired Kyla and me to find that book."

"So now you're going to take it from us," Levi said bitterly. "We shouldn't have told you."

Taking a deep breath, I reached for patience. "What do you think would happen between your Alpha and the unseelie king if he learned one of Nathaniel's pack members had his family heirloom?"

Levi gave a bad-tempered shrug, but I had a feeling I was getting through to him.

"You don't know what it's like," he said suddenly. "Our dads are wolves, our moms are humans. We don't fit in with the humans, but unless we're changed, we won't be wolves."

I raised one eyebrow. "No," I said dryly. "I have no

idea what that would be like."

Levi's mouth trembled with the hint of a smile, and he shook his head at me. "Fine. You win that one. All the adults say you smell strange, like different kinds of magic."

I winced. Did Nathaniel think I smelled strange too?

Levi must've realized he'd put his foot in it, because he backtracked. "Not strange like bad. Just different."

I cut him a break and changed the subject. "Sometimes fitting in isn't all it's cracked up to be. When I was a member of my coven, I thought I fit in. But a lot of those other members were lying to me."

Charlie's eyes went wide. "How come?"

"They were trying to keep me safe. But by lying to me, they made it so I didn't know I could protect myself. Now, I may not fit in anywhere, but I'm myself. Sometimes when you fit in, it just means you ignore serious problems because you don't want to risk being alone."

Levi chewed on that, and I surveyed the group of kids. "Why exactly were you so close to the seelie portal?"

One of the older girls took a step closer and cleared her throat. I'd met her before, and I was pretty sure her name was Phoebe.

"The book sometimes loses its power. Not entirely, but when we want to go invisible, it'll only do it for a few of us. But if we take it close to a portal, it recharges."

I thought about that. "It's a fae artifact. I'm guessing there's not enough of the power it needs in our realm. Can I take a look?"

Levi showed it to me, and I took a deep breath. The cover shone silver, as if it had been melted and poured over the book itself. And the book? It *seethed* with power. No wonder Finvarra wanted it back. For a moment, I felt bad for taking it away from the kids. Then I got a hold of myself. Not only was an artifact this powerful incredibly dangerous, but if anyone found out the kids had it, they'd be targeted. Besides, these kids could get into more than enough trouble without invisibility.

"You guys need to give it to me," I said.

A strange look came over Levi's face, and he thrust the book behind him. He reached out his other hand and shoved me.

I hadn't expected it. I fell into Charlie and twisted, attempting to catch him. But I was too late. He hit the ground with a thump, and we all heard the snap as his arm broke.

Levi looked down at his hands as if he didn't recognize them, the blood draining from his face.

Phoebe pushed Levi back. "What the hell are you doing? That's your brother!"

Levi stared at Charlie, who had devolved into sobs. I crouched next to him, taking a good look at his arm. It was bent at a bad angle. The kid needed a healer.

Levi swayed on his feet. He looked as if someone had reached into his guts and ripped them out. Something was definitely wrong. I stood, but Levi had already turned and sprinted away. With the book.

Shit.

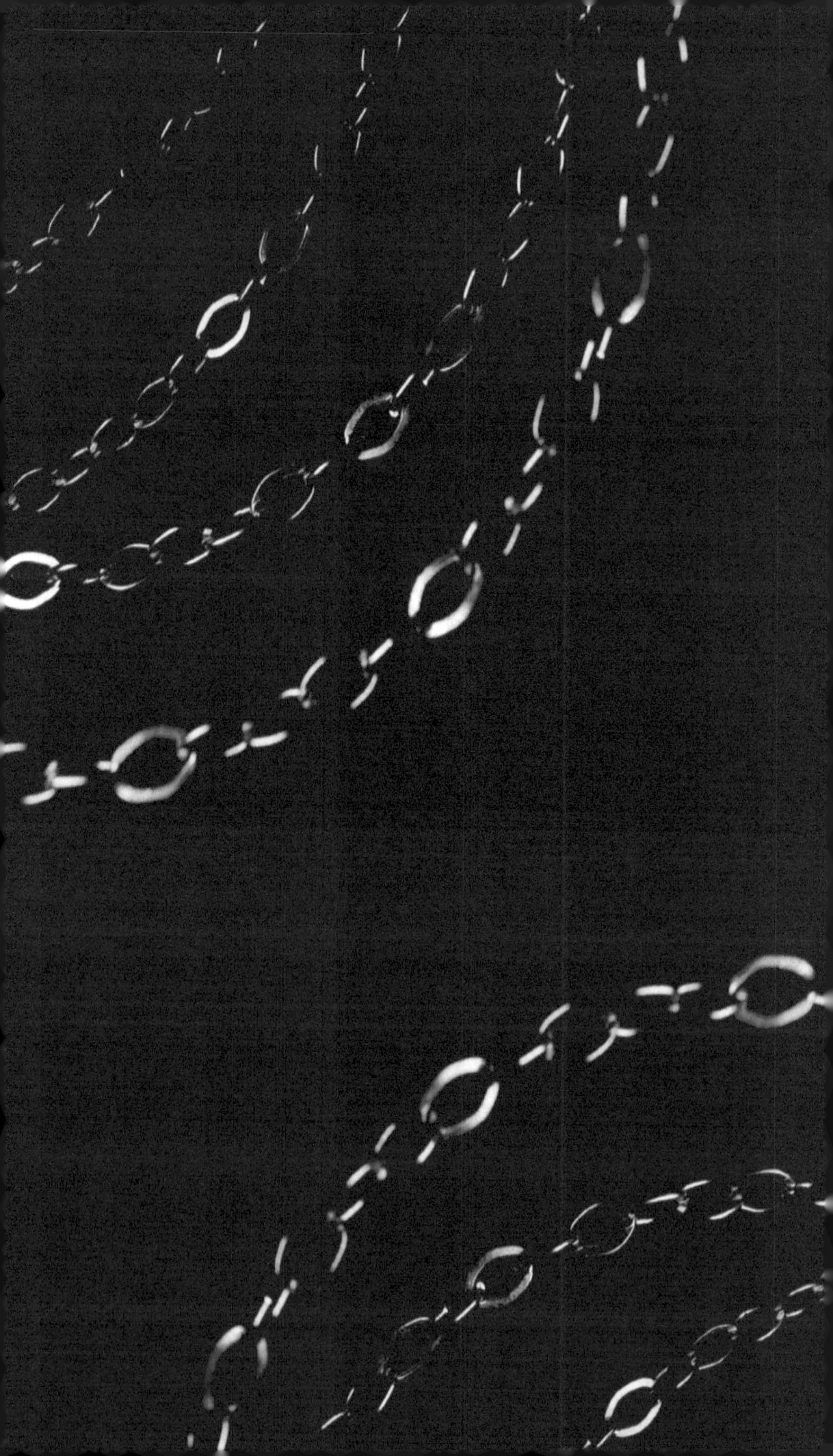

20

EVIE

I couldn't go after Levi until I knew Charlie was okay. The poor little guy was sobbing, asking me to get his mom.

"I'm going to take you to her right now." I raised my voice. "Okay, kids. Time to go home."

Loading Charlie into the car, I was careful to jostle his arm as little as possible. Each pained yelp and fresh flood of tears made me flinch. Three of the youngest kids came with me, and one of Phoebe's friends gave me a nod. "We'll take the rest of the kids home."

"Thank you. What's your name?"

"Erin."

"Straight home, Erin. No stops."

She nodded again. "I promise."

I drove slowly over any bumps. I couldn't imagine how much the jostling hurt Charlie's arm. Part of me wanted to take him to the emergency room, but they'd put him in a cast. Maybe even put him under if he needed surgery. A good healer could take care of the break today. Charlie would be tender for a few days, and then it would be as if he'd never broken his arm at all.

I called Nathaniel.

"Charlie has a broken arm," I said, putting him on speaker as I drove. "Do you have a healer there?"

"Our healer is away with some of our scouts."

"Shit." I slowed the car. "I'll take him to the emergency room." A sudden thought occurred to me. "Wait. Let me call you back."

I hung up on the Alpha, something that wouldn't please him. I could practically hear his growl of annoyance.

I called Aubrey.

"I need another favor."

"Of course."

I explained what had happened. "Samael took Eldan with him to the underworld. You know what he's like."

Aubrey laughed. "Yes, well, he *would* steal one of our best healers just in case his mate happened to bruise her toe or break a fingernail."

I smiled at that, slowing the car to gently go over another bump. "Do you know any other healers who could help?"

"It just so happens that I do," he said. "She can be in wolf territory within twenty minutes."

"You're amazing."

"I truly am." He cleared his throat. "Have you seen Selina lately?"

"Go visit her, Aubrey. She'd enjoy a visit from you." I'd definitely picked up on those vibes.

"Perhaps. My healer's name is Neana. Tell Nathaniel she's on her way, so the wolves don't eat her when she approaches their territory."

"You got it."

I hung up, called Nathaniel to relay the message, and then focused on navigating toward wolf territory. Charlie sniffled, and I took his unbroken hand with my own, giving it a squeeze.

"You're being very brave. The healer will get you all fixed up, I promise."

"Why was Levi so mean?"

"I don't know, buddy. But I'm going to find out."

Charlie's parents were already waiting when I pulled up outside Nathaniel's house. His mom opened the passenger door and pressed a kiss to his forehead, before moving out of the way so his dad could carefully lift him into his arms.

"Thank you," his mom told me when I got out of the car. "I'm Sarah, by the way. I'm not sure if we've been introduced."

We hadn't. Because she'd been terrified of me when she'd seen me using my magic in the playground.

"Evie," I said. "Did Nathaniel tell you a healer is on the way?"

She nodded. "Thank you for that. Where's Levi?"

"Truthfully, I don't know. He was devastated that he'd hurt Charlie. I'm not sure what got into him."

"He's been acting strangely, not listening to us for weeks."

"Do you know where he would've gone?"

"No." Grief tightened the corners of her eyes. "But he loves his little brother."

"I know. I've seen it. I'll ask some of the other kids if they know where he would've gone." Erin or Phoebe would be my best bet.

"Thank you."

A strong arm wrapped around my shoulders. Nathaniel dropped a kiss to my nose, and I attempted to control the heat that wanted to rise in my cheeks at the possessive gesture in front of so many of his wolves. Of course, after the way I'd let him carry me around the other night, that horse had already bolted.

I gestured for Nathaniel to follow me, and then I raised a silence ward. He arched one eyebrow, and I took a deep breath.

"I know how the kids have been disappearing. They have an unseelie artifact. A book."

"Excuse me?" Nathaniel looked truly stunned for the first time since I'd met him.

"Finvarra's missing family heirloom. They've been turning invisible just by touching it and making a wish."

The Alpha looked a little sick. "How exactly did

they end up with it?"

I explained, and his face went cold. "Human kids were chasing Charlie."

"Yeah."

"Most werewolf parents leave that kind of stuff for their kids to figure out. But if Charlie was terrified enough to run and hide, they need to step in."

"Nope," I said. "I'm going to have a little talk with the bullies."

Nathaniel gave me a long look. Then he smiled. "Something tells me you'll scare them more than a werewolf would."

"Damn right."

"I need to talk to Charlie's parents." Nathaniel pressed another kiss to my forehead, and I attempted to ignore what that did to my heart.

He stalked over to where Charlie's dad was holding him in his arms. They all disappeared into the forest, likely to wait for the healer in Charlie's house.

I jumped straight back into the car Nathaniel had loaned me. The area had cleared of werewolves, and the healer would look after Charlie. Levi would want to know his little brother was okay.

I called Kyla as I headed back out of wolf territory.

"I've found the book."

"What?"

I filled her in. She cursed. "It was right under my nose the whole time? In my own pack?" Her voice dripped with disgust.

"Yep. How's the search for Wim going?"

"He's here. I'm waiting for Finvarra's people to show up. They're going to catch him red-handed."

"Excellent. Be careful."

"You should be careful too."

I sighed. "I will."

"Where do you think Levi is?

"I caught the kids attempting to recharge the artifact near the seelie portal. Levi won't risk going back, but he's going to want to use the book. There are demons guarding the portal to the underworld, and they'd alert me if they saw a wolf kid hanging around. So I'm heading to the unseelie portal."

"Look after him, Evie. He's just a kid."

"I know. Don't worry. I've got this."

The unseelie portal was in Duke Gardens. Usually, the portal was surrounded by a twelve-foot fence, which prevented humans visiting the gardens from doing anything stupid.

Unfortunately, that fence had disappeared. I had a sinking suspicion that was thanks to the book in Levi's hands. If I knew one thing about fae artifacts, it was that they sometimes had a mind of their own. And if it had wanted to suck up power from the portal, it may have removed the fence itself.

Either that, or one of the unseelie had decided the fence was annoying them. And in that case, we were going to have words.

Levi was pacing back and forth in front of the

portal when I slowly approached him. His eyes went wide, and that was when I knew for sure that the book had him in some kind of thrall. Levi wasn't stupid. He had to have known I'd follow him here.

I could only hope that whatever effect the book had had on his personality, on his brain, it would disappear just as soon as he handed the book over.

"Go away!" he yelled, backing toward the portal.

I froze.

"Levi. Get away from the portal. You touch it, and you're dead."

His eyes were wild, but he glanced over his shoulder, taking in just how close he was to the portal.

"You can't have it," he said.

"Levi, listen to me. The book is from Finvarra's court. It's an unseelie artifact, and it's messing with your mind. Do you understand?"

His lower lip trembled, and for a moment, he looked years younger than he was. "I hurt Charlie." He stumbled back a step, and my breath froze in my lungs.

I kept my voice low, steady. "Charlie's fine, Levi."

"I broke his arm!"

"A healer has already fixed it."

"My parents will be so mad."

"They understand what's going on. They know it's not you. They know it's the book."

"The book?"

"It's a fae object," I said again, slowly and clearly. "It's messing with your mind."

Levi looked down at the book in his hands. Realization flickered in his eyes, and he held it out to me.

I inched closer to the teenager.

The air began to fill with a fog so thick, I could barely see. A chilling howl cut through the gardens.

And Fenrir melted out of the fog.

NATHANIEL

I would owe Aubrey a favor. Not only was his healer skilled, but she was gentle and patient, joking with Charlie and making him relax before she healed him.

Now, he was being doted on by his mom, while Gareth, his dad, paced back and forth, his wolf close to the surface.

My own wolf was antsy, urging me to *run*. I ignored it. Now was not the time.

"I don't understand," Gareth told me. "Levi's a good kid."

"He is. They found a seelie artifact, Gareth. That's why he's been acting out of character."

"My God." His face drained of color. "I need to go find my son."

"We'll go together. We'll find him, I promise."

My phone buzzed, and I pulled it out as we strode out the door. My heart stuttered as I read the message from Kyla.

Evie went after Levi. She's headed for the unseelie portal. Thought you should know, just in case something happens.

Of course she did. I should have known.

My wolf was furious, raging at me. He'd tried to tell me.

I ripped off my clothes and shifted. Next to me, Gareth did the same.

And then I ran.

I was distantly aware of Hunter and Xander falling into step with us, but all I could focus on was Evie and Levi.

It hadn't occurred to me to order Evie not to go alone. Even if I had, it was unlikely she would have chosen to listen.

Because she wasn't pack.

Because I still hadn't told her she was my mate.

This was *my* fault.

I left my other wolves behind me as I picked up the pace, leaving wolf territory. I didn't need Levi's scent. My wolf knew where to find Evie. And it was almost feral with desperation to get to her.

Virtus appeared on my left. I hadn't scented him behind me, but I wasn't at all surprised that he was ready to help.

My wolf urged me to run faster. Our bond may

be incomplete, but he could feel Evie, and he *knew* she was in grave danger. Which meant one of my pack members—little more than a pup himself—was in the same danger.

My wolf also knew we were going to be too late.

EVIE

"Oh fuck," Levi said.

Oh fuck, was right.

Fenrir was so large, he made the werewolves look like puppies. There were two holes in his jaw—where the sword had been planted. His fur was matted and bloody. He opened his mouth, displaying sharp, black teeth. One of his front teeth was missing.

I'd been right. If I lived through this, maybe I'd celebrate.

But that wasn't exactly looking likely.

Fenrir took a single step toward us, his body language making it clear that he had all day.

My mouth went dry. I needed to distract Fenrir long enough for Levi to use the book and go for help.

I focused, creating a ward a few feet from Fenrir, so we had room to move. There. That should give us some time—

He stepped through it, breaking my ward as if

it had never been there, and the resulting feedback knifed through me, dropping me to my knees.

I aimed my telekinesis at him, and he snarled, taking another step closer.

Fenrir was the son of gods. My power had no impact on him. I'd known it, but seeing it so blatantly was chilling.

I was dead. But Levi didn't have to be.

"Levi. I need you to use the book. When I distract him, you're going to turn invisible and run like hell."

He was shaking his head, and I turned my scariest scowl on him. He swallowed. "I'm not leaving you."

"You'll do what I say. Go for help. Get to Nate. Tell him…tell him…" There were so many things to tell him, and they all flashed through my brain at the same time. Why hadn't I said a single one of those things to him when I'd had the chance?

"Come with me, Evie. The book will work on you too."

"I can't, kid." I had to distract the giant wolf. "I'll go through the portal to the unseelie realm. It'll follow me there."

And if I lived, Finvarra would kill me for bringing it to his front door.

That little problem was for future Evie to deal with. I took a few steps away from Levi, giving myself space to fight. "I need you to listen to me. Get out of here."

"No."

"You're a distraction, Levi. I can't fight it if I'm trying to protect you, too. Now promise me you'll run."

He stared at me. "I-I promise. I'll get help for you, Evie." Sorrow coated his words. We both knew help would arrive too late.

I took another step forward. Fenrir showed me his teeth. Yeah, yeah, very sharp, very deadly. I refused to go to my death trembling. I rolled my shoulders and pulled my Beretta.

I longed for my Desert Eagle .50 caliber. I'd give a large piece of my soul for an Uzi. Or a shotgun. Hell, a grenade would be ideal at this point.

I had fifteen rounds. Time to distract the crazed wolf.

I took a deep breath and aimed. Slowly loosening my breath, I fired.

The first bullet hit Fenrir's flank. He snarled at me.

I fired again. The bullet went through his head. My chest lightened. I felt movement to my right. Levi. The book had enough power that he'd become invisible. Good.

Fenrir let out a blood-chilling howl. But it wasn't an "I'm dying" howl. It was an "I'm going to make you hurt" kind of howl.

The hole in his head closed up. My heart took up residence in my throat, my entire body seized, and every instinct urged me to *run.*

How had Fenrir healed that so fast, when he was still dripping blood from the sword that had been pushed through his jaw?

Gritting my teeth, I fired again. And again. I had one more magazine, but there was little point. All I was doing was pissing him off. Which was fine in the short-term, when I needed Levi to haul ass away from here. But it wasn't a good way to increase my chances of survival.

Fenrir's red eyes turned away from me, and panic exploded in my chest. I launched myself toward the wolf, but it was too late.

He lashed out with one paw, and Levi turned visible as he flew through the air.

He hit the ground and rolled, landing a few feet from me. I darted forward, standing in front of him.

"Are you okay?"

No sound. I risked one quick glance over my shoulder. Levi was conscious, eyes wide, mouth open as he let out a low groan. Winded. Winded was okay. Fenrir could have taken him out with that swipe of a paw. He was playing with us.

If Levi couldn't sneak past Fenrir, we needed a Plan B.

I didn't even have a Plan A.

"Where's the book?" I asked, keeping my eyes on Fenrir. The wolf wasn't attacking right now. I had a feeling it was *amused* by us. Unlike the other groups of humans it had slaughtered, it could take its time here.

This portal saw a steady amount of traffic every day. Why was it, when I needed *anyone* to walk through and provide the tiniest distraction, everyone seemed to be taking a nap?

"I still have it. Either it's not recharged from the portal, or that *thing* did something to it."

That wouldn't surprise me. Fenrir seemed to neutralize power. And he *ate* my bullets. I pulled my A-F.

"Get ready," I said. Levi got to his feet behind me.

I took one moment to mourn all the things I wouldn't get to say to the people I loved. But they knew I loved them. It was enough.

"Don't do it, Evie."

"You *promised*, Levi."

Fenrir trotted closer. He was less than fifteen feet away at this point. He wasn't giving me much room to work, with the portal six feet behind us. I just needed to make sure Levi was safe, and then I could dive through the portal. Surely Finvarra could help with the magic-eating wolf, right?

A rough growl trickled out of the fog. I went still. Fenrir tilted his head and turned as the beast appeared, his teeth bared.

I peered through the fog, taking in its tangled brown fur and rage-filled yellow eyes. It was the same creature that had attacked me in Nathaniel's territory.

My knees turned to jelly. I couldn't protect Levi from both of them.

The beast roared its challenge at Fenrir. It clearly wanted in on this afternoon snack as well.

Fenrir snarled and turned to face the beast, lips peeled back from his thick black teeth. This was the best chance we were going to get.

I wasn't sure how much the beasts could understand, so I couldn't risk communicating the plan to Levi. To be fair, it wasn't much of a plan.

"One, two, three." I lunged to the left. Levi shot to the right.

I hacked at Fenrir's leg, hoping to slow him down. He spun on me, and the other beast snapped at his leg.

Fenrir roared, slashing out at the beast. His thick claws dug into brown fur, ripped through skin. Blood sprayed.

I attempted to dart past Fenrir, but he wasn't paying attention to me. He'd turned once more. And Levi was in his sights.

No. Fenrir was looking at the book. And from the way his red eyes flared, he'd decided he'd quite like the fae artifact. Something told me it would make him indestructible.

The other beast stumbled in front of Levi. Fenrir growled at it, but it wasn't trying to eat him...

Our eyes met, and there was another moment of recognition. The beast didn't want to hurt Levi. It was trying to protect him. It wanted to protect me too, even as its lifeblood poured from the gaping wound in its side.

Fenrir snapped at the beast. It jolted back, but its coat was wet with blood, the pavement beneath it becoming a pool of red.

"Throw me the book," I screamed.

If Fenrir wanted the book, I'd be bait. Hopefully then, Levi could get the hell out of here.

Levi whirled, held up the book, and I saw the moment the book's hold on him won. He shook his head and backpedaled closer to the portal.

"Levi!"

Fenrir charged.

No. No. No.

I launched past the beast and threw myself at Levi. A scream ripped from my throat as I thrust every drop of my power around him.

We both fell through the portal.

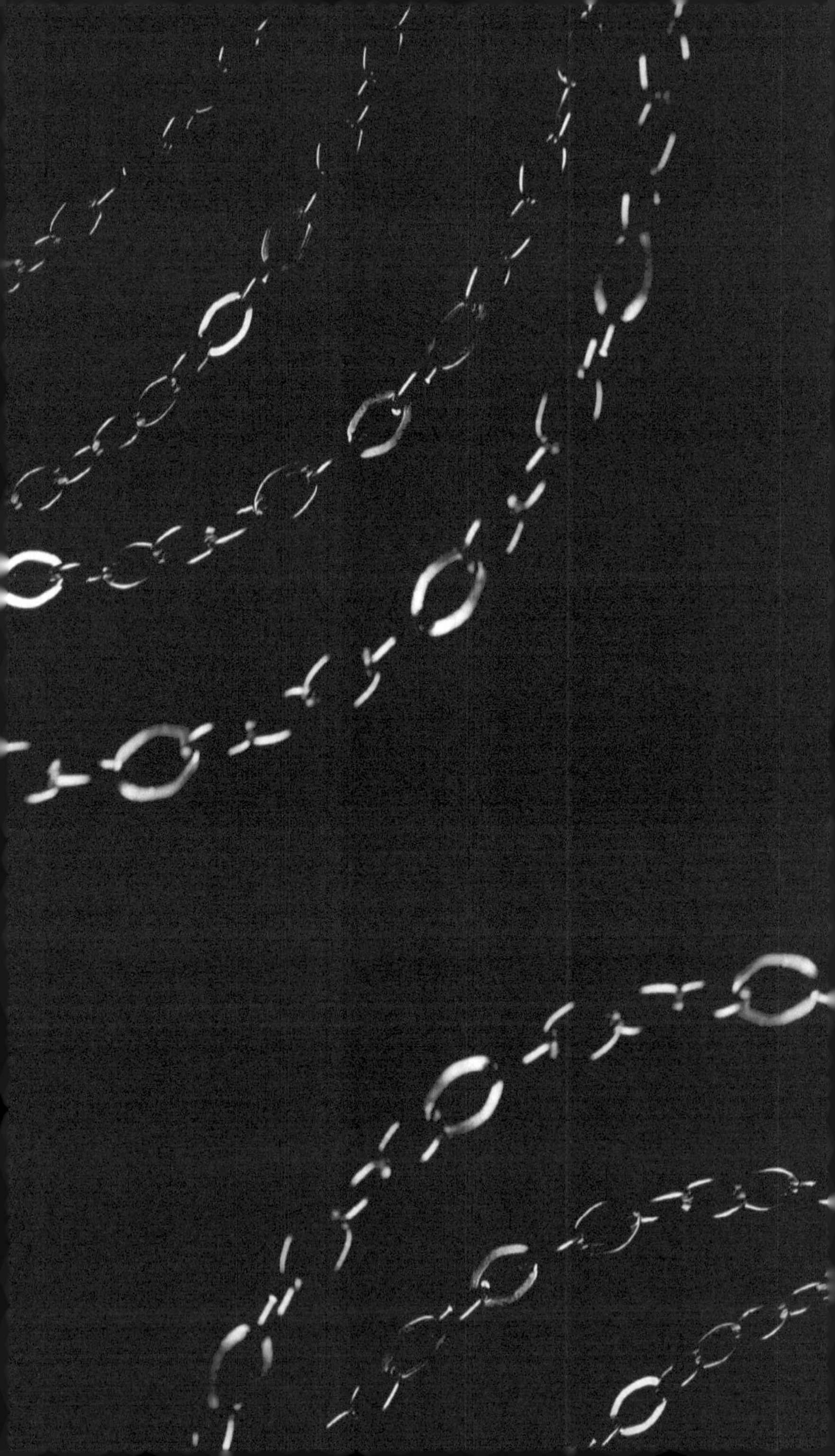

21

EVIE

Light teased at my eyelids.

"Evie."

My head pounded so badly, all I could do was let out a weak groan. I raised my hand to my temples.

My other hand brushed decadently soft blankets. My eyes shot open.

Nathaniel sat in a chair next to me. He let out a long breath and reached over, brushing my hair off my face.

"You scared the shit out of me."

"Where am I?" I croaked.

Nathaniel grabbed another pillow and helped me sit up, handing me a glass of water. Our eyes met and held. I didn't quite know what to do with the relief that poured off him in waves.

"Finvarra's castle."

If I was in the unseelie realm…

"Levi." I choked. My throat burned as my vision blurred. I was supposed to protect him, and I'd gotten him killed.

"Evie. Evie, stop. He's okay."

My breath hitched. Nathaniel got out of his seat and sat on the edge of the bed, wrapping his arm around me. I gave in to the urge and buried my head against his chest. "I don't understand."

"You protected him with your power," a voice said, and I shifted. Nathaniel tensed, and I could sense his wolf, unhappy with the way Finvarra had appeared in what was now considered his territory—however temporarily.

Finvarra merely smiled, then turned his attention back to me. He was watching me in a way that gave me goose bumps.

I glanced down at the sound of something tearing. Nathaniel's claws had extended, and he'd cut through the comforter around me.

"My apologies," he gritted out.

Finvarra shrugged.

"I don't understand," I said.

"Tell me what happened when you went through the portal."

Nathaniel slowly got to his feet. "You don't give her orders, fae."

Finvarra angled his head.

I swung my legs over the side of the bed, ready to jump to my feet if it looked like they were going to fight.

Unfortunately, my legs were bare. Someone had stripped my jeans off me.

Nathaniel's snarl ripped through the room. Finvarra rolled his eyes, but he kept his gaze on my face.

"We will speak of this when you feel up to it." *And when you're dressed,* was the subtext.

I nodded, and he turned, stalking out of the room. I glanced at Nathaniel, raising one eyebrow. He just paced to the window. Obviously, we weren't going to talk about it.

Fine.

"I can't feel my power," I admitted. "Any of it." My voice was very small. As much as I tried to push that power down, hiding it away...not being able to feel it waiting for me to unravel... It scared the crap out of me.

"Finvarra's healer said you burned yourself out."

"Will it...will it come back?"

Nathaniel turned, and I gazed into the eyes of his wolf. I dropped my eyes. I wasn't really up to a power struggle, and being in his enemy's territory was clearly making it difficult for him to stay in control.

"The healer said it will. You wrapped every drop of the power you could access around Levi. You saved his life, Evie."

Relief made my shoulders shake. Before I knew it, tears were rolling down my cheeks. I buried my face in my hands.

"Hey." Warm fingers wrapped around my own, and Nathaniel was suddenly there, pressing kisses to my tears.

"I thought he was dead. I really thought he was dead."

Nathaniel smiled. "You never would've let that happen."

"Who found us?"

"One of Finvarra's guards watched you both come through and land in this realm. Levi was screaming for help. You were unconscious." A muscle ticked in Nathaniel's cheek, and I raised my hand, automatically stroking him.

"Where did Fenrir go?"

"We don't know. We had no reports of any other massacres. He disappeared."

"And...the other beast?"

"Dead."

I'd thought so. There was no way it could've survived that gaping wound in its side. I knew it was out of control. It had killed a woman in my parking lot, after all. And yet a small part of me mourned it. "It was protecting us. It could've hurt Levi while he was close to the portal, but it didn't."

"Maybe it was saving him for later."

I'd thought the same at first, but... "No. I can't explain how I know, but it was on our side. I need to know what it was. Who took the body?"

"We did. It's in our morgue."

The wolves were pretty much self-sufficient. They could be cut off from the Triangle and not lose any sleep.

I sighed and swung my legs out of bed. My jeans were hanging over the back of a chair near the window, and Nathaniel threw them to me.

"There's something else," he said, turning to give me privacy while I pulled on my jeans.

I braced myself because, from his tone, whatever he had to tell me wasn't good.

I zipped up my jeans. "What is it?"

"We found this on you. It was on your arm."

Nathaniel turned back to me and held out a small silver coin. I frowned. "On my arm?"

He nodded. "As if it had been stuck there. It only became visible once you were in this realm."

"What is it?"

"I was hoping you could tell me."

I examined the coin. It radiated a dark power. A kind of power I'd never felt before. A sun was etched onto one side. On the other was a wolf.

I attempted to untangle the messy knot of my thoughts.

"I've never seen this before." How long had it been on my arm? *How* had it been stuck to my arm? And why hadn't I felt it? Not to mention, who could've gotten close enough to plant it on me without my noticing?

I went still. Nathaniel stalked closer. "You know who it was," he said dangerously.

I clamped my mouth shut. He just shook his head at me. "You won't keep this from me, Evie. Even if they hadn't come after you, they targeted my pack."

"I know. Just let me make sure I'm right about this."

He stared at me, and I sighed. "I promise I'll tell you just as soon as I figure it out."

"Fine." He didn't look happy about it.

Well, there was a lot *I* wasn't happy about right now, so he could join the party.

"I need to talk to Finvarra," I said. Nathaniel stiffened, and I gave him a dark look. "This overprotective shit is cute and all, but it stops here."

He let out a bitter laugh. "You believe I can control my reaction to learning you were in mortal danger?"

"You're an Alpha wolf. You can control your reaction to anything."

He leaned down and nipped the lobe of my ear. "That's where you're wrong, Evie Amana." His warm breath caressed the sensitive spot beneath my ear, and I shivered, barely restraining myself from rolling him beneath me.

He cursed suddenly, pulling away. "You're like smoke. The more I try to hold on to you, the faster you disappear."

I stared at him. I had a feeling Nathaniel and I needed to have a little talk about boundaries. But not while we were in Finvarra's territory and Nathaniel's wolf was already pissed.

"Go talk to him," he said finally. "We'll have our own conversation later."

NATHANIEL

Hunter and Xander filed into the room after Evie left. I'd left Ryker and Naomi in charge, but my wolf was itching to get back. To take Evie and surround her with my people in our territory.

"How is she?" Hunter asked.

"She'll be fine. Give me an update."

Xander took the empty chair next to the bed.

"We analyzed the blood from the creature that attacked our territory." His eyes lightened at the thought, and I watched him until he'd regained control. "They're working on the autopsy now, but we figured you'd need to see the preliminary results."

From the steady gaze he leveled on me, I wasn't going to like it.

"Give them to me."

He reached into his pocket and unfolded a few pieces of paper, smoothing them out before handing them to me.

I stared down at the report, struggling to accept the results. Finally, I lifted my head.

"No one speaks to Evie about this until I talk to her myself."

My dominants both nodded. I slipped the report into my own pocket with a low curse.

I took a deep breath. My wolf wasn't happy about waiting for Evie, but it understood that we couldn't be trusted around Finvarra at the moment. But knowing she was burned out, *vulnerable* in his presence...

"Nathaniel."

I let out a low growl. "Distract me. Update me with any pack business."

They complied. My wolf calmed when it learned of a new trade deal we'd set up with Harry. We had a large human company interested in one of our security packages. And two members of Frederik's pack were hoping to relocate.

"They're probably spies," Xander said. "We can't trust them."

"If I bond them to the pack, they won't be able to be disloyal," I reminded him. "Why would they want to join our pack?"

"He's not exactly stable right now. Rumor has it he has no problem with abusing his wolves. Even his submissives."

My own wolf wanted to howl at that.

"There's one more thing," Hunter said. Xander gave him a warning look, and I narrowed my eyes at him.

"I'm in control," I said.

Hunter took a deep breath. "Our spies say Frederik is *reluctantly entranced* by Evie."

I let out a bitter laugh. I knew just how that felt.

"And?"

"He's not planning to move on us any time soon, but he's been talking to the press. He knows we're not responsible for the massacres, but he's definitely implying that, if he were in charge of this territory, the attacks never would've happened."

I just shook my head at that. "Take pictures of the beast that was killed by the portal. Let them leak to the press. It's about time the humans in this territory accepted that there are creatures scarier than werewolves."

EVIE

Finvarra was waiting for me in his library. I hated the unseelie bastard, but even I had to admit he had good taste in libraries.

He waited for me on a chair that looked more like a throne. To his right, a fire burned. And in front of that fire, Virtus lay completely at home in the unseelie realm. I sighed. The griffin didn't discriminate when it came to paranormal factions. He seemed to love everyone. I slid the unseelie king a suspicious look as I took in the griffin's fur. It was ruffled along his head, as if someone had recently been petting him.

Finvarra ignored my smirk. A leather, hardcover book sat open in his lap, and he'd closed it as I arrived. He didn't even mark his spot. Bet he could find it again without even trying.

On the table next to him sat the silver book, looking far too harmless, considering all the trouble it had caused.

"How," Finvarra asked, "did my book end up in wolf hands?"

Since he wasn't offering me a seat, I turned and dragged one from the closest collection of chairs near the fire. I could've sworn I saw a trace of amusement in his weird gold eyes, but it was quickly banked as I planted my butt.

Even that amount of effort had exhausted me.

"Just a minute."

I lowered my head between my knees. A cold sweat had broken out on the back of my neck. It was a good thing Nathaniel wasn't here to see this shit. He'd probably throw me over his shoulder and haul me back to his territory.

When I finally managed to raise my head without puking, an unseelie was standing next to me. I jolted.

"You sure are quiet, huh?"

He held out a glass. Finvarra gestured for me to take it.

"What is it?"

"The healer instructed you to drink it upon waking. Unfortunately, your Alpha was too uncivilized to allow me to relay that message."

I gave him squinty eyes, but I took the glass. It tasted like flat Sprite, and I immediately felt a little better.

Finvarra's servant melted away.

"Obviously, you know Callula and Wimbar colluded to steal it. But one of the wolf kids found your book as it was being stolen. You could say it fell off the back of a truck." Close enough, anyway.

His eyes narrowed. "Explain."

His constant orders were pissing me off. I thought about being a smartass, but I didn't have the energy.

I filled him in. I'd been studying the unseelie king's microexpressions, and he was just as surprised as the Alpha.

Then he sat back in his chair, stretching his legs out in front of him. "How do I know Nathaniel didn't take it?"

I rolled my eyes. Thankfully, Kyla wasn't here to listen to this crap.

"Nathaniel doesn't want your fae artifacts. He has enough other things going on."

A ghost of a smile flickered across his face, and I stared. It wasn't often that I saw the dark fae king truly amused.

"Yes," he mused. "If his pack children are running around stealing fae artifacts and turning themselves invisible, it's obvious that he has more than enough to keep his hands full."

"They didn't steal it," I gritted out. "Charlie found it."

He waved that away.

I managed to keep my voice steady through

sheer willpower alone. "Want to tell me why Charlie's brother, who is otherwise known as a protective, loving brother, would have slowly turned into the kind of kid who breaks his brother's arm in order to hold on to the book?"

Finvarra raised one eyebrow. "It's an ancient fae artifact. Would you truly assume using it would have no consequences?"

"Explain."

His expression turned feral at my order. I took a deep breath. "These are kids, Finvarra."

He watched me. Eventually, he let it go. "There is a reason that book was hidden in an estate I rarely visit. It was given to one of my ancestors by the seelie." His full mouth thinned. "Just one of the many ways they have wronged our people over the centuries. The book *helps* its owner in many ways. The least impressive being the short-term invisibility it offers. My ancestor soon found that his council began to argue with him less often. His commanders no longer brought their own opinions to meetings. He slowly began to crave more and more power, until he was so paranoid, he was removing some of his lords from their own lands and returning them to his crown."

I swallowed. "What happened?"

"An unseelie ruler has ultimate power, but his rule was called into question by those who were temporarily outside of his kingdom. They could tell something had changed. Some people thought perhaps he had become mad. Others thought maybe someone close to the king was poisoning his mind.

"His son had been away, studying elsewhere, and was unaffected by the book. He returned, and when he saw the state of the realm, he killed his father. With the king's death, the son began his rule, and when he found the book, he took it to a seelie friend, who told him what it was."

Nerves fluttered in my belly. The book had influenced an unseelie king until his own son killed him. What would it do to a teenager?

"Will Levi be okay?"

Finvarra nodded. "If someone had taken the book from my ancestor and hidden it away, his son would not have needed to kill him. As soon as the book is not in one's vicinity, they will return to their usual self." He watched me out of those strange eyes.

"I'm guessing Wim didn't know about the side effects of owning the book."

"Some would assume the side effects are worth it for the power it can lend them."

"I want to talk to him."

"Why?"

"Because those humans may not have been the only ones he killed. Because there are other artifacts he stole. Because he killed Callula."

I'd assumed he'd taken his cousin's death with his usual calm indifference. But at the mention of her name, Finvarra's gold eyes blazed. I sucked in a breath.

It wasn't often that he showcased anything other than relaxed amusement or cold fury. This? This was fierce, protective wrath. He'd cared about his cousin. Her betraying him had hurt him. But Wim had killed her, so Finvarra was going to make him pay.

"I have already given the wolf permission to question Wimbar. She will likely fill you in as soon as she sees you."

Interesting that he refused to even speak Kyla's name. I gave him a knowing look, which he ignored.

"You have completed your side of the bargain and have returned my book. I will have the money owed transferred to your account."

"Thank you. Uh, how will Levi get back?"

"I can help with that."

"How? Humans can't travel between portals."

"Yes, as you've so recently proven, they can. Come now, surely you've heard the stories about how my dastardly ancestors liked to steal beautiful mortal women?"

I swallowed. "Of course. But they never returned them."

His teeth flashed in a feral smile. "That doesn't mean they *couldn't*. You did it yourself to save the human child's life. Although you burned yourself out in the process."

"That's how you do it? You...wrap someone in your power?"

An elegant shrug. "More or less. If you enjoy your

freedom, you won't allow anyone to learn that you can do such a thing. There are plenty of humans who would give anything to move to a paranormal realm—no matter how dangerous it would ultimately be for them to be powerless and at our mercy."

I shivered at the thought. I'd met more than enough dangerous humans who would use me as a mule if they could.

I'd keep it to myself. "Uh, there's something else."

Finvarra raised one eyebrow, waving one hand languidly in a "go on" gesture.

"I need your help."

His eyes sharpened. I'd managed to surprise him.

"For what?"

I filled him in. He considered it for a few moments while I surveyed his library.

"You will need to return the portal to me."

"Believe me, I don't want to hang on to it. Uh, just out of curiosity, what will you do with it?"

He flashed his teeth in a wicked smile. "My dear cousin will experience every moment of the pain and suffering he forced upon Callula. Then I'll destroy it."

I blinked at him. Half of me was cheering because— yay, vengeance. The other half was continually surprised at just how brutal paranormals could be. I supposed, after living for so long, you saw so much death and destruction, you eventually became numb to it.

"Okay, good plan," I said, because he was still watching me. "Nice doing business with you."

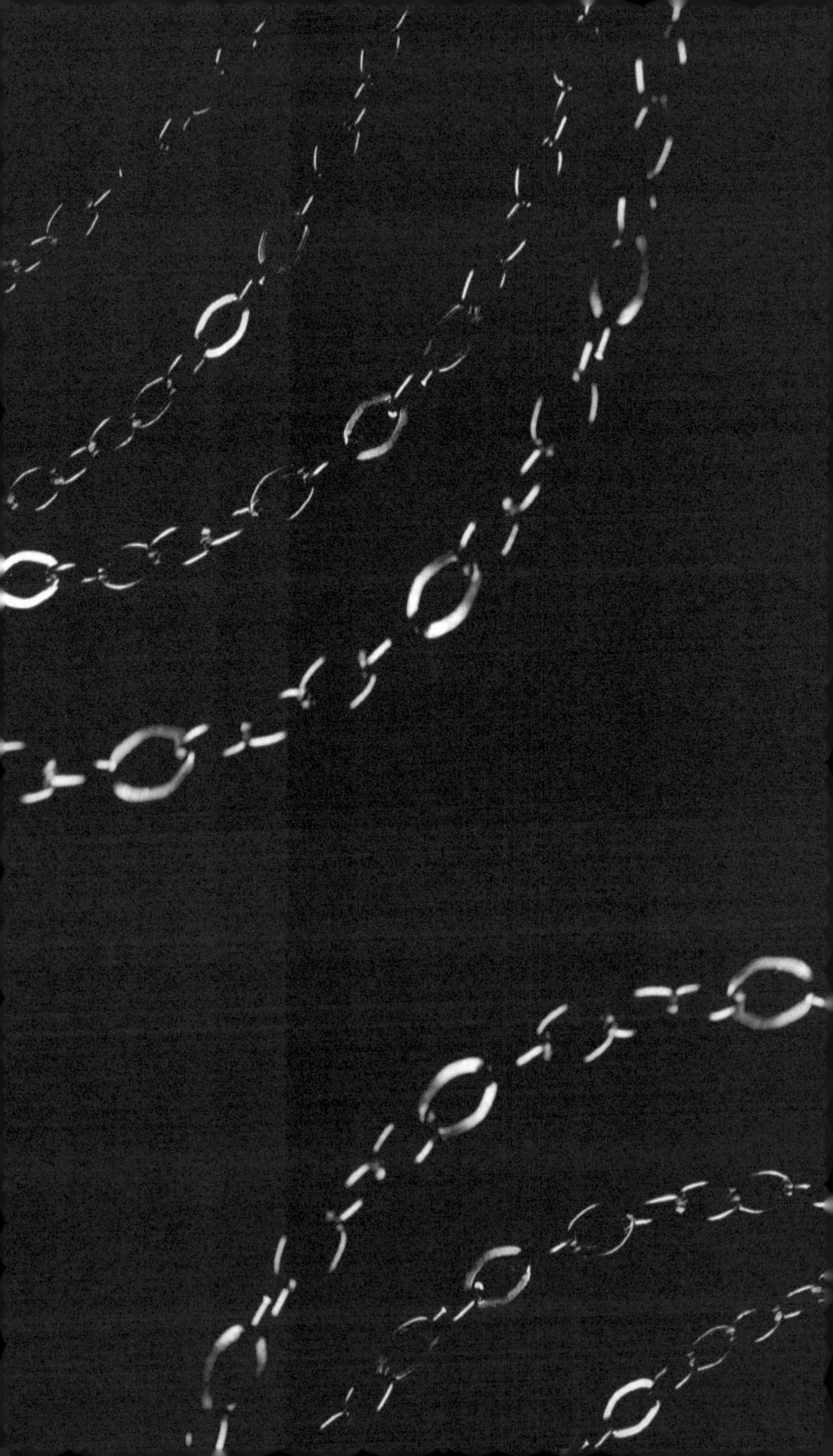

EVIE

One of Finvarra's guards escorted me back to the bedroom I'd woken up in.

"Thank you." I opened the door, finding Hunter and Xander deep in discussion with their Alpha. Xander gave me a searching look that made me slightly queasy, but they both nodded at me, getting to their feet.

"We'll leave as soon as Kyla is finished," Nathaniel said. "Make sure our people are ready."

They both left. I watched Nathaniel. "What's wrong? Other than the fact that you're in Finvarra's territory?"

"We analyzed the blood found at the scene."

I must have looked confused because he clarified. "From the creature Fenrir killed." He hesitated. "I need to ask you for something."

"What?"

"I'd like some of your blood."

"Why?" My voice was little more than a whisper.

"You know why."

"You think that beast was created in the lab. Like me."

He nodded, running his hands up and down my arms, as if he was attempting to ward off a chill.

I pictured the beast. There was no denying the connection between us, nor the wrath that had burned in its eyes.

"You think I'm…related to it."

"Related is a strong word. But it had power it shouldn't have had. Threads of different kinds of power. Like you."

If I hadn't already thought I was a freak, that would've done it. I took a large step away from Nathaniel and sucked in a breath.

He gazed at me steadily. "Don't pull away from me."

I didn't reply. He just shook his head. "We still need to have that talk when this is all over."

My pulse picked up speed, and I knew he could tell. Did he want to tell me he was tired of me? Maybe he was realizing just how much of a freak I truly was.

In that case, I'd be the first to leave. I was *done* with being abandoned.

"Evie? It'll be okay."

I opened my mouth.

"Are you guys in here?" Kyla's voice called.

She would've known we were in here, and she definitely would've known she was saving me from an awkward moment. Friendship.

"Back here," I said, my eyes still on Nathaniel. His own eyes had lightened in a way that told me he was on the hunt. I resisted the urge to bare my teeth at him. I was *not* his prey.

He smiled, as if reading my mind. "Have I ever told you how sexy you are when you're pissed?"

My cheeks heated, and his smile widened.

"Gross," Kyla muttered as she stalked in.

I grinned at her. "You delivered Wim to Finvarra?"

"Yup. The dickhead attempted to use his power on me when the guards showed up, but thanks to that ward you set, he couldn't do shit." Her gaze turned considering. "You know, you should monetize those wards. This could be a nice little side hustle for us."

"Did you get anything out of him?"

"We were right. Parila was in on it. She didn't actually *do* anything, but she knew what was going on. Finvarra has ordered her arrest."

"At least that's done." And Finvarra was going to make Wim pay.

"Any idea how we're going to kill a rampaging wolf who's bigger than us, faster than us, and impervious to magic?"

I slumped down on the sofa. "If we can't kill Fenrir, the only option is to trap him."

Kyla looked unconvinced. "Didn't the gods have

to try three times before they found a leash strong enough to tie him up?"

Yes. Yes, they did.

And when I found out who'd set him free, I was going to make them eat my fist.

"They did, but we have a secret weapon, thanks to our good friend, the unseelie king."

Kyla scowled. Then what I'd said must have hit her, because her eyes widened. "Evil. I like it."

"Thought you might. You'll also like the fact that, once we're done getting Fenrir through that portal and into that little slice of the middleground, Finvarra is going to do the same to Wimbar."

Her eyes widened. "Niiice."

Nathaniel placed his hand on my knee. "How exactly are we going to convince Fenrir to get into that portal?"

I sighed. "You're not going to like it."

I filled him in.

He didn't like it.

We argued the entire journey from Finvarra's castle back to wolf territory.

Kyla took my side—because friendship, but also because I was the best person for the job.

"If someone needs to play bait, I'll do it."

I hopped out of his passenger seat and glowered at him, hands stuck to my hips. Someone had arranged for his car to be delivered to the portal on our side, and he'd insisted on driving, leaving Kyla to take the car I'd been borrowing.

"Fenrir's not going to come after you," I snapped.

Nathaniel studied me. "It's the coin, isn't it? You took it when I wasn't looking. Where is it, Evie?"

I clamped my mouth shut. The coin turned invisible when pressed against the skin, which was why I hadn't seen or felt it. I could only take it off when my fingers brushed the exact spot.

Nathaniel was putting things together, and his claws shot out.

"The mages were targets, weren't they? I saw the list at the crime scene. They all had old coins with them. I'd figured it was some Mage Council bullshit. But someone targeted you too."

Nathaniel's face changed slightly. Kyla pulled her car behind his and strode toward us. He ignored her, his wolfy gaze pinning me in place.

"They tried to use a magic-eating godlike creature to try to take you out. Who was it, Evie?"

"I don't know yet. I don't," I said when he clenched his jaw so hard I heard something crack. I hoped werewolves could regrow their molars. "I have some theories, but I'm still poking at them. For now, we have an excellent way to get rid of Fenrir. Finvarra has even agreed to open the portal for us."

"Then *he* can be the one to lure it closer."

"You think Fenrir is going to try to target the unseelie king?"

"I think it's better to try than to have you risk your

life!"

"We'll only have one shot at this. Fenrir may be crazy, but he's still smart. The moment he realizes we're attempting to lure him into a trap, he'll never fall for it again."

"Someone else can do it."

I gave him a look. "I've done it before."

"With a roc. Not the same, Evie. Not even close."

"This is going to stun you, Your Alphaness, but I'm not a member of your pack."

"No, you're not," he said. "But that pack will lock you up if I tell them to."

My power flared. A ward formed around me. One so thick and so strong, I knew I needed to figure out how to replicate it in the future.

"Try it," I hissed.

"Whoa, whoa, whoa." Kyla held up a hand. She kept her gaze down, likely thanks to Nathaniel's dominance leaking all over the place. "There's got to be a way to compromise. Evie can lure Fenrir toward the portal, but we'll all be there too. We can provide enough of a distraction that he doesn't know what's going on. We'll all shove him into that portal if we have to."

I ground my teeth. "Fine."

A muscle twitched in Nathaniel's jaw as he watched me. "Fine."

EVIE

I wandered through the park on the edge of Nathaniel's territory for the fifth time. Of course, once we'd finally nailed down our plan, Fenrir had decided to disappear. There hadn't been another human massacre yet, but it was only a matter of time.

So here I was, for the third day in a row, wandering "alone" in one of the approved spaces on the outskirts of Nathaniel's territory. We'd made a list of places where we could attempt to trap Fenrir, and we were cycling through them. We needed locations that were far away from any humans, while also nowhere near the pack kids. Additionally, we needed them to have plenty of hiding spots.

Steve had come through with a wire, and Kyla had kept me sane by providing a running commentary of each member of Nathaniel's pack and the latest gossip about them. I was sure they were going to appreciate her big mouth.

"Are you limping?"

Nathaniel's voice came over the receiver in my ear.

"No. I stepped on a rock."

"Don't worry about him, Evie. He can't help

himself. It's a compulsion."

Nathaniel gave a low growl, but I could tell it wasn't serious. I smirked and began another lap around the park, attempting to ignore all the eyes on me.

We needed one of Finvarra's people to help with the portal since it required a dark fae to unlock it. Surprisingly, instead of sending one of his trusted inner circle, he'd insisted on attending to the matter himself. He obviously saw Fenrir as a large enough threat that he didn't want to risk anyone fucking it up. Especially since the portal had to be held open with sheer power.

Of course, he hadn't been following us around on this little jaunt. He'd given Kyla some kind of artifact that allowed her to call him. The moment Fenrir appeared, Kyla would call Finvarra, and he'd be summoned like a demon.

The fact that he'd given us that much power over him—even temporarily—spoke volumes for how concerned he was that Fenrir would turn his focus on the unseelie.

Hunter cleared his throat. "You're, uh...glowing again, Evie."

I felt my cheeks burn.

By burning myself out, I'd broken open whichever box inside me had been keeping the threads of my power neatly shut away. I could feel them now, desperate to find their way out. To cause havoc.

That power would be helpful, if we weren't up against a murderous creature who was impervious to that power. Instead, it was just doing random things like making my entire body glow like moonlight. I was willing to bet that came from the seelie court.

"When is this going to happen?" one of the other wolves growled. His name was Jarod, and I couldn't blame him for his impatience.

"You think you've got it bad hanging out behind that bush," Kyla muttered. "Poor Evie must be getting dizzy with how many circles she's walking."

The wolves began sniping at each other. Nathaniel allowed it. Likely because sniping was all they had, and at least they were blowing off a little steam.

It was only a few days until the full moon. After having their territory invaded and one of their kids almost die, the werewolves were hanging on to their self-control by a thread.

"How sure are you about this, Evie?" Another voice sounded, and I sighed.

Nelson.

I'd paid him a visit a few days ago to tell him what was going on and to let him know we had it handled.

He'd given me a disbelieving scowl when I'd filled him in.

"Like the giant wolf of myth?"

"That's the one."

He'd just stared at me, and I'd held up one hand, demonstrating my new fireball. "Before the portals opened, this was a myth too."

"You have a point. I want in."

And so, along with the wolves, a few scattered unseelie who were meant to keep an eye on us, and the seelie healer Nathaniel had talked into hanging around, we also had a group of cops stationed nearby.

It was basically a party.

"I have the coin," I muttered. But I *was* beginning to doubt myself. What if the coin was completely unrelated?

"The coin has a wolf on it," Kyla pointed out, and I realized I'd spoken aloud. "This is a good plan. We just have to be patient."

Ryker snorted in my ear. "*Kyla's* talking about patience. The world has turned upside down."

A dark, unnatural fog began to seep out of the trees surrounding the park. Adrenaline shot through me, and a chill slid over my skin as I forced my breathing to steady.

He was here.

Finally.

"Act cool, Evie." Kyla's voice was grim. "Remember, you're bait."

Nathaniel gave a growl so low, the hair stood up on the back of my neck. "Be careful," he said, and I knew it was his wolf speaking.

My power may be useless against Fenrir, but I'd used it to pinpoint every person in the area. And now I could feel them, slowly creeping toward me.

Fenrir appeared with an earsplitting roar.

"Finvarra will be on the way," Kyla whispered. "You've got this, Evie."

I gave Fenrir a shit-eating grin and let my hand wander down to my thigh holster. "This again? You didn't manage to do much last time. Let's go, puppy."

I wasn't sure if he could understand me, but he at least seemed to know I was taunting him. He snarled, revealing thick black fangs. Something moved in my peripheral vision.

"It's Finvarra," Kyla breathed, and Fenrir slowly turned his head.

I let out a sharp whistle. "Hey, big boy, check this out."

Shoving one hand into my pocket, I pulled out his tooth, holding it high. "You want it back?"

The growl he let out made me shiver, but I waved it as the shimmer to my right told me Finvarra had opened the portal. I slowly turned, then backed toward it.

I had no desire to be trapped with this beast in the slice of the middleground this portal led to. Although at least I knew for sure I wouldn't starve to death.

I sucked in a breath and took another step back.

And then Fenrir was there.

He'd moved faster than I could've imagined. In fact, he hadn't moved. He'd disappeared and reappeared at will.

I dove to the left as his paw slashed out, and the wind whistled as it shot past my face. That would've killed me for sure.

Distantly, I was aware of Nathaniel letting out a howl. And then the wolves surrounded us, half of them in their human forms.

Fenrir slowly turned, drool sliding from his wounded mouth as he took in the wolves. I could practically see him calculating. Shit. The last thing we needed was for him to disappear.

But I still had that coin.

I'd ended up back where I'd first been standing, thanks to my lunge to the left. I needed to get closer to the portal. I sidestepped once. Fenrir crouched, as if about to lunge.

Excellent.

One of the wolves leaped forward and latched on to Fenrir's leg.

Not excellent.

Fenrir let out a snarl, shaking the wolf off. He slashed out, and blood sprayed. I felt the moment the wolf died. Several of the wolves let out a mournful howl, and I caught sight of Kyla's agonized face the next time I turned.

Another wolf darted out. It was as if it couldn't help itself.

Nathaniel snarled, and the wolf froze, but it was too late. Fenrir lowered his head.

And I launched myself at him, my knife suddenly in my hand.

He couldn't target both of us at the same time. And for whatever reason, the coin made *me* the more important target. Fenrir changed direction at the last second.

He moved more like a bear than a wolf. His paw was twice the size of my head, and I heard something crack as he hit me in the side. I flew.

My head hit a rock, and the world disappeared.

No. I couldn't lose consciousness now. I had a job to do. I rolled, barely missing Fenrir's next hit. Some of the dark spots disappeared, until I realized one of those dark spots had a slash of silver down his back. Nathaniel was on top of Fenrir, his fangs deep in his neck.

We made eye contact, and his wolf stared back at me. It wanted me to get the hell out of there.

Nope.

I managed to stand. The ground seemed to tilt beneath my feet. I blinked a few times, and my vision steadied. That hit to the head hadn't been my favorite life experience.

Since the wolves were distracting Fenrir, I made my way back toward the portal. I noted where everyone was, my heart in my throat as Kyla launched herself at the huge beast. He shook her off, his attention still on Nathaniel, who was using his claws to dig deep into the monster's neck in an attempt to bleed him.

"Even I cannot hold this portal forever." Finvarra's voice was suddenly in my head, and I yelped. If I survived this, I was going to figure out how the hell he'd done that, and how I could make sure he would never do it again.

I flicked a glance at the unseelie king. He was holding the portal open, a strange black fog wrapped around him. His expression was as blank as usual, but I could see the hint of strain around his eyes.

We needed to finish this.

I sucked in a deep breath.

"Kyla, Hunter, Ryker, start herding him toward me. Nathaniel, you're going to have to ease up, so he'll decide he wants to eat me instead."

Nathaniel let out a vicious growl, but even he knew I was right. With a final slash across Fenrir's head, he jumped, twisting in the air so he could lunge at the beast's back legs instead.

The wolves worked together seamlessly. I swallowed, ready to do my part.

I may not be able to use my power on Fenrir himself, but last time, the wind had answered my call with the roc.

I lifted my hand, ready for the moment I could give him a nudge.

One of the wolves stumbled, blood flicking

toward my face. His body hit mine as he slumped, and I was suddenly six feet from the portal.

I could feel it, hot and deadly against my back. Fenrir shook off the wolves, rage burning in those red eyes.

He leaped.

I had nowhere to go.

I sucked in a breath and prepared to meet my end.

And then Nathaniel was there.

His body smashed into mine, and I flew through the air, landing with a thump. I flipped to my front and choked out a sob as Nathaniel latched on to Fenrir.

They tumbled through the air. Fenrir's claws dug into Nathaniel, and he roared as he flew toward the portal.

Fenrir was going to take Nathaniel with him.

Nathaniel struggled in his grip. He slashed out at him, rending a vicious slash across his muzzle. Fenrir yipped, and the portal slammed closed.

"No," I screamed. Fenrir was gone.

And so was Nathaniel.

Finvarra had closed the portal.

Someone was screaming. Bloodcurdling screams of horror and loss.

"Evie. Evie, he's okay."

I was the one screaming.

It took me a moment to stop as I stared

uncomprehendingly at Kyla.

My breath hitched, and I stumbled to my feet. Nathaniel was lying on his side, ten feet from the portal, Finvarra standing over him.

For all the unseelie king seemed to hate the Alpha, he'd obviously decided against leaving the wolves without a leader. He'd somehow managed to close the portal at the exact right time.

I knelt next to Nathaniel, still shaking. "You're a fucking mess." My voice came out raw. Fenrir's claws had ripped through him like a warm knife through butter. I could already hear his wolves calling for the healer. It was a smart decision to have the healer stationed close by after all.

He slowly got to his feet, pulling me with him.

"What are you doing!? Lie down."

He ignored that, obviously unwilling to show any signs of weakness. Men.

Nathaniel surveyed his people, noting injuries. "Kyla, get that leg seen to."

"Negative, Alpha. The healer's waiting for you."

Nathaniel raised his hand to the back of my head. He was painstakingly gentle, but stars still exploded in front of my eyes.

Now that some of the adrenaline was leaving my body, my ribs were burning so badly it hurt to breathe.

"Ah," he said. "I'll see the healer if you see her first."

I scowled at him. "You've been torn to shreds, you stubborn fool."

He grinned at me. "I can wait all day."

I blew out a breath but allowed him to lead me over to the healer. "Lean on me."

"I don't think so."

I ground my teeth. "We're going to have a talk after this."

"Dirty talk? I'm looking forward to it."

"It *will* be dirty, because as soon as you're not bleeding everywhere, I'm going to pound your face into the mud. You son of a bitch. What were you thinking?"

He just laughed.

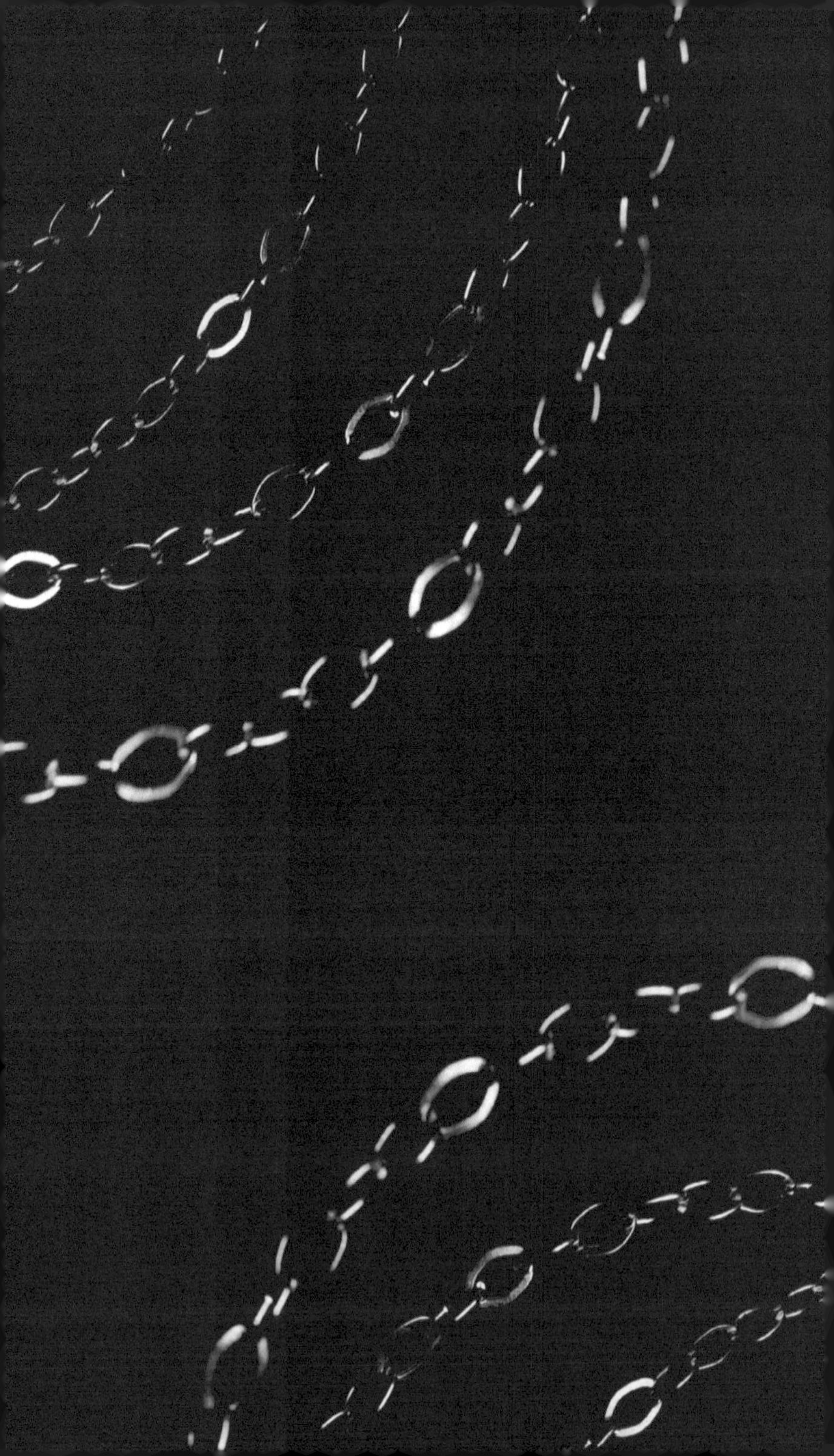

23

EVIE

It took two days before my ribs finally stopped aching. I'd made sure the healer only did the bare minimum, so she'd have enough juice for the wolves. And I'd sworn her to secrecy.

On the third day, I woke up in Nathaniel's guest room. He'd been busy mourning his pack member and making sure everyone was okay. I'd only met Rye once, but I'd cried at his funeral yesterday. He hadn't been an idiot. He'd just lost control of his wolf so close to the full moon.

I knew Nathaniel well enough to know he was blaming himself.

I sat up and reached for the coin on the bedside table. All the people who had died, all the grieving families, and for what?

A lust for power. And an attempt to take more of it.

It was time to tell Nathaniel exactly what had happened.

I pulled on a clean pair of jeans and a T-shirt, mentally thanking Tobias. As soon as I brushed my teeth, I felt like a new woman. The house was quiet as I stepped out of my room, and I glanced at my phone. It was quiet because it was eleven a.m. Everyone was at work, or at least getting back to their usual schedules, and it wasn't yet rush hour in the kitchen.

I could hear voices, so I began to pad toward the kitchen.

"When are you going to tell her?"

"Soon."

I froze. My instincts warned me that I didn't want to keep walking.

"Evie needs to know."

I sucked in a breath. Even though I was at the top of the stairs, I knew both wolves had heard me, because they both went silent.

"You may as well come down, Evelyn."

Ooh, he was *spoiling* for a fight.

I strolled down the stairs and into the kitchen. Tobias was nowhere to be found. Nathaniel was staring at Hunter as if he was wondering what his organs looked like...and considering disemboweling him so he could take a look.

Hunter sent me an apologetic look. "I'll just get out of your way."

Nathaniel watched him, and his eyes were all wolf.

I swallowed, my mouth suddenly dry.

"Whatever it is, you need to tell me," I managed to get out. "You've been saying we need to talk for days now."

Nathaniel turned his gaze on me. I went still.

"You're my mate," Nathaniel said.

The world spun around me, and I could feel the blood draining from my face.

"Don't I need to agree to that?"

He showed me his teeth. "Agree or don't agree, the fact remains that my wolf chose you the moment it first saw you."

Nathaniel took a single step closer. I stayed still, frozen. He raised his hand, as if he was thinking about tucking my curls behind my ear. Or perhaps he was considering resting that large hand on the back of my neck and coaxing me close the way he so often did.

I hated that a part of me wanted him to do exactly that. Hated that I craved his touch. Hated that I wanted to feel his warmth on my skin.

He fisted his hand and dropped it to his side.

My lips were numb. I'd come here to tell him something. I needed to tell him and leave. All I wanted to do was to be alone so I could lick my wounds in peace.

"Albert was behind the attacks. He was hoping to make the wolves go to war with each other, maybe even become convinced it was the seelie king behind the attacks. At the very least, he wanted the humans to turn on you. He was the one who set Ellen Harrison on the pack. He was paying her to be that unrelenting. He set his own mages up to die so they could lure Fenrir close. And when he realized I was investigating them, he had his mage plant the coin on me."

Nathaniel's expression darkened at that, but he shook his head. "We'll talk about that at a later time. Right now, we need to talk about us."

"There is no us. You *know* how I feel about lying." My voice hitched, and Nathaniel looked like I'd pulled out my knife and gutted him. I didn't let myself fall for it.

I'd opened up to him. I'd told him things I hadn't told anyone. Admitted how badly the coven had destroyed me when they'd abandoned me. Told him all about how everyone from my mother to my adopted family had lied to me.

And then he'd done the same.

He shoved a hand through his hair. "Tell me you wouldn't have run, Evie. Tell me you wouldn't have backed away so fast, you would've gotten whiplash."

Oh, *now* he called me Evie? I snarled at him. "You don't know that! How long have you known for?"

"Since the moment I met you. I convinced myself it wasn't true, until you had that chip removed, and I knew for sure."

He'd convinced himself it wasn't true. Because why would he want to be mated to someone he considered such a flight risk? I let out a laugh so bitter,

I almost choked on it.

"All this time," I marveled, my lips numb. "All this time, when I thought I was just getting to know you, when I was catching feelings—"

"Evie."

"Meanwhile, you knew I was your mate. Knew what? That your wolf considers me *his?*"

"Yes," he growled. "Exactly."

"Who else knew?" My voice was toneless. Distantly, I wondered if I was in shock.

And then it hit me.

"Danica knew. Didn't she?"

Her words flashed through my head from the last time we'd spoken.

"There are some things I can't tell you right now. But...I want you to know that anything I've done—anything I've kept from you—has been because I truly believed it was necessary. Because I love you, and I have your best interests at heart."

Best interests, my ass.

"Yes. She knew."

I took a step back, and he went still. Then his head angled in a way that was all wolf. "Sit down. We'll talk about this. I'll tell you everything. But either way, you're mine, Evie. Just as I'm yours."

I stared at him, at the wolf in his eyes, and I shook my head. "I don't think so. The man I'll choose will give me choices. He won't decide he knows better than me and then *lie* to me for months."

"You won't end up with any other man, sweetheart, so you can push that thought right out of your head."

I gaped at him. "Do you hear yourself?"

He merely stared at me. The Alpha had shaken off all pretenses of being a civilized man.

Panic rose, sharp and unrelenting. I felt like *I* was the wolf, with my neck caught in a trap. Nathaniel must have scented it, because he let out a hollow laugh.

"That right there, Evie. *That* is the reason I didn't tell you. You're so afraid of letting anyone close in case they abandon you again."

That wasn't it. Was it?

Either way, I was done. Done listening to him tell me how to feel.

"Does...does the mating bond make you want to spend time with your *mate?*"

He shook his head, but I could no longer trust him. It was all a lie. All of it. I may not have a spelled house changing my personality anymore, but I now had a mating bond that could do *anything*.

"You'd like to think that, wouldn't you?" His voice was hoarse. "You'd like to think that any feelings you have, anything that threatens your so-called *freedom,* is because of something out of your control. That way, you can lock those feelings in a box and never look at them again."

My entire face was numb now. I couldn't feel my fingers. But my chest ached like it had been cracked open. Like my rib cage had been pushed apart, leaving my heart exposed to the elements.

Nathaniel took another step closer. "You think I wanted this? I was doing just fine before you swaggered into my life. But now I know what I was missing, I'll do whatever it takes to keep you. Whatever. It Takes."

"Don't threaten me,' I hissed.

"Evie? Is everything okay?"

Liam walked in and froze. His gaze dropped to the ground. We both ignored him, staring at each other.

Another sob escaped my chest.

The biggest irony of it all was that I'd briefly felt like I belonged here. I'd imagined staying.

But if I'd really belonged, the whole pack wouldn't have lied to me.

I turned to Liam. "Can you give me a ride?" I asked. I just needed to get out of here.

Liam gave Nathaniel a wary look. "I'll wait in the car."

Nathaniel allowed him to back out of the room. But his eyes burned as he leaned close to me.

"You want him to die? Let him touch you again."

"You've never cared before."

"I just told you I'm your mate. Before doesn't matter."

"Fuck you, Nathaniel."

I stalked out of the house, slamming into Kyla.

She steadied me. "Jesus, Evie, what's wrong?"

"He said he's my mate." My voice was empty. I glanced up at her, and I saw it.

Guilt.

Gone in a flash. But I knew what I'd seen.

"You knew."

Oh God. Oh God, not Kyla too.

She didn't bother denying it. Her expression turned tormented, but I didn't care.

"How could you lie to me? *Why* would you lie to me?"

"Nathaniel ordered me not to tell you."

I let out a bitter laugh. "Oh, he *ordered* you? Since when do you take fucking orders?"

"It wasn't just a suggestion, Evie. He's my Alpha. I had no choice. I literally couldn't tell you."

My eyes burned, and I pressed the heels of my hands against them. Everyone knew. Nathaniel, Danica, now even Kyla. I'd been kept in the dark. Like a child.

I thought I'd felt betrayed when my mother took Danica and left me behind. I thought I'd felt betrayed when my coven kicked me out.

Now I knew what true betrayal was.

Everyone around me had known this secret. Had kept it from me. Because I wasn't to be trusted with the truth.

I backed up. Kyla's face creased, and she followed me.

"Evie..."

"Stay the fuck away from me right now, Kyla. I don't want to hear it."

Her eyes glinted. I'd never seen her cry, and I wouldn't watch it now. I turned and stalked past her, my throat so tight it felt like I could barely breathe.

It was time to talk to my lying excuse for a sister.

EVIE

Liam held out his keys as I approached. I wasn't sure where the car I'd been driving had ended up, but I wasn't going to be driving anything that belonged to Nathaniel.

"You'll have to take it. I can't drive you right now, Evie. I'm sorry, but..."

"It's fine. He's not exactly fucking reasonable at the moment."

Liam gave me a look that said I couldn't throw stones. I snarled at him and snatched his keys.

"Thanks."

My mind raced as I drove toward the portal that would take me to the underworld. Nathaniel had once told me he loathed using his power to keep his pack in line. He'd said he didn't want a pack of slaves. And yet he'd used that power to make Kyla keep her mouth shut.

I ignored the little voice in my head that told me how much that must've hurt him.

It was a choice. A choice he'd made.

I'd told him just how much I hated my choices being taken away. And how I loathed lies. I hiccupped and reached up, wiping at the tears.

No one spoke to me as I approached the portal. They seemed to know something was terribly wrong. Of course, I still had tears streaming down my face, so that might've tipped them off.

Danica was sitting on her throne next to Samael when I arrived, escorted in by one of the demons. A group of demons was standing in front of her, and she murmured something to her bondmate, then strode toward me.

Samael's eyes met mine, and I barely resisted the urge to flip him off. He'd known too.

He gave me a slow smile, daring me.

I raised my right hand.

Danica caught it in hers. "Not here," she hissed. "Say whatever you need to him in private, Evie, but he's the underking in this room."

Yanking my hand from her grip, I stalked out. "What about here?" I asked when we were standing in the wide hall behind the throne room. "Are you the underqueen here, Danica? Or are you my lying sister?"

She glanced around at the demons who were watching, wide-eyed.

"Follow me."

"Why? So you can lie to me some more? I just came here to tell you exactly what I think of you."

Hurt flashed through her eyes, and she opened her mouth.

I cut her off.

"You *know* how I feel about lying. I was lied to my entire fucking life. I thought you, at least, would never do this to me. How could you?"

"It was for the best."

For the best.

"Best for whom exactly? Because it wasn't best for me. I've been at Nathaniel's for *days*, Danica. I was enjoying myself, thinking we could have something fun. Thinking I could live my life as normal, but also be with Nathaniel. And then I find out I'm his *mate?*"

"When he told me, it was right after the coven was killed. You'd already left once without warning, after we found the lab. You'd been numbed for so long after the spell... He told me if you found out and left again, his wolf would've been compelled to find you. And he didn't want to do that to you. He was worried you'd disappear and HFE would find you before he could."

"So neither of you told me. For months."

"I'd thought he would've told you by now. I'm not sure why he didn't. Evie, please."

I ignored her and walked out.

I'd trusted my friend not to lie to me. I'd trusted my sister not to lie to me. I'd trusted Nathaniel not to fucking lie to me.

Clearly, *I* was the idiot here.

I barely even felt the pain when I crossed back through the portal. I was running on pure rage as I drove back toward Meredith's.

If Meredith and Vas also knew… I didn't know what I'd do. Where I'd go.

The bar was closed, but I knocked anyway. The door swung open, and Orin raised his eyebrow at me.

"Well, don't you look like something the cat dragged in."

"Thanks."

His eyes softened. "Get in here, and let me pour you a drink. Vas and Mere are too busy making out to do any *real* work."

Mere's musical laugh sounded. "I heard that."

Orin winked at me, and I followed him inside.

"What happened?" Vas asked as soon as he saw me. Both he and Mere were behind the bar, but he stalked toward me with a dark scowl.

I took a deep, shuddery breath.

"I need to ask you guys a question, and I need you to answer honestly."

"Of course," Mere said.

"Did you know I was Nathaniel's mate?"

Her mouth dropped open. Vas stiffened, and I watched him carefully.

"No," he said. "But…I guess it all makes sense now." He pulled out one of the barstools and gestured for me to sit. Mere got busy pouring me a drink.

"The werewolf Alpha, huh?"

I nodded. "Kyla knew. He made her vow not to tell me. We had a fight. I need to apologize. After all, it isn't really her fault. But…Danica knew, too. We had our biggest fight yet. She knows how much I hate lies."

Mere's expression softened, and she sighed. "I'm sorry, Evie. I know this is a lot, but there's something else you need to know."

I lowered my drink. "What is it?"

"Kyla went after the sword. I assumed you were going too, so I didn't stop her."

The world receded, until I felt as if I were floating above my body. "She went alone?"

Mere nodded, wiping at the same smudge on her bar, over and over. "She said she'd heard from Aubrey and the seelie king is moving up his schedule again."

Aubrey probably attempted to call me when I was in the underworld. When he couldn't reach me, he'd called Kyla, assuming she'd fill me in.

Instead, she'd gone alone.

"Of all the stubborn—" I got to my feet and pushed the stool back under the bar. "I'm going after her."

Vas went still. "I'm coming too."

"No," I cut him off. "You have a kid on the way. This is for Kyla and me to do."

Only, Kyla had obviously decided I wouldn't be helping her. She'd also obviously decided our friendship was over.

My memory provided me with the image of her wounded eyes when I'd confronted her, and I ran my hand over my face.

After the fight we'd had, I couldn't blame her. But it was stupid and reckless. We weren't prepared to put the plan into motion together, let alone by ourselves.

"I've got to go."

"How can we help, Evie?" Vas looked tortured. Next to him, Mere looked like she wanted to send him, but her hand had clamped around her lower belly.

"If we don't come back, let everyone know who has us and why. That's all I need. I've got this."

They let me go, but neither of them liked it. Unfortunately, that meant I had to return to the underworld.

My mind was looping around the same thoughts over and over again. We weren't prepared. We weren't prepared. We definitely weren't fucking prepared.

I stopped at Aubrey's. He paled when I told him what had happened. "She went alone?"

"Yeah. Don't worry, I'm going to kick her ass when I find her. If she's still alive."

Guilt stabbed into my gut. If she wasn't alive, it was all my fault.

"I gave her the map," Aubrey said, and I closed my eyes. "But I made a copy." He took my arm and led me to the closest chair, guiding me into it. Then he turned and murmured to one of his servants.

"I wanted to have a backup for my own records," he admitted.

"In case you decide to take the throne?"

He sighed. "A lot more would go into it than a decision to take the throne and a map of his castle, but yes."

The servant returned and handed me the map. "I need to go."

"Wait. I have a few things for you. I'd hoped to give these to Kyla, but she was a little...wild when she arrived, and I didn't get the chance."

Aubrey riffled through the hall closet and pulled out a backpack. He wandered away, although I could hear him muttering. When he returned, he patted the backpack twice. "There are a few things in here that should help. You'll know how to use them."

"Thank you. If we don't make it back..."

"You will. You better make it back, Evie Amana, and you better bring Kyla home with you, or I'm coming after you. And no one is prepared for war."

I nodded. Then I leaned up and kissed his cheek. His eyes glittered as he watched me turn to go.

"Good luck."

I drove to Gary's, where I parked my car and poked through the backpack Aubrey had given me. My mouth dropped open as my hand brushed a tiny jar of pixie dust. It could heal even mortal wounds if applied quickly enough. This jar was worth almost ten thousand dollars, although the human population had no idea it existed. If they learned of it, the next thing we knew, they'd be farming pixies for their dust.

I still had the key Entaris had given us. I shoved

it into one of the inside pockets of the backpack, then popped the trunk and pulled out the first aid kit Nathaniel's wolves all carried in their cars.

Gary watched me quietly while I stocked up on pain charms. I'd told him what had happened, and he was chewing on his gray lips with his sharp teeth. He loved Kyla too. I picked out some lapis lazuli, which was excellent for tracking spells if Kyla and I got separated after I found her.

"Thanks, Gary."

"Good luck, kid."

I got back into the car and drove toward the portal to the underworld. I didn't want to return, but I didn't have much choice.

This time, Danica was in the garden.

"Evie." A faint smile crossed her face, as if she thought I was here to apologize or some shit.

"Kyla went after the sword. Without me."

Danica paled. I ignored the horror in her eyes.

"I'll forgive you if you give me the ring," I said.

Danica glanced down at the ring, and I saw the moment she figured it out. "You think it'll help. You don't need to pretend to forgive me. Kyla's my friend too." She slipped it off her finger. "Here. Take it."

I didn't bother answering. I just pushed it onto my own finger and hauled ass back toward the portal.

NATHANIEL

I smiled at the mage.

It hadn't taken much for my wolf to hunt him. In truth, the monster inside me was almost disappointed by how easy it had been. He'd known I was coming and had gone on the run.

But no one could hide from me for long.

I watched as he raised his hand, and an ugly brown ward appeared.

Then I stepped through it.

He let out a choked sound that pleased my wolf. My people didn't make it known that Alphas could call on the power of the pack when necessary. There was no point tipping off our enemies. But my pack was large. Powerful. Angry.

I could feel them, all of them. Which told me my wolf was dangerously close to the surface. Regardless of how each of them felt about Evie as a person, they all felt the same violent outrage that the mages would dare come after my mate.

"How did you get in here?"

I shook my head at Albert. "That's not what you should be asking. You should be asking how much I'll make you suffer before you die for targeting Evie."

Surprise flashed through his eyes. He'd thought I had come here as retaliation for attempting to stoke a war between various werewolf packs. He thought I'd come to threaten him, maybe punish him, for the reputational damage he'd caused us among the humans.

I gave him a slow smile, and he trembled. "Evie is my mate."

His trembling turned to a full-body shudder, and my wolf silently howled his victory. We'd kill this threat to our mate. And then we'd convince her to return to our territory. To our home. Where she belonged.

I allowed the wolf to take over, only shoving him aside when I needed to travel back to my territory.

Hunter gaped at me as I stepped into the house. He immediately dropped his eyes, although not before I saw his own wolf peek out at the scent of the blood covering me.

"You killed Albert."

His voice was carefully neutral.

"Yes," I growled, still on the killing edge.

Ryker stepped into the room. "There's something you need to know. Vassago just called."

"And?"

"Kyla went into the seelie realm. Evie went after her."

That fucking sword. I'd always planned to be there to make sure they didn't cause a war—or worse, end up dead. But they went after it alone.

"You can't follow her," Ryker said. He stiffened when he felt my gaze on him and kept his own eyes down. "Tomorrow is the full moon. She's your mate. We just lost a pack member. There's no way your wolf will stay in control."

I watched him. My wolf pondered whether he should live. Hunter stepped into my line of sight. And that was how I'd chosen my dominants. Because they were loyal to me, but even more importantly, they were loyal to each other. That loyalty was good for the pack as a whole.

My wolf agreed. Ryker would live. But we *would* be finding our mate.

I'd known Evie would run. That was okay. I was going to prove we belonged together. Right after I saved her life, kissed her lush mouth, and spanked her ass.

I threw my head back and howled my fury.

THE END.

AUTHOR'S NOTE

Thank you so much to the curly-haired ladies in the Stark Society Facebook group who helped me with my research. Especially Raluca Enache, who helped me understand the curly-girl weather frustration, and Suzanne Ledford, who made me die laughing with her safeword quote.

The next book in the series is Unbroken Magic and it's a continuation of Evie's story. The final book in the Bargains with Beasts series is **Unending Magic** which is Kyla's story.